I0563512

A Death in Jericho

Lela Markham

Published by Breakwater Harbor Books

A Word from Lela Markham

Thank you for reading my book. If you enjoyed it, please take a moment to leave me a review at your favorite retailer. Only with your help can independent writers like me reach more readers. I appreciate it!

Wow, who would have thought when I published Winter's Reckoning that we'd still be dealing with Covid 19 (or is it Covid 21 now?) and that we would have witnessed the oddest election of our time. I swear, I'm not a prophet, but I definitely nailed the political intrigue of a president surrounded by questions and a potential replacement waiting in the wings just as I hinted in Life As We Knew It. I recently dug up my Gallup Strength-Finder results for a new supervisor and was reminded that I'm supposed to be good at drawing connections between past events and future trends. There you have it. Literary prophesy. Tampered with elections, global surveillance, media propaganda, viruses, censorship, and more. I still don't measure up to George Orwell or Ray Bradbury. I guess I'll have to continue practicing, reading the news and letting my imagination run free.

Why a murder mystery in the midst of the apocalypse? Why not? It gave me a chance to show both Emmaus and Mara Wells surviving the winter and Shane healing mentally and physically. And it set up the next book. Call it a transition—a deep breath between crisis, with a chance for Cai to shine beyond his brother's large persona. Don't worry, Shane will be back in the saddle with Worm Moon.

Watching the growth of Cancel Culture, particularly through social media, I've opened an account on LibertyandLiterature/locals.com so people will have a way to reach out to me if Facebook and Twitter decide I shouldn't have a voice. Locals has a commitment to not curtail freedom of speech beyond what the Constitution allows.

If you enjoyed this book or the series, leave a review.

Lela Markham

Thanks!

This book is dedicated to Miss Christine Smith, my high school Brit Lit teacher at Austin E. Lathrop Highschool in Fairbanks, Alaska, who made Shakespeare and Beowulf equally interesting to a bunch of bored 10th graders who just wanted to get a passing grade. She gave me an A because she made me want to learn what she had to teach.

No book is the work of a single individual. The author gets all the glory but standing behind every published writer is a host of support personnel. Thank you to Tim Poole, Luke Rudkowski, Sour Patch Lids, and Ian Crossland from Timcast IRL for all the thought-provoking conversations you host from a broadly libertarian perspective.

Because Delaney men are musicians, I always try to include at least one song. This book I need to thank the Eagles for *Take It Easy* and The Newsboys for *What If I Stumble*..

Table of Contents

"I should fancy, however, that murder is always a mistake. One should never do anything that one cannot talk about after dinner."

— Oscar Wilde, The Picture of Dorian Gray

A Death in Jericho

Book 7

Transformation Project

Prologue

Cold winter descended upon North America, wrapping Emmaus in snow. The pioneers called January and February the starving times because the supply routes closed and if you didn't have enough money to survive to when the first delivery arrived, you starved. Hard to believe we'd been reduced to such a state in just a few months.

We all took a deep breath and the world seemed to pause, frozen like bugs in amber. Frozen! There's irony for you. We hungered not just for food, but for news of the outside world, for warmth, for companionship from people who we'd lost. And, the days dragged on.

What happened to the body? Now there's a question worth asking!

So many people were dying of hunger, cold and the flu. Why should his death matter more than any other? Because someone else made him dead and we needed to know if he had earned it or not.

JT Delaney

January 1

Not A Turning Point

Jericho Springs Ghost Town, Jericho Township

Winter whistled over Jericho Ridge and slammed hard into Cai Delaney's back as he knelt in the snow behind the Jericho Hotel. What a way to start the new year, now barely two hours old. Not that the new year ever was a turning point, but he clung to a superstitious hope that New Year's Day represented a fresh start, out with the bad and in with the better — that naïve baby crawling to the future without the wrinkles and scars of the old-man past. Hogwash and the scene before him shattered that illusion like a hammer to a stained glass window.

Cai slid another polaroid into his pocket, swiping the back of a glove over his upper lip before the snot there could form a stalactite from his mustache. He'd grown a beard before, but he'd never hated it more. Those prior times had been choices, however ill-conceived. Forced to do it this winter, he loathed his facial hair now.

The body laid there a while — long enough to freeze solid so they couldn't unbend its arm. A dark woolen scarf pulled free of the dark ski jacket, dancing in the wind blazing past the living bodies examining the corpse. Snow had been piled over the body and tamped down. Whoever did this meant the body not to be discovered soon, but obviously wasn't concerned it would be discovered eventually. Else they were stupid. Cai supposed that possibility existed. The day before yesterday, the wind shifted and swept the snow from the body, freeing the scarf, which caught Joe's attention.

"When was the last time you were back here, Joe?" As the only trained police officer left in Emmaus, Joe became Police Chief when Bart Rawlson died in the City Hall Shelter incident three months ago, but Joe wasn't even 30 yet and had spent his entire four-year career in rural Kansas. He needed the mayor and the city attorney acting as detectives on this, which is why he'd backed away from the crime scene and called them. Cai figured to start with what they knew.

"Um, the day before the shooting out at Conopher's place. We started looking for and training volunteers then, so I haven't had time."

"And you came back here?"

Joe paused, considering his memory. Cai knew he had notes back at City Hall that he could refer to. Joe always journaled his day as Bart had taught.

"Yeah."

"Anything out of the ordinary." Cai wiped the snot off his mustache with the back of his glove.

"No dead bodies, if that's what you're asking." Joe looked up at the clear sky, which apparently stored his memory when his copious office notes weren't available.

"Shane had been here a day or so before – I could see his Jeep's tracks in the snow by the bridge and his footprints went to the backdoor to check the security system." He paused to review his internal notes. "One set of tracks in and out, nothing unusual about it. That could have been a day or two-old since we hadn't had a storm recently. I didn't do much that day, just visually scanned around the area because Alex's seed corn means life and death come spring and Shane's the one most likely to get through that door."

"Don't take this wrong. You sure you just didn't miss the body?" Murphy, a tall gangling former National Guardsman who served as Emmaus' temporary chief of town defense, let go of his AR15 to blow warm breath into his gloves. Cai imagined he could feel the temperature dropping by the minute.

"I know how to do my job." Joe came off like a country boy – *Mayberry* rather than *Law and Order*, and he didn't take offense easily, but Cai could hear the controlled irritation in his voice. "It was daylight. I don't know how I could have missed it."

"It was covered in snow."

"I've been back here a dozen times since the harvest, and I think I would have noticed something out of the ordinary like snow piled up right there, at least wondered why Shane would bother to pile snow up in one place like this."

Avoiding a urination contest seemed like a good idea.

"We'll need an autopsy to figure out how long he's been dead." Cai stood from his kneel and stomped his feet. Body detail for the last week erased his discomfort with corpses. He knew full-well his brother Shane fully embraced realism before it sucked him into a death roll. Cai had realism thrust upon him. Shane already broke. Could Cai survive the slow wearing away of his humanity until he felt nothing for the dead because they were no longer human? Could he somehow avoid that? "We can't stay out here much longer."

"I've seen him before." Murphy couldn't be much more than 22, but he'd served two tours in Iraq. He gave directions and ordered coffee in the same nonchalant tone as he glanced from the polaroid he held and then around the dark yard beyond the hotel. Jericho Springs got a lot of traffic for a ghost town. The back of Cai's neck prickled as if he felt observation from the woods.

"Where?"

"Border patrol about maybe a week ago. He showed up at the Lufgren Crossing gate, asking for, um, someone named, uh, Frazer – no, Faraday. Since none of us knew who that was, we told him to wait, and then he disappeared on us. Anyone in town named Faraday?"

Rob and Cai exchanged glances.

"My wife's maiden name is Faraday, but this isn't my brother-in-law or one of his kids and I don't know how they'd get here from Seattle. He say a first name?"

Murphy stomped his feet and blew on his hands some more.

"Um, Rick – no, Eric…I think."

Cai flinched. Rob's long-deceased brother had been named Eric and Cai's brother Shane combined the two names for a covert identity as a Central Security Agency operative.

"Can you remember the exact day?" Rob moved to direct attention from the situation.

"No. They all fade together now." Murphy sighed as if he mourned the days when it wasn't true. "It's all winter. It's always cold and I'm always on patrol. Else I'm sleeping. I can ask the guys who were on patrol with me. One of them might remember."

The National Guard guys shared a small abandoned house in town. The Army troop Cai brought in a month ago were quartered in another house whose owner hadn't been around when the Bombs went off. Rob shared with Cai that he hated using people's houses like that, but he didn't have a lot of options. He'd chosen houses whose owners would be understanding and he'd made sure those borrowing the houses knew not to trash them. Neither had. Had he done his job? Cai didn't know. He wasn't as wedded to the non-aggression principle as Rob. His grandfather Jacob had warned that political leadership always led to breaking the non-aggression principle. Jacob's prophesy proved right soon as the bombs went off and Rob struggled with that reality every day. Cai just tried to get through each day without fresh blood on his hands. The dried blood was bad enough.

The growl of a snowmobile came around the corner of the hotel. Vint Barrett dismounted well back of the crime scene and stomped through the snow to them, dragging a fold-a-sled. Snow collected on his short-cropped tightly-knit beard, making him look like one of those black Santas you find in cheap gift shops at Christmas time. Did those still exist? Santas and gift shops seemed from another era or a movie. Movies probably didn't exist anymore either. Hollywood sure didn't.

"Jeez. Who'd have thought we'd have a murder *inside* the wire?"

"People do incomprehensible things when they're hungry." Rob straightened. He looked tired and even old in the blasting wind.

"Like stash a body in a remote location." Joe pointed out to the darkness. "I'd be willing to bet there's evidence out there of how this got here."

"You don't think he was killed here?" Cai shoved one ungloved hand into his coat, seeking a warm armpit.

"Not enough blood and this is a weird place for anyone to meet. The only reason to meet here is if you wanted something in the hotel, but Shane's security system still won't let anyone in, so why would you kill someone if you hadn't got what you wanted?"

"That's a good reason to kill someone." Rob and Vint nodded in agreement with Murphy's statement – one hundred percent military mindset. Vint had only done one stint. Rob did twenty years.

"We're all only about nine meals from becoming barbarians. Are we ready to drag the body out of here?" Vint waited for instructions.

"I think we should wait for daylight." Rob looked at the sky where stars twinkled like diamonds around the icy fingernail moon. "I think Joe's right that there might be some evidence that survived the storms and we should look for it while we can see. Since it doesn't look like it's going to snow more, leave the body in place until dawn."

"It's getting colder." Cai switched hands in his armpits. "It's going to be hard to stay out here much longer."

"Yep. Let's go over to the fishing cabin. I'll fire up the woodstove. We can take turns guarding the body until sunrise."

"I'll take first shift since I just got here." Vint scanned the woods for unseen threats. "Instructions?"

"Don't walk around. You might destroy evidence." Joe became better at giving orders the longer he'd been the chief. "If you need to pace, stick to the trail you just made."

"Sounds good."

"Someone will be back to spell you in an hour." Rob turned toward the path out of the slight hollow the Jericho Springs Hotel sat in. "Maybe we'll all think better in the warmth with some coffee."

"Coffee? What's that?" Joe's joke fell flat.

Cai followed Rob toward the vehicles, then Murphy and Joe a moment later. The wind sighed over the ridge and churned snow in their path.

Milking Shed

Andrew Bennett Farm, Jericho Township

Dawn grayed the sky as Andrew Bennett entered into the milking shed to find the nanny goats gamboling about the large space broken into stalls. He pulled up when he saw the bucket of spilled milk lying next to the stool.

"Matthew?"

A nanny complained about her full udders. Milk-bearing animals relied on their humans in a symbiotic relationship. They produced milk for their herders to relieve the pressure.

"Dammit, kid, we need every resource this farm can produce."

Andrew righted the bucket and set it next to the plastic milk crate they used for a stool. Matt uncharacteristically didn't show. Josiah had gone to cover the town guard, leaving Andrew to keep the farm going with the younger kids. Matt was the best of them, but they weren't adults yet. Andrew called a little louder and he heard a grunt from one of the stalls. Matt sat on a straw bail in the storage stall, his head back against the slat wall and his eyes squeezed shut.

"What's up, kid?"

"Headache."

"Migraine?" The 16-year-old got those occasionally, but not since the power situation had banned video games.

"It feels like there's an icepick in the back of my head."

"Well, you're no use out here if you can't see. Go on up to the house. Send Luke down."

Matt sighed and opened his eyes. One pupil was enormous and the other was a pinprick. When Andrew held out a hand to help him up, he missed it.

"Your vision doubled?"

Matt rubbed the eye with the outsized pupil. Andrew reached down and intercepted one of his hands so he could help him up.

"Go take a nap."

Matt stumbled as he walked out of the storage stall.

"Sorry about the milk. I needed to puke and – and --." Sudden tears flowed down the boy's usually ruddy cheeks. Andrew caught him around the shoulders and led him through the harrowing west wind to the house. Colleen Bennett turned from the stove where she made breakfast Thank God they'd not sold off their extra animals yet when the Bombs went off. The extra milk, eggs, and pork kept them fed without eating cornmeal three meals a day. Matt pushed his mother out of the way to puke in the sink.

Colleen pinned Andrew with a look he couldn't analyze.

"Migraine."

Colleen went to stand beside Matt and asked him to look at her. He winced from the light. Meanwhile, Andrew directed 14-year-old Luke to go milk the goats.

"What about feeding the pigs?"

"I'll worry about that. The pigs can go hungry for a while. The goats are in pain. I got the cows already. Go."

Colleen directed Matt to sit in a chair and used her eyes to communicate that she wanted to talk to Andrew alone. They withdrew to the laundry room off the kitchen and he closed the door.

"That's not a normal migraine. I've never seen his pupils do that before."

"I can take him into the clinic, I guess." He'd just finished a drum of ethanol. He could afford the fuel for the truck – though that meant he'd have less later.

"No. I mean, Dr. Callahan can't do anything about this, right? There's no treatment."

"For a migraine?

"Drew, we have to be prepared. He had the flu. Kix, Calvin, the Mapes boy, Alex's brother-in-law."

"I think you're jumping to a conclusion."

Colleen pulled on her waist-length braid while staring at the door.

"I don't think so." Her soft affirmation worked more strongly than a shout. Andrew's gut settled into his feet. They stared at the door a moment longer before Andrew stirred.

"I'll help him up to bed. He's not going to want to eat, but something tells me you should make him." Colleen nodded. "Try to keep your worry to yourself. No need to scare the kids before we know for certain." She nodded again. Andrew opened the door. Matt's head rested on his arms folded on the table. "Come on, kid. Let's get you somewhere dark, see if this stops soon."

Sarah, their 12-year-old, brushed past Andrew at the bottom of the stairs.

"Go relieve Luke from milking the goats."

"I'm feeding chickens."

"He can do that after he feeds the pigs. Where's Anna?"

"Collecting eggs," Colleen called from the stove where she rescued breakfast.

"Go do what I ask."

Matt stumbled on the third step. Andrew glanced down to see his toes catching as he tried to mount each step. In the boys' room, Matt sprawled onto his bed with an arm across his eyes.

"Call if you need anything?"

"Yeah." Matt oozed exhaustion and pain, so Andrew pulled the curtains across the windows and left him to nap, praying it was just a migraine.

Alaska Calling

Delaney House, Emmaus, Kansas

Everything hurt this morning -- a clear sign he'd overdone last night, according to Jill.

"All I did was sit up in a wheelchair for an hour – less than, really."

"And you can't do that right now." Her green eyes admonished him. Shane shifted against the pillows and his entire right side seized. Sweat broke out on his face and he feared he'd hurl.

"I don't mind helping you."

"I mind being helped."

"You don't mind is the problem." Shane stared at her for a long moment before he recognized it was a joke.

"Sorry. In too much pain to laugh."

"I'll get breakfast ready. Take a nap. It'll help."

Shane napped more in the last week than at any other time in his life. He closed his eyes and listened to the distant clatter from the kitchen and the quieter sound of wood burning in the stove next to his bed. Static interrupted the quiet. Click Michaels set up the radio station in the living room this morning. So far, just the basic ham radio rested on the table over by the stairs and now it erupted in a burst of static, resolving into a broken string of words.

"EMMAUS (static) CAP, (static) Arctic KC-135R (static) ANG (static) Alaska. Anyone there?"

Click left a while ago and Shane lacked the energy to get out of bed. After the message repeated three times, Jazz came into the room and stared at the offending unit.

"Should I turn it off?"

"No. Answer it." She gave him an instructions-please look. "See the button on the mic stand? Push that down when you want to talk and repeat after me. Whoever it is might be cycling frequencies, so they may not answer you right away, but they clearly want to talk to someone in Emmaus."

Jazz gave him a half-grin and turned toward the unit.

"Mic button pushed."

"Emmaus KC-432R, Kansas CAP. Responding to ARCTIC KC-135R, AK ANG Elmendorf AFB AK. What can I do for you? Over."

Jazz repeated segment by segment after Shane. Dead silence.

"You let go of the button?"

"Oops." Static burst from the speaker. Shane rolled his head on the pillow. After a moment, he told her to send out the same message again.

"Emmaus (static) looking for (static). Can you advise? Over."

"Tell them they're breaking up and to please repeat."

"(Static) Sullivan (static). Please advise. Over."

"I'm sorry, ANG Elmendorf, I can't understand what you're asking. Please repeat. Over." She let go of the button and looked at Shane, who wished he could get up off his bed on the floor to take over but knew he couldn't. "I don't know what to do."

"Try tuning it. The second button from the right, I think."

The static cleared a bit and Jazz tried her message again.

"(Static) Emmaus (static) skip not quite in (static) landing strip (static) week? Over."

Jazz looked at Shane.

"He's acknowledging transmission difficulties, trying to skip the signal off the atmosphere to get hold of us. He probably can't hear you any better than you can hear him. And, I think he wants a landing field. Ours is covered in feet of snow. Tell him that and ask him what he's flying."

"Elmendorf ANG, this is Emmaus CAP." Shane laughed and nodded at how quickly she was picking up the lingo. He braced his ribs against the muscle spasms, resisting curling around them. "Emmaus Airfield is uncleared – repeat not cleared – of snow. What are you hoping to land here? Over."

Static with intermittent words followed.

"Tell them to try at night. We're just wasting battery power right now and that's a lot of time somebody has to spend on the stationary bike." Jazz relayed the information.

"Write down the frequency range and maybe we'll be able to reach them later." Shane hissed, trying to find a comfortable position. He could hear voices in the kitchen.

"Sounds like Alex." Jazz stood. "You up for a visit?"

"A really short one." She disappeared from view. In a minute or two Alex showed up and he and his hired hand Mark sat down on the sofa against the front wall so Shane could see them without twisting.

"What's up?"

"Pete has that flu aftermath." The tall blond farmer stared at his big callused hands.

"Crap. I'm sorry, man." Shane directed this at Mark since he was Pete's father.

"You know he and Poppy got married at Thanksgiving?" Shane stared at Alex for a long minute.

"I did know, but lots of things are foggy right now because of the concussion. I don't think I still have it, but it's just taking time for things to heal."

"Understandable." Mark glanced at Alex. "Maybe this isn't such a good idea."

"He's the only one I know who might be able to help us."

"With what?" Shane wanted to shift positions again, but he knew it would hurt and his pain seemed to freak people out, so he didn't.

"Calvin Johanson stopped breathing. I had an aunt who had polio back when my grandfather was a kid and she needed an iron lung for a while. Remember, we talked about it when we were reading those old magazines a long time ago?"

"Yeah, I actually do remember that. She wouldn't have used that kind though. She would have gone to the hospital and used an actual iron lung. That magazine had a wooden box that did the same thing."

"Do you remember how it was constructed?"

Shane stared at Mark.

"Um – from an article I read when we were 12? No. But we were poking around in my grandfather's library." He pointed to the door at the bottom of the stairs. "Jacob never threw away reading material, so it's probably in there."

"Could you find it?"

"I can't even move, Alex. I don't know how much help --."

"I can look for the magazine." Jazz sat down on the couch by Shane's head. "Would that help?"

An expression of profound relief passed over Mark's dark face and Alex smiled.

"Maybe if you had that to jog your memory, the engineering would make sense." Shane stared at his best friend, gut twisting.

"I don't know." Shane rubbed his forehead, which really hurt now. "I do know it's going to need to be airtight and – I think there were some pumps involved, and …."

"You need to take a nap after your mom gets some food in you and you two need to go because his energy is limited." Jazz touched Shane's bruised shoulder ever so lightly before she stood and ushered them out of his presence. Shane closed his eyes against letting tears fall while she was gone. Jill returned with a bowl of food when Jazz came back.

"Bacon and grits."

"Corn mush." Shane might be overly emotional, in pain, and wanting to sleep for a week, but he still preferred reality to fixing things up with window-dressing. His voice came out husky from the tears and he cleared his throat.

"This is not all on you." Jazz put her hands in her rear jeans pockets. "I'll find the magazine and then we'll go from there. Jace Welton can probably figure it out. You need to rest and heal. We'll work this out without you."

"I want to help. The only thing I can do right now is think, so this should be right up my alley – once I've had a nap."

"And, food." Jill spooned up some of the mush. "Open up. Don't make me do 'airplane-into-the-hangar.'"

Shane sighed and complied because he didn't have the strength to do much more.

Dead End

West of Emmaus, Jericho Township

The relentless wind whipped over the ridge and scoured the snow behind the hotel as Cai Delaney and Joe Kelly wallowed through the drifts toward the ice-encrusted Jericho Well House. Rob took Vint and the body to town, and Murphy headed out on patrol, leaving the city attorney and the police chief as the CSI team. You went to war with the army you had, according to Rob. Cai never planned to be a soldier.

"Hey, over here." Joe's call caused Cai to alter course toward Jusilla's Creek, which now carried the flow of the artesian well that blew its valves after the Pulse fried all its controls. Lower than the surrounding ground, the creek bed barely passed notice, but Joe pointed a gloved hand to follow the marks of a snowmobile that had stopped just shy of the bridge.

"See the footprints? He came up the bank there and merged with Shane's footprints."

"Looks like." Cai tightened the closure on his hood as the cold wind invaded his coat. "Where did it come from?"

He and Joe scanned around the blue-white landscape. The low sun peeked through the taller trees on the Lufgren Farm, casting purple and white bar codes across the snow. Jusilla's mostly ran dry without the spring's contribution, but it once formed part of a vast network of prairie streams, now mostly plowed into fields. Cai let his gaze follow the depressed snow like snake tracks. It turned southward in the patch of woods that embraced the toe of the ridge. He and Joe exchanged glances.

Preparing for this investigation, Cai asked Vint to leave his snowmobile and borrowed one of Alex's. Jusilla's formed one leg of the spring's outflow and another creek followed the toe of Jericho Ridge. The CSI team followed the creek, pausing occasionally to assure they still had the snowmobile tracks in sight. The stream ran behind the Jericho Springs B&B and then along the foot of the slope. No similar tracks joined the single trail as it rounded the end of the ridge. The trail then disappeared under the new bridge at Wolf Creek. Joe pointed to where the trail ran up the bank and followed Old 24. Cai led the way across the snow-covered bridge as they turned westward.

Free of the ridge's deflection, the wind now battered them, made worse by the forward movement of the snowmobiles. Cold soaked through Cai's coat and sweater and settled into his left shoulder. His right hand on the steering yoke grew numb. The trail turned northwestward across fields and continued for some time before it crossed County Road R and disappeared into scoured snow. He powered down.

"What do you think?" Joe stared out across the snow, looking like he'd love to go chasing phantoms. Cai's head felt stuffed with ice and his lips barely moved. This field belonged to Shane, he thought. Out in the unbroken snow, Cai watched the first murder of crows he'd seen since the fall rains circle something, their raucous cries echoing across the snow. Death lay at every turn.

He shivered as much from unaccustomed dark thoughts as the icy blast of winter.

"You and I won't pick up a trail. Lots of people using snowmobiles these days."

"Sorry, the wind. What did you just say?"

Cai rotated his shoulders, feeling his bad one pop. They needed to get in where it was warm before his parents had two hypothermia patients to nurse.

"We're done." His lips felt less wooden. "We won't pick up the trail – not one among dozens. I'll ask Ed Greyeyes to come take a look. He might be able to see what we can't."

A fringe of frost coated Joe's dark eyelashes as he considered the wide expanse of wind-blown snow. Red flared across both cheeks, stark against a fringe of black hair where it worked lose of his cap. Everybody needed a barber these days.

"Does it bother you that a stranger died here, and we aren't going to be able to figure out who did it?"

"Of course, it does, but all we can do is try. Let's head back to the fishing cabin, get warm, compare notes."

They turned wide along the road and chased back toward Jericho Springs. Cai's teeth chattered and his thumbs burned with cold. January's killing time pressed on every side.

Where Is the United Nations?

SullCorp Hub, Columbus, Ohio

UN Evaporated Like Sugar in Rain.

"Where'd you find this article?" Despite the destruction of so many major cities, Julian Raines and his team of hackers and IT specialists worked slowly and resolutely to reestablish the Internet. So far, none of his crew encountered living users, but more archives opened every day.

Connie O'Halloran glanced at her tablet.

"Mises Institute."

"Who are they?"

Connie frowned, consulting her memory which seemed to be in her right frontal lobe.

"Libertarian, Austrian Economics think-tank out of Alabama."

"So not part of the Republic of Afrika?"

"No, not so far. Why do you ask?"

"Well, it sounds like a conspiracy theory. Why would the UN go away?" The computer node for SullCorps

Columbus hub stood quiet with almost everyone gone to lunch. Connie and Julian usually ate later.

"You need to look at the photos and read the article."

The article claimed to be written by a survivor of New York City who reported cannibalism and showed photos of widespread destruction – buildings that looked to be bombed out, including the UN.

"The UN General Council evacuated the city three nights after the Bombs. Other personnel relocated to an undisclosed location before the Pulse. The UN building itself burned the night of the Pulse."

The photographs showed helicopters over the roof of the iconic Manhattan structure which was still intact at that time. Then other photos showed the building with its windows blackened by soot. Whoever Jon Drasines was, he had balls of steel, photographing citizens clashing with Knight Industries black shirts and cops and sometimes other citizens.

"The website also has video. New York City has devolved into a hell hole."

"Not really surprised. I only spent a couple of weeks there. I met some nice people, but I also met some evil monsters. And there were buildings on fire when I left the night of the Pulse. So, this is Manhattan. What about the other boroughs?"

"No idea. Why?"

"Kate's from Brooklyn or Queens." Connie's generous lips smiled easily. "What?"

"I'm not sure if I'm surprised you don't know where her hometown is or if it makes total sense."

Katharine Sullivan, the wife of Joseph Sullivan, a scion of one of the richest families in the world, lived up to her reputation for being cold and aloof. The closest Julian had gotten to her was during their walk out of New York City after the Pulse and he could only guess she was from one of the eastern boroughs based on the accent she'd let slip when she had a mugger under gunpoint.

"She's…mysterious. I might have gotten you a way to get your family here."

"But not for me to get there?"

"Fred doesn't want to let your skills go and he feels you'd all be safer here since SullCorp contracted with the Knights."

"I like my house…my dog."

"Your dog can come. I've seen quite a few people with their pets."

"At this rate, the third floor will just be residential apartments."

"Likely. This is the most defensible place possible." Connie frowned. "What?"

"I guess I don't like collective solutions to anything. I thought I did, but – I trust Fred, but I don't trust the situation."

Julian found himself nodding in agreement.

"We can't go until Joseph is completely well, but yeah --." Joseph Sullivan developed secondary pneumonia as a sequela of what was being called the Lakeland flu. Julian sighed. "The tea leaves hold dark omens if you know what I mean."

"Columbus is our home, but yeah. I feel like my husband is on the dark side of the moon and like the ROA will come knocking on our door any moment."

"That's why I agree with Fred that your family should come here. He's arranged a phone call for you – or, he's working on it anyway. He'll reach out as soon as it is arranged. Provided you agree, he's got two rooms on the third floor for you and them—get you out of the dorm."

"That's good. They took Alexandra's boy to the infirmary last night, you know?" Julian stared into her toffee-colored eyes. "He woke up yesterday with a headache. It just got worse. That's the second one."

"Supposedly it's happening out in the city too. All we can do is what we can do." Julian indicated his screen. "Can you find me any corroboration for this? Has anyone on the node been able to pick up Europe yet?"

"No, which I think is weird. The geo sync satellites should link up to Europe, right?"

"They should. Maybe that should be my focus." Across the room, Merat sat down at his computer, the first one back from lunch. "I should go meet Andrea for lunch. Don't forget to eat."

"I won't, I promise."

"Keep looking for stories like this. We need to find out what's going on out there."

"Will do. Hey, Julian, do you think it's a bad thing the UN went away?"

While Julian contemplated his answer, Merat turned in his chair.

"Since when has the UN ever done anything worthwhile? My parents lived through Kosovo. The UN is useless. Was and will be if it still exists."

"Screwed up in Korea too," Connie added.

"I don't know. I'm not a very political person." Julian thought better than to mention that as a convicted felon still on parole, he'd not been able to vote in nearly a decade. He'd never gotten a chance to vote since he was only 19 when he went to prison. "I don't know what they could have done anyway. Merat, what are you working on?"

"Trying to connect with New England."

"A worthy goal. If you find Canada in that...."

"Sure."

"Do you know anyone in Kosovo?"

"Um, yeah. I have cousins. Why?"

"We're trying to connect with Europe." Connie jotted something in her notebook.

"I could try sending an email. I haven't thought to check my Hotmail account to see if it's there. I'll let you know if it is. What should I say to them if I'm successful?"

"Checking in. Let them know you're okay, condition of the fam, ask for news."

"Okay." Julian wondered if Merat, who was around his age, would make a good node manager if he decided to pull stakes. Connie would as well, but she sounded like she might want to bug out too. Merat's mother worked for SullCorp and she and Merat shared an apartment on the third floor. Merat's father, a US Army soldier, had been gone to Miristan when the bombs went off. They'd want to stay here so he could find them.

"Better run." Connie nodded at the clock on the wall. "Andi's going to kick your skinny white-boy butt."

"Yes, ma'am." Julian hurried off to meet his suitemate, thinking about the possibilities of trying to reach Europe.

Short-Circuited

Lake Washington, Seattle

Freezing cold water washed down his back, rolled him over, tumbled him in the surf. The sky briefly flared blue and then faded to gray. Was it the sky? Might it be a ceiling? He remembered making sheet forts with his brothers and they always liked the blue one because it reminded them of the out of doors. He remembered their freckled faces and brandy-wine hair, the gales of laughter. He tried to think of their names, but the stubborn words wouldn't come, and the icy water washed over him again, stealing his breath and wiping away all memory.

The bright light might be the sun, baking his brain in the noonday heat. He couldn't close his eyes against it as a headache threatened. He'd felt this way in a faraway land, waiting behind a boulder on a beach for it seemed like days. What had he been waiting for? Time to pass, people to come, blood to spill. In memory, he'd spent the time scanning the horizon. Now, he tried to look around, but his eyes wouldn't cooperate, so he only saw the blazing sun as the hours ticked by.

Cold and dark, time to tell. Sinking lower. Air to breathe. Don't forget to breathe.

January 2

Coroner's Inquest

Emmaus Medical Center

Marnie Callahan, MD, defacto lead doctor of the Emmaus Medical Center. called in Amisi Ceylon and Nick Kletti as her coroner's inquest panel and they'd spent the night before pouring over the evidence for this early morning meeting. Ami was a virologist with emergency room experience who had coincidentally rolled up to Emmaus after the Bombs. She'd been helping at the EMC. Nick had been a neurologist in another life and currently lived in an enclave within the greater Emmaus community. The three of them stood on the far side of the body, wrapped in heavy jackets. Rob, Cai, and Joe huddled in their coats on the other side of the gurney. The coal stove at the other end of the building just couldn't get heat to this far exam room. Marnie supposed the lack of heat would keep the body fresh for a bit longer. She resolved to make her report brief so everyone could warm up by the heater.

"To start – he's John Doe. No ID. So far, nobody has recognized him. He's a mixed-race male, approximately late 30s – Asian and black. Medium height, medium build – good musculature and he's been eating regularly, which makes him a unicorn." Her audience didn't laugh so she kept going. "He has several interesting scars – bullet and stab wounds and I'm going to guess that a parent used a cigarette as a punishment."

Cai winced. Joe sighed heavily. Rob just waited for her to continue.

"He was rendered unconscious by blunt force trauma to the right parietal lobe and then he was smothered. I found pillow material in his airway. I've got Sharon McLaughlin trying to figure out what fabric it might be. That may help."

As a quilter and fiber artist, Sharon's forensic investigation represented the closest to CSI they had. Marnie glanced from Nick to Ami, inviting them to join the presentation.

"He would have died from the head injury," Nick explained. "There was penetration of bone fragments into the dura mater and subdural bleeding into the brain tissue of the right parietal lobe. By the size of the hematoma, I would guess whoever struck him took up to an hour to decide if they should kill him for real, but he would have been disabled by that level of damage regardless of what followed."

Nick glanced at Ami.

"We're none the three of us a medical examiner or forensics expert, but there were defensive and offensive wounds on his hands and forearms. He fought back. I think there might have been at least two assailants – one right-handed and the other left-handed. That much I can tell from the pattern of bruising. I found one identifying mark. She tapped a finger to the photo that a tattoo with a star and a circle formed of two crescents."

"Any idea what it means?" Rob passed the photo to Cai.

"None. I'm not a tattoo person."

Cai shrugged and passed it to Joe who just frowned.

"It was high up on his forearm, inner elbow. I think that's all I have." Ami leaned back against the counter, shoved her hands into her coat pockets.

"A lot of what might have been forensic evidence was destroyed by lying in the snow for a few days and the body freezing." Marnie just wanted to make that clear.

"Joe, you got anything?" Marnie figured the police chief should be entitled to a report.

"I don't think he was killed behind the hotel. We found a snowmobile track by the well house. Whoever it was dismounted and, hard to tell, but maybe deposited the body behind the hotel. Maybe that's just because I think he was killed somewhere else and then dumped there. Hard to tell with the comings and goings of tire tracks and snowmobiles in the area, but there weren't signs of a struggle in the yard there."

"That's consistent with the freezing pattern." Nick leaned against the counter. "I think he was dead when he was set outside."

"So where'd the snowmobile track go afterward?" Rob jotted a note.

"It backtracked on itself." Cai sighed. "It rounded the end of the ridge and then followed along the creek northwest. When it crossed a road, we lost track of it. I asked Ed Greyeyes to take a look. He says he'll get back with us."

"Anything else, Joe?"

"I didn't study for this. We always figured the state cops would take over if we found a dead body. Or the county sheriff. I can't tell you anything about bodies that you don't know from hunting and serving in the military. There's no doubt evidence out there in the snow that a CSI could uncover, but I'm not one."

"I understand. You're what we have, and Bart couldn't have done any better. Cai, you got anything besides the snowmobile?"

"Um, I'm completely new to this. I took a criminal law class, but it didn't prepare me for a homicide investigation, but – there are no labels in his clothes – not even his shoes. Along with the missing ID – I tried to fingerprint him, and I don't think freezing after death would remove the fingerprints entirely."

"I thought it was something akin to freezer burn," Ami announced. "What else could it be?"

"Some classes of criminals remove their fingerprints with acid." This came from Nick. Marnie assumed he'd learned that during his years in prison.

"It's like a Le Carre novel." Rob frowned at the sheet-covered body.

"There is that possibility, right?" Father stared at son a moment before Cai continued. "Shane's not the only one hiding secrets. No offense to you, Ami, but several of the people at the B&B are spooks, right?"

"I probably shouldn't confirm that, but I don't know this man and that means he's not from the B&B."

"Could others be hiding somewhere else in the community?"

"Not to my knowledge and – well, frankly, the others speak rather freely in front of me and I think if there were another safe house here, they'd have let it slip by now."

Cai picked up the sheet to look at the man's face, setting the sheet back in its place, tongue playing with a chill blain on his lip.

"I suggest I start interviewing everyone in the area. Use my legal skills. Joe and I can each work on it in the course of our duties and see what we find."

Rob nodded. Marnie shifted on her stool. Easily sanitized, metal stools sucked the heat right out of a body, even a pregnant one. She'd love to share that terrible pun with her husband, except Cai's face held a Golden-Retriever-focused-on-a-duck look that meant he wouldn't get the joke.

"There is one possibility you might want to consider." Nick frowned at the sheet. "Suppose this man came from outside the community."

"How would he get here?"

"Don't know for certain, but perhaps the same way I got here from the compound – snowmobile."

"Then his assailant kept the machine?" Cai looked thoughtful as Nick nodded then shrugged.

"But why would he come to Emmaus?" Rob fingered his beard. "We're barely feeding ourselves, it's cold, we're not near anything."

Nobody said anything for a fist of heartbeats, then Cai spoke up.

"Spooks convention, maybe."

All five of the other heads in the room raised. Rob opened his mouth and closed it, swallowed.

"Ami, how did you know to come to the Sullivan house?"

"Javi told me to."

"How'd he know?"

"Grant Rigby is his handler, as he was Shane's."

Now Cai straightened.

"They had orders to come here?"

"I really wouldn't know. Javi didn't trust me at first, so he didn't tell me his thinking." She stared at one of the glass-fronted cabinets. "That's not exactly true. When we got here, they vetted us, so I don't think they expected Javi to roll up there, and they certainly didn't expect me."

"But this is a CSA property and that means Spook Central." Cai still stared at her as if asking a question.

"I don't think so. Grant seems to have come here as a safe zone for his family. He let Javi in, but I don't think he *wants* anyone else." Marnie mulled over the stress on the verb. Were there others at the B&B that Rigby didn't want? Perhaps Ami's slight accent caused her to think that. Ami grew up in Egypt but lived in the United States for more than half her life. Her accent was difficult to pin down.

"And Shane?" Rob looked tense.

"I don't know your son except in the most casual of ways. He's come to the house a few times. They go secret, behind closed doors, and he doesn't stay long."

"Include the B&B on your canvass list." Cai and Joe nodded. "How long can we hold this body at low temperatures?"

"Maybe a week." Marnie swallowed bile. "I'm not sure what more we can get out of it. We just don't have the equipment."

"Try to hold it for a few days. We'll bury it when we have to." Rob looked from Cai to Joe. "When Shane's awake, show him the photos."

"I was thinking about showing him the clothes too. Maybe Rigby, Chavez, or Shane know this guy."

"I can ask them." Ami held out a hand for one of the polaroids.

"Given how close the B&B is to the Hotel, maybe someone there saw something – comings and goings." Ami nodded at Cai's suggestions. "We should also ask Alex."

"I'll go up and ask Ren if I can check around his property. It's possible someone came through his estate and dropped down over the ridge. There'd be snowmobile tracks possibly."

"I think if I ask nicely, mayor, Ren would allow me to do that." Joe's mild voice reminded he was supposed to be the local constabulary. Rob nodded. Marnie abandoned the stool.

"Cai, you want to help me put him in the furnace room?"

Cai pushed and she pulled. Because of the heating situation, the furnace room was the farthest from the coal heater and the coldest thanks to the cold-air makeups for the furnace that stopped working after the Pulse.

"This was a brutal murder. Be careful of who and how you ask questions."

Cai paused, cocking his head at her.

"Yeah. It's a dangerous world we live in now."

"And, much as I wish it weren't true – finding a dead body behind your brother's hotel and Shane isn't involved – pretty long odds on that."

"Yeah, I don't want to have that discussion. Guess who I found in Beulah yesterday?" She waited, not really in a mood to play 20 Questions. "Win Reese took over one of the abandoned houses there."

"What happened to Bob?"

"No idea. Win found a pantry nobody had raided and he's okay for a while. He says he's moving on as soon as his leg's up to it."

"What about his wife and kids?"

"She's putting out at Liberty's soiree."

"My father the pimp." Marnie sighed trying to contain her judgment, unsuccessfully.

"How's your mom?"

"Stubborn. The flu has her laid pretty low, but she's still independent as the day is long – and somehow she isn't out of cigarettes yet."

"Smokers. Did I ever thank you for quitting before we started dating?"

"Nope, but I figured you were grateful." When she and Shane dated, he'd said just kissing her was sometimes like licking an ashtray. She couldn't mention that because it caused division between the brothers. Cai slid his hands into her jacket and pulled her close, lowering his head to kiss her.

"Honey, not over the dead body."

He winced, then quirked a weird smile.

"I guess you can get used to anything." He'd been on body duty--cleaning out the dead from houses—since before Christmas. "Let's take this to the lounge."

As they emerged from the freezing furnace room to the chilly hallway, Marnie sneezed.

"Danged change of humidity." She rubbed her belly where she distinctly felt something growing. "I'm serious, Cai. Don't risk your life asking the wrong people questions."

"I won't. But who do you mean by the wrong people?"

"Ami's partner is scarier than Shane who can't hurt you right now. I can only assume the man he works for is also. Those guys out at the Compound. Hell, even Rafe Conopher has gone over to the dark side since he killed that USDA officer on his lawn. How's Dell, anyway?"

"I think he and Leisha are adjusting to killing their neighbors on their front lawn."

"And Kix?"

"It's got to be painful to see your kid unable to move. Any closer to a treatment?"

"No. That's Ami's bailiwick. He'll recover or he won't. We're just lucky the cannabis oil seems to be working on his seizures. I'm pretty sure we have two other cases – a kid with a paralyzed arm who seems to be stabilizing and Poppy's husband who has the same symptoms that killed Cal Johanson."

"Oh, no! That's -- ." Cai shook himself. "We don't know yet, right? You haven't had enough of these cases to know for sure."

"You're right. Better not to be doomsayers just yet. His symptoms are progressing much slower. Maybe we'll figure something out before he can't breathe or maybe he'll recover before that happens. Hope plays better than darkness."

They hugged. The building seemed quiet this time of night since they had no patients onsite. Marnie and her staff were stretched too thin to give 24-hour care to any but the most critical. She anticipated that as the secondary flu cases stacked up, she might never go home.

"I'm off to interview people. Remember to eat."

"I will. The baby doesn't give me the choice anymore."

"You work too hard."

"That's also not a choice. I love you. Take care out there."

He kissed her and let himself out the door. Given the time of night, she flipped the lock to closed and turned to the pile of charts from yesterday that hadn't been processed because actual patients intervened.

Hospitality

Sullivan B&B, Jericho Springs

"It's so great to be out of that room." Captain Elena Brousard took a plate from the stack on the counter. "I understand why you were reluctant, but after a week in four walls, it's nice to see other faces." Her honeyed accent assured Grant she hailed from New Orleans just as her bio claimed, but he still didn't entirely trust the two soldiers who'd appeared out of nowhere just a week ago.

"I'm right here." Sergeant Kevin Perez cast a sheepish smile at his superior officer. Grant supposed they might be lovers. It wasn't unusual on long stakeouts for men and women to pair up – hence, Chavez and Dr. Ceylon, although Grant suspected they held more depth of feeling than either of them would admit. Chavez looked lost without her, sitting by the window blinking out into the morning brightness. Emily asked him if he wanted juice. Unless you knew what to look for, Javi faked seeing fairly well, but with extra people in the kitchen, he was naturally nervous to move around. He asked for eggs and bacon too. Jim laughed.

"You got something against my pancakes?"

"Nope, just felt like trying something new."

"I should take a plate down to Ron." Grant began spooning eggs and bacon.

"I'll do it." Eden held out her hand. "I'll tell the girls to come upstairs for breakfast."

Jim grabbed the butter dish and began slathering butter between pancakes, singing under his breath. Grant smiled to hear him feeling lighter. He'd been sad since his wife's death and it seemed like he'd gotten older in the space of weeks, but he seemed to better today, and Grant rejoiced to see it. Eden laughed, turning toward the door to the hallway where the stairs to the basement were.

"Grant, can you take plates to Brian and April? I wonder --." Emily's question was lost as something punched Grant in the shoulder, throwing him back against the counter. Emily screamed as smoke trailed up from Perez's silencer. Broussard drew her gun and Travis hit the floor like a dropped 2x4. Perez's 9mm clattered to the floor as he choked, scrabbling at Javi's hand gripping his windpipe. Emily moved toward Grant, eyes wide at the blood blossoming from his shoulder. Every instinct screamed to stop Broussard as she moved to follow Eden, but Grant was in the grip of bullet shock and Javi wasn't close enough. Jim flowed toward Broussard, surprisingly quick for one so old. The door swung closed as he struggled with her, butter knife aimed into her ribs. The door swung open to give them a brief glimpse as a deft sweep of the knife caused dark red blood to spurt.

Eden screamed. Javi dropped Perez into an innervated twitching heap on the linoleum and moved to catch Grant as he wobbled.

"Dad!" Emily turned toward the door and Grant's heart thudded in fear. Through the open door, Grant watched as Jim lowered Broussard's twitching body to the floor. Javi assisted Grant to the hallway where Broussard gasped in a spreading pool of blood.

"What the hell?" Grant dropped to his knees.

"They can't --." Broussard choked. "The old order must die. They had to …."

Her eyes grew unfocused as blood soaked through Grant's pants.

"What in the world?" Ron Patterson demanded, appearing at the basement door, 9mm in hand. "What happened?"

"Where are my girls?" Emily moved toward him, but he held up a restraining hand.

"I put them in the bunk room, told Miranda to stay put."

"We'll explain it to you … later." Grant wiped the sweat off his forehead. Javi stopped checking Broussard's pulse.

"She's gone."

Far out in front of the house, they heard banging on the gate.

Groceries

Emmaus

A single sustained blast of wind swirled ice particles in the air by the off-ramp as Ren Sullivan dismounted his chestnut Morgan gelding. He'd spent the last couple of days rounding up Count Chocula and assuring the townspeople he had trucks of supplies on the way. The young man who exited the lead truck pulled his hood with both hands and snapped it closed before redonning his gloves. It had to be -20 degrees. Thank God the wind calmed from yesterday.

"Sir."

"Where are the other two trucks?" Ren stared at the four he could see.

"No idea, sir. We lost one two days out and the other yesterday. There are marauders on the highway. Both trucks were the last ones in the convoy." Ren sighed. "And the roads are pretty hairy between Hutchinson and here, sir. I was stationed in Delta Alaska for three years and the roads there were better."

"Yeah, Alaska DOT had working plows." Ren decided to hold a sense of humor about the lost trucks. You couldn't make an omelet without breaking some eggs and the "marauders" were probably as hungry as the people in Emmaus. He'd get more trucks on the road and make sure they traveled with heavier armament. He hoped the drivers were safe. He'd told everyone to look to their own safety over the food supplies. If they showed up, would he put them back to work as drivers? Well, with partners he could trust. Truth to tell, in times like these, the truckers might simply have turned out of line to sell to the highest bidder.

The town guards at the gate wakened him with a radio call when the sun wasn't yet up. They required his presence to let the trucks in because Rob kept tight border security. Most towns along the way barely had the strength to wave hello and goodbye, but Emmaus experienced a confluence of lucky breaks and Rob hadn't tried to collectivize the food stores, so folks here were doing a bit better than many other towns. Hence, border security here required Ren to vouch for his drivers. These guards were Army personnel and they seemed kind of bossy, but National Guardsman Murphy told them to allow it. Ren wondered what might develop in the coming months if the Army didn't want to comply with Rob and Shane's leadership. He'd had Knights to fight back against the Army in Wichita, but here in Emmaus, it was just townspeople and a handful of National Guard.

A half-hour later, Ren stood in the back warehouse of Huffman's Market talking with Jos Osimowitz, grandson of the owner. A big coal stove barely warmed the cavernous space to above freezing. Rob Delaney's brilliance showed here. Unwilling to play God with the food supply, he'd set up a system of taking large windfall shipments to Huffman's so that people could trade for it. The Osimowitz family took a cut of the shipment in payment and managed a circulation of the available goods in the community. Private enterprise in the apocalypse probably wasn't flourishing, but it still functioned. That the teenage grandson of the owner wore a gun in a shoulder-holster even inside the warehouse suggested not everyone in the town wanted to trade for food.

"Where's Mae?" he asked as Jos told Canaday, the lead driver, where to deposit the goods. "Ty, after you get unloaded, maybe you could help this young man stock the shelves."

"Of course, sir."

Jos looked like Ren punched him in the gut.

"You all right, son?"

"Granmae died."

"What?"

"Yeah. Of the flu."

"I'm sorry. She was a fine woman, a sharp business mind. How you doing here by yourself?"

"She trained me well. It's a big empty building though."

Ren nodded. He remembered his house feeling like that after Lottie died. Even though Joseph, Katharine, and Allison were there, the house echoed.

"It helps to have something to do." The boy looked older than his years. "How's Allison?"

"I just tracked her down out at Vance's. So much has changed while I was away. Hard to believe. A world without Huffy." Jos nodded, sucking in a deep breath. "Should I ask where your mother is?"

"She was in Atlanta, I think. Can't imagine that she wasn't."

"And your uncle Stan?"

"Mara Wells, I think. He was swinging by every few days to check on me and then the storms started, and I guess he can't get through."

"I've got a Tucker." Jos's young eyes narrowed. "It's like a giant snowmobile – enclosed. I can take you over there if you want."

Jos grinned, shaking his head.

"Why? She's been dead nearly a month and I'm taking care of what needs to be taken care of."

"How old are you?"

"Fifteen going on twenty-five, sir. I think we're all growing up fast. I think you're going to be surprised at who Allison is now."

"No doubt. Let me know if there's anything I can do for you. That Tucker will be here for a couple of more days and then it's swinging over to Garden City. Might take a bit of time for it to return."

"Noted, but someone has to be here to run the store now that I have stock. Don't hold the – whatever a Tucker is – on my account."

"Tucker's like a giant snowmobile with a cab."

"Ah. Interesting. I better get to supervising or things will be a mess and I hate messes."

"I'll get out of your way then."

Ren headed toward the door into the alley, thinking he really should go see Allison now that he had a moment to breathe. Jos's warning that she might be different now echoed in the scared parts of his soul.

Taste of Lies

Sullivan B&B, Jericho Springs

The morning air tasted metallic as Cai Delaney slid out of the Subaru to bang on the gate at the Jericho B&B. The autopsy filtered through his mind. Even if the murder victim shouldn't have been in the township, nobody had a right to deprive him of his life. Unless he was hurting someone and then that might be different, but then why would the person who killed him hide the body?

The hope of a productive interview faltered as Cai waited, shivering in the still air. Maybe they all slept, or they ignored him to cover up a murder. He just didn't know enough to be certain and when he'd tried to ask Shane, his brother had said "They don't really like visitors" as if that solved the basic question. Shane kept pushing himself too hard and then needed a full day of sleep to recover. New Year's Eve had been too much and Alex and Mark visiting yesterday had just wiped him out. Couldn't people just figure out that Shane couldn't help them right now, not when he needed to recover from his injuries?

A woman finally came to the gate, her blond hair mostly hidden beneath an indigo knit hat and a big jacket.

"What can I do for you?"

Cai introduced himself and explained why he was there. Emily Rigby pulled her coat closer around her body. Defensive or cold? Cai felt cold and her nose glowed pink. He didn't want to believe people were defensive around him.

"We don't know anything about that."

"Can I come in and ask questions, please?"

"Is this an official investigation?"

He sensed a 4th amendment challenge shaping up. He supposed Rob could issue warrants in the absence of a judge.

"It is. We don't suspect anyone here, but I still have to ask the questions."

They entered by way of the side kitchen entrance. He could see the front door was used, so his curiosity piqued. A familiar horse and cart waited in the side yard as did a snowmobile.

"Brian or April Halloran here?"

"April is working with our son Dylan right now and Brian is about somewhere."

Brian knew Javi from the raid that freed April from sexual slavery a couple of months ago, so that was plausible. Cai stashed his gloves in his coat pocket and pulled out his notebook, remembering that Dylan was the Rigbys' son who Ami referred to as Patient Zero for the neurological disorder that appeared to be sweeping through town. The kitchen felt pleasantly warm from a wood stove in the corner. Fitted out as a high-end kitchen from a bygone year, the room looked and smelled clean, as did Emily Rigby. Although embarrassed that he hadn't bathed since before New Year's, Cai understood it to mean the Rigbys had running water and electricity, even if he couldn't hear the generator running right now. He smelled something incredible as he inhaled the warm air.

"Would you like some coffee?"

"*Real* coffee? Oh, God, thank you. I'd *love* that."

The house felt like people inhabited it in utter silence. While she hung up her coat and cap, Cai sat at the table in the bay window. Someone cleared the breakfast dishes, but there were still crumbs on the table. Soon he wrapped his chapped hands around the steaming mug as she offered sugar and powdered milk. Heaven!

"Have you seen any activity over by the hotel?"

"People come and go. Shane Delaney – I guess he's your brother." Cai nodded. "He's so much darker than you."

"He takes after our uncle and grandmother – Greyeyes blood. I got my coloring from the Delaney and Faraday sides of the family. Go on."

"Shane usually stops by when he's checking on the property. We haven't seen him since he got hurt, of course." Something flickered behind her golden-brown eyes.

"Would that cause you to spend more time looking at the hotel?"

"It wouldn't cause me, but it would cause Grant and Javi. They haven't mentioned much though."

"Are they here?" Cai saw the flicker again.

"Javi is. Grant's out. I don't know that I can help you. I can get Javi for you if you need me to."

"I'd appreciate that."

"Stay here."

She fled the room. Cai felt a palpable sense that she didn't like him in her house. Chavez's formidable gun skills kept him from following her, although his sense of mystery wanted to. While he waited, he tried to stretch his hearing. He knew from Brian that there were two younger children here as well as the grandfather. How could a packed house be so silent? Also, how was it that the table hadn't been wiped, but it looked like someone had run a mop over the floor in a couple of places?

Javier Chavez followed Emily into the room. Tall and panther-like, Chavez always appeared ready to kill any threat that might present itself and he considered the whole world a threat. He leaned against the counter, muscular arms across his built chest.

"What do you want?"

"We found a dead body over at the hotel."

"She mentioned. You ask your brother about it?"

"It's been since he was hurt so not really. I kind of have a hint of what you do here. This guy had no labels in his clothes and his fingerprints were burned off."

Chavez's eyes twittered.

"So you thought you'd ask the intelligence agency? That's deep cover shit. CSA just manipulates the cyber records so we don't have to mutilate ourselves. No idea who he is."

"Maybe this will jog your memory."

Cai held out a polaroid. Chavez blinked at it, reluctantly took and stared at it with narrowed eyes. Cai swept his gaze down the assassin's body, taking in the clean shirt, the flecks of what might be blood on his jeans.

"Still don't know him." He passed the photo to Emily who shook her head, clearly communicating with Javi. She passed it back to Cai.

"Ami has a copy. Maybe you could have Rigby and the others take a look?

"Sure. Look, we notice when there's activity over at the hotel, but it's not our main focus, and we haven't seen anything in the last week."

"What is your main focus?"

Chavez straightened from the counter.

"None of your business. We're kind of busy right now. I'll ask the others to look at the photo, maybe run it through a database, but you need to go now."

"I should talk to the others."

"Everybody's gone." Emily didn't move to block the door to the rest of the house, but she clearly wanted to.

"You said your son was working with April."

"Yes, but Dylan wouldn't know anything, and he couldn't tell you if he did because of his speech disability."

Cai looked from one to the other and realized they'd closed ranks. He wasn't getting anything more out of them. He drained the coffee cup, savoring it to the last drop. Thanking them for their time and heaven in a cup, he put his notebook back into his pocket and left by the side exit.

Brian Halloran fed his horse some hay and seemed startled to see Cai. Enslaved together at Hutchinson, they became fast friends. Brian's walnut-colored skin looked pale out here in the cold.

"Hey."

"Hey. Anything been going on around here I should know about?"

"Like?"

"Suspicious activity at the hotel or even over here." Brian glanced toward the hotel on the other side of the creek. You couldn't see it through the high fence. Why had nobody ever noticed the B&B had cut itself off from the creek that was its best feature? Brian frowned.

"No, nothing."

He breathed out entirely too much fog. The cold didn't make Cai's hair stand on end that way. Spidey-senses?

"What's going on, man?"

"Nothing I can share. You know, medical stuff." Cai stared at his friend for a long moment, considering all the possibilities of why Brian would hide stuff from him. He didn't have a clue.

"Right. Well, I guess that's it then." Cai couldn't force Brian to share, although he hoped Brian would be more forthcoming when he visited him at his house tonight.

And maybe Ami would be more forthcoming. The Land Rover in the driveway suggested she was here. Something was going on and it felt … current, but he guessed asking the same questions over and over again expecting different answers was insanity. He'd have to wait to get the right people alone in a different setting.

Wicked Witch

Seattle

The wicked witch cackled and flapped as he stared unblinkingly at the sky. Time out of time. Sometimes he was home with the familiar people with their brandy-wine hair and sometimes he was floating in cold, staring at the sky, watching the wicked witch preen. He felt his life ebbing away beneath him, trickling away into the sand as cold water enveloped his body. Other times, darkness wrapped him in nothingnesss and he only knew the sound of droning, interspersed with the measured tones of his mother as she soothed him through a fever. He couldn't feel her hand upon his forehead, and he wished she'd give him a drink of water, but he couldn't begin to ask – floating away in icy water, chest heavy and growing heavier.

Breathing Box

Lufgren Farm, Jericho Township

"People come and go from the old townsite all the time." Alex applied a strip of oakum to the edge of the plywood box he and Mark built, tapping brads into place. He became Cai's brother-in-law when he married Keri the summer before, but they'd known each other their whole lives. Mark Ramirez was a relative stranger but had become family when his son married Alex's sister in November. "Shane seemed pretty wiped. Anything we can do to help with that?"

"Ask Marnie or Mom. I'm not sure. So, you just don't pay any attention?"

"One of the pleasures of not being a townie is that I don't have to care about my neighbors. Except for the B&B, the closest are the other side of the airfield and the far side of the ridge. I can't see them, I can't hear them, and it would be silly to pay a lot of attention to them." That seemed odd since most of the farmers west of Beulah Ridge were Alex's cousins. "I've got work to do."

Mark applied another strip and Alex moved on.

"What are you doing?" Cai tried to imagine what the box might be for. So far it was three-sided, about half as long as he was tall and open at both ends.

"My son is getting weaker. The paralysis is moving higher. The Johanson boy died of respiratory failure." Mark's explanation didn't help Cai any.

"I had a great aunt who had polio back in the day, so I got to thinking about the iron lung she used while she was recuperating." Now Alex's explanation began to make sense. "If we can get him through the hard part, maybe he'll live."

"What are you going to use for a pump?"

"We don't know yet. That's why we visited Shane. When he and I were kids, we read this article about the wooden iron lung and how it worked. It said it used a pump, but it didn't explain how it worked. Or we don't remember. Jazz is going to look in your grandpa's library and Shane said he'd think about it between naps."

"I'm driving around town asking questions about a murder. While I'm at it, I can put the question to the mechanics among us."

"Sounds good. Sorry, but we need to finish this. It needs to be ready if the worst happens."

"I'm going up to the house to ask Keri and Alice if they've seen anything."

They nodded, but their attention was on their work and Cai understood that. Keri folded laundry when he came into the kitchen.

"It must feel like joy to live with running water and electricity." The "coffee" was soy, however.

"I don't want to lord it over you, big bro. What's up?"

Cai explained. Keri and Alice listened and answered his questions. Alice ground corn while he talked. Neither of them had seen anything.

"Lots of people in and out of there lately." Keri finished the basket of laundry and poured herself a cup of warm nutty liquid. "Josh Callahan is the only suspicious one I've seen."

"When and how often?"

"I think he's meeting with the head of that group at the B&B. They usually meet over near the well house."

"How do you know that?"

"There's a trail of sorts along our fence line that parallels the Jericho Road. I go running that way."

Cai considered the flecks of blood on Chavez's jeans. He needed explanations, but Marnie's warning echoed loudly in his mind.

"You ever hear what they're talking about?"

"No. I don't get close enough and you wouldn't either. Josh isn't the same kid he was before, you know?"

Cai nodded. He turned at the loud clatter of feet on the stairs. Poppy came from the living room, her blond hair loose around her torso, a scowl on her face. She waved at Cai and started signing to Keri.

"I'm sorry. She's going too fast." Alice looked expectantly at Keri, who signed a few questions to her teenaged sister-in-law.

"Pete has pooped himself and the smell was too much for her."

The smell was too much…for the quintessential farmgirl?!! Alice got up to take care of her son. Keri signed something and Poppy signed back. Emmaus had a large Deaf community because of the extended Lufgren clan, so Cai knew some sign, but he couldn't keep up with a free-flowing conversation.

"She says the lights were on all night over there last night. Do you know about the helicopter that landed at the airfield a week ago?"

"Helicopter?" Cai knew nothing about that. With Shane down, the aviation buffs were in short supply suddenly. "What sort of helicopter?" Keri interpreted, signing just moments behind what Cai said. Poppy glanced at him with an expression that said he was stupid. "I don't know, but it was painted like the military. Maybe Shane can help you."

It was more than the hearing members of the family had been able to provide.

"Would Pete have seen anything?"

"Pete's head hurts all the time," Poppy said through Keri. "And he can't even sit up, so no, he hasn't been looking out of windows."

"*I'm sorry for Pete*," Cai signed. Poppy nodded and rubbed blood-shot eyes. "I'd better go. I've got a lot of miles to cover before dark. If you hear or see anything…."

"Of course." Keri left off interpreting for Poppy to walk Cai to the door. Brother and sister hugged one another. "I hope you'll pray for us too. We're working against the clock and he's getting weaker."

"You know I will. I wish there were something more I can do, but I'll let the local mechanics know there's a need."

"Thanks."

The wind scoured the driveway, piling snow against the side of the barn. Cai stared around at the familiar yard, thinking he'd never seen so much snow. The storm barn's arc roof was ... yeah, he couldn't see it. Even the sauna was now barely visible, hidden in feet of snow.

Winter had to break soon before the cold and snow ended them all. Cai shivered, feeling the wolves surrounding them. So many people dying of starvation, cold, and disease, and yet the murder of a stranger sucked the hope out of him. To keep ahead of the dark thoughts, Cai kept moving, kept asking questions, kept gathering evidence. He *needed* to find out how this man died because nobody deserved to die alone and unmourned.

What Happened

Inside the Sullivan B&B before Cai Arrives

She'd stopped the bleeding, although she couldn't be sure about internal hemorrhage. Travis shivered as Eden sponged his forehead. Her hands shook slightly, but the girl didn't cower from blood or stress. With Ami's instruction, she helped to roll him on his left side, backboard, and all. That his legs weren't moving told Ami a lot that she wished she didn't know.

"Call if his condition changes. He might need to puke. Some people don't handle blood transfusions so well."

Eden nodded. Her young face displayed an indomitable will. They built them tough in Alaska. Some of it might be the Aleut bone structure – powerful jawline and broad cheekbones. Her eyes looked worried.

Ami stripped off her exam gloves and went to the bathroom off the central hall where Emily and Javi dressed Grant's shoulder wound.

"What the hell happened here?"

Ami spent the night at the clinic for Marnie's coroner's inquest and she'd arrived home to find mayhem -- Brian,

April, and Eden trying to stop Travis from bleeding out and Javi loading two dead bodies into the motorhome. Unusual activity even for the Jericho Springs B&B. The soldiers who'd sheltered with them for over a week died suddenly and brutally.

"We'll have an after-action review once we're past the crisis." Grant's uninjured hand gripped the edge of the vanity with white knuckles as Emily followed Javi's instructions for stitching his back closed. She'd already bandaged the front.

"No, I think we need to discuss it now."

"Get out," Grant hissed. "This isn't a democracy. You don't get included in the management decisions. Leave the room."

Ami prepared to argue, but Javi captured her arm with a big hand and dragged her out of the bathroom.

"Let go of me!" She tried to jerk her arm from his grip, but her efforts proved futile. Circling the blood pool in the hallway, he stopped when they got to the living room, but he didn't let go.

"Shut up! You don't know what happened and your doctor-god complex is showing."

"You broke that man's neck, Javi."

"That's what I do when people try to kill me or my team. You weren't too unhappy with those skills when we first met, and Travis probably doesn't object that the guy who put a bullet in his spine died slowly suffocating over a minute or two. He deserved it!"

Ami sobered. She knew this side of Javi. She'd seen him do this before they even knew each other. She'd grown complacent to the ice-cold assassin she increasingly loved. Which was the real Javi? The warm lover in her bed who laughed at her Egyptian-flavored jokes or the human Terminator who refused to be stopped even as he was going blind. Did it matter?

"I'm right about his legs, yeah?"

"I think so, yes. Could be shock, but…. What happened?"

"I don't have time, Ami. We can't keep those bodies out there. We don't know they don't have trackers on them. I--."

They both turned toward the door as they heard banging on the gate. While they decided what to do, Jim came halfway down the stairs, his shirt and pants still covered with blood.

"It's Delaney's brother." He'd knifed the female pilot. Ami assumed he'd gone for the splenic artery. They'd have to scrub the hallway floor. She tried to remember the chemical that removed blood trace evidence. Emily came out of the bathroom, scanning her hands.

"Can you handle this?" Javi asked. "I need to go change my shirt before I interact with anyone." A smear of blood ruined the gray t-shirt.

"I'm going to tell him that most everyone is out. Ami, can you get Grant upstairs? Jim, tell Eden she has to keep Travis quiet."

"Where are the girls?" Ami asked.

"Still in the safe room." Emily steeled her backbone, sidestepping the bloodstain on the wood floor, heading toward the kitchen. "Ron's staying with them. Jim, I need this floor clean. It's the only place to meet with him."

The swinging door revealed April and Brian Callahan were already taking care of the kitchen floor, their young faces set in grim determination.

This just keeps getting worse. Now a convicted traitor is babysitting. Ami headed to the bathroom to get Grant while Javi headed upstairs on Jim's heels. Grant met her at the door, his face grey and hands shaking.

"Who's out there?"

"Cai Delaney. It's probably about the murder they found behind the hotel. Did we have anything to do with that?"

Grant raised an eyebrow at her. He looked ready to fall down, so she slid in under his right arm and guided him around the bloodstain to the stairs.

"I didn't have anything to do with it and Javi hasn't left the property in days, so no, I doubt *we* had anything to do with it." Halfway up the stairs, he paused to steady himself. "I'm sorry I snapped at you. You got the edges of my pain and anger at letting my guard down. I should have known better."

"And I'm an outsider, so I'm one of them, right?"

They continued up a couple of steps.

"Is that what you think?" She didn't answer. "We set up a lab. We let you in on our family meetings. We didn't lock you in the attic. You're as much a part of this group as

Jim." They got to the door of the room he shared with Emily. "I've got it from here. Can you go check on my girls, please?"

"After I check on Dylan, yes. Did he witness any of this?"

"He no doubt overheard it. April did."

Sweat sprung up on Grant's forehead. His light brown hair grayed at the temples since she'd met him.

"Go lay down. I'll take care of it."

Dylan's door swung open as Ami approached, causing her to startle back from it. Dylan's right side convulsed with spasms and his lopsided posture said he'd gotten himself into the chair on his own. A tray lay on the floor beside the bed, flashcards carelessly splayed across the wood.

"Bbbang." Dylan's whisper said it all. He wanted to know what was going on. Ami pushed his chair back from the door and closed them off from the hallway.

"Shh." She tried to remember what April said about Dylan's speech comprehension. He couldn't say a lot of words, but what did he understand? "Listen." He took a deep breath and let it out slowly. He did it a second time before he focused on her face. His affected foot settled awkwardly on the rest. "Everybody's okay." Should she tell him specifics? Would he understand or become more agitated? Her gaze fell on some of the flashcards at her feet – photos of his family with their names printed under. She gathered them up and slowly went through each picture. She figured he'd be able to figure out Grant's injury without her telling him.

"Bang?" His speech was monotone, but Emily heard a question in there. Whatever his limitations, he knew a silenced gunshot when he heard one. She held up Grant's photo and pointed to her left shoulder.

"He's okay."

He screwed up his face, clearly searching for words.

"Bang …out?"

She frowned at him, trying to convey that she needed more information. He pointed to his right shoulder and then touched behind his shoulder. His arm spasmed more.

"Yes, the bullet went through. He's sewn up. The bleeding has stopped."

Dylan's lips twisted.

"Bbbblllood?"

"I'm sorry. I don't understand."

He tried to find words, his arm getting tighter. Then he pantomimed someone knocking as if on a door. *My God, even brain-damaged, these people think about mitigating their profile.*

"Your mom and Javi are dealing with it. It's okay."

Dylan's mouth pulled over to the left in an attempted smile.

"I need to go." She considered whether to tell him she was checking on his sisters, but that might fan his agitation. Before she could decide, the door opened, and April came in. With long, blond flyaway hair and light blue eyes, the speech therapist reminded Ami of street waifs in Cairo when she was young. Her eyes still didn't trust easily.

"I'll stay with him. The girls don't really know me."

Dylan frowned, but Ami left the room before he could produce a question. April could handle it. She would need to because Ami had other duties, none of which she was trained for.

She turned toward the basement stairs as Emily came into the hallway again, this time carrying a bucket of water. Javi came right on her heels. Ami stopped in her tracks.

"He's satisfied for now, but he won't stay that way." Javi's rich voice still held a hint of his native Columbia. "I need someone to help me dispose of those bodies. I think we need to do that quickly, before he circles back, or someone launches a surprise on us."

"I can scrub the hallway." Ami held out a hand for the bucket. Javi's gaze shifted toward her voice. She doubted he could see her as much more than a foggy blob anymore. "Hiding dead bodies is not an activity I want to share with you."

"She's right. We killed them. She didn't." Emily set the bucket down. "How's Grant and Dylan?"

"Grant's lying down, Dylan is concerned about you guys. April said she'd explain it to him."

Brian Callahan now joined them in the hallway.

"Is someone going to explain to me why I'm lying to my best friend?"

Ami sighed.

"I'll do my best while I clean this up. You two go take care of what you need to take care of." Javi nodded. "I don't want to know where you're taking them, but on your way back, you need to swing over to the compound, ask

Nick to come to examine Travis. Tell him that a corner of my lab is set up to do sterile surgery."

"Patterson can get hold of the compound. I'll let him know so Kletti can get here faster."

Emily nodded then and she and Javi departed, leaving Ami with one gruesome chore and a tap-dancing performance of a lifetime.

Gathering Eggs

Vance Farm, Brady Tanks, Jericho Township

Allison navigated the stairs pretty well with the leg brace. When Ren last saw her, she'd had her leg in a cast and needed crutches to get around. She limped to him and leaned into her grandfather's chest as a scatter of tears washed down her face. She smelled clean. Her hair trailed down her back in a single braid, so unlike the young fashionable girl he'd left behind a couple of months ago.

"It's okay, now, baby girl. You had a time of it, but you're safe now."

She pulled back, her delicate features now twitching with laughter.

"I was worried about you, ninny. You were supposed to be back that night and then you weren't."

"Got tied up. Thought I could get Lewis straightened out, get the trucks moving again – and then the Pulse happened, and all shades of trouble commenced. The Army thought they could force me to be the warlord of Wichita. Turned out, I don't like to be told what to do, but I'm a fine leader when it's my choice."

"So everything in Wichita is settled?"

"No! Big city like that, there's always something about to blow, but I left good men in charge. I knew I needed to get back here. What the USDA did here, though --."

"Oh, that seems like so long ago." Allison looked up the stairs where a tall boy with dark hair descended hanging onto the railing with one hand while the other arm fisted against his side. He stopped at the bottom of the stairs and stared from Allison to her visitor. "David, this is Ren, my grandfather." The boy gazed intently at her face as she spoke, while she also used the signs for "friend" and "grandfather".

David grimaced and his throat convulsed before he whispered "hi." Then he signed "bird".

"Yes." Allison nodded too. "You can keep talking to me if you come gather eggs with us."

Apparently, Allison – daughter of Katharine Lansing Sullivan – now did farm chores. She helped David don his coat and assisted him across the yard to the smaller of the two barns which apparently was a goat-and-chicken shed.

"I want to thank you for winterizing the house. You did good, little girl."

"If I'd known you'd be back, I would have done something different, but I had to be practical. This leg keeps me from doing a lot of things. Where you staying?" Her mother never would allow her to speak in vernacular, but apparently, Trish Vance had more important concerns.

"The groom's cottage. Plumbing froze, but there's a woodstove. We could work out the sleeping arrangements."

David tossed a chicken out of its nest and handed eggs one at a time to Allison who put them carefully in a wire basket.

"Um, I – don't think – well, I've got a job here and Trish -- Mrs. Vance – needs my help. So does David."

Ren blinked at her as she followed the boy to the next stack of nests. David's right leg dragged, and he had limited use of his right arm, but he seemed to know what he was doing with egg-gathering.

"You like it here? Looks like kind of hard work."

Allison glanced over her shoulder at him. She wore faded dungaree overalls and a red bandana contained her bright hair.

"I like working with David and I'm learning stuff that might be useful if the world doesn't right itself. I love you, Granddad, but it's not like you need my help."

Ren felt a momentary sadness, but then he laughed. Of course, that was true, it was just a shock hearing it from Katharine's daughter. He wanted her company, but that wasn't the same as needing her help. Watching as she took eggs from David, Ren wondered if perhaps she had feelings for this boy.

"Can we talk alone?"

Allison gave him a sidelong glance before sputtering with laughter.

"I guess you don't know because you weren't here. The USDA hurt him and damaged his brain. He doesn't understand much of what anyone says. He understands me better than most. So if you want to talk behind his back, go ahead. He won't understand it anyway."

"And you're okay with that?"

Her mouth quirked up in a half-smile.

"You mean spending all day hanging out with someone who can't carry on a conversation?" Ren nodded. "I like that he's coming back because I'm working with him. I feel…um, useful. I'm learning how to do therapy – and farming. And, I like Trish and his brothers. They're a real family."

Her blue eyes seemed wistful a moment. She sighed and straightened her spine.

"Mom and Dad?"

"They made it as far as Columbus. I don't know more than that."

"At least they're alive. Perry did his job."

"Apparently. I've forgotten what I meant to strangle him for when they left."

Allison smiled at him.

"Perry's not one of those Friday pay-check guys."

"Nope, he's not. Gotta do something special for him when he gets them all back here. I'll be around to visit and you're certainly welcome to come visit me whenever you want. I get that you want to be useful. It's a time in this world when usefulness bests almost everything else. If there's anything I can do for you or the Vance family, just let me know."

"They have resources. I think they're pretty well fixed but thank you for the offer. I'll let Trish know. And,

Granddad, I'm glad you're back and I hope you're not too disappointed."

"I'm not disappointed, baby girl. I'm proud as I can be of you."

They hugged. David waited with an egg in his hand. When Ren said "goodbye" his mouth twitched and his Adam's apple bulged before he croaked "bye."

"I'd walk you to your horse, but he can't do this by himself, so I'll say 'bye' now." Allison and Ren hugged again, and he headed toward the door to the yard. The wind slammed him in the face as he clung to the door to keep it whipping off its hinges. He dragged himself around the edge of the door and put his weight on it to close it. Looking to the west caused his eyes to pour, but the sky looked blue and hard. Count Chocula shook his bridle as Ren approached.

"Sorry, boy, we have things to do today. I promise you some oats when we get back home."

The horse bumped his broad forehead into Ren's chest as if to say they remained partners. There were certainly more comfortable ways to get about – if only he had a working car. He pulled his hat further down on his ears and turned Count toward his next destination.

Coffee with the Fam

Liberty Trucking, Jericho Township

Back in the days when Kansas was the buckle of the aviation belt, Liberty Trucking's main building had been a warehouse and loading dock for the Delaney feed store's distance business. Cai had been in grade school when his grandfather leased the land and buildings to Jason Breen. Before the Bombs, Liberty truckers could choose to live on-site in a strip of small rooms on the second floor, but most didn't. Now truckers, their women, and their kids stuffed the building to the rafters. Jason converted some of the outbuildings to a grow shed and brothel. Donna Reese cast Cai an embarrassed look as she headed toward the old beater truck she drove. He nodded and smiled like they passed in the grocery store. He didn't have a better solution to offer her.

Jason frowned when Cai turned down his offer of whiskey.

"You a 12-Stepper now?"

"I've never said yes, and nothing has changed recently. I'm good, thanks. Besides, I'm here in a professional capacity." Jason's expression subtly shifted. Cai the cop triggered suspicion as all cops did.

"About?"

"Your guys are out and about still, right?"

Jason's crags eased a bit.

"Much as the weather allows. The roads keep us close to the hearth."

He sounded almost apologetic, a rare Jason moment.

"Yeah, that's not --. I'm not criticizing your efforts to keep us resupplied and, per the mayor, we don't want to know what you do outside of the town line unless there's a possibility it will come to visit us."

"How do you feel about that?" Jason's eyes held challenge. Cai usually ignored those challenges. His father-in-law's oppositional personality reminded him of Shane's but while Shane would simply go for a long run or a horseback ride, Jason's opposition could turn nasty when the mood struck him.

"I don't want to know." Jason arched a skeptical eyebrow. Cai sighed. "Hutchinson made me a lot more practical."

A week of slavery woke a man up. Killing a man set that in stone. Jason's gaze weighed and measured him and maybe didn't find him quite so wanting.

"Anyway, I'm wondering what your guys have seen *inside* the wire lately."

Jason stared at the coffee cup he'd given to Cai who tried not to feel self-conscious as he took a sip. Keurig? Where did Jason get this stuff?

"I'm not sure. They haven't mentioned anything, but it's not like they think I care."

"Not at all?"

"Well, if Rob does something that might affect us, I want to know. I was sorry to hear about Carl, by the way. I liked him."

"You did?"

"Yeah. When I was a kid getting picked on by the likes of Rafe Conopher, Jace Welton, and Mace Kettridge, and then getting treated like I didn't exist by Joe Sullivan when my mother cleaned his house and my father drove his father and his sorry ass around – Carl came to my rescue a few times. He was the first one to tell me I controlled my worth." His crags moved up and out. "He didn't say it quite that sanely, but – ." Cai laughed with him. "You know about Jacob paying my defense for the Murder 1 trial, right?" Cai nodded, sipping more coffee. "That was Carl's idea and your grandfather always said it was funded out of his trust fund. Carl would never take thanks for that. And when Jacob and Ren helped me buy my first truck, they both claimed it was Carl's idea too. You know he and my dad were friends?"

"Before my time." Technically Jason was Cai's father-in-law, but Cai struggled to think of him as such. Seventeen when Marnie was born, he didn't act like a dad and he treated Cai like he was some lesser-form of human.

"Never will know if the stories he told were delusions or not. Even then they sounded like they were reality, you just couldn't be sure." Cai nodded. Jason rubbed his jaw, which needed a shave. "I'm thinking you're not here to talk about Carl. You're here as a cop, right?"

"An investigator, I guess. We found an unidentified body inside the wire day before yesterday."

"So?"

"He was murdered."

Jason paused in taking a sip of coffee. He smiled into the depths.

"And that's our problem, why?"

Typical Jason answer. Cai drained his cup.

"Emmaus' problem or Liberty's?"

"Either. I mean, if he's not part of the community someone probably killed him for a good reason. And, Liberty doesn't care about stuff that doesn't affect us."

Cai pulled out a photograph and laid it on the desktop.

"Is he, uh, frozen?"

"That's how we found him. I have a photo from when we unthawed him, but it's pretty gross."

Jason considered the photo.

"I don't know him."

"Can I show it around?"

"Sure. I'll even go with you so my guys will answer you straight. But, I'm serious. Why waste resources trying to solve this guy's murder. If he's not from town, who cares who killed him?"

"Do you know who might have?"

"No, but people coming from outside the wire – could be anyone, and folks might have axes to grind. What my guys do to resupply this town tends to piss people off and your brother and his friends at J Springs might have enemies – not to mention the guys over in the militia compound. Where'd you find the body?"

Cai hesitated. What details should he let out? Was he trying to corner Jason in a lie, or did he think Jason was a relatively honest man who was falsely accused of a heinous crime 25 years ago? He opted to treat him like he was Marnie's father.

"Behind the Jericho Springs Hotel."

"Obvious suspect?"

"No. Marnie says the guy was still walking around the last time Shane was still walking around."

"And my daughter is a forensic scientist now?"

"No, but she's a doctor, so she's the closest thing we have. She brought Drs. Ceylon and Kletti in on it. They agree."

"Because both are unimpeachable sources? Do you see the hypocrisy in that?"

"Potential conflicts of interest no matter how you look at it, but we're not in a situation where we can call Las Vegas CSI, so.... Any chance I can get another cup of coffee while we do the interviews?"

"Sure, since you won't take my whiskey. Your mother want more cannabis oil for Shane?" He opened a cabinet in the corner to reveal the Keurig.

"My mother might, but Shane said 'no'. Marnie reports it's working on some of her patients."

"Good." Jason winked at Cai. "I always wanted to be a medical philanthropist. I guess this is my opportunity." He raised both eyebrows and winked again.

"Are you ever serious about anything?"

"Sure. You endanger my life and I'll get real serious real fast. But, serious about the community treating me like I'm a good guy -- ." He snorted with derision. "That would make me as delusional as Carl."

"For what it's worth, I don't think you're such a bad guy."

"Why, that's right white of you, counselor." Jason laughed as Cai tried to work out the reference, getting tangled up in woke politics and accusations of racial supremacy. "Sorry, it's something my father used to say. Since Carl's death, I've been thinking a lot about him. Not very PC, my dad."

"Yeah. Losing Jacob set off similar thoughts for me."

"How's Shane doing, by the way?"

"A lot of pain, real low energy, surprisingly not depressed."

"I thought about dropping by, but I didn't want to risk carrying the flu to him. It doesn't sound like getting sick would be good for him."

"No, it wouldn't, but being bored isn't good for him either."

"I'll check my temperature and bathe thoroughly before dropping by. How's Marnie and the baby?"

"She's showing. No longer feeling sick. We think the kid's due April or May."

"Good. You know if it's a boy or girl?"

"The ultrasound was too early to be certain and Lila couldn't get a good view."

"Do you care?"

"Nope. After being freaked out over it not being planned, I'm happy to become a father."

Jason laughed.

"That was not *my* first reaction. It wasn't until my sister made me go to Beulah to see the kid that I fell in love." That kid was Marnie.

"Yeah, well, I'm 12 years older than you were. Were all your kids born by the time you were my age?"

"I was 24 when Josh was born. Then I went to prison for two years and Maggie wasn't talking to me when I got out. By the time we reconciled, she was closing in on 30 and didn't want more kids."

"Were you the walking-the-floor type? I mean, you didn't live together, right?"

"We did so. From the time Marnie was about two days old until I went to jail. Not since I got out though. I tried, but she likes her independence. And, yeah, I changed shitty diapers and burped the little puke bags. Those are some of my fondest memories. I'd have wanted six of them if things had been different. Mind you, I had no way to support that many kids – not then anyway. What about you?"

"I plan to be a hands-on dad, yeah. Income-wise – who knows where this mess is headed?"

"It's not the end of the world and we will adapt to whatever we're being transformed into." Jason held out the warm cup of coffee. "Just so you know, kid, if you hurt her, I'll kill you, but you're starting to win me over."

Then they went out into the main room and started asking questions about a body nobody seemed to know anything about.

Confession of Feeling

Kansas Prairie South of Jericho Township

Javi leaned forward to shout into Emily's ear.

"What's that ahead?"

Emily let up on the gas.

"A barn and a house."

"Is there anyone around?"

"I don't see anyone and there's no smoke coming from the chimneys. Should we swing around?"

"No, we need to check it out. Abandoned farm is as good as any place to dump the bodies."

Emily grunted, still uncomfortable with the messy business her husband's associations put her in. Her next breath came deep and slow and then she started the snowmobile going forward. As they neared the house, Javi smelled char and Emily eased off the gas again. Javi couldn't see the details, but he guessed from what little he could see, smell and hear. The barn had been painted red, but black timbers groaned in the prairie wind. The white house looked hollow-eyed, smoke staining the siding above the blown-out windows.

"What do you think happened here?" Emily whispered like they visited a graveyard.

"Looks like it happened a while ago. Snow's built up on the timbers. Some houses in Emmaus caught fire during the Pulse. Maybe that's what happened here. Stay here. If anything happens, take off. I'll be okay."

He swung off the back of the snowmobile and walked up on the porch of the house. The floorboards groaned under his weight and felt warped beneath his boots. His training taught him to use all his senses. Going blind made it a necessity. The roof had enough openings in it to let light into the interior. He figured anyone who didn't know he was going blind would try to hide and he could still see movement and contrast. He scanned what he could see. The snow built up on the carpet assured him it was a good place to leave the bodies. He returned to the snowmobile and grabbed the first of the plastic-wrapped bodies to carry inside.

"Do you need help?"

"No. I killed him. I'll dispose of him."

She powered down the snowmobile while he struggled through the snow and across the porch. Rigor set in and Perez's height made his body unwieldy. The metal door warped in its frame from the fire. If he got it open, he'd never be able to close it and that would potentially attract attention, so Javi dumped the body through the opening that had been a picture window before the fire. He paused at the steps going into the yard, listening. The prairie sighed. Something black landed on the peak of the destroyed barn.

"What is that?" Javi pointed. The crow cawed before Emily could answer.

"Won't they … you know?"

Javi picked up Broussard and turned to slog back through the snow. When he returned to the sled, Emily wiped her cheeks like she might have been crying. All he could see of her was her brown snowmobile suit and indigo cap, but he assumed that movement wiped away tears.

"It doesn't matter." He meant it. His childhood taught him life was cheap and he'd dealt his share of death, had failed to stop the death of millions. "We all die in the end. Whether it's worms or crows, something eats us."

"You're not helping." She sounded like she might be crying again.

"This is the world now. I used to be out-of-step with everyone else. Turns out I was just ahead of my time."

"We can't forget we're human. That renders us no more than animals. Is that who you want to be with Ami?"

Javi fumbled around to find his water bottle and took a long drink.

"She makes me feel." A hollow opened in his chest at that admission.

"What do you feel?"

"Anything. Don't get me wrong. I enjoy sex…with women…but I've never felt much for them beyond that…until her."

"Love?"

"I'm not sure I'd recognize that. But I was glad she wasn't there this morning and then glad when she showed up to save us all. I wanted her to come with me for this, even though I knew she wouldn't."

"She didn't kill them. This is our responsibility."

Javi closed his water bottle and stashed it in his pack on the sled.

"We should head back. The sun's past noon and it gets dark early. We need to see to find our way back."

"Could you, if you had to?"

"Find my way back to Emmaus?" Javi scanned the snow behind the sled. A light bit of fluffy snow fell from the grey sky, creating a carpet of sparkling powder that reminded him of Christmas ornaments for some reason. "No. I can't tell much." He blinked stinging eyes as he scanned the horizon. "That way?" She sighed. His heart twisted. "I'm wrong, aren't I"

"About 20 degrees off."

"So I'd wander until I ran out of gas and then freeze to death." He pulled his beanie over his ears. He got through life by not embracing what he couldn't change. He couldn't afford to change now. He needed to live as long as he had life. "We need to go. I can't make out the details of the horizon, but I can see how close the sun is to it." He pulled on his gloves while she restarted the snowmobile. Swinging over the back of the seat, he arranged his long legs so he would be comfortable going forward and then he settled a hand on her shoulder blade to let her know he was ready to go. She turned northeast and drove forward, the wind brushing his eyelids, causing tears to well in his eyes.

Waiting

Seattle

He floated in nothingness, sometimes in the bright light and sometimes in darkness, crushed by cold and scorched by heat, but these told him nothing at all. His head hurt and light made his eyes flinch behind their lids even as he tried to drag them open to see around.

He knew no time, no distance, no past, and he couldn't grasp a future. There was just him in a tucked-away corner unable to understand the wicked witch. He couldn't see her anymore, just hear her cawing and cackling. His headache radiated from everywhere, pulsing the world beyond his lids and flinging off into the icy darkness.

Oblivion tempted and yet when he would lose his grip on consciousness he'd sense losing his grip on something more precious than he knew. Don't sleep. Hang on. Wait for what will come … though he had no notion beyond just breathing in and breathing out and waiting.

Loss of Motion

Lufgren Farm, Jericho Township

Poppy Lufgren stepped out of the shower, hanging her damp towel over the laundry basket and squeezing water from her long blond hair before reaching for the clothes she'd set out on the back of the toilet tank. Dressed in her clean jeans and sweatshirt, she braided her hair before folding her farm-work clothes and setting them atop her work boots to carry them into the room she shared with her husband. She'd need them tomorrow.

Pete's dark hair looked stark against the white pillow and his pale face. He'd complained of a worsening headache this morning, his fingers clumsy as he'd signed left-handed to her because he said his right hand was numb now. She'd let him sleep when she'd come in from the farm, been surprised when he hadn't reacted to her getting her clothes. He'd become so sound-sensitive recently and tiptoeing was something the Deaf struggled with.

He turned his head when she entered the room, clearly fighting against weakness. His lips moved.

"*What?*" she signed.

His face tightened. His shoulders shifted slightly on the pillow, but his arms didn't move. Well, his left arm twitched a little. His lips moved again, and tears welled in his dark-brown eyes.

"*Wait,*" she signed and stepped out into the hall. Putting a hand to her throat to assure she was making sufficient sound, she called "Help" down the stairs. She ran back to the room. Pete looked terrified as Poppy asked him how he was feeling, what she could do for him.

Her sister-in-law Keri pushed into the room. Poppy dropped Pete's limp hand to sign to her, but she could feel the mattress vibrate as Pete spoke.

Keri signed for Poppy to move. She waited by the dresser while Keri examined Pete and asked him a bunch of questions. Poppy assumed she was asking questions since she was touching Pete at various parts of his body. Finally, with tears in her own eyes, Keri drew Poppy to sit next to Pete on the bed.

"*Interpreting me.*" Keri signed while Pete spoke. "*Move arms, can't. Weak this morning. Progressed. Sorry, I can't talk with you. I love you.*"

"*Okay. You better soon.*"

Tears poured down Pete's cheeks. Poppy wiped them for him.

"*Love you.*" Pete nodded, speaking. Poppy glanced at Keri.

"*Keep fight.*"

Poppy looked into Pete's chocolate irises and saw doubt. He was slipping away, and he knew it. He spoke again and Keri pushed Poppy out of the way to prop him on a cushion.

"*Wrong?*"

"*He feel chest-tight.*" Keri slid Pete higher on the cushion and he seemed to relax a bit. She stepped back again. "*I go, tell mom-dad. You stay. Calm.*"

Poppy started to crawl into the bed with her husband, paused, and moved his arm so she wouldn't lay on it. His chest felt hot under her hand as it vibrated with whatever he said. She couldn't understand him. What if he never got better?

God, what I do? What you want me do?

She told herself not to cry and smiled as God provided her a vision of learning to read lips so she could understand her husband. She'd never bothered because it was hard and you missed so much, but for Pete … yes, for Pete.

Glint in the Sun

Sullivan "Shack", Jericho Township

Joe Kelly pulled to a stop in front of the single-story blue bungalow where Ren Sullivan lived currently. The Shack along the driveway stood solemn and empty-eyed, while smoke wafted from the chimney at one side of the bungalow. He pulled the collar of his coat up around his neck and knocked on the door. He waited for a response, but nobody answered, so he walked along a side path to the stable. One of the stalls had been set up for Ren's Morgan, but the piles were cold and nearly frozen, so they'd been gone for a while. As he left the stable, he glanced down at the trail and saw a wide-tracked snowmobile pattern. Curious, he followed it in one direction, which led to a trail from the woods that dropped off the side of the ridge. He pulled out his binoculars. North to the militia. Through intervening trees, he could see the blue metal roof of the modern main building.

"Don't go jumping to conclusions." Mom always said that to him whenever they'd read a mystery together. *"You need the evidence before you catch the bad guy."* Tears in this blasting wind were a fool's idea, but they threatened nonetheless.

He followed the trail back along the path. He expected it to continue into the trees south of the Shack and drop down to Jericho Springs. Instead it rounded the corner of Ren's cottage and ended at a woodpile.

"Did Ren give wood to someone or is someone stealing Ren's wood?" His voice wafted off into the icy air. No way to know without Ren's witness. Joe wriggled the toes on his right foot. He'd been out here long enough they felt cold. He wrote a note and tucked it into the door of the cottage. Glancing at the woodpile again, he saw the wink of something beside the chopping block. He walked back to it and kicked at the snow to reveal a strip of metal about two inches long with a bracelet chain on both ends.

"A medical alert bracelet." They no longer used these old metal styles. He warmed the metal with his breath, brushing off the snow. "Cameron Hotsey, bee sting, epipen." The number on the tag wouldn't do him any good and he had no idea who Cameron was. Maybe from Mara or Beulah, possibly one of the refugees who'd stuck around when the rain trapped them in Emmaus and after the Pulse rendered their vehicles useless. He'd include it in the evidence. Or ….

"Don't jump to conclusions."

The bracelet might belong to someone connected to Ren. He'd hang onto it until he could ask. It was only evidence if it related to the murder. He returned to his vehicle and turned the heat up as high as it would go before heading back off the ridge to continue his patrol.

Brother Secrets

McAuliff Militia Compound, Jericho Township

Cai looked around the McAuliff Compound's main room. Built over a missile silo that had been converted to survivalist apartments, this glass-and-wood-skin-over-concrete structure completely surprised Cai on his first visit. Light filtered in from some upper windows, so even though plywood still blocked lower windows, the space felt light and airy. Families gathered on the balcony, apparently working on schoolwork.

Dan McAuliff and Ron Patterson both looked at the photo with scowls.

"Don't recognize him. Mind telling me what you think we might have to do with it?"

"I'm not thinking you do. I'm just trying to ask as many people as possible."

McAuliff and Patterson exchanged glances. Patterson's non-expression worried Cai.

"Where'd you find the body?" McAuliff asked.

"Jericho Springs."

Yeah, that shift in Patterson's posture could be considered the ex-con equivalent of a flinch. Cai almost wished he'd brought Frank Giffin with him as an analyst.

"That's the last place I'd stash a body." McAuliff didn't seem to notice Patterson's behavior. "I could kill a man if I had reason, but I'd never set someone else up as the fall guy."

"Who are we talking about?"

"Your brother, of course."

"You do hold some grudges against him, then?"

"Sure, but unlike him, I wouldn't fabricate evidence against someone else."

"I don't think Shane would either."

McAuliff and Patterson both snorted.

"Water over the dam, but ...." McAuliff shrugged. "We weren't doing some of the things they claimed we were doing. Someone fabricated that evidence. Shane is the most likely candidate. But I let it go because this is a different day and he was as much a pawn of the statists as anyone else." McAuliff handed the photo back. "You know who you might want to ask." Cai quirked an eyebrow. "Josh Callahan – er, Breem. He's been doing some work for the CSA guy at the B&B. We don't see him now that he's moved back to his dad's compound, but this looks like how messy he might get."

Good to know. His brother-in-law hadn't been at Liberty when Cai asked the questions there. Maybe he'd be a source – but someone other than Cai would need to question him because Josh still held Cai responsible for Marie's death. Somehow, no matter how much Cai repented of that one stupid act, he could never really rectify it.

"You folks seem to have settled here."

"We have." McAuliff scanned around the big space. "It's becoming what it was always meant to be – a community."

"If that was the purpose, why did the FBI target you?"

"You ever read my book?"

"No, sir. Grandpa had a copy, but I never got around to it."

"You might find it enlightening, given the times we're living in now."

"Were you a prophet?"

McAuliff laughed and rubbed his chin.

"I got close as a hand-grenade. I don't think the government wanted anyone thinking the way we were thinking, but it was exactly the right way to think because this is what they were planning."

"Nuclear attacks?"

"No. Starvation, population reduction, economic degradation."

A shiver ran down Cai's back, so he reached for his coat on the pretext of leaving.

"I'll have to scare up that book."

"We have lots if you need another copy." Patterson grinned. "Hard-backed. Betcha he'd sign it."

"You're a jerk." McAuliff sounded amused. They shared some common experiences, a common belief, and a common enemy. Of course, they were like brothers. Cai wondered if there was any hope he'd ever grow that close to his biological brother. Shane's recent near-death experience worried at Cai's conscience like a cattle dog.

"I'm headed out. Thank you for speaking with me. Could you let Nick Kletti know I'd like to speak to him at some point?"

"Sure."

As they passed through the large crescent of the kitchen, a dark-haired young man looked up from the bread he sliced. Cai glanced around. He'd always supposed libertarian societies were pretty white – kind of like rural Kansas -- but now that he thought about it, he saw a lot of diversity around this room – still majority white, but also black, Asian, and American Indian – about like America had been.

"Your people homeschool?"

"We originally planned it that way and now it seems like the only choice."

Cai nodded, pulled on his scarlet cap and gloves, and headed out to continue his interviews.

Apocalyptic Adulting

Huffman's Market, Emmaus

Ren Sullivan stamped the snow off his boots while Jos Osimowitz added a bit of firewood to the stove in the corner. The front area of the grocery store had been closed off with sheetrock.

"Come to collect your cut?" Jos asked.

Truthfully, Ren didn't need the cut. Allison had done a good job of husbanding his pantry. He merely followed Rob's guidelines.

"I don't need it until you're done selling it all."

"That'll be tomorrow."

"What?"

"I'd say 90% of the stock you brought already went out the door, less our cuts. Word gets around fast and people were lining up at the door when we were still stocking shelves."

"My goodness. People were really hungry."

"Or just desperate for something else to eat. Ground corn gets old fast. I'm glad to see canned fruit myself."

"I'm a bit surprised at how quickly the food sold out, but I'll get on the horn and try to order some more. If the weather holds, we might be able to get it here by the end of the week."

"It would be great if we could get regular resupply."

"I'll try. There's still a lot of road between Wichita and Emmaus."

"I appreciate it, sir."

Jos pulled off his cap and ran a hand over his disheveled hair. The last time Ren had seen him, he'd been a clean-cut young man, but nobody in town looked like they'd seen a barber in a while.

"Do you have running water here?"

"Nobody has running water, sir. It's the apocalypse."

"I'm just learning what's been going on."

The boy gazed at him. He looked tired beyond his 15 years.

"All due respect, sir. I don't need you to assess my needs. I'm good – better than most. I usually get some food. And, age – that doesn't mean much anymore. I drive. I own a gun. I do time on the border patrol. I run one of the few functioning businesses in the town. I'm an adult as far as anyone else is concerned."

Ren opened his mouth to argue and remembered Allison telling him that she had made a decision and he didn't need her. Jos didn't need Ren.

"I'll call Wichita, see what we can do. Good night then."

His horse, Count Chocula, liked cold weather, but Ren felt half-frozen before he reached the Delaney house. Jill answered the side door, her hands covered in flour. Ren stomped the snow off his boots and entered the mudroom.

"I heard your family took control of Carl's radio. I guess that old tower of Jacob's brother still works."

"Kind of. I don't know much about it. It's Click and Rob's baby. Neither of them is here right now. Can I help you with something?"

"I'm looking for a radio that can reach Wichita. I know Carl could."

"The only one here who could help you is Shane and he's not up to it right now."

She wiped her hands on a dishtowel.

"How's he doing?"

"In pain, wore out, not used to resting. As his body heals, his mind races, which wears him out."

"He'll be okay." Ren didn't know Shane well, but he'd been impressed by the young man in the few days surrounding the Bombs. Not much rattled him. Jill drew a loaf of bread from the oven of the coal stove. It looked to have a lot of cornmeal in it, but it was still a pretty loaf. Ren missed Lottie who'd made bread often before her stroke. "Any chance Rob has time to talk to me tomorrow?"

"Sure. Choose a time and I'll make sure he's here."

They settled on late afternoon and Ren let himself out the back door, walking past the warm glow of the lantern-lit garage window to mount Count and head toward his lonely new home. To the side of the Heights Road, houses stood empty, no smoke from chimneys, as his flashlight sparkled off snow drifts that winked like diamonds. For all that society felt to be dying, the world remained a beautiful place, though it was hard to remember it during this killing time.

Loose Ends

Delaney House, Emmaus

Jazz ran a curry brush over Rocket's side while Cai asked his questions. Tasked with stable work today, she'd been at it since well before sunset. Rocket deserved a rubdown for being such a good horse. Since Shane's injury, Jazz rode her everywhere and had decided the mustang's reputation for being cantankerous was overstated.

"I never went anywhere near the hotel that day." She turned to look at Cai, her green eyes direct and calm. "I was on the interstate and south of it, but there was no reason to go to the Springs."

"You see anyone when you were out there?"

"Other than Shane, no. There was a helicopter at the airfield. I thought that was weird. Besides that – nothing, really."

"What sort of helicopter?"

"Single set of blades painted Army camo."

"Parked at the head of the commuter?"

Cai checked the airfield on his way to the trucking company.

"No. Against the trees by the road. I couldn't see the commuter past the hangars."

Cai's neck hairs stood on end again. He resisted the urge to look over his shoulder to see who stared at him. He knew it would be Belle the cat or maybe Macky the bay gelding.

Jazz finished checking Rocket's hooves and patted the horse's neck. She'd been riding Rocket a lot since Shane's injury.

"I heard you found a body out behind the hotel."

"Heard? From who?"

"Jos Osimowitz."

"Who'd he hear it from?"

"Don't know. Didn't think to ask. Is it a secret?"

"No. How likely do you think it is for someone to come in through the wire?"

"Pretty danged easy with the flu and the weather. We patrol, but – if someone can approach the town without detection, they can easily evade us. Mind you, it's hard physical exertion if you enter away from the checkpoints, but Shane and I both crossed out of the wire that day without detection."

"We're not doing a good enough job."

"I don't think we can. I think we're exhausted and hungry and there's not enough of us. And there's nothing moving out there, but with Jacob's death, the duster isn't flying, and we don't have any idea what is going on outside of the range of our binoculars. We're still pretty armored against large groups, but individuals – not so much."

"How are those Army guys working out?"

"Murphy's irritated by them, but okay, I guess. They got that whole branches-of-the-services-pissing-contest thing going on. Murphy's been putting them on their own checkpoint, so he can keep his guys and the town folks away from them. Your dad, by the way, doesn't think that's a good idea, but Murphy's all he has until Shane is on his feet again. How's the community patrol going?"

"A bunch of amateurs. I guess it's better than no police but just."

They ducked into the mudroom, closing the door behind them as quickly as possible. Rob looked up from the stove where he stirred a pot.

"Where's Mom?"

"Medical center. She took my truck. Go get yourself cleaned up. Dinner will be in 20 or so."

"I need to ask Shane some questions about our investigation."

"Wash your hands before you go near him."

Cai finished thoroughly washing his hands with a combination of grease and salt before going into the living room where Shane lay petting Glister. His brother looked over his shoulder as Cai settled on the sofa. Shane shifted carefully onto his back.

"So what's up?"

"You know about the dead body we found behind your hotel?"

"Not officially, but you guys forget I can hear you when you're in the dining room. And, that's all I know – far as I know."

"That day – could anything have happened?"

"That big? I'd probably remember killing someone – or at least have nightmares about it."

"You do have nightmares."

"About old stuff. So, I don't remember anything like that."

"How close to the airfield did you get that day?"

"Went through Alex's south 40. Too many trees to see anything."

"No helicopters?"

Shane blinked at him.

"No."

"Not even when you topped the interstate?"

"I don't think I looked. I was chasing deer."

"What about a single-rotor military copter?"

"With a weird ball on top of the stack?"

"Uh, maybe that was what Poppy was describing."

"I encountered a Kiowa somewhere over near Colorado Springs. Could be that."

"Why would they be interested in Emmaus?"

"No idea." Shane settled his head back onto the pillows and stared at the ceiling. "My phone is up there on the end table. I can try texting Rigby."

"I already talked with Emily, Dr. Ceylon, and Chavez and they stonewalled me."

Shane stared up at Cai as he tried to hand him the only working cell phone in Kansas. For a moment, Cai worried he'd lost focus.

"Chavez being hostile isn't weird. You didn't talk to Grant?"

"He wasn't there."

"Now *that* is weird." Shane took the phone and used just his left hand to formulate a text and send it.

"Arm hurting?"

"It still needs support. It's getting better. I'll hang onto this." He put the phone on the floor beside his mattress. He shifted his shoulders. "Anything else?"

"Not about that. Um, I spoke with McAuliff." Shane's eyes drifted left.

"And?"

"Did you – this is probably none of my business." Shane gave him an uh-what-do-you-think expression. "Did you manufacture evidence against the militia?"

Shane sighed and swallowed audibly.

"No. The reason they are armed now is I didn't tell my handler about the second silo with the weapons. By that time, I was beginning to realize they were being railroaded, so I kept quiet. Figured I wouldn't add another layer of dirt to their burial mound."

"Were they guilty?"

"Of?"

"Treason or whatever?"

"I honestly think they were guilty of thinking outside the box, but no, I don't think it was treasonous. Or maybe it was by current interpretation of the law, but the Founders would have invited them to dinner."

"That sounds like Jacob."

Shane nodded, then closed his eyes and breathed out slowly.

"You jar something?"

"It just hurts off and on. So, is the hotel still locked up?"

"Yeah. If the batteries have run down, why can't you just breach the door?"

"And, do what with Alex's seed corn?" Shane looked at him through narrow eyes. "It's safest where it is – for now. Nobody can steal it there. I need to take a nap, so I can think about how to help Alex with a wooden iron lung."

"He told me about that. Is that really a thing?"

"Yeah. It was in an old magazine in the house library when we were kids. Unfortunately, while I remember reading it, I don't remember the details."

"You think it's the concussion?"

"I hope I'm just exhausted. The problem is, I'm always exhausted right now. But Jazz is looking through the library. It's not like Jacob ever threw away reading material."

"That's true. So you're probably not up to looking at the evidence on the murder?"

Shane sighed.

"I want to, but my head and hip both hurt today. Let me take a nap and then, maybe. And if Rigby calls me back, I'll let you know what he says."

"I wish there was something we could do for you."

"There isn't. I need steroids and painkillers and there aren't any. And it's getting better – or was before I overdid it. I'm going to nap and then I'll let you know if I'm up for it." His eyes blinked. "Although whatever is cooking is tempting to stay awake for."

"I'll make sure we save you some. Although, I'm headed to meet up with Joe to compare notes. And here's your buddy."

Glister licked Shane's hand and settled on the floor with a resigned doggy sigh.

"Yeah, somebody has to keep me warm, fella. Go." Shane aimed that at Cai, his hand on Glister's back so the dog wouldn't misunderstand him. "I'm fine. Go."

Cai grabbed his jacket from the hooks in the mudroom.

"Where are you headed?" Rob pulled a mixture of some kind of bird meat with potatoes from the old coal oven. Testing the meat, he decided it wasn't done and slid the pan back into the heat, closing the door with a rag.

"Joe and I are comparing notes at his house."

"This has nothing to do with Shane, right?"

"No. This guy died when Shane was mostly unconscious. We're not sure of much, but that's not in question."

"Good. You be careful out there. And, if you would, swing by the med center and tell your wife to come home. My grandchild needs rest."

"I'll do that. Always like spending a moment with my bride."

Hugging his father, he headed out for yet another stage in a long day.

Daring Times

Sullivan B&B, Jericho Springs

Ami watched while Nick Kletti performed a neurological exam on Travis Meyer, the son of the last constitutionally-elected president of the United States. Travis stared at the wall as if something there terrified him.

"Eden, can you stay with him while I confer with Dr. Ceylon?"

The girl nodded. Nick jerked his curly head toward the kitchen. Ami followed him.

"He's got no feeling or movement from T8 down. You were right to catheterize him." He rubbed his neck. "I'm not a neurosurgeon. That bullet probably does need to come out, but I risk doing more damage or even killing him if I muck around in there. It's possible this is shock and his feeling and movement will come back as the swelling goes down, but not if I sever his spinal cord while trying to remove the bullet."

"I'm more worried about infection. I tend to think he'll be paralyzed, or he won't, and either way, bacteria spreading in his abdominal cavity is a bigger issue."

Nick scrubbed a hand through his hair. He hadn't practiced in at least a half-decade. Doubting one's skills after so long a hiatus seemed natural, but she couldn't afford not to be bold.

"I'd be willing to assist you. I'm assuming you don't want Marnie Callahan to know."

"I don't. My sister Chris can scrub in as nurse. But what can we do for anesthesia?"

"We've made some ether out at the compound. There's a woman there – Gail – she is a surgical nurse. I'll have her bring it and scrub in. Do you know how any of this happened?"

"I can't tell you."

Nick blushed.

"Of course, you can't. I'll make that radio call. My apologies for delving in where I don't belong."

"Not necessary. I'd tell you if I didn't think it was dangerous for you to know."

Nick pulled the radio from his coat pocket in the kitchen. Ami left him alone while he talked to his comrades. She wished she had time to conduct the next round of experiments in her lab. The one good thing about what had happened here today was that she'd gotten viable blood from both deceased soldiers before Javi and Emily had taken them to an undisclosed location from which they had not yet returned. Now that she had a moment, she recorded the donations. She should type and cross-match them. Travis no doubt would need blood for the surgery and the more blood she could access for her experiments the better. Isolated at Cheyenne Mountain since the Pulse, Broussard and Perez gave a rare opportunity to test blood that had never encountered the novel virus Ami called Samira's Flu.

"Let's check out this operating theater of yours." Nick stepped down into the garage and looked around.

"That sounds much too grand." Ami directed him to the small space she'd surrounded with shower curtains joined by Velcro closures that had been Madelyn's last act of kindness before her death. "I've got Lister's solution to paint the walls before we start. It's the best I can do in the situation."

"It'll have to do. I compliment you for doing this. I created a first aid room, but I resisted the thought of doing surgery."

"I was kind of hoping I'd never have to."

"The crowd you live with though…."

"*Ay-wa.* Some part of me knew it would come to this eventually. Is the ether on its way?"

"Yes. Have you ever used it?"

"I saw it used in Egypt. Some of the doctors who work with the extremely poor still use it."

"I reviewed a video on it. And Gail is part of a medical historical society, so she's familiar. Will Chris join us soon?"

"She's on her way, just getting off a shift at the medical center."

"Then we should think about how to get him in here without moving his spine or restarting the bleeding."

"I've got an idea for that. Let me consult with Grant and I'll get right back with you."

Grant turned out to have already thought of that. She found him in the basement safe room, talking with Josh Breem on the telephone.

"He'll be here within the hour to help Eden move Travis into the surgery." Grant wiped a hand over his forehead. "How long have Javi and Emily been gone?"

"Three hours, thereabout. Is Emily good at driving on ice and snow?"

"She grew up in California, so no, but Javi seems able to drive when it's not dark out."

"He's a good actor, Grant. He can distinguish light and dark and colors now, but he can't see details."

Grant sighed.

"I'm beginning to wonder what we're doing here." He rested the elbow of his good arm against the table, looking exhausted.

"Well, I've never known, so aren't we a pair?" Ami laughed nervously, then sobered and straightened. "I need to get things ready for the surgery. She's not going to want to, but Eden needs to be elsewhere."

"I'll handle it."

"And you need to rest at some point."

"I'm aware. Worried about Em for now. And my girls. I'm going to head upstairs to check on them."

"Don't blame me if you pass out."

"I won't. Ami, thank you. You kept a clear head today and I appreciate it."

"I did spend three years in the Baltimore ER. The beautiful tragedy of the American physician training system is that you learn a lot about going without sleep and staying cool under fire."

"It showed today."

He wobbled a little as he gained his feet and she put out a hand to steady him. He cast her a grateful smile before walking away, clearly in pain but choosing to ignore it.

Losing Friends

Greyeyes Allotment, Jericho Township

The eastern sky sprayed with indistinct diamonds as the sun disappeared into the west. Cai urged Ronin up the road through cleared cornfields. He technically owned this land. Jacob granted it to him in his will. A boarded-up bungalow sat at the end of the road. Cai dismounted and walked his horse to a door in a small hill near a stable. From the small shed, he heard a horse nicker a greeting to Ronin, who he left tied to a hitching post before knocking on the door.

April glanced out the window beside the door before opening it. Cai had to stoop to clear the lintel and step down onto the linseed-oiled floor.

"Hey!" Brian took Cai's coat and hung it up on a pegboard near the door. The soddy had been hollowed out of the hillside by a Greyeyes ancestor who never would have built a house like the one out front. GPa built that for his part-white wife who wanted to live above ground. The hill formed three of the soddy's walls and the front wall, where the door and window were, was made of sod bricks. Unlike some sod houses, a framed roof rose above the level of the prairie it had been dug from. Cai doubted it was original. Most soddies still around didn't stand proud of the prairie. Over the years, subsequent inhabitants plastered the walls and built a side bedroom that was now a storeroom, and added a bathroom. Cai suspected the floor was for GMa in the early days of their marriage before the bungalow had been finished. Nobody lived here for years, so Jacob couldn't provide the Callahans with running water, but the approximately 16 by 20 space was cozy, warmed by a corn cob stove, and dry. A barrel in the corner of the kitchen gave them water for everyday needs. A white iron bed with an antique quilt occupied one corner of the room.

"What brings you here?" Brian drew Cai over to the table while April hastily made the bed. Marnie would scramble to do the same thing.

"What's going on at the B&B. I know you weren't saying what you knew."

Brian stared at his hands, full lips tightening, then ran a hand over his curls.

"Frankly, I can't tell you. There's rules."

"You're not a doctor and HIPPA, I'm pretty sure, no longer applies."

"All due respect, Cai, but ethics aren't governed by laws." April came to stand behind Brian. "Ask them what's going on. Don't put us into a position of having to break our ethics."

"Seriously? We find dead bodies and you're protecting them?"

Brian shifted uncomfortably.

"Maybe there's nothing to protect with regards to the dead body you found. Maybe what happened this morning is not related." His rich voice vibrated with tension.

"Brian, you and I are friends and I don't want there to be a division between us, but I need to sort out this situation."

"We can't help you." April sounded firm. "And, Cai, pulling the 'we're friends' card won't change our stance."

Cai didn't know her as well as he knew Brian. Hutchinson separated men and women and April spent weeks in sexual slavery in Hays. He didn't know what made her so firm, but his court training said she wouldn't break. Brian might, but not with her standing at his shoulder. While he considered his next move, he realized that they'd both showered recently. The Jericho Springs B&B was one of the few places in Emmaus that had running water. He'd lost this argument before he even began.

"Fine. I'll keep poking around, maybe get myself killed by Chavez, and if I live, I'll figure it out."

"Javi isn't that dangerous." Brian's blue eyes held secrets Cai couldn't fathom.

"If you say so. So, lighter note – how are things going for you two?" He deliberately met gazes with April who nervously tucked a blond lock behind her ear.

"We're doing okay here. It's a nice place. You'd almost not know it was underground." She giggled.

"We can't tell you about our patients. Does Marnie share?"

"Sometimes. I'm kind of on the supply staff, you know?" Brian nodded. "I know you're working with Nate Sherwin and you're both working with David Vance and

Emily Grant's son. Do you think this illness is entirely new?"

"I've never seen the symptoms before." Brian stared at his hands again. "And it does seem to be tied to the flu. Everyone who has been paralyzed had the flu. I'm not a virologist, so I'll defer to Ami – Dr. Ceylon's – expertise."

April glanced toward the woodstove where a pot of something that smelled like fish bubbled. The medical center accepted payment in food, so the staff there were fairly well-supplied. The farmers were doing better, but they were doing the best of the non-farmers.

"We need to get back to making dinner."

"Of course. Well, thanks for the visit. You know Ren Sullivan's caravan arrived this morning. The food should be available tomorrow."

"I've already set aside my trade goods. Thank you for reminding us."

April walked him to the door as Brian stirred the pot. She dropped her voice to a whisper.

"Don't pull this again, Cai. We won't open the door if you continue misusing our friendship."

He stared at her, surprised at her sting, then glanced at Brian who wouldn't meet his eye. Okay, then, message received.

Holistic Medicine

Conopher Farm, Jericho Township

Marnie parked her Subaru in the rutted driveway of the Dell Conopher house. Like most of the farmhouses in the area, the blue-clapboard house sat in the middle of a field of corn stubble that couldn't be seen under feet of snow. A big barn to the right and behind the house probably held a few farm animals and a lot of now-useless equipment. Bullet holes marred the paint on the front porch. Marnie held her coat closed with her free hand as she waited for someone to answer the door. It seemed her belly got bigger every day. The skin on her abdomen started to stretch.

The door opened and Rafe Conopher, brother of Dell, swept her with an icy gaze. He'd always been an angry man from the first time she'd become aware of him when Shane tossed him out of Nick's Pizza on his first day of work. Local rumor had it that his wife Cady had changed him for the better.

"Well, howdy, Dr. Quinn." An old joke that Marnie was inclined to ignore.

"I'm here to see Kix, and I hear some of your kids might have the flu."

"My kids are fine." His jaw tightened and his eyes grew petulant. "I'll get Leisha for you."

Marnie supposed that meant to wait there by the door. The heat from the kitchen wafted toward her as the door swung open and closed on its hinges. Leisha came out a moment later, wiping her hands on her apron.

"Thanks for coming." She offered to hang up Marnie's coat and then led her upstairs. Kix, her teen son, collapsed and quickly lapsed into a coma a couple of weeks ago. He lay on his left side, propped with pillows, eyes closed, drooling, his right hand fisted under his chin. Leisha helped Marnie roll him onto his back, which caused his right leg to convulse in spasms. The stoma that made it possible to feed him looked good, his urine was pale yellow and there were no signs of skin erosion. His left limbs were still curiously limp with no deep tendon reflexes. His eyes reported the pressure on his brain and there was nothing Marnie could do about it under the circumstances. His temperature said he was still fighting whatever it was.

"His labs showed a significant drop in hematocrit. He's anemic. I brought a unit of his blood type. Are you okay with a transfusion?"

"Yes, of course. Will it help him fight the infection?"

"Possibly. It's all experimental at this point." Leisha nodded. Marnie relaxed. "Keeping him as healthy as possible can't hurt." If Ami's hypothesis was correct, Kix's immune system inflamed his brain seeking to eliminate the flu his body fought off weeks before. Nobody knew anything for sure.

"I'll have to wait around a while for it to be delivered." Marnie hooked the blood bag on a ceiling hook, which they probably used for the thrice-daily stoma feeding. "Let's roll him on his side in case the transfusion makes him sick." On his left side, Kix's right limbs convulsed even more though supported by pillows.

"Do you need to stay right here with him, or would you like to join us in the kitchen?"

The kitchen was warm and inviting. Dell and the other children were working today while Leisha and Cady washed clothes in the warmth from the coal stove. Out of the large windows, Marnie could see Rafe going in and out of the soddy Cai said his family lived in.

"How are things with your kids?" Marnie hoped Cady would be more forthcoming, but the strawberry blond winced and shook her head.

"They're all down with the flu, but Rafe won't let you examine them. He's convinced you're somehow causing this paralysis."

"Do you believe that?"

"No. It's just the flu and then there's something else that happens to some boys."

Boys? Well, yes, maybe. Marnie couldn't think of a single girl who had developed the brain swelling. Boys? She'd have to ask Ami.

"Would you like a warm beverage? We've quit calling it coffee." Leisha looked exhausted, but Marnie supposed humor helped.

"Sure."

Leisha spooned some brownish grounds into a pot of water and put it on the stove.

"How's your pregnancy going?"

"So far good. My mother had easy pregnancies too, so I'm hoping I've inherited it."

"They're all different. Any signs of this flu ending soon?"

"No. It probably won't until the warmer weather has us outside again."

"Margaret Shillinger was saying we should all be wearing masks." Cady spread the shirt she was scrubbing to check for missed spots.

"It really doesn't do any good. If you can breathe through a mask, a virus just passes right through. It's like surrounding your porch with chain-link fence to keep out mosquitos. Ami says virologists wear fit-tested respirators. Wash your hands and don't touch your face."

They both nodded. Marnie asked for permission to help them and set to squeezing water out of the clean garments. She felt comforted dealing with mundane laundry rather than life-or-death illnesses.

"Where do you dry these?"

"In the basement. I hung lines. No, sit down. We can do that. I'll get your beverage."

The baby stopped kicking at the introduction of warm liquid. The little alien swam laps like it thought Marnie was a pool. Outside in the yard, Rafe and Dell looked to be arguing. Marnie had never seen Dell agitated before.

"We're so glad to be here." Cady looked at Leisha as she said it.

"I know. Rafe may eventually wear out his welcome but you and the kids can stay. I promise and I've made Dell promise."

Marnie looked at the watch she wore. It belonged to Vi Delaney – a sensible old-fashioned face to replace her cell phone that had died in the Pulse. She excused herself to check on Kix. She thought he might have fallen asleep as he didn't spasm so much when she removed the needle from his arm. She put a hand on his shoulder and prayed a simple prayer silently.

God, grant me the wisdom to know how to treat him and give him the strength of body to overcome this disease.

Of course, nothing happened, but Marnie felt marginally less depressed and overwhelmed. She gathered her instruments into the backpack she used as a doctor's bag and went back downstairs.

"I'll be back around next week. Call me if anything changes. For now, he appears to be stable and that's the best news possible under the circumstances."

"We thank you so much for everything you've done." Leisha hugged her. "I know it must seem hopeless compared to all the technology you had just six months ago, but God's got this. Somehow, it'll all work out."

Marnie nodded. She believed that – in theory – but Leisha was right. In the post-Pulse world, medical treatment felt a little bit hopeless – like a teenage boy going up against a giant.

On her way back to the house, she passed Cai as he walked Ronin along the snow-narrowed road.

"Hey, how's your day?" he asked when she rolled down the window.

"Long, but I'm headed home now. How was yours?"

"Still don't know anything."

"Sorry. Hey, Rafe Conopher is acting weird."

"That would be normal behavior for Rafe. Weird how?"

"I don't know how to describe it. Angry. His wife described paranoid ideation."

Cai looked out across the neighborhood.

"Don't know." Fog iced the air in front of him. "I'll swing by there tomorrow. How's Kix?"

"Same as he's been. I worry that the pressure on his brain is liquifying it, but there's nothing I can do about it, so -- ." Headlights appeared in her rearview mirror. "I'll see you at the house."

He waved and she pulled ahead, closing the window as she went.

Getting Caught Up

Delaney House, Emmaus

Shane and the dog both looked to be in deep REM when Rob suggested they adjourn to the den. People talking in the dining room disturbed the kid, and Rob figured if the only medicine they could offer was sleep, then they shouldn't disturb it. Jazz stood on a rail ladder to access the upper shelves in the den which was lined with bookshelves.

"Any luck?"

"Not so far. I'm about done with this room." She pointed to the next section of shelves. "And then I'll move to the basement. Hopefully, I won't need to brave the attic."

"Do you need help down from up there, young lady?" Ren Sullivan held out a hand. Rob doubted Jazz needed any help to dismount the ladder, but she grinned and accepted Ren's support.

"I'll start again after I've eaten dinner."

"Sounds good." Rob tossed wood into the parlor stove. "Shane eat anything?"

"Yeah and then he fell asleep."

"He needs it. Sleep is healing."

She nodded and exited the open door which Rob had left open for the heat.

"I'm trying to get hold of my headquarters to bring in more food. I'd have asked Carl for help by now, but ...." Ren looked momentarily sad, but like all who had been as close as Carl allowed, Ren expected Carl's death. "I know he left the radio to – what's his name?"

"Click."

Ren raised an eyebrow, then laughed. He didn't go by Warren. How could he expect anyone else to go by an embarrassing first name?

"Anyway, can he do anything?"

"I'm not sure. Let me see if he's downstairs and try to raise him on the handhelds if he's not. Just enjoy the peace and quiet."

Click was actually in the garage-barn skinning rabbits when Rob found him after a brief detour to the basement. He hung the rabbits up to drain and followed Rob into the house.

"He'll join us in just a moment." Rob took the old leather chair by the desk. It felt weird. Even after Jacob and Vi moved to the ranch, he'd not felt comfortable taking what had been Jacob's seat. "He wanted to wash his hands."

"That's fine. Do you ever remember a winter with so much snow and cold?"

"Not really. Pa said there were some when he was a kid, but yeah, pretty severe weather right when we don't need it."

Click came into the den and took the remaining seat. A medium height man in his late 30s, his thick hair now flopped over his forehead. Everybody needed a barber, and none were to be had. Ren explained what he needed. The newsman nodded his understanding.

"Sure. If the skip's in, I can get Wichita easy, but it's probably going to be at night during a cold snap."

"So it's not like dialing a cell phone?"

"No, sir. Could take a few days to make a connection."

"Everything ready to go?"

"Yeah, mostly. I wish I could get the big radio going. We could broadcast and pick up from all over the region. Well, actually, the world if I had the power."

"What's preventing it?"

"The region? I don't think anything now. Carl wouldn't share all of his tech and so what I needed for the big radio wasn't available. Now it is – but with no heat up at the station, it's going to have to wait."

"I can maybe fix that. I can probably order it."

"Seriously?"

"Yeah. I'm rich that way, right?"

Click laughed. His hand rubbed across his sand-paper whiskers.

"Starting to feel like we'll never see the 21st century again."

"We may not – at least not as we knew it, but I think we can edge into the 20th century with some thought. The first thing would be to get more groceries headed our way and then to get heat up in the radio station. This inability to communicate needs to be overcome as quickly as possible. We might be able to pull a woodstove out of one of the abandoned houses. I got a lot of wood up at the Shack. Thought I'd be heating the whole house, but I won't need it for the groom's cottage."

"Allison didn't know what else to do after the USDA attack." Rob rubbed the back of his neck. "Mothballing the house seemed like the best way to go about things."

"She did good. The groom's cottage would be tight for the two of us, but she's decided to stay with the Vances for now."

"Trish will appreciate that. She's feeling the loss of Kitty and Dick."

"That whole incident – I wish I'd been here."

"No, you don't." Rob took a deep breath and let it out real slow. Click stared at his boots. That was a part of town history best not revisited.

"Just so you know, if nobody's said, you've done a great job leading this town through a trying time."

Rob sighed, looking at Click, who swallowed before speaking.

"About 30 percent of the population has died since October 1."

Ren's expression sobered.

"That's about what they've lost in Wichita. Hutchinson said they'd lost 20%. I heard rumors the cities that survived the bombs lost way more than that – some from starvation, others from cholera and the flu."

"Any estimate on the death toll?" Ren stared concernedly at Click. "I'm a reporter. I'm supposed to ask questions like that."

Ren fiddled with the tag on his jacket zipper.

"I've heard estimates of 50%, but I don't think anyone knows. I got that bit of speculation from Knight Industries in Seattle, but they admit they can't get half the country on the phone, so --. Heard a rumor that they're eating one another in Pittsburgh and the Old South is enslaving white people this go-round."

"Shit." Click's whisper barely rose above the crackle from the stove.

"What he said." Rob thanked God silently that Emmaus hadn't come to that yet. Nobody wanted to eat corn again, but nixtamalization kept them alive.

"You get that tower up and running for me, and I'll pay with food. I've got plenty."

"Thank you."

"You got your father's binder, I see." Ren pointed to the binder on the shelf behind Rob. "You start reading it yet?"

"When I have time. Could be a great treatise on how to build a community around the non-aggression principle."

"I've read parts. The man was prescient. Sorry not to be here when he passed."

"He wouldn't have been." Rob smiled. A weak cry carried through the open door. Rob stood, almost bumping chests with Click.

"He's probably just having a bad dream. I'll check on him."

"Thank you."

Click ducked into the living room.

143

"That happen a lot?" Ren frowned toward the door.

"Being a contractor doesn't protect you from the realities of fighting a war. You just get paid better for it."

Click came back in.

"Jazz is seeing to him." He sat down, a goofy grin on his face. The two older men realized the meaning after a moment.

"Young couple in dire circumstances will be drawn together." Ren smiled as if at a fond memory. "How long do they think he'll be down?"

"Depends on who is giving the prognosis." Rob still looked at the doorway thoughtfully. "Marnie says spring and she's uncertain he'll walk again."

"Because?"

"Lack of technology scares her. Ami – have you met her?"

"I've heard about her – Dr. Ceylon, right?"

"She's more optimistic as is the physical therapist. He was here earlier today, which is probably why Shane's in so much pain and exhausted."

"My sister had polio when we were kids. She was completely paralyzed for a while – couldn't even swallow on one side. She recovered though. Some days it seemed like she'd pushed herself as far as she could go, but a day or two later, she'd be pushing herself again. The human body is an amazingly resilient machine."

Rob vaguely remembered Ren's sister. She'd been an adult when he was a teenager. He'd never thought of her as a polio survivor.

"Good to remember that. Just so you know, Allison faced some pressure to just distribute your pantry to the community. She refused, but as people get more desperate, you may find them on your doorstep."

"That's part of the reason I want to get more trucks headed our way. When I left, BNSF had cleared a mile of rail and gotten at least one locomotive working."

"How'd they manage that?"

"Found an antique diesel that didn't fry in the Pulse."

"Where they going to get the fuel?" Click looked intrigued. Reporters!

"I had a mothballed refinery down in Louisiana that was pretty easy to restart – compared to the ones with all their electronics torched, anyway. Can't heat the whole country, but I could supply some trains. And I've got crews working forward from there – trying to resurrect the oldest refineries first since the technology is more readily available."

"American innovation. It's an amazing thing." Click nodded to Rob's observation, then he laughed, which got the other two men looking at him.

"I used to be one of those trolls who thought America had never been great –just lucky and pushy. But my wife – her dad was an entrepreneur. He showed me American greatness in small businesses and I mostly stopped being a troll. I still figured we were just lucky. Now I see folks rising to this challenge in the unluckiest of times and I kind of think it's something in the DNA of Americans to strive to overcome obstacles."

"It's something in my DNA, I know that." Ren stretched his hands toward the woodstove. "I think we were in trouble. A lot of people thinking they could live a life of leisure on government benefits. Those people are either dead now or they've changed their minds. The folks who survive this will be resilient, hard workers. I'm not saying it's a good thing that maybe 100 million people have died in three months, but that the future might turn out okay because of the reordering of society that will occur because of it."

Rob considered that statement. Ren and Shane shared realism as a personality trait.

"That'll be a good thing…if we live."

Click nodded, no doubt thinking of his wife and kids who died in the fireball known as Chicago.

"Just trying to find a bright side in all of this." Ren stood. "I should get going. I'm hosting the truck drivers for a few days. Know of anyone who has freight to haul back? They'll be hauling some salt and Jos is rebalancing his inventory, but the trucks are still half-empty. Go figure that nobody wants to give up their corn."

"If you can get to Mara Wells, the MacArthur Dairy was branching into wind turbines. I don't know how far they got because it started snowing and we couldn't keep the road open with a 50-year-old plow burning biodiesel."

"Hmm, and Stan's crew isn't digging from the other side?"

"No radio transmissions either."

Ren looked thoughtful, shrugged, and headed for the door with Rob following. Shane reclined on pillows while Jazz read *Oliver Twist* aloud. Rob followed Ren to the backdoor. Click joined them.

"I'll make an effort to get through to Wichita tonight. Who am I looking for?"

"Phil Luiken at SullCorp. Or Crispin at Knight Industries."

Rob stirred from a thought.

"I forgot to ask – have you heard from Joseph yet?"

"I heard from backdoor channels that he made it as far as Columbus, but communications haven't really been reconnected, so that's all I know."

"Well, I'm sure he's fine. Perry's a good man."

"Absolutely. I'll keep the faith on that. You folks have a good night now."

Rob closed the door. Click had doffed his coat, but still wore the clothes he checked his trapline in. He jerked his thumb toward the annex of the mudroom that now served as a hygiene center.

"I'm going to go get cleaned up. Can you save me a bowl of whatever that is on the stove?"

"Of course. Um, Click …." The reporter looked at him, pushing his bangs back from his eyes. "I'm glad you're here."

Click grinned and nodded.

"Thank you. I'm glad to be here too."

He ducked through the curtain and Rob turned back to the stove. Jazz's voice drifted in from the living room.

"Easy. If you're in pain, let us help you."

Shane's voice sounded muffled. Glister came tapping into the room and stood by the back door.

"You gotta wait, boy. Click will be done soon." The Lab looked at him like he understood and settled down on the rug to wait. Alicia lumbered up the basement stairs, holding her belly with both hands.

"That smell's great."

"Sit down, I'll get you a bowl. You want some bread with it?" The darkly pretty woman nodded her head and lowered herself into one of the chairs at the kitchen table. Rob sliced off a generous portion of bread from a fresh-baked loaf and ferried a bowl of venison and vegetable stew to her. "Enjoy. We have maybe two more meals of venison left. We won't have any meat for a while after that."

"Will your friend get more food?"

"He'll try. He's a resourceful man, but these are trying times."

"I wish we could have brought all Mami's stash, but …." Alicia's young face turned downward. She pressed a hand to her belly where her t-shirt rippled as her baby moved. "If Mike survived, he'll figure out a way to get it to us." Her voice quavered.

"There's a lot of bad road between here and Santa Fe. He might just be waiting the other side of it." Rob hadn't gotten to know Shane's mercenary partner well during the few weeks he'd stayed with the family, but what he'd gotten to know he'd liked. And he thought Alicia was a fine and resilient girl who would figure out how to support her baby even if her husband never returned. She shook off the sadness to dig into the food. Nobody wasted food these days. The concept of not-eating because you weren't hungry no longer had a reality. "You feel up to grinding more wheat and corn?"

Before Shane's injury, he'd been the primary one to ride the stationary bike that charged battery-powered items and ground wheat into flour and corn into meal. Cai and Jazz picked up some slack, but they had other duties.

"Yeah, I can do that. How's he doing? He's been asleep pretty much whenever I check on him."

"He's in pain now that Brian is getting him moving and I think he overdid New Year's Eve. But he's healing, I think."

"How's the depression?"

"That seems to be under control. Maybe a little too early to say that certainly, but he's at least talking to me."

She nodded, wiping her bowl with the crust of her bread. She leaned back in her chair, sighing.

"I think how we used to take a simple stew for granted and I never would have eaten deer meat. I wonder if I'll look back on these times when my daughter is my age and miss such simple pleasures."

"My parents did. Just sitting on the back porch during an autumn evening or a dance at City Hall. Our era had become so busy. Maybe it's good to settle down and just breathe." Rob took her bowl to carry it to the pan of hot water on the coal stove. "I just wish we could do it with food, electricity, and heating oil."

She flashed white teeth and nodded, levering herself to standing. She paused before going into the dining room where the exercise bike along with its jerry-rigged attachments occupied one corner

"We're alive, so we're not doing so badly."

They both nodded more or less to themselves and then she turned toward her task and he turned toward his.

Dreams A to Z

Delaney House, Emmaus

Everything changed, his soul as numb as his hands. He'd split knuckles cage-fighting and rock-climbing before, but he'd always felt those pains before. Maybe it was the tequila. He poured himself another shot and tossed it back. His stomach turned ominously and sweat broke out on his forehead. The fetid air in la cantina stank of cigarettes and warm cerveza. Brick's face, as it turned to hamburger, rose with nausea. Shane swallowed it down. Behind him, someone called something out, but he didn't care. He poured himself another shot. It would be his last. If he drank it, he'd throw up, something he ordinarily tried to avoid. It wasn't that he couldn't hold his liquor but drinking on an empty stomach was never a good idea. Plus, though he'd paid a nice amount of money for the bottle that said it was Seco Herrerano, he doubted it. There were likely no government agencies checking on the purity of anything, let alone alcohol, in San Miguel.

"You Faraday?" The tall, broad-shouldered Hispanic guy leaned in way too close given the circumstances of the evening.

"Who wants to know?"

"Mike Sanchez. The CO said I should crash at your place tonight."

"You just in?"

"Yes, but I've been here before. You?"

"*A week …a lifetime. Not sure. Eric.*"

"*Ric?*"

"*Sure.*"

Mike laughed.

"*Why not, right?*" *He pointed a big paw of a hand at the Seco.* "*You sharing?*"

"*Please.*"

Mike reached over the back of the bar and snatched a shot glass.

"*So where you from, amigo?*"

"*Midwest. You?*"

"*California.*" *He said it with an exaggerated Chicano accent.* "*Been a while. You?*"

"*Since I've been home?*" *Mike tossed back his first shot.* "*Months.*" *Shane reached across the back of the bar himself, grabbed a water glass, and filled it with the faucet.*

"*You might want to watch that.*"

"*I've been here long enough it doesn't bother me anymore. You?*"

"*Like I said — not my first rodeo.*" *Mike's gaze lingered on Shane's knuckles, but he didn't say anything.* "*You know, that's like insulation.*" *He shifted his gaze to the back of Shane's head where he'd bundled his long hair after his morning shower in the back alley behind the barracks.*

Shane grabbed the tie that held it in place and released the still damp mess to cascade its curls over his shoulders and down his back.

"*Wow! That a bet?*"

"*It drove my father crazy.*"

"Here's to driving our fathers loco." When Shane didn't react, Mike lowered his shot glass to tap against Shane's water. "You drinking any of this?"

"I think I've had enough."

"Good because I'm just getting started."

Shane looked up from the water glass as the lighting changed from smoky dimness to New Mexico winter light. Mike stood beside Alicia's papa's old blue Ram, his eyes sunken into his sockets and sweat dampening the bit of hair that had grown out of his close cut.

"Take care of her, amigo!" And as he said this, a long white worm wriggled free of his right nostril.

"Shane – Shane – wake up. Shane!"

He flailed, trying to push his attacker away and pain lanced through his arm and side. The shaking stopped, but the hands remained on his shoulders. Jazz's face floated above his, eyes narrowed with concern.

"You okay?"

His heart galloped in his chest. He stared around the room. A shadow behind Jazz shimmered, pulled, and dissolved. He wiped the sweat off his forehead with the back of his hand.

"Was I screaming?"

"Muttering." She offered him his water bottle. He stared at it, chest still heaving, which hurt his ribs and shoulder and threatened spasms in his hip.

"Can you help me sit up?"

He'd been pushing himself up to sitting for a few days now, but pain ruled his life today and he wanted to avoid any more. Jazz grinned and slipped an arm behind his back to bring him far enough up to drink without drowning himself. Any other time he would have enjoyed the proximity to her breasts, but he just wanted to drink his water and lie back down.

"Thanks." He let her lower him to the pillows again. She set the bottle on the floor beside his mattress where there was a gap with hers. She lowered her butt onto her own mattress. "What time is it?"

"Evening. Sun's going down. Do you want some dinner?"

His hip throbbed and his back answered in counterpoint.

"I need to get on my side."

"You hurt yourself by overdoing?" She helped him roll onto his right side. This position was hard on his sore shoulder, but his back preferred it and he could feed himself. She brought him a bowl of vegetables laced with bits of venison. His left hand became more coordinated with practice.

"Brian and Ami both thought I was ready. Marnie thinks I just pushed it. You should see my hip. Purple as an eggplant. Brian dropped by earlier to put me through range-of-motion and it hurts. He said it would and just go with it. Mom says she'll let me out of bed tomorrow if I feel up to it."

"And you will." She grinned at him as she settled onto her mattress again.

"I don't know. I've never been a coward about pain, but this time…." He wanted to shrug, but he was learning not to move when he didn't have to.

"You're pretty hurt. It's okay to feel weak right now."

"It's not me."

"Do you always have to be you?"

Shane sighed. He had no idea. None of the touchstones in his life made any sense right now. The emotionality that seemed to be part of the head injury and pain of his other injuries further messed with his self-identity. He set the fork down and held his hand out to her. She took it.

"Thank you for keeping me from panicking."

"Sure. You'll be you again – well, maybe a little different."

"Because I accepted Christ?" She nodded. "I guess it was kind of obvious the other night."

"I don't think anyone objected."

"No, they've been banging on the door to heaven for me for 20 years." Laughing hurt his ribs a little less when he was lying on his right side. "How old were you?"

"I walked an aisle when I was 10, but I don't think my heart and mind followed my body. I count my salvation from when I was 17."

"Why?"

"Life speed bumps made me analyze my relationship with Christ. What about you?"

"I think Jesus visited me while I was dying." Her hand tightened on his and a beatific expression illuminated her face. "I was dreaming but it felt real."

"Probably was real, and because you were in distress your brain made it seem like a dream."

Shane sighed with relief. He'd kind of feared whoever he confessed to would say he was crazy. Hadn't that always been his fear since he was 14, that he couldn't be considered rational if he accepted what many people considered to be a fairy tale? Cai and Jazz were well-read, Marnie was a doctor, his parents didn't seem so dumb anymore. He hadn't sought God, but God found him amid a maelstrom and helped him hang on until rescue came.

"Did you acknowledge Him?" He'd drifted. She brought him back.

"Kind of hard not to. I kind of thought it was GPa Joseph – Vi's father – but then I accepted it was Jesus and – He knew stuff about me that nobody else knows. It's tempting to say that was my psyche giving me comfort, but – when I woke up – woke up alive – the feeling isn't going away. A lot of times when I'm lying quietly, I'm praying. I *never* prayed before. And – okay, I have a concussion so what I read doesn't stick well, but it's like I keep finding answers to my questions whenever I read the Bible." She nodded. "You too?"

"Yes. After I went through … what I went through, I had lots of questions and when I asked Him to answer them, I found those answers in the Bible. Still do."

"I'm just kind of scared."

"Of?"

"I don't want to lose myself."

She smiled.

"You won't. Jesus can transform your soul, but it's always voluntary whether you let Him change your mind."

"Did you let Him?"

She laughed now, tinged with ruefulness.

"He and I are still working on that."

"Still?"

"I bet if you'd asked Jacob in the last days of his life if he and Jesus were still working on him, he'd have confessed the truth."

Shane remembered some conversations from sharing a bed with Jacob in those last days. He nodded, then sighed.

"I should get the rest of this down before I fall asleep again. How goes the search for the article?"

"Very methodical. That room is wall to wall and floor to ceiling books and magazines. And, wow, the political philosophy section – I keep reminding myself not to linger." She laughed. Shane smiled. If his mind ever shifted back to earthly things, that section might capture his attention too. "I'll find it if it's there. Click says there are more bookshelves in the basement and out at the ranch."

"And in the attic. Keep searching. I—are there still books in the school library?"

"Yeah. They transported all of it to City Hall since the building wasn't secure. Carl Sullivan spearheaded that."

"How is Carl?" Something flickered behind her eyes. She stared at him for a long moment. "Yeah, concussion.

He died, right?" She nodded. "And, I'm getting tired again, so the symptoms get worse. Can you sit with me until I fall asleep?"

"I will." She shifted off her mattress and, still holding his hand, sat down on the floor with her back against his mattress. "Get some sleep. And if you wake up later, I'll just be in the den. Okay?"

He nodded. They sat there for some time, just quietly holding hands until his eyes grew heavy and sleep dragged him under into a meadow of prairie flox nodding in the sun and a roan mare waiting nearby.

After-Action Review

Sullivan B&B, Jericho Springs

Ami read the blood pressure cuff numbers and Chris recorded them on the clipboard. Beyond their sterile stall in the corner of her lab, she heard the door open.

"They're back," Jim reported. "We're meeting in the drawing-room."

"I'll be out in a few minutes."

Nick sighed and eased down his surgical mask.

"I think that went pretty well without the usual instruments. Respiration's good, blood pressure is steady. Chris, Gail, and I will wait here with him. You deal with that out there."

Chris flashed her older sister a reassuring smile, her teeth white in her swarthy face. Ami slipped out of the cubical, resealing the closures, dumping her surgical gown, hair wrap, and gloves in the laundry bin by the door. She washed her hands, ran water over her face, and headed to the sitting room where the others gathered.

"...nobody will find them until thaw." Javi sounded certain. "That's what took us so long, finding a place that wouldn't attract attention for a while."

"You and my wife hid bodies, Chavez. You can see why that might concern me?"

"Frankly, I can't see a whole lot anymore, Grant, but my expertise and her eyesight worked together."

"We removed anything that would identify them and bring it back to us." Emily didn't sound as certain, but Ami supposed it was her first carcass hiding. "We did the best we could."

"To cover up the murder of two Army officers." Ami didn't care if they shouted her down. Someone had to state the obvious.

"It wasn't murder." Emily's eyes snapped blue fire.

"Really? Perhaps someone could enlighten me as to how it wasn't."

Grant grimaced, shifting on the couch.

"I screwed up. I wanted to trust them. Their story checked out as best we could ascertain. So we decided to let them out."

"We?"

"I opposed the decision." Javi leaned against the wall by the patio doors.

"I pushed for it." Emily sighed, shaking her head. "I should have listened to you." She stared at Grant.

"Not worth fighting over now." Jim's crags etched deeply into his face like grooves in granite. "Errors of judgment occur. We dealt with it."

"How's Travis?" Eden hadn't asked and Ami blinked at Javi in amazement.

"It'll be a while before he comes out of the anesthesia. Can't tell how long because ether is not an exact science. We're packing his spine with snow, trying to mitigate the damage as much as we can. We'll know more tomorrow. At least he didn't bleed massively. We only used a unit of blood."

Eden wiped tears from her eyes. She'd kept a brave face until now.

"What's the extent of the damage?" Javi remained a realist.

"We don't know yet. That might take a few days. Nick's going to stay the night. He and Gail. Chris is going back to the med center, so we don't attract attention. I still don't understand how you ended up killing them."

"They seemed friendly enough – we were having breakfast and – well, my theory is they were here for Eden and Travis."

"Why?"

Eden cleared her throat, wiped her tears as Grant and Emily exchanged glances.

"My mother is Francine Maracle and Travis is President Meyer's son."

"Ah, so they're assassins, then?" Ami knew Javi couldn't see her glance his way, but he and Grant both nodded.

"They had weapons, guns. Must have been secreted in their packs. They shot Travis and me and they would have killed us all if Javi hadn't …."

"Thank God the girls were still downstairs." Emily cried now. Jim put a comforting hand on his daughter's shoulder.

"And, Jim, thank you! I couldn't have taken both of them. I couldn't even see her." Jim nodded at Javi. "So are we done?"

"Far as I'm concerned, yes." Grant stood, pushing with his good arm.

"What about the helicopter?" All eyes turned toward Eden. Her gaze made a slow circuit of the older adults in the room.

"Nothing to be done. None of us can fly it and Shane is down for a while, so.... It's not perfect, but let's just hope nobody comes asking questions we aren't prepared to answer." Grant looked around the circle to see if anyone had any.

"They will, though." Ami clasped her hands together in her lap. Just half an hour, she'd been wrists deep in a teenage boy's abdomen. "Cai Delaney will ask questions – of us, of everyone and anyone who might know anything about that murder behind the hotel."

"Then I need to reach out to Shane, see if he can call the bloodhound off. We didn't have anything to do with that and we got our mess out of their town as quickly as we could."

Grant turned toward the door, stretching a hand to brace himself on the doorframe. Sweat broke out on his forehead.

"That'll have to wait until tomorrow." Ami pinned Emily with a commanding stare. "He needs to rest. Javi, maybe you and I can send this message to Shane."

Grant and Javi exchanged glances. Well, probably not. Javi's pretense of sight grew more thespian every day.

"Go ahead." Javi lifted his chin at Grant's permission. "Don't tell him what went down here, just that we had nothing to do with the hotel and we need his brother to back off."

"I can try. I'll need your help, Ami."

Emily took Grant by the arm to lead him away. Javi dropped a hand on Ami's shoulder. Although he could get around the house fairly well on his own, he struggled when the lights were low. Eden stood.

"Can I go see Travis?"

"Yes, so long as it's okay with Dr. Kletti."

The girl nodded and disappeared toward the kitchen.

"What aren't you telling me?" Ami kept her voice low as she and Javi headed toward the basement stairs.

"Nothing. Nothing I can tell you anyways."

Ami stopped and turned toward him. His swarthy face lay bathed in shadows, the only light being from the glass-doored woodstove in the adjacent living room.

"Is this where you pull the 'no sex until you tell me' gambit?"

"No. I enjoy sex too much for that. It's one of the chief reasons I'm not a Muslim." Ami laid her hand on his chest. "I'm glad you weren't hurt today, which concerns me. You're the longest relationship I've ever had."

He felt for the opening frame into the living room and guided her toward one of the sofas. He pulled a long leg up onto the sofa so he could face her.

"You're the longest for me too."

In the low and shifting light, she could just make out the conflict on his face.

"I don't know if we should talk about the future or not."

He swallowed audibly.

"Don't be afraid."

"Of what?" She couldn't think of any reason to be afraid other than that Cai Delaney might push too hard and get himself killed for his efforts.

"Of what happens to me if I don't have your help."

Ami quit breathing for a handful of heartbeats, just stared at her lover – a man who did not do vulnerable and yet was standing in the middle of a freeway at rush hour.

"I'm not here out of obligation. When we started our relationship – before your eyesight started to fail – did you feel obligated to be with me?"

"No. I thought you were sexy, and it never really occurred to me that it might become more. Though I – well, I kind of have felt a connection with you since about the second day – that night at the motel – but I never figured it to last as long as it has. Three months is – about 11 weeks longer than I've ever sustained a relationship closer than Confidential Informant. You?"

"I dated another intern for – two months."

"What happened there?"

"He had a meltdown from the stress of working in the ER and withdrew from the program." He chuckled, which Ami found endearing. Javi didn't do meltdowns. "I find your unflappable attitude much less frightening. And your one-week relationship?"

"I was on leave and she was a fellow tourist – German. I don't remember much else about her. We saw some tourist sites in Istanbul and rolled in the sack like twice a day for a week. And then she went back to Munich and I went back to the Mirage."

"So do you think if we'd met under different circumstances we'd be lovers?"

"I think I would have wanted to be lovers. It's the future that has me stumped. Would we still be together if I weren't going blind? Or if we weren't living in the same house? I mean, I've never been this honest with anyone, but –I just don't know."

"Why are we having this conversation?" Ami had never been so honest with any boyfriend before and she didn't know where it might be headed.

"When Travis went down, and Grant started to bleed – Eden and Emily both became tigresses. And I thought 'would Ami do the same for me?'" He shifted, started to stand, muttering. "It was stupid."

Ami caught his arm, pulled him back onto the sofa before he got all the way upright.

"I don't know how I would react because I've not been in that situation. But when I walked into the kitchen and saw the blood all over Jim's clothes my first thought was 'Is

Javi okay?' Followed quickly by 'who needs my medical attention?'

"The Hippocratic Oath takes precedence over wild sex anytime you want it? Who saw that coming? Let's go. I'm exhausted. We need to send that message before I can't think."

"This fatigue a new thing?"

"I think it's connected to the blindness." He drew her up from the sofa. "Staying functional requires a lot of effort and, at the end of the day, I feel like I've run a marathon."

"You'll adjust and hopefully it won't be forever."

"That's what Brian says." They reached the basement stairs, but he turned to face her before going down them. "Thank you for being concerned about me. Turns out my skills still work when I can't see." He kissed her on the mouth and headed down the stairs ahead of her.

Coupling

Delaney House, Emmaus

Cai and Marnie slowly settled back on the pillows, pulling the blankets over them. They'd go down to sleep in a few minutes, but some alone-time in their bedroom every few days allowed them to be a couple. Cai noticed the other day that Rob and Jill disappeared like that sometimes too. Amid tragedy upon tragedy, love needed nurture to remain sweet.

"How's this going?" He put his hand on her belly. At five months along, even a tall long-waisted woman like Marnie began to show.

"Far as we can tell, I'm good. We have a whole stream of pregnancies coming after us, by the way. Lots of failed birth control."

"Without Netflix, what else are people going to do unless they have a murder mystery to solve."

"How's that going?"

"Don't know. Nobody knows anything." Her hair used to smell of strawberries and apples and now he just smelled soap and a scent he thought of as her. "It's like this guy fell from the sky."

"I didn't find fall injuries." He knew from the timbre of her dark voice that she joked.

"Shane says he'll look at the evidence tomorrow...if he even feels like sitting up. How is he...really?" She sighed into his chest.

"He's healing, but it will take time and I hate to be a Debbie Downer, but there's a chance he won't walk again."

Cai lifted his head from the pillow to stare to meet her gaze. The cold room clawed at him.

"You're kidding?"

"No. Hip injuries are tricky, and his hip was reset by a veterinarian without an MRI or even an x-ray. He seems not to have any nerve impingement and if anyone can suck up the pain and surprise me, it's Shane, but these sorts of injuries used to regularly cause permanent disabilities."

Cai settled back on the pillow, drew her back into his chest.

"I'm going to stay in denial about that for now."

"Of course, you are. Nobody does optimism better than my man." She giggled and then sighed again. "You know, Rafe Conopher isn't the only one losing it. I've had a half-dozen women come in with bruises. Some of them I'm not surprised, but others – I never would have thought those men would hit their wives."

"Hunger messes with your thought patterns. Desperation makes it worse. I'll talk to Rafe tomorrow – maybe sound Dell out too. I can't promise anything though. We're just trying to keep neighbor from looting neighbor.

We're not actual cops who can interfere in domestic disputes."

"Putting someone in the town cells right now would add a new dimension of putting prisoners on ice, I guess."

He kissed her on the forehead. They at least still had a sense of humor. Doctors get paid well even if it was in food. The Delaney household wasn't eating as much as they might like, but they weren't starving…yet.

"We should go downstairs before the blankets freeze."

"Just a few more minutes. You're curled up with a pregnant lady. You shouldn't need to worry that you'll freeze." Her fingers brushed his lower abdomen where his tattoo hid. It seemed like another lifetime ago that he'd marked himself with the guilt he thought would never end.

"You do make a great bedwarmer."

"That's so rude." She poked her fingertips into the ticklish spot at the top of his ribs and he twisted to get away from her.

"Hey, not fair! You know how ticklish I am!"

She sat up, reached for his sweatshirt that she'd worn today because her clothes were quickly becoming too tight.

"I'm exhausted."

Deprived of her warmth, he reached for his pants.

"We all are. The days are getting longer though, so that'll help."

"Optimist now, optimist forever."

"You know it. Thanks for telling me the truth about Shane."

"Sure. Your mom already knows."

"Does he?"

"I've broached the subject. The world's foremost realist already knew, but he's choosing not to let it consume him."

"So the depression probably really is gone?"

"He's turned a corner on it, I think. Plus, how many challenges has Shane faced that he didn't overcome?"

"None that I know of. Bring your hairbrush. I'll re-braid your hair for you."

"Sounds lovely. A hundred strokes?"

"Sure." He loved brushing her long, thick hair. Pregnancy thickened it further and it was at least a hand longer than it had been when they married in July. Dressed, they headed back into the warmth and embrace of family, a little closer as a couple than they'd been this morning.

January 3

Reviewing the Evidence

Delaney House, Emmaus

Shane spread the evidence across the table as far as he could reach. Cai sat down at the end of the table and waited while Shane examined the clothing, the photos, and the jewelry, then read Cai's notes and the autopsy results. He rubbed the back of his neck where dark curls now sprung.

"Do you need to lie down?"

"Soon." Shane braced his forearms on the wheelchair arms to shift his weight. He still didn't have enough strength in his shoulder to do seat presses. "So, this guy was anonymous. A shadow man. No fingerprints, no labels in his clothes. Nothing weird about what he was smothered with – Sharon found evidence of cotton-poly, which would mean a sofa pillow, she thought."

"Do you recognize him?"

"No. Contrary to popular belief, there are no spook conventions and he's not alive to show me the secret handshake." Cai laughed nervously. Shane's smirk grew larger. "I'd say he's spent some time in sunny climes based on his tan configuration. Probably military training."

"How do you get that?"

"You can tell a lot about a man with how he treats his boots." Shane pointed to the heavy pair of black leather boots. "Standard issue military and that polish is something you learn in officer candidate's school. It's been a while, though. Traveling rough." He tried to shift his weight again. "Take me back to bed. We can talk once I'm horizontal."

Cai helped him onto the sofa and settled under blankets.

"There's one thing that doesn't make sense – it's out of place. The tattoo. It's pretty distinctive. A C and three stars. A guy like that would have it removed because in the old world it could be tracked. A guy like that wouldn't risk wearing something memorable like that."

"It was on his forearm. I mean, my tattoo is on my lower abdomen, so it's only visible to certain people."

"You have a tattoo?"

"Don't want to talk about it."

"Love tag, huh?" The teasing glint in Shane's eye almost cause Cai to share, but he didn't want to bring up painful memories for either of them.

"Something like that, not really. So, he wasn't keeping it a secret. Which means?"

"No idea."

"Any ideas for who would drop a body in your backyard?"

"A few. I thought I'd mended most of my relationships since I got back, but Josh Callahan comes to mind – some of the guys at the militia might still hold a grudge."

"I think the B&B are acting weird."

"Rigby insists they didn't have anything to do with it. And it's one of those things you don't want to push too hard into. They won't mess with you so long as you don't mess with them, but you are edging toward messing with them."

"Why is your boss meeting with Josh Callahan out by the hotel?"

"He's not my boss and I'd guess he needs some muscle with Dylan down."

"What about Chavez?"

"He doesn't work for Rigby either." Shane grinned at Cai's skepticism. "We're contractors, not employees."

"It's a fine distinction." Shane shrugged, rubbed his shoulder, then grinned at Cai's frown. "You really aren't going to tell me what I need to know?"

"I really don't think I know what you think you want to know. Rigby came here to protect his family. Yes, he's monitoring whatever is out there to monitor. Yes, Chavez and Rigby both have killed people. Probably Dylan has too. None of the three of them have a reason to frame me. Josh Callahan might. But I don't like him for this."

"Why not?"

"I don't think Josh started out as a killer. And I'd be surprised if he has killed anyone. If he were going to do it, however, he'd do it with a gun, not up-close and personal with whatever bludgeon and then with a pillow."

"Kletti thinks the head injury might have been an accident."

Shane nodded. Glister shoved his big head under Shane's hand and he distractedly rubbed the dog's ears.

"Josh would have shot him to put him out of his misery. He's just not a pillow kind of guy."

"How can you be sure?"

"Because *I'm* not a pillow kind of guy. That guy I killed up at the Shack – I accidentally broke his larynx and I tried to save his life soon as I realized what I'd done. I didn't want to kill him. Prison changes people, but I don't think Josh's basic nature has changed. He wouldn't put a pillow over someone's face like that."

Cai opened his mouth to ask more questions and then just stopped, sitting down on Jazz's mattress instead.

"Do you have any idea why this guy was looking for Eric Faraday?"

Shane stared at him.

"That shouldn't track to here."

"It did, apparently."

"CSA are – were masters of building identities and manipulating records. Eric Faraday is in Phuket."

"Only he isn't."

Shane sighed, shrugged with his good shoulder.

"I'll ask Rigby to look into it, but … I don't know. It shouldn't track back to here."

They stared in different directions while Glister cleaned Shane's left hand with his long tongue.

"You okay?"

"Yeah. I just don't want to overdue again and set myself back."

"No, I mean – did you try to hurt yourself?"

"Maybe. I don't remember." Shane's green eyes shifted to Cai's gaze. "You don't have to worry about me. Things are better now."

Cai wanted to believe that, but Shane's bluish waxen features the night they found him still haunted him and Shane's gaze still shifted behind him at times as if someone was standing there in the empty room.

"It's called PTSD." Shane stopped petting Glister to push himself up against the arm of the sofa. "Things from other places and other times pop into my mind now and then, and it's like it's happening right now."

"I know what PTSD is. How does almost dying make it better?"

"Not … but come on. I came to Watch Night."

"Yeah. Is that your version of walking an aisle?"

"It's the closest I can come right now." Brother stared at brother. "I'm done running. He's real to me now."

Cai nodded. They'd argued so often about this when they were teenagers. It seemed anticlimactic now.

"I guess you're going to do this your own way."

"Don't I always?" Cai snorted.

"Okay. So, I've got places to go. You okay here on your own? Dad said you are, but Marnie's still pretty certain you need to stay down."

"I'm probably going to crash five minutes after you leave anyway. And you don't have to worry about my hurting myself. I just reached the end of myself and found God waiting there for me – where He'd always been if I'd just stopped running long enough to find that out."

"Okay. If you come to any conclusions about what the B&B might be hiding, will you share?"

"If it has anything to do with the murder – yeah, probably."

Cai laughed.

"That's so you. And, yet, not."

"Let me handle it. Chavez *will* kill you if you push into their business, so let me handle it."

The hairs on Cai's forearms stood on end. He imagined standing in the B&B kitchen drinking a cup of coffee while talking with Chavez, who seemed so relaxed – like a big cat ready to pounce on an antelope.

"How did you get into that – that line of work?"

Shane's gaze twittered. He must be used to lying about that question. But then his gaze settled on Cai's – well, not his face. Somewhere lower – collar bones maybe.

"Bad company. I was supplementing my income in college selling pot."

"I knew that. That doesn't bring you up on the government's radar generally."

Shane sighed.

"One of Jason's guys talked me into hauling a shipment to Arizona on my way back to school. I dropped it off. No problem. But the house was under surveillance and my roommate's father was high up in the DEA. He recognized me and called off the agents. He warned me that at some point, I would owe him a favor. Three days before graduation he called it."

"Spying on the militia?" Shane nodded, mouth working.

"That made me *persona non gratis* here, so I headed to Cali to work for Grandpa's friend. Turned out his kid was hauling all kinds of illegal stuff into South America. When they picked me up, I was terrified. That's when I met Grant. They embedded me back with the company. My job was simply to fly planes, do whatever was asked, and take a lot of mental notes. When they broke the owners, Knights Industries swept in to buy the company's assets and they offered me to fly for them. I thought I was leaving the CSA behind at that point, but Grant showed up a few weeks into it and informed me that I was still an agent."

"But you'd quit when you came home?"

"More or less. I wasn't doing well. War follows you. The shit you do in war follows you."

A soldier dying in front of him while the gun slowly cooled in his hand flashed through Cai's mind.

"And you feel okay now?"

Shane frowned, then shrugged, then chuckled.

"No. I feel like I've got a dislocated hip and shoulder and cracked ribs." Cai laughed too. "But, yeah, I think I see light at the end of the tunnel now. And, all this lying around, which would have been dangerous for me before, is giving me time to think and stow some stuff."

Cai rubbed the back of his neck.

"So how are you still mixed up with them?"

Shane sighed.

"That's the part I can't tell you. Sorry."

"I'm worried about you."

"With them?"

Cai nodded.

"Well, right now, if Chavez decided to kill me, he could. But he's got no reason to want to do that."

"Does he need a reason?"

Shane's eyebrows arched and then he laughed, grimacing, bracing his ribs.

"He's not a rabid dog that attacks randomly. Yes, he needs a reason."

"How did he end up in that line of work then?"

'My guess – probably an angry young man who learned early to control his reactions. That's who they like."

"And that's why you aren't passionate anymore."

Shane sighed, cocked his head, then shrugged with one shoulder.

"Depression sort of dulls all other emotions, I think. But, yeah, I'm probably never going to get as excited as I used to be about stuff. And, now, I need to go to sleep and you need to go do whatever it is you gotta do. And, Cai, don't worry – you're not turning into us. You've got to kill a whole lot more people than you've killed before you start to feel so little about it."

Cai nodded, then a thought occurred.

"Who says you don't feel? You feel those deaths so passionately you went off the rails and nearly killed yourself."

He squeezed Shane's good shoulder and then, steeling his backbone, walked away from him to the kitchen because he needed to trust Shane sometime and that time was well-past.

Forging

Delaney Ranch, Jericho Township

The warmth of the forge slapped Andrew Bennett in the face as he pulled the shed door open. The forge in the middle of the building warmed all corners of it, casting a mellow amber glow on all the old wood surfaces and infusing the air with a tang of hot metal. Nevada stood with her back to him, dressed in overalls and a welder's shield, her hammer coming down on a piece of strapping iron. Andrew circled along the wall until she saw him and stopped pounding.

"Hey." She stripped off the shield and idled the input on the forge. The bright cherry of the coal dulled. "Nice to see you. What can I do for you?"

Nevada Randolph was in her mid-30s with dyed-blond hair now growing out at the roots. She was slim, with surprisingly muscular arms, and tended to show entirely too much skin for Emmaus society, although truthfully, it made sense in the forge's heat.

Andrew heaved a deep sigh and stiffened his spine. He didn't fear much, but he feared saying this aloud. Verbalizing would make it real and Andrew wanted to deny Matt's reality, though he knew he couldn't.

"I've got a problem. My son appears to have the secondary flu."

"Oh, shit. I'm sorry, Andrew."

He felt tears creeping up behind his glottis.

"Matt's legs already won't hold him though he can still move them a little."

"Progressive?"

"Yeah. He can move his arms, but they're getting clumsy and this morning he was out of breath. I got this idea. I saw it on a television program many years ago." Andrew pulled out a drawing Faith had done, based on his description. Nevada wiped dark-rooted blond hair from her face and joined him at her side bench to talk.

"It's like a cuirass." He smiled that she knew what it was.

"Yeah, it's based on old armor. It's called a biphasic cuirass. It uses vacuum pumps to work a vest that is inside the cuirass."

"Acting like a diaphragm."

"Yes. I hope it doesn't come to it, but I want to be ready if it does."

"We can try. You bring measurements?" He flipped the paper over so she could see them. She looked over at a discarded car hood in the corner. "I have the materials and I'll prioritize it. It'll take a while – days. Fortunately for you, I worked with a creative anachronism society for a while, so I've made these before. I'm not a leatherworker, though. You have the vest worked out?"

"Yeah, Hiram Shore says he can help me. He's got a kid where it seems to have stopped at his hips, so he gets it."

She nodded. Hiram suggested Nevada because he'd made the apron she now wore and touched as if she remembered it too. She must be about four months along now, still slim, but maybe the apron didn't fit quite so loosely in the front now.

"Of course. When he's done, bring it here and I'll adjust as needed and then we'll need to fit it on Matt. I can probably make it more comfortable with thinner material across the back. What's this?" She pointed to a square at the bottom of the figures.

"I found the proposed measurements for the cuirass. I figured you'd appreciate the calculations."

"Absolutely." She scratched an eyebrow with a thumbnail. "I don't want to scare you, but you probably need to have extra materials to fill in gaps that will appear when his arms and legs start to lose mass."

It felt like she kicked him in the guts, but he nodded, swallowing the lump in his throat. Matt's legs were still muscular even as they weakened, but it had only been a day. Of course, atrophy would set in if he couldn't move. Shore's son's legs already looked stick-thin after only a week.

Andrew drew a steadying breath.

"Sorry to have to say that," Nevada said. "I know it would be hard if someone had to say that about Kim."

"Thank you for your honesty. You're the first to mention it, but you're absolutely right. We need to prepare for the worst and hopefully be surprised by the better. I'll leave you to it."

Andrew fled the forge without even talking about price so he wouldn't cry in front of her. Matt, paralyzed, was not something he was prepared to accept and yet, he knew in his heart of hearts, that's where they were headed. He got into his truck and leaned his forehead against the steering wheel, weeping.

Mechanical Problem

City Hall, Emmaus

Ice rimed the windows as Jazz perused the stacks. The heating system for City Hall fried in the Pulse, so Rob conducted Mayor business out of the house. Joe worked out of his car. If the fire department were called up, they'd shovel snow on the flames. Thank goodness someone thought to bring the old-fashioned card catalog to City Hall and she'd not forgotten how to use it. Jazz blew on her left hand while her right trailed along the spines. She found the three-book section she was looking for and took them to a table by the window so she could scan through them, turning off her headlamp to preserve the battery.

Forty-five minutes later, a frustrated Jazz locked the library behind her and trudged through the snow to where Rocket the mustang waited. She rubbed the mare's neck, talking to her in low friendly tones before mounting the saddle and turning toward home. She flinched as a compact and muscular chestnut gelding appeared from her left.

"Afternoon, young lady. What are you up to?"

Ren Sullivan looked different in a heavy winter coat with a blue beanie pulled down low.

"Um, I'm using the library."

"That's why I'm asking. I thought we'd abandoned the building, but then I saw the horse when I rode by earlier. Why hang out in a freezing cold building looking for books when you live in arms-reach of the Delaney private collection?"

"Because what I was looking for isn't there. But it wasn't in this library either."

Ren wiped snot off his upper lip.

"Can I ask what information you're looking for? The Shack has an extensive library too."

"Alex Lufgren is trying to build an iron lung for his brother-in-law."

"This secondary flu?"

Jazz nodded, pulling Rocket's reins to keep her from biting the chestnut gelding. Could horses be alphas like some dogs were? Her family had once had a terrier who acted like Rocket.

"And they're needing something they don't have?"

"Expertise. They built the box. Alex says he's pressure tested it and thinks it'll work, but they don't know how to make it breathe."

Ren grunted, then stared at the horizon. Jazz waited.

"My sister had polio when I was a kid. She spent six months in an iron lung, and I liked mechanics, so I studied it. If I'm remembering correctly, it's two vacuum pumps that operate in sequence – one to add pressure to the box and make the lungs exhale and the other to remove pressure so the lungs can reinflate."

Jazz considered what that must have been like, to have a sister paralyzed, but she didn't know what to say. Ren gave her a grin.

"She recovered – well, mostly. She had some weakness in her left arm, but she didn't let that slow her down much."

"She still alive."

"No, she died about – a decade ago now. Cancer. She lived a full life though. Travel, career, marriage, kids."

"Good for her. So vacuum pumps – like from a car's air-conditioner?"

"Or a floor vac. The change in pressure doesn't need to be that great. Brenda used to take a break from the lung by laying on this thing called a 'rocking bed'. The rocking action would move her diaphragm up and down to simulate breathing. After she graduated from the iron lung, she'd sleep on the rocking bed. Eventually, she didn't need it, but it took time."

"Good to know. Thank you. I was thinking of it as a medical challenge, but it's mechanics."

"It is. What fascinated me was the timing. One pump has to turn off and the other turn on and then cycle like that and if the timing gets off, it's pretty distressing to the patient."

Jazz nodded. Thanks to her father and brothers, she'd grown up learning mechanics and she could visualize the two vacuums with the timer to keep the cycle going.

"Thank you so much. I'm going to head to the house and see what Shane thinks."

"Well, you're most welcome, young lady. I'll head on now and you let me know how that turns out. Sometimes it takes a community to solve problems."

Jazz smiled and turned Rocket toward home. Shane opened blurry eyes when she came into the living room.

"How are you?" he asked after she'd spent several minutes sketching what she thought would work for the wooden lung.

"I learned something about iron lungs today." She shifted so she could sit on the floor in front of the sofa and show him her drawing.

"What do you think?"

"Theoretically, that would work." Shane's mouth tightened as he handed back the sketch. "Sucks that my brain doesn't work right now."

"You think you're still concussed?"

"No. I'm just exhausted. I feel clearer when I'm awake, but some stuff, like the mechanics of this – I just don't have the energy to expend on it." He rubbed a hand over his face. "What's the weather like out there."

Jazz got up to add another load of wood to the fire. The main floor of the Delaney house stayed fairly warm with the coal furnace in the basement and the coal cooking stove in the kitchen, but the living room cooled off if the woodstove wasn't going.

"Cold! Must be 20 below. Rocket doesn't seem to mind though." The coal bed in the bottom of the woodstove glowed red through a thin crust of ash. She fully opened the chimney damper, laid one quarter-round on the left side and another on the right, leaning so they touched above the coals. She then left the airtight door open a crack and dialed open the air intake.

"No, she's wild at heart. What about you?"

"I miss my car's heater."

"And here I lie in the lap of luxury, not even expected to load the woodstove."

She turned to look at him, holding the airtight door slightly open.

"Could you?"

He grinned and shook his head.

"I'd probably sleep through freezing to death."

Flames started flickering, so Jazz closed the door, levering the handles closed.

"You hungry?"

"What time is it?"

"About 11."

"No, I can wait for lunch."

"You know, don't you?"

"That food's going to be tight until spring? Sure. Hard to miss that."

"Ren Sullivan brought in a shipment and it's already gone."

"People snap up what's available while it's available."

Jazz glanced at the stack temp and reduced the air intake and adjusted the stack damper.

"You read about that in history – how the pioneers would show up right after the train or supply coach was unloaded, but I never thought I'd see it, let alone live through it."

"Yeah."

"Injuries like yours…having to boil water before we drink it…heating with coal that we shovel into the furnace. It's just…. Historians always want to visit the past times, but we're living it now."

"For now. The technology we knew still exists, it's just not accessible currently, so this is a vacation at best."

"Vacation?! This is a sucky timeshare. Why didn't we pick Kauai circa last year?"

"Yeah. The Garden Isle would be nice and warm about now."

Shane raised his left hand to touch her cheek, eyes warm and full of an emotion she couldn't interpret.

"If we were on Maui right now…and I weren't hurt."

She smiled at him, then took his chapped hand in both of hers.

"You need to answer me something, though."

"What?"

"You and Marnie?"

"Water under a long-ago bridge."

"You sure?"

"For me, yes. I assume for her. We have to be nice to one another but I'm not even sure we would be friends if the situation were different."

"And there's no other women?"

Shane's gaze turned away toward the woodstove and Jazz's heart skipped a beat.

"I haven't been a monk, if that's what you're asking, but my heart doesn't belong to anyone else anymore."

For a heartbeat she considered his full lips, but then he yawned, showing that he had no fillings before extracting his hand from hers to cover his mouth.

"Sorry."

"No, it's fine. Take a nap. It'll fill in the time before lunch. I'm going to go ride the bike, charge up the radios so I can take one with me when I ride to Alex's house this afternoon."

Shane yawned again, but then caught her hand.

"I promise, I'll stay awake when we can have a real date."

A real date? In a world that had been off-kilter for months, it seemed as if dating would never come around again. The ultimate realist suggesting a future stunned her and she thought it lucky that he closed his eyes for sleep so he couldn't see the tears of hope that sprung into her eyes.

Sons & Brothers

Conopher Farm, Jericho Township

Dell Conopher ducked under the lintel at the top of the stairs. He'd finished the morning chores early and decided to spend some time with Kix. He usually came up to sit with him after dinner, but what time he could give his oldest son seemed precious. What if his lungs grew weak? Death seemed so much worse than paralysis. Dell resolved not to think that way in front of his son.

Kix lay on his right side, facing Dell, limbs limp and propped on pillows, eyes closed, as he'd been for the last month. Dell used a washcloth to wipe drool off his cheek. His fever broke yesterday, Leisha reported.

"Hey, Kix. How you doing today, buddy?"

It had been weeks since Kix acknowledged their presence with so much as an eyelid flicker. Dr. Callahan thought he was comatose. Dell figured it didn't hurt to talk with him even if he was sleeping. He pulled a chair over to the bed and picked up Kix's left arm to massage and stretch each joint while he told him about the farm, his siblings, the town, anything that came to mind.

"Geneva really looked funny holding that nanny goat off with a pail."

Dell walked around to the far side of the bed, pausing at the window. Rafe stood in the driveway talking with Cai Delaney. Neither man looked happy to see the other. Near as Dell could remember, Rafe had been a senior when Cai was a freshman. They'd never been friends, though Cai played on their softball team this summer.

Dell rolled Kix onto his back, gently arranging his arm on a pillow. His stick-thin left leg remained limp, easy to stretch and move. Dell put a pillow behind his knee to ease that joint. Kix's right leg had been twisted and spastic for weeks, but today, it moved easily under Dell's big hands and the toes didn't point down so much, nor did the limb twist with spasms like usual. He draped that leg over the other half of the pillow. Kix's right hand remained fisted under his chin. It didn't do any good to arrange it on a pillow. It wouldn't stay. Dell did place a pillow between the boy's chest and upper arm because that seemed to help his hand relax a little.

"Getting pretty skinny there, kid." They fed him twice a day through a feeding tube and then a longer feed at night. Leisha boiled vegetables and pureed them to mix with the protein powder slurry that was his main meal. Still, Kix kept losing weight, his limbs becoming more atrophied with every day.

Dell peeled back Kix's left eyelid. The eye still turned in toward his nose. Dell placed a couple of drops of eyewash and then moved to the other eye. This one twitched instead of turning inward. That was new. Did it mean something? Dell administered the drops and arranged the pillow under Kix's head.

"Well, you're probably tired and I've got work to do. I figured we'd read more of *Watership Down* tonight. That sound good?"

Kix's right eye twitched behind the lid, but otherwise, he wasn't giving away any secrets. Cai Delaney waited in the living room when Dell went downstairs.

"Walk with me to my horse."

Dell followed him out the door. The cold moderated overnight, so the wind didn't take away his breath.

"What's up?"

"I just wanted to let you know that Rafe is scaring me. I tried to ask him about some mechanical issues, and he is paranoid."

"Yeah." Dell didn't want to admit it, but Rafe's behavior had been obvious for weeks now.

"How long has that been going on?"

"He's always had a temper, but it's been growing since he killed the USDA cop. I don't know how to help him. Makes me hope that whatever brain damage Kix is left with includes amnesia for the men he had to kill."

"Yeah." Cai stared off across the fields, his blue eyes cast into dark places. He sighed. "I heard a couple of his kids have the flu. Anything Marnie can do about that?"

"He's convinced Marnie is causing the paralysis, calls her Typhoid Marnie."

"He needs not to do that to my face."

Dell chuckled. Cai never gained a reputation as a brawler, but Shane's kicking Rafe out of Nick's was town

197

legend, so Cai's mild manners might just be the sod over a banked fire, hiding fury.

"Let me know if you need any help with this."

"I will, but – well, provided we stay off certain subjects, Rafe's been a big help around the place. And his family is safer here than in town."

"I get it. Just don't be a hero, right?"

Dell nodded. Rafe's mental condition concerned. He was drinking a lot and Dell suspected he wasn't buying his booze from safe sources. He'd seen bruises on Cady. He knew something needed to be done, but other than talking with him – well, Rafe was family and family didn't always make sense. They fed Kix every day even though he couldn't move even an eyelid. It seemed like you could justify all sorts of toleration for the right people.

Waking

Seattle

Whoosh, hiss. Whoosh, hiss. The dull beep-beep-beep of a backhoe. Whoosh, hiss.

"...horeme...acose?"

The woman's voice sounded like someone talking through a closed window. He tried to peel his eyes open but failed. A vague sensation of floating, of changing position in space, enveloped him as a whining buzz pulsed somewhere under him. He tried to listen to the woman.

"...plump shadafis an sullinoval ... recalled a ... patron of arts ... pleasant smile ... lips."

She read and he felt it somehow familiar, a book his parents read aloud to them when he was a child. It remained hard to hear through the door, over the whoosh-hiss, and backhoe. He thought to ask her to speak up but couldn't feel his tongue or lips.

Realization clawed at him. He couldn't feel ... anything. He might be suspended in the air, touching nothing. There was a movie a long time ago with the premise, from the guy that wrote the dinosaur cloning movie. Was he in a coma? That would explain the inability to move or talk. Wouldn't it?

"God, these bloody English! Bursting with money and indigestion."

The door remained closed, but with an effort, he could make out the words. He knew this woman, he thought, but he didn't know from where.

Hello? I'm here. How do I let you know?

The floating sensation enveloped him again with the whirring of some kind of hydraulics. He remembered a guy in boot – or maybe it had been BUDS – who fell off a high wall. When they'd visited him later, he'd been in this bed that moved on its own. Might that be the case? Geo didn't know and the uncomfortable thought of what such a bed meant caused him to flinch.

Geo…his name? Yes, he remembered. The woman said his name and he heard some shuffling and the voice grew closer for a moment.

"How's he doing today?" The male voice sounded equally muffled, not to mentioned slightly blurred by the Ozark accent. Ozark? East? He remembered traveling through mountains.

"…ver's down. …number … vous system."

"…miracle he survived. …all thanks to you."

"…licking his hand." The woman sounded amused. Geo couldn't feel what she meant. Maybe they weren't talking about *his* hand.

"Hey, man." The man's voice moved closer to his ear. "Hope you don't mind my letting Duke lick you, but he seems to get pleasure from it, and maybe you can feel it. Anyway, we're not supposed to stay long." What he said next got lost in the whirring of the bed moving. "…heroine. She got you back here, kept you alive." Whoosh-hiss. "…raided Kenmore…captured…some…but Echo Lake was empty…." Whoosh-hiss. "…knew we were coming." Whoosh-hiss. "…figure who did this to you."

Sherwin stepped back, called to Duke. It became harder to hear him.

"…still…ur dog."

Geo remembered the big black Lab who he'd inherited quite by accident.

The woman's voice moved closer to his ear.

"I know you're in there. You have to show them. If you want to live, you have to show them."

Tracking

Delaney House, Emmaus

Ed Greyeyes scratched ice from his scraggly mustache as Cai poured him a cup of what they called coffee. Cai allowed him a moment to commune with the hot beverage before asking the important question.

"Were you able to follow it?"

"Better than you and Joe did." Ed donned his reading glasses to look at the map between them. "You lost it right about here and I followed it to here." He drew a line with his long callused finger. "It's a wide-track, probably an Expedition SWT."

"Mountain ride? Here?"

"Someone must like to play in the powder. Or they were prescient. I mean, we got nothing but powder this year. I saw one a while back – last winter, on a trailer."

"Whose trailer?"

"No idea. I even gave that a thought. The license plate was local though."

"Beulah County?"

"Yeah. I admired this machine I could never afford and moved on." Ed laughed. His sled was older than Cai. In a testament to Ed's mechanic's ability, it ran better than the one Cai borrowed from Alex. "Anyway, I think it was headed to Mara Wells, but I tracked that way for a while and didn't pick up the trail again."

"You didn't go all the way?"

"No! That west wind was blasting my face off. It's probably why the trail wore away. The snow is more sculpted going west."

"Yeah, that's why Joe and I stopped too. Vint says it gets visibly colder as you go west, and the biodiesel ices up the lines in the grader."

"Sorry I can't give you better news, but at least I can tell you about the sled. It was heavy going to and lighter going out, so yeah, could have been carrying a body...else two riders."

"Thanks for doing it. I felt weird about hitting you up for tracking."

"It's what Tonto's good for." Ed gave him a toothy grin. "No, I owe you for loaning the Rez the Army guys and aiming us toward the USDA facility. Most of us won't starve this winter."

"Good for you. So you won't starve. How's the flu?"

"Yeah, I keep hearing about that. Don't know about it though."

"What do you mean?"

"We haven't had it. Which is weird because flu and Indians – wasn't a good match in times past, you know."

"You haven't had it? At all?"

Ed shrugged, laughed.

"Some people have had colds, but no – no flu."

Cai stared at his cousin, contemplating the significance of this revelation.

"You had it?"

"No Nobody here has – well, Alicia when she was in Santa Fe. Lots of people in town have had it, though."

"Could it be a family thing? We're immune or something?"

"I don't know, but Amisi Ceylon – the doctor working with Marnie – she's going to want your blood."

"What if I don't want to give it?"

"It's for science, man."

"Huh." Ed grunted, staring into his coffee cup. "I'll swing by the clinic when I leave. I mean, I'm all about the science."

He flashed laughing eyes at Cai and they chuckled. Ed drained his cup.

"You want some more?"

"Nope. Don't want to grow man-boobs and I should head back. It's harder to see when it's dark. There's no road signs. All buried in the snow." He started donning his clothes again. "You know, there's lots of Greyeyes and Wyandot blood round here. It seems kind of weird that nobody on the Rez has been sick and not in your family either. Should I talk to that doctor about that?"

"You should. It might not mean anything, but if it does – and it can't hurt for her to be thinking along those lines. She says she's open to suggestions."

Ed nodded, pulling his bomber's hat down around his ears and dragging on his snot-back gloves.

"Gotta jam if I'm giving blood. Tell Shane he needs to be awake next time so I can have a real visit."

"I'm standing right here, man." They laughed together and Ed turned toward the back door.

"Tell your dad I finished a barrel of high-quality ethanol and he can have some of it if he comes to the Rez."

"I'll do that. Only him?"

"Only him. Us cousins got to stay in touch, you know."

Ed walked out the door, ending the conversation. It wasn't a white people way of doing things, but Cai didn't think it was rude. It was just a different way of conducting civilization. Man, he sounded like Vi now. His grandmother always sought to reconcile the two sides of their family to the greatest extent possible, and while sometimes other ways of doing things could be frustrating, Cai thought he managed to honor her legacy on most days. Indians didn't say "goodbye". They simply walked out, which made goodbye self-evident. It made sense that Ed hoped to talk with Shane, who wasn't much for wasting words either. They were more alike than Cai was to either of them…something he regretted.

Outside the Compound

Columbus, Ohio

Julian Raines doubted this was the smartest idea he'd ever had, but Connie asked him to come with her to collect her family and he couldn't manage a reasonable excuse not to. Andi tagged along because the compound wore on her. Perry joined because he said he wanted a look around. Kate didn't care about anybody but herself and Joseph, who had just been released from the infirmary after a nasty bout with pneumonia, so they stayed behind at the tiny apartment they all shared.

Andi's hazel gaze scanned the streets as they wended their way toward Connie's home. Julian knew the romantic thoughts he harbored for her were a dumb idea. A native of Georgia who lost her parents in Atlanta, she still worried about white folks in the Republic of Afrika. He wouldn't travel there with her and he doubted she wanted to go anywhere else.

The SullCorp truck drove through streets narrowed by broken-down vehicles, casualties of the Pulse, and a lack of fuel. People walked now unless they belonged with an outfit like SullCorp. Columbus had gasoline a month ago, but the snow cut off the supply lines. Food dwindled and everybody worried about when spring would reopen the roads and rails. The anticipation wrestled with the fear of the Republic of Afrika in Julian's heart.

The post-World War 2 houses here reminded Julian of the neighborhood he grew up in. He hoped his parents were okay. He hoped Connie's family fared well.

The driveway they turned into fronted a two-story house painted a sunny yellow. Connie climbed out of the truck and, per arrangement, Julian followed her. Her husband met them at the door – a tall, gangling white man. He crushed her to his stomach, and they wept for a moment.

"I'm bringing you to the Sullivan compound. We need to get you packed and – where are the boys?"

"Kevin's playing with one of the neighbor kids." Parker spoke with a twangy Australian accent. Derry's…. Honey…" Connie froze, staring at her husband, Parker. "He's in hospital. He had the second part of this flu."

"Oh, God! How is he?"

"He's getting better now. They think the damage is done."

Julian's gut clenched and hair stood on his forearms under his coat.

"How bad is it?"

"I just, uh,…."

"Tell me!"

"His arms are paralyzed. The left side of his face is paralyzed. He can breathe. He can move his legs. They don't know if he'll get better."

Julian settled a hand on Connie's shoulder as she wiped her hands across her cheeks.

"We need to get you to the compound. Do they say when Derry can come home?"

"They aren't saying. They have to feed him through a tube because he can't swallow."

Connie wiped her nose.

"Get packed. We won't have much room, so just some clothes. Julian, do you think we could swing over to the hospital?"

Perry had come in behind them. He pulled out his radio.

"I'll call Joseph and see what we can arrange. We've already got a couple of these kids at the compound. That would be easier for you."

An hour later, they pulled into the parking lot off Olentangy River Road where the futuristic blue-and-white Methodist hospital was.

"We need to go with them," Perry told Julian as the younger man settled down for a wait. Andi nodded like she knew that and slid out of the truck to stride after Connie and Parker, her light brown hair ruffling in a blustery breeze.

"Why?"

Perry tapped the earpiece for his radio.

"Joseph's made the arrangements, but Connie and her husband don't have the weight my SullCorp ID does. And the more of us the better."

Perplexed, Julian followed Perry to catch up with the three that went before them. They were sent to the pediatrics wing. Here, as they walked down a long corridor, Julian glanced into rooms and saw what looked like iron lungs three to a room in at least six rooms.

"This is horrible," Andi remarked as she waited with Perry and Julian in the corridor while Connie and Parker talked with a stressed nurse in a room. Connie disappeared from view and Parker continued talking with the nurse. "These poor kids."

"Those iron lungs represent only a small percentage of these kids." Middle-aged, fit, and still as straight-backed as during his years of Air Force service, Perry didn't ruffle easily. "I've been hearing there's hundreds."

"Like polio in the 1950s." Julian remembered black and white photos about that era from a book he'd read in high school. This hospital had quite a draft.

"Kind of. It seems this illness only affects adolescent boys."

Julian snapped a glance at Perry but couldn't follow the topic further because Parker came out of the room.

"Connie's spending a minute with Derry while we wait for the doctor. The nurse doesn't think we can take him."

"If he's not on life support, we *can* take him," Perry assured. He hunched his shoulders and spoke in a lowered voice. "Word from Wichita is we should spare no effort. They're trying to figure out what causes this and learn how to treat it."

"Aren't the hospitals doing that?" Andi frowned.

"I assume, but the more brains at work on this, the better."

Connie's eyes were puffy with tears when she joined them in the corridor to talk with a young, darkly handsome doctor who said her name was Dr. S. Ibrahim. She spoke with a Middle Eastern-flavored British accent as she grabbed a chart from the rack on the door and scanned through it.

"Taking him home may be a logistical nightmare for you. He requires tube feeding, he's on a catheter. Although he's escaped pneumonia so far, his chest wall and diaphragm are weak, so he has difficulty keeping his airway open. With antibiotics in limited supply, he's at risk of death. He also can't sit up, he has no head control, nor use of either arm. Are you sure you're up for this?"

Parker glanced at Connie who glanced at Perry who nodded definitively.

"Yes," Parker said.

Dr. Ibrahim notated on the chart.

"We can have him ready for transfer tomorrow at this time. I wish more parents were as brave as you. Many of the young men on this floor will eventually require triage if they don't improve and, uh, Derry is weeks past cessation of active symptoms without return of function. Although we can't make definitive statements with such a novel disease, you may need to prepare yourselves for this being as good as it gets."

"Our son is a fighter." Dr. Ibrahim nodded firmly at Connie's objection.

"This may be an enemy he can't fight. It may seem cruel to say it, but you shouldn't be in the dark on what this disease does."

"What do you know about something that only started a couple of months ago?"

Dr. Ibrahim gazed inward over sad scenes. Julian thought she couldn't be much older than him and yet her eyes held an old soul.

"I know far more about it than I ever wished to know. I'll put in the order. If you'll excuse me."

She didn't wait for permission to walk away. Julian sort of thought she fled without running. That draft touched his back.

"I'll have the med department at SullCorp call for his records." Perry turned toward the stairs. As they turned by the elevator, the freight elevator opened, and two orderlies pushed a bulky wheelchair into the hall. A boy sat cuffed in the chair, legs restrained, and mouth muzzled. His bright brown eyes, twittering back and forth, glowed with fury and paranoia. Julian had seen guys from Mike Mod in prison restrained thus. He met gazes with the two orderlies. The nearest man barely nodded in affirmation at Julian's unspoken question. And then the kid started twisting against his bonds and roaring through the muzzle.

"Wrong floor, man." An orderly called down the corridor. "We can't take bizerks here. Next floor." He pointed up.

Julian stepped through the stairwell door as the elevator closed.

"You saw that?" Andi nodded toward the door.

"I don't know what disturbs me most – that this disease creates violence in some or that it happens often enough that they've invented a term for it."

"What disturbs me more is the rest of us unaware that they exist." Perry turned to follow Connie and Parker to the ground floor. "We better get back to the compound. Sun's almost down."

"And?"

"There's been reports of roving bands of robbers. It's just better to get going so we don't have to worry about encountering them."

They took their time reaching the compound however because Perry didn't want the vehicles of their convoy to become separated. In the alleys and backyards of Columbus, Julian saw shadows gathering and cold washed over him like an avalanche. Andi caught hold of his hand.

"It feels like death stalks us, doesn't it?" She barely spoke audibly. Julian nodded. "My grandparents would say the blessing of God has left this place."

Perry turned his head to talk to them from the front seat.

"Do you believe in God?"

"No, sir, not after Iron Town, but I think I understand what they were after. Don't you feel it too?"

Perry frowned, eyes on the sidewalks.

"Yeah, but that's just dread – the fear that grows when you don't know what to do. We'll find our way and turn things around the right way in time."

They rode about three blocks before any of them said what was on their minds.

"If we live that long." Julian hated to be the realist in the group, but this felt like the night before an impending riot. That nobody corrected his pessimism shot another shiver through him.

Alaska Calling Again

Delaney House, Emmaus

The clatter from the kitchen receded as Shane pushed the wheelchair into the living room. He paused to roll his shoulder, then rubbed the joint before continuing toward the couch. He felt – well, not great, but better than he had that morning. Sleeping most of the day helped. He'd gotten up a couple of times to use the bathroom, but his body had been sore enough that he hadn't wanted to stay up. After eating dinner, he felt ready to lie back down, but he could wait until the rest of the family were done cleaning up.

"You okay?" Jazz stood behind him, so he pulled on the left wheel to turn around.

"Yeah. Just too much noise still."

"Do you need help lying down?" She held a dishtowel in one hand, and he could smell salt-water.

"Soon, but I'm good for now. The dishes are more important."

"Okay. You yell if you need something. Don't push yourself again."

"Yes, ma'am." He saluted her with his left hand because he couldn't get his right arm up that high.

Giggling, she disappeared back into the kitchen. He couldn't hear the words Jill used, but he guessed the question was "Is he okay?" He smiled and turned back toward the living room. Enough room at the bottom of the mattresses allowed access to one of the couches if he needed to lie down, but he wasn't in pain yet. He felt strong enough to transfer if he needed to. It was the mattress on the floor that might as well be on the moon. He could just read while he waited for the family to be done.

The radio by the stairs crackled.

"EMMAUS KC-432R, Kansas CAP, (static) Arctic KC-135R (static) ANG Elmendorf Alaska. Anyone there? Over."

Shane turned the chair, judged the clatter from the kitchen loud enough Click wouldn't have heard it, so wheeled to the table.

"Emmaus KC-432R, Kansas CAP. Responding to ARCTIC KC-135R, AK ANG Elmendorf AFB AK. Over."

"Emmaus CAP, good to hear from you. Solar storm interfered with transmission the last few nights. This is Sergeant Casey Llewellyn, Alaska National Guard. Who am I talking to? Over."

"Shane Delaney. Over."

"I'm hoping to speak to someone in leadership there. Over."

"My father's the mayor, I'm the head of the town defense force and I own the local airfield." He'd been pretty out of it the day they read Jacob's will – still hungover from getting drunk as his way of grieving – but he remembered that much. "Over."

"Good. Great. We're looking for an airfield. Our database says yours isn't big enough to take a DC-3 though. Over."

"It's not and it's feet deep in snow. Wichita might have cleared its runways. Over."

"Not interested in Wichita. We need to land near your location." Static growled. Shane adjusted the frequency and it settled down. "…for that? Over."

"Say again, Elmendorf. Atmospheric skip must have hit a hole. Over."

"You have an interstate, right? Over."

"Yes. And you're right. Some straightaways could be used as a runway. When are you wanting to come here? Over."

Sensing movement behind him, Shane glanced over his shoulder to see Rob standing there.

"Hang on a minute. Need to ask."

"Who is that?"

"Alaska is getting back to us. They need to come to this area for some reason and they need an airfield. They're suggesting the interstate."

"I caught that. We can't. We've got people barely eating enough to sustain life and two working plows that ice up every time the temperature drops."

"Emmaus, they're hoping for next week. There's … forecast break … storms along the entire corridor. I talked to a woman before. …she relayed that we can provide food and medical supplies in exchange for …? Over."

Shane continued to stare at Rob, whose lips twitched. Shane saw the calculation in his blue eyes.

"Emmaus, you still there? Did we lose the skip? Over."

"Hang on, Elmendorf. The mayor is being apprised of the conversation so far." Shane turned back to Rob as a tinge of pain throbbed from his hip. "We can't turn down food, right?"

"Ren says it'll be February before he can get another shipment to us. I've got people starving. No, we can't turn down the food, but I don't know how we're clearing a runway in a week with the exhausted people in this town."

"That's up to you, Dad. I obviously can't help with that."

"I can." They both looked at Cai. "I think so anyway. Offer Jason and his guys a cut and they'll make it happen."

Rob cut a glance at Shane.

"What he said. DC-3s use remote runways in Alaska, so they don't need a perfect tarmac."

Rob scratched his scraggly beard.

"Tell them we need to examine our resources, but we're tentatively on board with it. If we could aim for at least a week, maybe two out. We need that break in the storms to do the clearing."

Shane exchanged a glance with Click. It was technically his radio.

"Do you prefer…?"

"Carry on."

"Elmendorf, this is Emmaus. Over."

"Go ahead, Emmaus. Over."

"Per Mayor Delaney, we're on-board for food and medical supplies, but we're resource-challenged. We're going to need to martial what we have for this project and that means asking volunteers to shovel out from people who haven't had adequate food since October. We're going to need at least a week, maybe more to clear the interstate as a runway. Over."

A long pause ensued as the ache in Shane's hip began driving an ice pick upward into his torso. He needed to move his leg to ease the cramp starting, but he knew he wouldn't be able to talk for a minute if he did that.

"Emmaus, we require a runway in your area. We understand your resource challenges. Can you get back with us when you know? Over."

"We can. Atmospheric skip allowable, we'll have an answer --." Shane glanced at Cai and Rob, holding up two fingers. They both nodded, though neither with a lot of confidence. "Day after tomorrow, Elmendorf. We'll let you know if we think we can do it at all and hopefully have a timeline. We're going to need some of that storm break to clear too. Over."

"Of course, Emmaus. Will await your return call. Thank you. Over."

"Talk to you then, Elmendorf. Over and out."

Shane rolled back from the table.

"I need to lie down."

Cai and Rob rushed to get him settled while Click powered down the radio.

"So much for an evening broadcast tonight...unless someone is willing to ride the bike."

"I'll get on that." Jazz turned into the dining room. Marnie insisted upon checking Shane's vitals before she would allow the conversation to continue. By the time she was done, the entire household except Jazz gathered in the living room.

"You are remarkably resilient, but you can't push yourself." Marnie let Cai pull her to her feet before she sat on the sofa. "How's the hip?"

"Now that I'm lying down, I'm okay." Shane rubbed a hand over his face. "I'm fading fast, though. Ask the guys at the militia too. They have food, so they might be feeling better than the townspeople."

"Go to sleep." Cai winked at him. "I've got this covered. You're not working right now."

"I hate that, but my body isn't cooperating."

"I'm doing a radio broadcast. Man, she's empowered." Click got up to power up the radio. "Jazz, can you keep this up?"

"Yeah. I'm good."

"People of Jericho Township, this is Click Michaels, your town crier, bringing you news from Emmaus, Mara Wells, Beulah, Brady Tanks, Wyandot Reservation, Donovan and Luther. And as I have it, I'll report on what we know about the world beyond our borders. It's 7:30 pm and all is … well, not good, but where there's life, there's hope, right?"

Shane wanted to stay awake for the first community-wide broadcast since the Pulse fried KERB's main transmitter, but with the warmth from the woodstove and the general exhaustion that plagued him all the time, he drifted off into sleep before the end of the 10-minute broadcast.

January 10

Infirmary

SullCorp Hub, Columbus, Ohio

Merat found Bosnia, but his cousins hadn't emailed back as yet. Julian had found a tangle of code in the Cloud that made him wonder if the United States government's fabled kill switch had triggered. Assuming a terrestrial-based AI would no longer be functioning, he'd spent the morning trying to tease out the lines of code. Europe was out there. He just needed to make contact. But it was time for a break. Nobody could code 24/7, not even him.

The node's windows looked out over the SullCorp parking lot and the weather outside looked frightful, apocalyptic snow and winter lightning. Julian shivered. Snow felt like a death sentence to a boy that grew up in Seattle. He associated snow with prison and frankly, he felt trapped here. Joseph's ongoing respiratory treatments meant they couldn't leave yet, but as soon as they could – Perry agreed with him. Columbus felt unsafe for reasons neither of them understood.

Julian wondered if Andi would stay behind or go forward with them. Her family had been in Atlanta, so there was little chance she would find any of them alive, but her heart lay in Georgia. He'd let his heart get tangled up with the hookup. There was no reason to believe she'd go with him when he went. Maybe he needed to be honest with her, but the sting of his breakup with Jenna remained. He feared Andi would reject anything more than the sex they were regularly engaged in.

"I'll buy you lunch if you come with me."

Julian shifted his gaze from his computer screen to Connie's face.

"Excuse me?"

"That must be some fascinating code."

Julian laughed.

"I love untangling Gordian knots."

"Don't you have a sword?"

He frowned at her, confused. She giggled.

"Alexander the Great solved the unsolvable puzzle knot by simply slicing through it with his sword."

"Oh? Yeah! No sword. This is high-level NSA code. I suspect it has a sword that might come right out of the monitor and stab me in the chest."

"As good a reason as any to come with me."

"Where are you taking me?"

"I want to visit Derry in the infirmary. I want you to come with."

"Why?"

"I don't know. I just feel like company. Parker's working in the motor pool, and Kevin is in school. I just don't want to go alone."

"How's he doing?"

"They say better. The hospital had discontinued nutrition a few days before."

"Triage, right?"

"Yeah. It's just so strange to see him like this."

Julian nodded. He didn't know. He'd never seen Derry before the virus took his mobility.

"Sure, I'll come with." He locked his screen and stood, stretching for the ceiling. "Andi's working today too."

They left the computer node. With the growing need for an infirmary, the small medical clinic expanded to take over a cluster of offices at one end of the same floor. Nobody stopped Connie as she went to her son's bedside. Derry lay slightly inclined in a hospital bed, thin arms propped on pillows, head rolled over to his left shoulder. A tube ran into his nose for feeding. He'd kicked the blankets off, so the catheter was visible. Connie pulled the blankets up to his chest again.

"How are you today?"

The boy's right eye focused on his mother and then swept toward Julian, who smiled at him and stepped away. He'd been in the infirmary a few times, but this was a new room set up for the encephalitis patients – six teenage boys, all suffering from some form of paralysis. A couple were still in pain or unconscious, still exhibiting raging fevers. Two used wheelchairs to get around. One had a withered arm.

Julian sensed the movement before he actually saw it. Peripheral vision was a survival skill in prison, and he'd survived. He flinched right as the chair whizzed by his head and then he backed up, judging the boy didn't have the strength to swing it again. An attendant bustled across the room to take it from him.

"He's here to eat our souls."

"Now, Chris. We've told you that's not true. Let's get you back to bed."

Julian kept a wary eye on the pair as the attendant put Chris back in bed, settling his useless arm on a pillow.

"It's rare." Carmen was an RN who had joined the SullCorp medical staff recently.

"What?"

"The paranoia. That's the second patient I've seen. The paralysis is more common."

"Good to know, I guess."

"Hopefully those symptoms ease after the fever breaks. The other boy died."

"Hopefully. Do you know how much of the population this encephalitis affects?"

"Thousands in Columbus alone. The hospitals are overrun. Most of the ones with respiratory issues are allowed to die for want of vents. Derry's lucky he continued breathing, but they stopped feeding him two weeks after the active symptoms abated."

"Will he be okay?"

"He's getting the food he needs, but we don't know about his future."

A tray clattered to the floor over by Chris's bed.

"We may need to restrain him if this keeps up."

Julian's hands turned to ice as he remembered the kid in the hospital thrust up like Hannibal Lecter.

"He's still running a fever?"

"Yes. It might just be the pain."

"Is there pain?"

"In their heads and backs, yes. Until the fever breaks. Did you have the flu?"

"Andi and I didn't get it. Not yet anyway."

Derry's face contorted and for a moment, Julian wondered if maybe he was also angry and paranoid, but then he realized Connie was smiling. Mother and son were sharing a joke and Derry only had half a working face. He sounded like he was choking, but that was laughter.

"I think if you didn't get it when others in your apartment had it, you'll not get it. Some people are immune or at least resistant."

"Good to know."

Connie wiped Derry's mouth and cheek with a cloth.

"My husband is working on a brace to help him sit up," Carmen reported. "He's a plastics engineer."

"Cool." Julian hated that his compassion grew thin. Prison taught him weakness killed and Derry's weakness seemed impossible to overcome.

"He won't be able to walk though because the paralysis affects his hips."

Julian frowned, watching Connie rearrange the blankets again.

"But not his lower legs?"

"Right. Most of the paralysis resembles either encephalitis or a spinal cord injury, but his is an odd pattern. There are signs of encephalitis, but the scarring is in the nerve plexus."

"How do you know that?"

"The hospital has an MRI."

"It survived the Pulse?"

"It was powered down and disconnected from the power source for maintenance."

"Right! It's the long-line transmission that kills stuff."

"Unfortunately, the power situation prevents them from scanning every patient, but Derry's pattern was so different, they decided it was worth the resources. They included the images in his file."

"But then they were going to let him starve to death?"

"I think they felt they had learned all they could from him."

"Triage?"

"Yes."

The hospital draft followed him to SullCorp.

"You ready for lunch?" Connie asked.

Julian stared from Derry to Chris.

"Yeah. Let's go."

They didn't talk until they were almost at the cafeteria.

"Something on your mind?"

"I worked for B&W."

"You mentioned. Computer security, right?"

"Usually. You know that Carson Wilson has a passion for spinal cord injuries?"

"His brother's a quadriplegic, isn't he?"

"Yeah, a bicycle accident when they were kids. I was asked to work on some code for a nanite project."

"Nanites? Aren't they just theory?"

"Kind of. It was a while back and they had a working model that was about an inch square. I got it to do some cool things. And their robotics unit was headed to a breakthrough when I went on vacation."

"And, you're telling me this because …?"

"Maybe nothing. I just…. Maybe I just want to give you hope."

"Wouldn't that project have fried when everything else did?"

"Maybe. Did you know Methodist hospital has a working MRI machine?"

"I saw the images in Derry's file."

"So, theoretically, B&W's nano lab and the source code I was working on are well-protected. I don't know how close they were to actual repair of spinal cord damage. I heard rumors of animal trials, but there was no way they were ever getting a human trial passed the FDA."

Connie turned to stare at him.

"Which no longer exists – right?"

"Or B&W might feel they no longer need to ask permission to try their technology on volunteers."

A smile wavered across Connie's face and then she sobered.

"We need to get through this winter before we get our hopes up."

"We do, but I just thought you might want in on that secret. It's between you and me, right?"

"Yes. I won't even mention it to Parker. He's much more hopeful for Derry than I am."

"Good. So what did you work on this morning?"

"I found the email address of that reporter from Mises. I'm hoping he replies to me today."

Julian smiled. They might just be writing and detangling code, but their efforts to reconnect the world would someday all be worth it.

Shadows of Darkness

Conopher Farm, Jericho Township

A scream followed by loud angry words issued from the soddy as Dell came out of the barn. He saw Leisha come out on the back porch as he strode toward the soddy door. Cady bent over Elizabeth while Max clung to Rafe's back like a tiger. Cady's nose bled as Rafe tried to pull Max off him. The boy bellowed as Rafe grabbed his arm and then Dell stepped in.

"Cut it out!" He had half-a-head on Rafe and though not a brawler, he could throw a punch if he needed to. He caught Max as Rafe backed off.

"They won't listen." He bellowed like a bull in rut.

"Yeah, well, a lot of people don't think fists say much important. What is *wrong* with you? You're supposed to love your family."

"I do!"

"You have a weird way of showing it. Go for a walk. Stay gone until sunset. If I see you, I'll shoot you."

Rafe shot an uncertain look at Dell, grabbed his jacket, and stormed out the door.

"He's just so afraid," Cady said.

"So he makes you and the kids afraid? We're all talking tonight. Geneva can take care of the kids so we can discuss this. This is not happening in my home."

Cady nodded, looking as scared of Dell as she'd been of Rafe a few minutes before. Conopher men were big and loud when angry and Dell was angry, as well as scared, for his brother and the family that came with him.

"I got work to do."

He slammed the door closed behind him, took three long strides toward his house, and stopped. Rage coiled up between his shoulder blades and tightened his neck, pulling his head toward his shoulders. He took a deep breath, relaxed his jaw, rolled his neck, and lowered his shoulders. He rolled his neck again, then his shoulders. He balled his big callused hands into fists before relaxing them to fall by his thighs. His head felt the cold again. He took another deep breath and let it out ultra-slow before walking toward the blue farmhouse, refusing to kick snow as he crossed the yard where Leisha waited in the kitchen.

"It's getting worse."

"I noticed," she said. "Want something warm to drink?"

"Maybe when I come down. I promised Kix I'd visit him during lunch."

"That's good. Listening to his breathing is very relaxing. I'll have food ready for you when you come down."

"We're having a family conference tonight."

"Good. He needs to hear that nobody is on his side, so he'd better straighten up."

Dell gave the strength of his life a brief hug and headed up the stairs. Kix hadn't moved of course. Leisha had rolled him from one side to the other sometime since Dell had been here to help her bathe him. Dell supposed one side or the other was just the same to someone who was comatose. No, he wouldn't think like that. Kix was still in there, just unable to respond.

"I brought the book. You want to sit up a little for this?"

Dell arranged three pillows against the headboard and gently rolled Kix onto his back. The boy's limp limbs offered no resistance. They felt like skin and bones, but at least they weren't burning hot with fever. Dell blocked Kix's head from rolling with a towel to catch the drool and then sat down in the side chair to start reading *Watership Down*.

"The rabbits became strange in many ways, different from other rabbits. They knew well enough what was happening. But even to themselves they pretended that all was well, for the food was good, they were protected, they had nothing to fear but the one fear; and that struck here and there, never enough at a time to drive them away."

Dell paused, reaching for the water bottle he'd set on the nightstand for when his throat grew dry.

"Funny. That reminds me of what the world had become before the Bombs. We knew something was coming, but we pretended the signs weren't an omen. You agree?"

Dell looked up, expecting to see Kix as he'd been for months. The blue of the boy's eyes struck him behind the heavy lids.

"You awake, kid?"

Winded

Donovan, Northwest of Mara Wells

Kris Lawson hadn't realized Emmaus, Kansas had so many trees until they pushed west of Jericho Ridge toward Donovan and the trees dropped away. McArthur's Dairy had a small grove of trees around the outskirts of the yard, but one was going to die from the fire that had scorched its branches after the Pulse. Snow covered the charred timbers of the main production building, but Mac McArthur had moved his remaining cows into what must have been the old barn and set up turbine production in a shed that probably held vehicles before his change in business plan.

Kris could smell the tang of metal in the air. Someone had been welding.

"Wow, that's a great machine." The tall dairyman lingered by the open door a moment before closing it and turning to his guests. "What can I do for you, gentlemen? I got to tell you, I have regular customers for my milk and cheese and none to spare currently."

"No, that's fine. I hear you're building wind turbines."

"I am. Now there's something we could talk about. I've got a few finished, but there aren't any takers. Emmaus might be more interested than the starving people of Mara Wells, but I can't get there without a rig like yours."

"I've got food and salt if you want to make a trade."

"I've got four turbines finished besides the one on my house, which I'm not giving up."

"Right. Two bags of salt for each and I'll toss in a flat of canned fruit and another of veggies."

"Done. How are things in Emmaus?"

"People are hungry and there's a flu that's causing paralysis in teenage boys."

McArthur nodded, sighing.

"Yeah. We've had a few die. The flu itself seems pretty weak, but then they can't move their legs. One stopped breathing. I hear the other simply stopped eating."

"It's horrible."

While Ren and Cai talked, Kris walked around the worktable that contained the parts for a wind turbine.

"That – uh, cage – what's it for?"

"It's a shroud. Turbines with unshrouded blades slice and dice birds and I figure they're going to need all the help they can get to come back from the rad rain. I kept modifying the shroud on my home turbine until I figured out how to get maximum efficiency. You a mechanic?"

"Yes, sir."

"Well, if you're can show me your skills, I'll hire you. My hope is once spring comes, this factory is going to be humming."

"I'll think about it. I have family in Garden City. I'm going there to check on them and I'm sure the folks will want me to stay, but I will definitely consider your offer."

"Sounds good. Let's get those turbines loaded. I saw you were optimistic, even brought a tow sled."

"I was." Ren grinned. "I'll unload the salt and food while you two load the turbines."

"Thanks." Mac started donning his outwear. "Any idea when regular food deliveries might start? We're okay here, but Mara is suffering."

"I'm trying. These storms don't make it easy."

"I get that. You ever wonder why no relief planes showed up to drop food to us?"

"Well, I know why that is." Mac lifted a brow in question. "UN decided America didn't need rescue until we'd exhausted our own resources and then the UN wasn't around by the time that happened. It's me and Brian Wilson trying to feed the whole country. Rumor has it Gates and Melinda bugged out for Hawaii with Zuckerberg and the Bezos."

"So much for the compassionate wealthy, I guess. Glad the greedy capitalists decided to hang around."

Ren laughed. Kris hadn't given a lot of thought to politics except when his father would go off on one of his rants, but it did seem interesting that the great philanthropists of his generation were nowhere to be seen right now. Mac flipped the tarp back from the turbines laid head to foot in a row.

"Grab the bottom end there." Mac's wingspan was impressive, so while Kris suspected he carried the heavy end, Mac carried the blade head that was bulky. Kris wondered if his parents' windmill still worked. He guessed he'd find out when he got there.

Growing Suspicion

Southwest of Emmaus

Cai stomped his feet, trying to bang blood back into his toes, half-listening to Murphy's report about repairing the town fencing. What good would it do to repair unmanned fencing and only on the Emmaus end? Dangers could still come in over by Mara Wells and then come to Emmaus.

The scene before him mattered more, even as he pretended to listen to Murphy. Now that Shane was awake most of the day, he wanted to know what was going on with the town defense forces, and this would be something to report. He'd be more interested in the runway project too. Using roof scoops, shovels, and a cobbled-together snowblower, the combined crews from Liberty Trucking, the McAuliff militia and the salt mine had cleared about three-quarters of the 3,000 feet of interstate required to land a DC3. Now they worked to clear 150 feet from the right-center line to accommodate the wings while a group of teenagers Jazz had rallied chipped through the hard pack to finish the last quarter of the makeshift runway. Given the cold, they made great progress. The cold meant it wouldn't snow – he hoped.

The wind swirled around the site, scattering icy snow that felt like diamonds scraping his skin. He longed for a warm fire and a cat curled up on his lap. That wouldn't happen any time before spring, not the way his life shaped up. There had been times when Shane's capability completely annoyed him, but now his abilities were greatly missed.

"Thanks for taking care of that." Cai didn't know another way to shut up the national guardsman and he wanted to think rather than talk. "I got places to be. Shane's feeling a lot better, so you might want to start swinging by the house to give him your reports."

Cai swung a leg over his borrowed snowmobile and turned east along the interstate. Razor-sharp ice crystals whipped across his face and encrusted his beard. His hands grew numb from the cold and his lips turned to blocks of ice.

He paused at the top of the slope dropping down to the airfield. That helicopter bugged him every time he thought of it. Where did it come from? Where did the occupants go? Now buried in snow, it made clear it had been abandoned by its owners. Who were they?

Along this section of the town, the "wire" consisted of the interstate itself and intermittent fencing. Cai edged the trucking company property and ran his machine the length of the Emmaus Field runway. He wondered if Shane's inheritance would be worth a dime come the new world. Would airplanes still fly? He supposed Shane could make them if he could find places to land. The guy wasn't meant to be anchored to the ground any more than Jacob had been.

He paused at the end of the road before turning onto Old 24, considering his next move. A man died horribly within the wire of the township and he hadn't been able to find the killer. The guilt burned in his guts. Maybe he'd been a disconnected product of an abusive childhood, feeding off the secrets others kept, but he'd been a human being who shouldn't have had his life taken from him so cavalierly.

While Cai thought, he saw a snowmobile turn into the Jericho Springs road. Long, black, powerful, not the tired iron Alex kept around for farm chores. Cai shook out the numbness in his fingers and goosed the gas to send the old Polaris across the roadway. He didn't need to aim for the ditch because the road hadn't truly been plowed. He worked to keep from slipping into the ruts caused by the big farm trucks. He turned into the Lufgren Farm road, but he didn't stop at the house, shooting past to follow the old road to the back corner of the property where Alex had his active woodlot. He watched as the big Ski-Doo Skandic turned into the B&B. He steered the snowmobile out the back entrance of the wood lot and dismounted to investigate the treads left by the Skandic. Wide like the snowmobile that had transported John Doe's body. Those treads were long buried in the snow, but Cai had photos. Not that he needed them. He'd stared at them so many times he knew what they looked like.

He remounted his snowmobile and crossed the bridge to the hotel, stomped through the snow, scanning the area with fresh eyes. Had there been a turnoff from the B&B that they'd missed? Chavez certainly could haul John Doe up that bank and deposit him here behind the hotel. But why? Not that Chavez called anyone "friend", but Shane said he had no reason to mess with him. They were allies. Maybe just a convenient place to store a body until he could get rid of it?

"Chavez will kill you if you dig in where they don't want you."

Yeah, but Shane, I can't ignore murder. Can I?

Something winked in the sun as he kicked a snow clod aside. He tracked the movement with his eyes, then dug his gloved hand around in the area until he found a hard, metal circle. He brushed off the snow and stared at the red and brown stone with stylized writing engraved around it. A class ring?

Creeping Dread

Andrew Bennett Farm, Jericho Township

Andrew paused at the door of the bedroom, settling his nerves. He'd felt confident yesterday when Brian had gone over this with him, but now he worried he'd break something.

He knew it needed to be done, but it still brought him to tears to think that Matt needed someone else to move his legs for him. Matt shifted his head on the pillow, grimacing. His ongoing headache got worse when he moved his head.

"Hey." His voice barely registered. He shifted his head back to what must be a neutral position. "Here to move the manakin?"

"None of that, boy."

"Why not? I'm like a Gumby doll."

Andrew folded back the blankets to uncover Matt's legs, just as Brian had shown him. The boy stared at the ceiling. He couldn't raise his head from the pillow anymore. A tube snaked from under the blanket to a bottle under the bed. Matt would one day be a tall man and he'd been on his way to being as muscular as his father. Now Andrew could encircle his calf with his hand.

Start with the largest joint first. Andrew bent the leg at the knee, pushing it into the abdomen, feeling the stretch in the flabby muscles across Matt's buttocks.

"Mom tell you?"

"About you struggling to breathe this morning?"

Matt nodded weakly.

"We just need to be careful to keep from putting stress on your diaphragm."

"I was laughing."

"Yeah. How is it now?"

"I can't breathe in deeply. I've been trying and I just can't."

Hence the whispery voice. Andrew continued stretching him.

"I dozed off earlier and I woke up dizzy, gasping."

Don't pause. Don't scare him.

"You have a falling dream?"

"I don't know. I think my chest is becoming paralyzed." A tear trickled down Matt's temple. "I can't move my arms anymore. Yesterday, I could feel my hands and today I can't. I don't want to die, Dad."

Andrew set Matt's leg down and gathered his son's limp body against his chest.

"It's going to be okay. We've got help coming. You just have to hang in there. It'll be here soon."

Careful the Cage You Poke

Delaney House, Emmaus

You need to find out what they know.

Or else Cai Delaney would end up dead, was the unspoken warning. Unaware of the camera by the gate, Cai inspected the imprint of the snowmobile in the road where Grant and Javi could observe him. It seemed likely his suspicions were now leveled at the B&B.

Fortunately, it had been a month since Jazz Tully gave blood and her being a universal donor made her blood critical for the Medical Center.

"You want mine too?" Shane sat in the wheelchair near the window, a book in his lap.

"No. You're still healing. I do want to take a small vial for test purposes. I've got a theory I'm trying to falsify. How's your leg, by the way?"

"Stronger." Shane maneuvered over to her bag and rooted around it to take his own blood sample. "It still aches a lot and hurts some when I try to move it, but I'm doing okay with passive range of motion. Brian and Clem say another two weeks and I can start putting weight on it."

"Good. It takes longer without cortisone and painkillers, but the body does heal itself."

Shane produced his blood sample while the blood pouch filled. Ami pulled the needle and had Jazz hold gauze to the puncture wound.

"Can we talk?" Shane rolled toward the dining room where Ami had left the small cooler. She nodded, casting a glance at Jazz.

"Don't worry. I can't hear what I'm not supposed to hear." The American girl seemed remarkably suited to the man she now looked at with affection. She laid back on the couch.

Shane closed the doors anyway, both to the living room and kitchen, though no one was in there.

"What is going on at the B&B? Cai is suspicious and even flat on my back, I know something is up."

"No." She lied, and she only hoped her voice didn't betray her. "Javi is suspicious of everyone and Cai senses that, but we aren't up to anything." *That you need to know about.*

Shane evaluated her with his emerald eyes. She waited, hoping he couldn't read her mind.

"Tell Grant I need to actually talk with him. You guys can't pull crap inside the wire."

"We didn't."

"I don't believe you, and neither does Cai. If there's more stuff to be hidden, you'd best get to doing it, because he will come looking. And, if Javi kills my brother, he'd better run. Might take me some time to catch up, but I will, and he knows it."

"I hear you. I'll have Grant call you. Is your phone...?"

"Yeah. So's the tablet. Either way. I just need to know what's going on so I can help keep the attention off you."

"I'll tell him. We had nothing to do with the body behind the hotel."

Shane looked skeptical. He pushed over to the kitchen door to open it. The Delaney's dog ran up to him for affection. Ami would never understand the American obsession with domestic animals. The cat made sense. It caught rats. What did the dog do?

Shane caught her wrist as she packed her bag.

"Seriously? Grant has my loyalty only so long as he doesn't pit me against the best interests of my family. Got it?"

Ami felt the cool touch of the firm pressure on her bones and nodded. The canned heat that came with men like Javi and Shane could not be tempered, and she did not wish to get burned.

"I'll talk with them and have Grant call you."

Shane let go of her wrist and rolled out into the living room.

"You okay?" He paused at the couch where Jazz stared at the ceiling.

"I'm fine. Starting to get good at this whole giving blood thing and it means I get to eat full meals today."

"Is that the secret to not fainting in the middle of the street?"

"It is, Mr. Delaney."

They were giving her leave to go, so Ami gathered up her supplies, donned her coat, and headed for the Land

Rover to continue home where she would have to tell Grant that Shane and Cai were suspicious.

Friends

Emmaus Medical Center

Cai banged snow off his boots before entering the med center. A dozen people huddled in the lobby, many of them coughing, all with the hollow faces of the chronically hungry. Cai wondered how many would be dead by spring thaw. Rumor had it, they were stacking up bodies in the now deserted caretaker's house at Beulah Cemetery. Nobody knew how they would open more ground before thaw. Nobody wanted to waste the wood or coal, not even for their own loved ones.

Marnie leaned back against him as his arms went around her.

"Who is this?" she asked mockingly. "Surely it's not my ultra-busy husband."

"Here to hug my ultra-busy wife."

"What brings you here?"

"I don't know. I just felt the need to hug you. I found this in the snow behind Shane's hotel and I figured I could ask you about it and get some loving."

He held the ring so she could see it.

"Know anyone who graduated that year who had this stone."

"No. It doesn't ring a bell. Ask Shane. He knew more of the guys than I did."

"Yeah, I'll do that." Cai put the ring back in his inner coat pocket. "How's our little one?"

"He's a linebacker in the making. Maggie says babies go to sleep when you're moving around, but that's not his MO."

"Mom always says Shane was like that, just cantankerous and contrary."

"Oh, no, that's not a good sign."

"We won't need sleep. Love will act like caffeine."

"You are such a dork. Hey, Brian."

Cai glanced over his shoulder. He and Brian hadn't really talked since their exchange over what the B&B might be hiding and Cai hesitated to bring it up again.

"How's it going?" Brian started filing sheets into patient charts.

"Not bad. Shane is getting antsy."

"He's got another few weeks where he's just going to have to put up with the boredom. I keep telling him that. Is he being stupid when my back is turned?"

"No, he's surprisingly good, but I can tell he's about to blow."

"You guys have a great library. I suggest he gets familiar with it."

"He has. So – look – I'm sorry about the other night. I was out of line."

"You were, but April also came on kind of strong. She has her opinions about confidentiality."

"Right. I get that."

"How's your mystery going?"

"Not well. I've interviewed pretty much everyone this end of the township and I don't know – I have no real strong suspects."

"I'm pretty sure it's not the B&B. They're just close and suspicious acting, so you think they look guilty, but they're not dumb enough to dump dead bodies where they could trace back to them."

"Mmm," Cai grunted. Brian shrugged.

"My two bits, for what it's worth. Let's not talk about it anymore so we don't feel compromised."

"Agreed. Do you and April have enough corn cobs?"

"I think so. How much longer can winter last, right?"

"Ever read Laura Ingalls Wilder? This winter reminds me of one of her books."

"My sister used to read those. Back then, I thought it was so-not our lives. I should have paid more attention."

"I can loan them to you if you and April need something to read."

"She might like that. Thanks for understanding why we can't share medical details with you."

"Yeah. Thanks for understanding why I need to solve this mystery."

They embraced, slapping each other on the back before breaking.

"I gotta get going. I'm expected on community patrol soon. Marn – you get off your feet sometime day, right?"

She waved at him but was headed toward a patient and he knew better than to get in the way of that.

Who You've Always Been

Delaney House, Emmaus

The vibration of his phone pulled Shane from sleep. Jazz breathed heavily next to him. He untangled himself from her warmth to reach for the phone. His hip complained at the stretch as his fingertips grazed the phone. He hooked a fingernail in the otterbox and dragged it toward him.

Rigby. No surprise there. Who else with this number was still alive?

"Hey. You got my message, huh?" He whispered, hoping Jazz would stay asleep.

"I did. Threatening her isn't your style."

"I didn't threaten her. I threatened Chavez."

"You like to live dangerously. Can you even walk yet?"

"Nope, but I figure you won't let Chavez kill me until you have those thumb-drives out of my safe and I don't trust you enough to give you the combination."

"I figured. So you want to know about the body behind your hotel?"

"I just want to keep my brother from getting killed by investigating it."

"I'm not stupid enough to kill your brother, Shane. Especially since we didn't do anything. The body behind the hotel wasn't ours."

"Hang on. I'm sending you a photo."

Shane sent the copies he'd made of the Polaroids. He waited while Grant looked it over.

"Messy."

"Do you know him?"

"Why would I?"

"No fingerprints, no labels in his clothes."

Silence. Shane plucked the fabric of his sweatpants to shift his leg and forestall the cramp growing in his hip.

"We'll run face rec and get back to you. We had nothing to do with him being dead, but it's possible he was here for us. Can you keep your brother off our backs?"

"I can try. He doesn't listen to me, but I'll try to warn him off."

"And he'll only get the same answer I'm giving you. We didn't kill this guy and we didn't stash him behind your place."

"I believe that. Get back with me about the face rec."

"Will do. I'll also run this tattoo. It's ringing a bell, but it's a distant one. It didn't mean anything to you?"

"Same as you – a bell too distant to be of help."

"Glad you're feeling better. You know how much longer you'll be down?"

"No. I can sit up most of the day now, but they still won't let me put weight on my leg. But that's supposed to be soon. What's going on out there?"

"Not much. We keep hearing rumors, but they don't develop into anything. But spring may change things. Historically it's war campaign season."

"Gee, you're a ray of sunshine."

"I'm who I've always been. Hang in there. I'll get back to you."

"Sounds good. Tell Ami there's no hard feelings."

"She's a realist. Talk later."

Shane put his phone on the end table and laid his hand on Jazz's shoulder.

"You can quit pretending to sleep now."

She rolled against him, turning her face up to him.

"I figured you'd prefer I'd stay out of your conversation.

"By listening to it?" He grinned at her and she chuckled. "I don't care." He chuckled now too. "We fell asleep and I need to move now."

She rolled up to sitting, which gave him enough room to shift his leg. Pain spiraled up and down from the joint.

"Sorry. I kind of forgot."

"No problem. I enjoyed that. I think it's the first time I've ever slept with a woman without sex being involved."

"Oh, really? I bet you used to snuggle with your mom without sex being involved."

"I bet I was wriggly and annoying."

"Wild one, huh?"

"Oh, definitely. I don't want you to think I was promiscuous, though. Much more of a serial monogamous."

"I didn't ask."

"No, but I figured from cuddling comes questions."

"Are we really doing this?"

"I don't know. I'm kind of enjoying just feeling each other out."

"*Feeling?*"

"It's like the Pennsylvania Dutch – bundling."

"Um, that involves being sewn up in a sheet in some contexts."

"Definitely couldn't do that right now, but – Look, I'm not up for anything just yet, but this getting to know each other thing – I like that."

She smiled and looked sidewise at him.

"Me too."

She turned her head at clattering from the backdoor.

"I better go help with that."

Shane watched her disappear into the dining room and wondered why he was risking his heart in yet another battle zone, but truthfully, he didn't think he could stop himself.

Intervention

Conopher Farm, Jericho Township

Rafe's rage filled the living room, seeming to pound against the walls and bounce back to batter them all.

"They're *my* family!"

"We are *all* family." Leisha's cheeks flared with her own high emotions. "You cannot beat your wife and children without our interfering."

"Those kids need discipline."

"You mean like Dad used to discipline us?" Dell wanted to stand up to go chest-to-chest with Rafe, but he knew that would only escalate the situation. "That worked out so well for Trey. Look, Rafe, I get that we're all on edge and you're not sleeping. Leisha's had trouble sleeping too. It's not something any of us wanted on our conscience. But you can't take it out on your children and Cady."

"If it bothers you so much, I'll just move them back to town. I'm not having my kids disrespect me."

"It's not safe in town. You moved out here because it wasn't safe in town."

"And we couldn't keep the house warm." Cady spoke scarcely above a whisper. "We were all going to catch our deaths."

"And, there they go getting the flu here."

"The flu is everywhere." Leisha corrected Rafe. "It's dangerous stuff, viruses."

"I don't like you giving my wife ideas. We're moving home where we belong."

"No, no, we're not." Cady's wavering voice rose above Rafe. "We're not safe with you, not like you are now."

Rafe wheeled on her and Dell stood, blocking him with his shoulder.

"You're not doing this. You can stay, but you can't abuse them."

"Your kids treat you like an ass."

"Yeah and Leisha is the most-disrespectful wife on the planet." Dell grinned at his wife of 20 years, who had sprung to block any blows from landing on Cady. "I don't always like it, but I always love and respect it."

"You want a second wife?" Rafe's spittle sprayed Dell's face.

"Don't be like that, man."

Rafe grabbed his jacket from the hook and slammed out the door, rocking the house with his fury. Cady burst into tears. Leisha hugged her.

"You and the kids are sleeping in the house tonight." Dell watched as Rafe strode down the rutted driveway. "Just in case he's still angry or drunk when he gets home. Geneva and Lace can share a bed so you can be comfortable."

Cady wiped her cheek with the back of a shaking hand.

"What would we do without you two?"

"It'll be fine. When he doesn't get what he wants, he'll start to listen to reason. He didn't used to be this way, right?"

"No. It started after the USDA."

"Then he just needs to remember who he is. I'll talk to him tomorrow. It'll be fine."

Dell wished he didn't feel like he was lying, but that hollow feeling in his stomach, that was an untruth told.

"I'm going to go help Leisha."

He headed upstairs to the linen closet where Leisha was sorting through the sheets, tears running down her cheeks.

"You okay?"

"Some days – God, are we being punished for Mace?"

"What? Honey, that's silly. Yeah, things are tough right now. You rightfully feel guilty, but you were protecting our kids. Imagine if we'd let them take the food, where we'd be today? Mace was the one in the wrong and he forced you to take an action you didn't want to take. So, stop thinking like that."

"But, Kix and Rafe and ...."

"Leisha Hope Schoenfeld Conopher, you stop that right now. Rafe is an idiot who didn't choose to avoid our father's path and Kix is just a victim of a virus. You know God doesn't pull strings like that. And you also know that as a child of God, you're forgiven for what you repent from. So, you want to go into the bedroom right now and kneel to pray? I'll make the bed up. But you gotta stop blaming yourself for things you had to do and above all, you know God is not responsible for Mace Ketteridge deciding to

steal our food. So, go on. Take care of yourself for once."
He gave her a gentle push toward the bedroom and then
turned to choose sheets and be about the next task at hand.

Spy craft

Sullivan B&B, Jericho Springs

Pain sliced through Grant's concentration as he stretched his shoulder while listening to Ron Patterson's report.

"So, you know Bill Gates owned a bunch of fields north of town going to Wyandot Lake?"

"No, I didn't know that. Why should I care?"

"He sold them – well, transferred them – to the government this last summer."

"And, that matters why?"

"I got through a USDA firewall and transferred ownership to me. Would you like in on this deal? You're eventually going to need resupply, right?"

"We can talk about it. It would depend on the field."

"Sure. I just promised I'd keep you apprised of my activities."

"Don't be too egregious about it because you don't want to attract attention."

"I backdated it and ran it through some dummy companies. And Bennetts and Lufgrens will remain the largest landowners in the county."

"Good. So what else?"

"Your dead guy from the hotel – I found him – or a cover identity anyway. Kenneth Qualls. It says he's a real estate developer who sold some fields to Joel Rhys a couple of years ago."

Grant stopped torturing himself to stare at the tall computer hacker with rapt attention.

"The only thing of interest about him is that tattoo. The three stars with just a single crescent is connected to the Nation of Islam. The addition of the mirror crescent may be connected to this weird group out of Atlanta that was connected to this 1960s/70s utopia scheme called the Republic of Afrika."

"The what?"

"Yeah. It's not been a thing for half-a-century – except – Atlanta is no more, of course, but in the communities around there's been a revolution. Call it the apartheid state of the South."

"Crap! White people enslaving black people again?"

"Nope. Try the other way around and they're calling themselves the Republic of Afrika."

Grant literally needed to remember to close his mouth.

"How many people are we talking about?"

"Millions. The southern version of this flu, which is being called variously New York and Lakeland's flu, is much more deadly, particularly to white people. And, they've experienced some of the same hunger issues people around here have. So, it's about two million blacks enslaving about the same number of whites. They waited until they got sick, stripped them of their weapons and food, then turned them out of their homes with just the clothes on their backs. They disrupted families. And they executed a bunch of people in public spectacles. They targeted well-to-do neighborhoods."

Ron opened a screenshot of a group of white men with metal collars chained to a post. One man's back was to the camera and his torn shirt was brown with dried blood.

"Oh, my god!"

"Yeah. So, this guy Qualls --." Ron tapped a few keys. "You know him?"

Grant stared at the photo of a living and unfrozen Qualls.

"No, although he seems familiar. Can you blow that up and brighten the image, so maybe Javi could see it?"

"I'll work on that. When do you want it?"

"He's upstairs right now."

Javi blinked tears out of his eyes and surprised Grant by finding just the one spot where he could still see somewhat clearly.

"Jordan Quinn. Black father – Korean mother, I think. Mom died when he was a kid, dad became an abusive alcoholic. He ended up in foster care with me. We didn't know each other very well but when the agency was looking for recruits, I looked him up. As I remember, they were very impressed with him. He was assigned to deep cover about the time I went into the Neharis Network."

"Do you remember what deep cover?"

"No, but Shane might."

"Why Shane?"

"He was on a stateside break and he field-trained the guy."

"As Eric Faraday?"

"Yeah, of course. You weren't in on this?"

"I vaguely remember it. Thanks. Maybe Shane knows more." Javi massaged a temple and rubbed the hams of his hands into his eyes. "You okay?"

"The whole dark into light and find that one spot where my vision is still mostly clear works, but I'm starting to get headaches when I use it."

"I'm sorry."

"Yeah. So, Ron said there were more tapes out of Santa Fe and Mexico. I'd better get to listening." He sighed deeply. "Death's never bothered me, but the people dying at the border – it's actually making me angry."

"After everything the US has done for Mexico…. I get it, but it's the situation we're in and we can only adapt to it."

"The one thing, though – there's no flu in Mexico, far as I can tell."

"So, the wall might not be such a bad thing after all … if they'd airdrop some food on the north side."

Javi nodded and fumbled for the doorknob into the monitoring room.

"This whole thinking thing – I'd really rather go back to being a field agent."

"Then we'd have nobody to translate Spanish. Go translate Spanish, please."

Grant paused for the door to close and then he dialed Shane.

"Hey."

"You okay? You sound weak."

"You woke me. What's up?"

"Do you remember Jordan Quinn?"

Shane stayed silent for almost too long.

"I trained him. That's where I know the body from."

"Yeah. That tattoo is connected to an outfit called the Republic of Afrika. It's a black supremacist group that died out in the 1970s but revived after the Bombs. They've taken over Georgia and a loose affiliation around there." Grant went on to explain the whole slavery thing. Shane asked a few questions, but mostly let Grant talk. "What do you think?"

"Maybe he was headed here for refuge. He didn't seem like a bad guy unless you got between him and his target."

"Like Javi."

"Sure. I assume Javi wouldn't enslave us if the opportunity presented itself."

"I don't think he would. So you don't think Jordan would?"

"I didn't know him that well, but he didn't seem particularly woke, and he agreed to the assignment."

"Which was?"

"A black supremacist group. Only it wasn't called the Republic of Afrika. I don't remember what it was, though. Give me a name and I probably could confirm it."

"Good enough. Thanks for your help. Now, will you convince your brother to stay off our backs?"

"I said I'd try. I know, he's like a dog with a stick, but I think he's starting to admit defeat."

"Well, I want Quinn's murderer brought to justice too now, just so long as he lets go of us."

"As I said, I'll try. No promises."

"How much longer for you?"

"No idea. Brian got me up on my good leg this morning and I passed out, so --. Something – orthostatic hypotension – it's when you've been sitting on your butt for far too long."

"You'll get past it. Is that why you were napping?"

"Yeah. But I'll keep trying. How's Dylan by the way?"

"Um, yeah. He's realizing the extent of his disabilities and starting to get depressed." A long silence issued from the other end of the line. "You don't know what to say to that, do you?"

"Not to you. Depression sucks. My sister-in-law is here with a blood pressure cuff, so I'm assuming I need to stop talking now."

"Thanks for the information."

"No problem. Don't count him out yet. He's still healing."

"Is that what they say to you every five minutes?"

"Pretty much. Talk to you later."

"Uh, Shane!"

"Yeah?"

"Be careful. I know you've got a plane coming from Alaska soon. Someone might want Francene Maracle dead."

"How do you know that?"

"Can't tell you."

Grant could hear a woman's voice in the background during Shane's silence.

"I'll keep it in mind. Bye for now."

Grant hung up and walked out into the monitoring room where Javi listened to headphones and Ron ran five screens. In the main basement, Miranda and Lainey were playing hopscotch and singing this cute song. He almost wanted to linger, but there was firewood to bring in and it was his turn to feed Dylan. He could get so caught up in spy-craft that he sometimes forgot to attend to ordinary life and there was far more ordinary life than there was spy-craft.

January 20

Usual Suspects

Delaney House, Emmaus

Marnie paused as she entered the room. Cai looked up from the collection of items and photos arranged on the bedspread.

"Still trying to crack the case?" She pulled out several pairs of pants, holding them up to her outsized body.

"No matter how many times I go over it, it doesn't add up. Shane's the only connection."

"Shane was flat on his back when John Doe died and he's too smart to stash a body where it would be connected to him."

Cai grinned at her. He'd been jealous of her past relationship with Shane, but the last month convinced him that she held no remaining feelings for Shane. She still admired her competition for valedictorian of their high school class, and he could live with that. He'd be suspicious if she didn't admire Shane's intelligence and willingness to risk injury or even death when necessary. It seemed like they passed a test in their marriage where he no longer needed her to prove herself to him. As for Shane ... he seemed increasingly admiring of Jazz Tully, though still in too much pain to do anything about his attraction.

"Except for Josh, everybody in town seems to not be connected."

"How is my brother connected?"

"He and Shane's boss meet at the well house from time to time."

"Yeah, but that doesn't mean he killed John Doe."

"I don't seriously suspect Josh. I think it's suspicious that I keep missing him, though."

"It's not. He doesn't like you, so of course, he's avoiding you, even more so now that you're playing cop, which he *really* doesn't like." In the mirror, she saw Cai acknowledge the truth of her statement. "So, you're saying you have no viable suspects?" Marnie stripped off her dirty pants and slid the yoga pants over her underwear.

"No, I'm – I still circle back to the B&B. They have a snowmobile and their connection with Shane is solid. And something is going on out there. I can feel it."

"I just don't think Ami would let them kill a man and stash him in Shane's backyard."

"Why not? Does she even really know Shane?"

"My point and – well, she's a normal person. She has morals – well, ethics, anyway."

"I just need some evidence that points me in the right direction. Can you talk to Ami for me?"

"I'm – well, I can, but –you know I can't make her tell me any truth, right?"

Cai caught her, pulling her into a backward hug.

"I trust your wily ways, you witch!" His smile warmed her neck. "Did you eat?"

"I did. This baby insists upon it." She turned in his embrace, kissing him. "I'll do my best, but really – I don't think there's anything to find. Yes, they would be out of place in the world as it was, but now – we should be glad they're here and willing to share their information with us."

Cai pulled back, staring at her. Why would she protect the B&B people? They weren't members of the community and he had a mystery to solve.

"Honey, do you know something I don't know?"

Marnie's smile faded.

"I know that she's the only other doctor in town and I'm about to give birth to our baby."

"So … you're worried about what happens if you go into labor without another doctor? Mom can deliver the baby – I think even Jazz has delivered a baby."

"She's not a doctor."

"So you're worried something might happen?"

"My first delivery in med school was a normal pregnancy until she went into labor. She died of a cerebral hemorrhage on the table and we had to take the baby by Caesarian. I don't want to take any chances."

"You'll let a murder go unsolved for fear's sake?"

"No, but you need to know what I'm thinking."

"So do you. They're the only suspects I have and I need to be able to interview them under the force of law, so I intend to ask Dad for warrants."

Something passed behind Marnie's eyes, a shift of perception that he wasn't sure he wanted to analyze. She came over and slid between him and the evidence, her hands on his shoulders.

"You're frustrated by being stuck. Ask Shane to give it one more try, and I'll try to talk with Ami about it. Maybe they're your strongest suspects just because you suspect them." He frowned at her. She kissed him, turned, and left the room. He sighed, remembering the sweet scent of her, and turned back to the evidence on the bed. "Hey." She showed up at the door again. "You need to help me make the bed. And you remember it's the big day, right?"

Arrival

Delaney House, Emmaus

Morning dawned ice cold and crystal clear. Rob Delaney stood on the front porch of his family home, anticipation singing through his veins.

"I wondered where you were." Jill mounted the step. "Shane just got off the radio with the Alaska flight. They should be here in an hour." Fog billowed from her mouth with every word and her cheeks grew pink with the cold.

"Good. Jos reported that people are asking him when the next shipment of food would be in."

"I heard some of the mine guards came back from an expedition empty-handed."

"Jason says there's nothing left out there. We *need* this." They went back into the house via the front door. Cai and Marnie were making their bed preparatory to stacking it with the others in the corner so Shane could get around while they were gone. Shane gave Jazz a radio lesson while that occurred. Click came from the kitchen, carrying a camera and his cellphone. Most cellphones fried in the Pulse along with the towers they linked with, but his still worked as a recorder. Shane was the only one that Rob knew who could still make a phone call.

"Where's Alicia?"

"Neatening up downstairs." She lived in a corner of the main basement and Click lived in the storm cellar. Both were close enough to the coal furnace so they didn't freeze to death. Click spoke to Jill now. "I skinned those rabbits. Looking forward to stew tonight."

"Me too." Rob kissed his wife and looked around the group. "It's a big day. If we can establish a relationship with these folks, we might have a steady source of food and medicine. I feel like the pioneers must have when the rail line came through."

Shane rubbed a hand across his chin. He needed to shave which was hard without cream but still refused to grow a beard. He'd settled for shaving every other day. When they'd run out of modern blades months ago, he'd switched to the daisy razor. Rob supposed he needed to show him how to use a straight razor sometime soon.

"Something?"

"Just – there's something they're hiding from us – whatever business they have in this area. I wish I could go with, but obviously, I can't, so stay frosty." He scanned around the entire group. "All of you. Click, I'm sure we've got a gun we can loan you."

"I was a combat reporter and I didn't carry a gun, so …thanks for caring, but no."

Shane laughed, shaking his head, and rolled over toward the couches to get out of everyone's way.

"What's the word of the day?" Rob checked the mag in his gun and holstered the weapon.

"Brandenberg. And the flash for the day is three long, two short, one long." Click volunteered to make up a code word every day so that they'd have the means to identify someone if needed.

"Marnie and I are going to the medical center." Jill moved toward the kitchen. "Alicia too."

"Click, Cai, and I are headed to the runway. Jason's offered his place as a warmup shack." Rob followed his wife.

"I'm on patrol." Jazz followed him into the kitchen. "Murphy asked Keri and me to take up a position in a water tower out by Shane's fields. I'm borrowing Cai's Savage."

"That's Shane's paranoia wearing off on him."

"I think it was his suggestion and we know he knows stuff he can't share. I also know it seems like a good idea."

Rob nodded. His instinct was to trust this faraway offer of help, but Shane had good instincts too. For all that he was young, so did Murphy.

Even with all the traffic to the runway, the road bogged down, and it took time to drive to where they expected the plane. Shane had them on the radio, and he kept Rob apprised via the handheld.

"They just passed overhead. They'll circle back to head into the wind." Rob looked at the blowing snow outside the cab of the pickup. The prevailing wind was from the northwest, ice-cold and steady. The plane would land going west. He supposed that was better than with a tailwind. "They point out we need to provide light for them to take off when this is all done. Over."

"Jason says they've got it covered." Cai rolled his eyes at Rob who tried not to laugh aloud. "Thank you for handling the radios. Over."

"Shove it, big brother." Shane sounded good-natured about it, but they all knew he wanted his mobility back. "Over."

They struggled through the snow to stand next to the plow Vint Barrett ran down the runway this morning. He had built a small warming fire for them to wait by.

"What's that joke Pa used to say about DC3's?" Rob wasn't surprised that Cai grimaced with confusion, so he asked Shane.

"A collection of spare parts flying in loose formation. There's still about a thousand of them operating around the world, a lot of them in Alaska. They are workhorses and since Douglas Aircraft is probably disbanded, I say we reverse engineer the existing ones. Over."

"You do that, son. It'll give you something to do while you're laid up. Over."

"Believe me, I am working on it. So freaking bored. Over."

"Here it comes." Cai pointed to a dot in the air east of them.

The silver plane's propellers created a blur of snow as it touched down on the tarmac barely a plane length from its beginning. The pilot went full flaps almost immediately, feathering the props as he braked straight to about three-quarters of the runway. Rob hadn't told anyone outside of his closest associates when the plane was due and Joe,

Murphy, and the Army group blocked the road from town to keep looky-loos from getting too close.

The Emmaus greeters held by the fire while the plane powered down. The door about halfway back on the plane dropped open and a group of three people emerged from the 75-year-old aircraft. Rob started forward, flanked by Cai and Click. For the first time, he felt his daughter's scope on the back of his neck. He trusted Keri. He trusted Jazz. They wouldn't shoot unless something went wrong. After everything they'd been through in the last five months, Overwatch felt more comfortable, even when you realized the area could go hot any moment.

The shortest of the Arctic-expedition-clad delegation held out a heavily-gloved hand as they neared. The ruff of the coat obscured her face until their hands touched and he found himself smiling into the face of Francene Maracle, Speaker of the US House and the constitutional President of the former United States.

We Need to Talk

Emmaus Medical Center

Marnie met her at the door of the clinic. Ami knew something was up when Marnie immediately flipped the lock to closed and dragged her into the staff "lounge" where the coal stove kept the building from freezing.

"What is it?"

"Cai plans to go to Rob tomorrow, after all this stuff with Alaska is over, to tell him he believes the B&B was responsible for John Doe's death."

Marnie's pregnancy had rounded her face and put color in her cheeks. She was a lovely woman even in her husband's clothes, but her blue eyes filled with dread.

"I need you. You'll be the only doctor when I have the baby."

"Well, thank you for thinking of me." Marnie frowned, thought through what she'd just said, and started to rephrase. Ami laughed. "There's no offense taken. I've been afraid of this from the beginning. What would your father-in-law do?"

"The same thing he's been doing with everyone else – banish you. There's a growing little community in Beulah, huddling in abandoned houses."

"Me as well? Even though I'm working on the encephalitis?"

"I think so. Why was he killed?"

Ami took a deep breath and considered her options.

"I don't know. We didn't kill him. We didn't know who he was."

"Do you now?"

"Yes, but you wouldn't know the significance. I don't myself. Grant assures me he had nothing to do with the B&B."

"But you are hiding something, aren't you?"

"It's a house of government operatives. Of course, they're hiding something."

"If you want my help, I need to know what that is."

Dread filled Ami's chest.

"How would that help?"

"I'd tell Cai and he'd back off you."

"No, he probably wouldn't."

"How do you suppose?"

Ami remembered washing blood from the wood floor. If she didn't tell, they'd be banished and probably die in a huddle in Beulah. If she told, they'd be banished and die in a huddle in Beulah. Murder dealt consequences and she saw no safe place with which to avoid them.

"You might be able to get away with telling Shane. Cai senses Shane isn't getting straight answers from the Rigbys and so he's going to keep pushing. But if Shane could definitely say he knew what happened, he could convince Cai to back off."

Ami sat down on the sofa here and buried her face in her hands.

"Your brother-in-law scares me."

"You can outrun him."

True, at the moment.

"I'll go there and tell him then, but – you may not like what I have to say."

"I don't care what you've done. I need another doctor in this community and so you could ax-murder a family of five and I might not vote for banishment."

"I hope you're joking."

"Not so much. I had to tell the Bennetts I have nothing to offer their son by way of treatment. Trust me, that sort of reality turns your heart cold."

Ami knew that full-well. She reached for her gloves and then her cell phone rang. Marnie looked stunned as she answered the call.

"Yes?"

"This is Ron Patterson. I think the house is going to need you."

"What? You need me – ."

"There's a plane landing from Alaska. I think the kids will need you."

An Alaska plane? What was going on?

"Yes, well, I – I'll be there as quickly as possible."

She pocketed the phone.

"How is that working?"

"The same way Shane's works, and that's about all I know. Listen, I've no time to go talk to Shane now, so I'm going to tell you and you can tell him or Cai, or whatever you think will work." She took a steadying breath. "We had some soldiers show up from Cheyenne Mountain and they tried to kill us. They shot Grant. We took care of them – killed them. We hid them far out of town, however. We kept our business in the house so as not to affect the community. And we had nothing to do with that fellow behind the hotel."

Marnie looked stunned, silently rubbing her ribs with one hand.

"Now I have to go. There's an emergency at the B&B. I'll be back as soon as I'm able."

She left her fate in the hands of a woman who, she hoped, cared enough not to treat it cavalierly.

Caribou Barbie

Delaney Airfield, Jericho Township

Some people called Francene Maracle a bimbo. In her mid-fifties, she remained tall, slender, and attractive. Rob held mixed feelings about her. She played what Jill called "lipstick" feminism very well in that she was comfortable in her female skin. Married with five children, she'd worked her way up through local and state politics, been selected as the VP candidate for a very popular Republican politician who had blamed her for losing the election. She'd finished her two allowed terms as governor of Alaska. When the long-time representative of Alaska stepped down for health reasons, her former Lieutenant Governor appointed her to fill his seat. When she won the seat in her own right a year later, the House came together to select her as Speaker of the House. It was unprecedented and within two years, she found herself dealing with a president nobody elected and then a terrorist attack nobody expected.

Before the Bombs, Francene Maracle was the exact reason half the country didn't trust the mainstream media. If you saw their coverage of her, you thought she was Grizzly Bear Barbie – a dumb bimbo who had to have slept her way to her position. If you saw her on Newswire or one of the newer alternative media, you suspected she might be the most intelligent and down-to-earth member of the House. The reality was she was both and neither.

"Thank you for keeping this private." She'd shed several layers of cold-weather clothing in the office of Jacob's hangar at the airfield. Rob was glad he'd thought to come fire up the oil-drip stove and warm up the small space.

"No problem. My sons are trying to coordinate the meeting. Do I get to know what's going on?" Rob held his hands out to the stove to warm them. It wasn't bad duty, VIP entertaining while Jos and Anders McAuliff honchoed moving the goods to town. Francene's gaze flitted toward Click who sat in the corner.

"This part is off the record?" He nodded, flashing a reassuring thumbs-up. "My daughter Eden was in Wichita working for Ren Sullivan when the Bombs went off. We didn't know how to get hold of her until I got a message from Ren before Christmas. We knew we couldn't just fly into a commercial field, so it took me time to gather what I thought would be a good haul to entice you folks to help us out."

"Doing it over an open radio could have attracted marauders, but so far our overwatch says we're good. The cold has probably discouraged everyone who could manage a raid."

"You get many of those?"

"We're pretty well-armed, so no. Only a couple. What's going on out there?"

"You think I know?" She laughed, pushing back a lock of grey-shot honey hair. Her hazel eyes twinkled as she cast a glance to Click. "We can go on record now." He held up a thumb to show they were now officially exchanging information. "I'm not the president. I don't want to be. There's no rescue coming."

"Yeah, I knew that in October. What's going on out there?"

She sighed, holding her hands out to the stove. They were strong hands, long-boned, capable.

"California is all burned-out cities and empty farmland. They encased most of the bombed cities in concrete, but Los Angeles had two hot spots so California was more complicated. Portland got hit too, but the Willamette Valley farmers are reorganizing now that the radiation levels are dropping. Bunnell & Wilson is in charge in Seattle and things are stable there. In the southeast, Georgia, that area, blacks are enslaving white people."

"No!" Rob exchanged an incredulous look with Click who scoffed.

"Yes! It's weird. They're calling themselves the Republic of Afrika. They put out regular videos and articles – lists of the sentences given to people for 'systemic racism' and 'failure to provide proper respect'. Death is a common sentence, but so are 'indenture' and 'reeducation'. They claim the flu didn't hit black people like it hit whites and it's that southern strain that's killing so many people. We hear it's not so bad up north."

"It's hasn't been so bad for us, but there's a secondary effect – an encephalitis that seems to affect teenage boys."

"Yes, that's what we're hearing too, mostly out of Columbus. Seattle has been protected by winter and so far doesn't have the flu." She sighed again. "In the Southwest, the southern strain has been particularly deadly. I don't know if it affects Hispanics less, but so many people have died, who knows. The population there always was majority Hispanic and they've taken control under the auspices of the American military."

Rob raised an eyebrow. He'd heard she was a racist and never believed it. She was married to an Aleut, for heaven's sake. Still, her calm assessment seemed strange after years of feeling he had to apologize for looking white. Technically, he was more Indian than Shane, but Shane's dark hair meant he never had to prove his blood. Francene sighed, then laughed lightly, before sobering.

"I know how it sounds, but it's what we're hearing. The northern tier states are struggling – starving, freezing, dying. New York collapsed after the Pulse. It's like a Snake Blitzkin movie. They're eating people in Pittsburgh. Columbus seems to be hanging onto civilization."

Rob shivered. Ren mentioned the cannibalism and Rob thought he exaggerated it. Now? He didn't know. There was no reason to believe Francene more than Ren.

"What about the world around us?" Click asked that pertinent question while Rob checked the coffee pot on the stove. He'd been surprised to find a can of actual coffee on the shelf as if Jacob might walk in at any moment.

"Some US troops pulled out of Europe, South Korea, and the Middle East and are supposedly headed back here, but there's no Pentagon, so who knows when they'll get here or if they'll be on our side when they arrive. I think there might have been an expeditionary force arrive in

California before the Pulse. Nobody knows where they went."

"Any idea who did this?" Click wasn't going to give up on the larger-world story.

"Lots of ideas. None of them confirmed. Some blame Iran or North Korea. Supposedly US forces out of Miristan bombed the Shalamar province in October. I mean, big bombs, but nobody has taken credit for bombing us – US cities -- and there's a rumor the fissionable material might be of American origin."

"What?!" Rob felt gut-punched.

"Not verified. We may never know. If the information wasn't uploaded to actually space storage, it was wiped by the Pulse."

Rob sat down in Jacob's chair, rubbing a hand over his face. She poured him a cup of coffee. Click got his own as she sat down on the edge of the desk.

"You got anything you want put in that?"

All day, every day!

"No, thank you. You wouldn't like me drunk."

She arched a perfect eyebrow. He remembered something about her husband getting a DUI when he was very young. Rob supposed he'd stayed home with the younger children. She sipped coffee.

"Strong like camp coffee." It was hard to tell if she admired that or was disgusted. She sipped more of it. "The Middle East is a tinderbox. Some of the Arab nations attacked Israel, but they set off a small nuke in Tehran and that scared everyone into backing down."

"They shot a missile into Iran?"

"No. They already had a suitcase nuke there. They'd planned ahead."

"And the Arab countries accepted that?" Click recorded her now.

"I think they're glad Iran can't threaten them anymore and OPEC has discovered it can't make a profit without the US, not with Alaska coming into the world market as a direct player." Click's eyebrows disappeared into his beanie. "Thirteenth largest proven government-owned oil reserve in the world. We're creating our own OPEC with some countries that don't particularly care for the House of Saud. That's mostly what I've been doing with Governor Sheridan."

"Where's the UN in all this?" Rob figured he could ask questions too.

"The what?" Francene rolled her eyes. "They dissolved like snow in the hot sun after the EMP. The UN building burned. We hear rumors, but nothing too concerning. I think they're done. The US provided most of the funding for their shenanigans."

Rob sipped coffee, which stopped him from shivering.

"North Korea tried to attack Seoul with troops and conventional weapons and South Korea is now in control of the entire peninsula. I hear alternatively Jung has been executed or that they're keeping him in the manner to which he has become comfortable so that they don't create a martyr."

"China didn't come in on North Korea's side?"

"Without the US as its primary market, it's facing a deep recession, scrambling to direct its energies elsewhere. The premier demanded the US repay its loans, but Marshall Ellerby, the designated survivor, told them 'no'. Then Anna Beyers out of Cheyenne Mountain also told them 'no'. You know about there being two governments for half-a-second before the Pulse?" Rob shrugged. What did it matter? "Yeah, Colorado and New York both went dark after that and so I think there's no government anymore." Francene sipped some more coffee. "Some people think China might try to occupy the Pac Coast, but B&W and Knight Industries will have something to say about that and they're integrating the American military at a phenomenal rate."

Rob gulped the last of his coffee like a shot of whiskey and rose to fill his cup again. He filled hers too. Click waved him off of his cup.

"What about Europe?"

Francine stared at the wall calendar. It was from the previous year because Jacob died in November and nobody was publishing calendars this year.

"The historic lines of tension reasserted themselves. Germany – yeah, she never learned not to take over the continent. She was just biding her time. They declared Germany is the head of the EU – the GEU, I guess you could call it. Russia got its back up about that. There are troops in the Ukraine and Poland rattling sabers. Sweden, Norway, and Iceland formed a new Scandinavian coalition and told the GEU to leave them alone. I think Denmark wants to join, but they're shaking in their boots. The UK, Ireland, and Scotland are demanding autonomy. The

Balkans are rioting amid runaway inflation. Switzerland and Liechtenstein closed their borders. We'll see how long they hold out."

"God. It's a nightmare!" Click looked like he wanted that stronger stuff to put in his coffee.

"I don't know about that. Give it a year and they'll either have destroyed each other or remembered that war has consequences. We have bigger issues to worry about here – well, you do. Alaska is protected by the Great Barrier Reef of Canada."

"How are they?" Rob figured full information worked best.

"Chill as always. A new coalition of conservatives took control not long after the Pulse when the former premier proved unable to cope. Much easier to deal with than the leftists who were in charge for so long. They let us fly over their country, after all. Even let us land and refill."

"What else?"

"Marshall Ellerby's dissertation – well, supposedly his, has been circulating. Pretty scary stuff – all about a multi-point terrorism attack that could take out the transportation and communications grids and cause the balkanization of the United States." Rob raised an eyebrow. "He was a 26-year-old graduate student when he wrote it, and it's all conjecture and nobody knows what's really happening. Most people aren't on the radio or the Internet to brag. And Ellerby probably died during the Pulse. It would seem that the US is going to break up – well, has already broken up. The northeast is pretty devastated except in the rural areas, so is Tidewater. Florida's gone. The Old South is now the

Republic of Afrika. The rest of the South are forming a loose coalition to defend themselves against them. There's some sort of government forming in Columbus Ohio that's calling itself the United States, but near as I can tell, nobody is joining them. I suspect Seattle will absorb Oregon. There's that mess centered around Albuquerque. Texas and Louisiana seem to be getting married. Don't know about the Midwestern states. The Dakotas are mostly deserted or dead. You folks were lucky, though. Food and a much shorter winter."

"Yeah. I expect we'll lose 40-50% of our population, mostly to disease and inadequate heating, some to hunger, but if we make it to spring, there's a good chance we'll survive."

"Except, I think there might be civil war after all the starving is over."

"Not with so many fighting-age men paralyzed. I just don't see how that works."

Rob and Francene froze at Click's observation. Cai came in the man-door with a swirl of wind-driven snow.

"Shane says the B&B won't shoot us if we show up at their gate."

"He's talked to them?"

"That's what took so long. I guess they were a little paranoid. Click's picture convinced them."

"Well, then, Francene --."

"Frankie, please. I'll get dressed." She moved to where she'd shed her layers.

"How'd she end up at the B&B?"

"Shane might know." Cai shrugged. "She going to step up?"

"No." Father and son locked gazes. "I didn't think she would. I'm kind of glad she won't. It leaves us free to rebuild the right way."

"There's going to be war."

"Maybe. Let's not give the future power to destroy our present, okay? Are we ready to go? You're driving, son."

Cousins

Delaney House, Emmaus

"Hello?"

Shane lifted his head off the pillow, reached for his 9mm. Rigby's warning that someone might want Francene Maracle dead rang in his head.

Who the heck left the door unlocked?

"Hello? It's Ed. Anybody home, Glister?"

"I'm in here." Shane pushed himself up against the arm of the couch, rubbing a hand over his face. He'd been running the radio for hours, his hip slowly tensing and hurting until he needed to lay down and then he fell asleep.

Ed came through the dining room opening.

"Your dad around?"

"No."

"He doing something with that DC that landed this morning?"

Shane gave him an embarrassed look and Ed laughed.

"Tonto see far, breed." Ed flashed a big grin and flopped onto the end of the couch. Shane stared over his knees at him. It hurt, but he was trying to keep his weak leg from leaning against the back of the couch. "You going to put that gun down?"

Shane checked the safety and tossed it on his bed, which was the only one not stacked against the wall.

"What brings you here?"

"I brought a barrel of fuel. Figured he might trade for some of that cider."

"He probably would. The jugs are upstairs, and I can't go there."

"I can. What's the exchange rate?"

"No idea. I've been mostly sleeping for the last two months."

"You know, they could have asked me for some product."

"If I'd wanted it, they would have, but I can't do that to myself."

"What? Float away on fluffy pink clouds dreaming of unicorns or whatever? I grow some good stuff."

"I know that, but I stopped in college and I don't want to start again."

Ed grinned, spreading large hands, palms up toward Shane.

"Okay, your choice. I'm not a pusher. So whatcha do all day?"

"Stretching exercises, nap, charge the batteries, nap, grind corn, nap. Mostly a lot of napping."

"So pretty much like hanging on the Rez in winter? Why do you think I grow pot?"

"I'm so freaking bored."

"How much longer? A few weeks – a year. Somewhere in between?"

"Brian says I can start limited weight-bearing next week. We'll see how it goes from there."

"You have a high pain tolerance. I remember that time you separated your shoulder. Rode your horse back into town and let Dr. Vashon reduce it without pain meds." He sobered. "You know walking will be harder?"

Shane wanted to argue, but Ed didn't do serious except when it was truly serious.

"I plan to follow instructions. It's against my instincts, but I've learned a lot lying on my back staring at the ceiling."

Ed's gaze flickered, then he nodded. The radio crackled behind him. Shane reached for the wheelchair.

"Should I stick around, or can I grab a jug of that cider?"

Shane did the transfer and then rolled toward the radio.

"How big is this barrel of fuel?"

"It's a barrel. 55 gallon."

"If there are more than 10 jugs, you can have two. If there's less, you can have one."

"I'll take one and come back for the other if your dad agrees."

"I don't have a concussion any longer, but okay, treat me like I'm addled." Shane realized he sounded annoyed, so he pulled a face so Ed would know he was kidding – mostly. Ed laughed.

"Emmaus base, can you get Ren Sullivan on the radio for me? Over." Shane turned to his father's channel.

"Pathfinder, let me see what I can do. Greyeye's Raven wants to exchange a barrel of generator fuel for cider. How much does 55 gallons buy? Over."

"Two jugs. Remind him not to drink it until it warms to room temperature. Frostbite of the esophagus is a thing. Over."

Ed laughed and headed up the stairs. He wasn't much of a drinker. Shane suspected the cider was for trade, just like it was for the Delaneys.

"It's in the hall?"

Shane nodded. With the handheld, he tried to call up Ren.

"I'm here, Maverick. What do you need? Over."

"Pathfinder wants to talk to you, Ren. I can patch you to Channel 9. Over."

"Sure, patch me through, Maverick. How are you doing? Over."

"Better. Tired of people feeling they need to ask that question, but thanks for asking. Patching through now." He switched to Channel 9. "Pathfinder, I've got Ren on the horn. I'm patching you through now. Over."

"Ren?"

"I'm here, Pathfinder. Over."

Shane turned the volume down and glanced at Ed who was coming down the stairs.

"You okay here on your own?"

Shane shifted his weight in the chair. He'd probably gotten up too soon, but his strength was holding out.

"Sure. I'm just a radio call to someone for help."

"Well, then I'll be on my way. And, you know Leroy Red Fox has a ham. You can get him on Channel 19 most evenings."

"Good to know. For now, this is the only communication system we have, so … if he hears anything out there, tell him we'd like to know."

"Will do. You lay down if it starts to hurt – you hear?"

"I hear, but I don't always listen."

Shaking his head and cackling like a hen, Ed disappeared around the dining doorframe, leaving Shane feeling unexpectedly alone.

Miracle Tech

Emmaus Medical Center

What to say to Cai to get him to leave the B&B people alone? Marnie didn't know. She could only hope that he'd listen to reason if it came from her. Ami was too important to the community to lose her and it might be possible that the overwatch function of the B&B was too important to lose as well.

She scanned down through the chart in her hand. Matthew Bennett seemed to be weakening. She wished she could give better news to his parents, but she wasn't prepared to deal with respiratory failure. Ami said she'd circle over that way in a day or two to see how things were working out. Marnie hoped Matthew would still be alive.

The lobby door jangled, and she looked around the corner to see Anders McAuliff and two men she thought were mine guards muscling a crate in the door.

"What's up?" She pushed the door closed behind them, frowning at the crate.

"It's a gift from that VIP. We were headed to the grocery but figured we'd stop on the way to give this to you. It's medical equipment."

"Meds?"

"We're pulling that off the truck now, but this is some stuff I don't recognize."

"I'll figure it out. Can you put it in the staff area?"

Anders signaled his guys and opened the door for three men carrying large boxes. He pushed the door closed against the wind.

"We might make it to spring with that, right?"

"It's better than if we don't have it."

Anders opened the door for two more men carrying boxes.

"That's it. We're headed to the grocery with the rest. You need help unpacking everything?"

"I've got staff. They're just not here right now. It'll be fine until they are. Thank you so much."

"It takes a village." The slight mocking tone in his voice made her laugh. She pushed the door closed behind the mine crew. Then she keyed her radio. "Nile Princess, you got your ears on? Over."

Complications

Sullivan B&B, Jericho Springs

Travis looked stunned as Eden asked her question. He showed some voluntary movement in both legs, though he was not recovered by any stretch of the imagination. The biggest impediment to recovery was that his spinal fracture couldn't be fused in these circumstances by the inadequate medical team available and so he was stuck in bed until something could be done about that or until it healed on its own.

"Alaska? You asked me before, but you know, things are different now."

"No, they aren't for me. Are they different for you?"

Ami tried to act like the view from the window fascinated her.

"I may need a wheelchair and I can't pee, so yeah."

Eden cast a distressed look Ami's way.

"I'm not a neurologist, but you should continue to make progress now that the swelling's going down."

"You need physical therapy beyond what I can manage here and a spinal fusion to stabilize that fracture." Brian leaned against the wall by the door. "It's a good place to go. They still have a functional modern medical system."

"And what if it doesn't get better?

Brian's eyes flickered, then narrowed. He straightened from the wall.

"Out, both of you. Travis and I need to discuss something so he can make an informed decision."

Eden frowned as something occurred to Ami. She touched Eden's shoulder.

"Let's go sit at the end of the corridor. It's a big decision. Come on."

Eden still frowned even when they sat down on the loveseat in front of the windows. Her mother's voice filtered up the stairwell, Grant's deeper voice throbbing at intervals.

"Do you know what they're talking about?"

"Downstairs or Travis and Brian?"

"Travis."

"Yes. I know you two are intimate."

"Shh, she'll hear you."

Ami laughed softly.

"My mother would feel the same." Now Ami sobered because it was a difficult topic. "Spinal cord injuries have consequences. We have to do things for Travis that he can't do for himself right now."

"Like the catheter for him to pee?"

"Yes."

Ami waited for it to sink into the girl. She blushed, then went pale when it did.

"He can't…."

"Not right now and the future of that is uncertain. He's improving, but he might still be a paraplegic. Most male paraplegics resume a sex life after they heal, but it may need to be adaptive. And he's scared he won't be able to. That's the conversation Brian is having with him right now."

"He thinks – what – that I'd stop loving him if he can't --."

"It's just a really hard time for him and he doesn't know what he doesn't know. He's scared. He's in pain. He's feeling helpless. The idea of a trip to Alaska probably feels overwhelming. And being his age and contemplating not being able to perform in that way must be terrifying. And, I won't lie to you. Even if this is temporary, it will take months of really hard work for him to get back to full strength."

"I'm not going to leave him."

"You might want to when the anger hits. And it will. He'll get frustrated and it will spill over."

"Does it with Javi?" Her lover's ice-cold exterior covered a lot of emotions.

"Javi is a special case. Most people in Travis's situation will experience frustration and anger and it will spill into your relationship. Just remember that he's frustrated with his situation and he's not so much angry at you as he's angry at the situation and you're handy."

Brian stuck his head out the door and waved for them. Travis looked calmer, and in less pain when they entered. He took Eden's hand.

"I explained it to her." Ami saw no reason to keep it a secret. Secrecy just left everybody in the dark. Look at the mess secrecy created with the town.

Travis's gaze dwelled on Eden's face.

"Do you understand?"

"I do. We'll get through it. You'll heal or we'd need to find new ways of doing things. That's not why I love you. It's just part of you and whatever disabilities you're left with will be a part of you too."

"I just don't want to trap you."

"You're not. Come to Alaska, get surgery so you can get out of bed, and physical therapy so you can maybe walk. And if you don't, we'll adapt. I promise."

She wiped the tears from his cheeks. She was an incredibly strong woman.

"Yeah, yeah. I'll go. Thank you. I love you." More tears flowed from her now. "Does your mom know?"

"About?"

They stared at each other a moment and then laughed. Travis winced with pain. Ami excused herself. She left the medical center quickly when Javi radioed her and she needed to get back. She needed to know if Marnie would help them.

Happy Valentine

Huffman's Market, Emmaus

Nothing says "I love you" quite like looting and killing.

Jos set down his pencil after circling February 14. He'd been just as glad as any to see the Alaska shipment come in, but his calculations brought him to a grim conclusion. If everyone rationed carefully, this food would last the current population of Emmaus about 24-25 days.

Maybe that would be enough for Ren to get his next shipment through. Nothing in life was easy or secure right now. It reminded him of a football game, victory won in yards. Only this game didn't have a quarterback. It just had a teenage grocer calculating calories and wishing his town's mayor would step in and mandate sharing. But no, people would come tomorrow and snap up whatever was available, and he'd sell it for whatever they had to offer. Increasingly, people offered family heirlooms as payment, which he wasn't interested in because Jason Breen wouldn't be paid that way. Ren Sullivan had said to not worry about paying him a cut, but that made bookkeeping complicated.

Capitalism kept him fed better than most people in town, but it hurt to have women offering their bodies to him for a bit of food. Some days he just wanted to throw the door open and let people take what they wanted. Why couldn't he do it? This food hadn't cost him anything.

He remembered a story Granmae told him about how the Pilgrims originally were communists. They were supposed to share everything in some kind of Christian commune. It didn't work because some people didn't work. Why should they if they were getting fed while others put in the effort? The governor eventually allotted plots to each family and that gave everyone incentive to produce for themselves. Mayor Delaney believed that scenario and Jos noticed that the desperate people were not farmers but had been online salespeople and computer programmers who had never planned for such a disaster. The farmers were mostly willing to hire them and pay them in food. They didn't need to be desperate.

Someone banged on the door. He'd enclosed the front of the store so he'd have a warm space to work, though he still stocked the shelves in the poorly heated back. The glass front of the store had been enclosed in plywood and insulation board, so he couldn't see out the door. He paused with his hand on the lock.

"Who's there?"

"Gen Conopher. My dad sent me."

Jos unlocked the door to let her in. She was a tall girl with dark brown hair and chocolate brown eyes. They knew each other from school, but not well. He hesitated to lock the door behind her, but since he sat on the motherlode, that would be dumb, so he overcame his discomfort.

"What can I do for you?"

"Potatoes." She set the sacks of spuds on the floor. "For canned goods."

"Technically not open until tomorrow."

"I'll come back. I have twice this. I'll go unload them."

"Do that. I'll let you get what you want."

"Thank you. We missed the last shipment."

"We cleaned out like that." He snapped his fingers. He opened one of the bags to assure the spuds were in good shape. "Nice."

He manned the lock while she carried in the spuds. *Blasting cold wind.* Then he escorted her into the back to select canned fruit.

"No vegetables?"

"We had a truck garden. Lots of carrots and canned green beans. How are you doing?"

"Living the life." He gestured to the cavernous space around them. Hard to believe this had once been a thriving grocery store.

"Lonely?"

"At night, yeah."

"It's cold in here. How do you sleep upstairs?"

"I don't. I'm sleeping in the storefront. I just drag the cot into the back for the day."

"Wow. What happens to your plumbing come spring?"

"Jace Welton winterized it for me. How's Kix?"

"His eyes opened this morning."

"That's great, right? He's coming out of the coma?"

"The doctor's coming to check on him. It's hard to tell. He's not talking or moving."

"Yet. He'll get there."

"You – have you had the flu?"

"No. Should have. Granmae did." That made him sad and he didn't want to be sad when a pretty girl was here.

"It was a horrible few days, but it didn't seem that bad. Until Kix couldn't move."

"I've heard there are at least a dozen guys down with this second thing. Some seem to have passed the worst of it."

Gen nodded as she grabbed a couple more cans.

"Thank you for letting me do this."

"No problem. So your parents are letting you drive now?"

"My dad's been letting me drive on the farm since I was 12. I waved at Sheriff Joe on my way here."

"He's a funny guy. You'd expect him to be all law and order, but he isn't."

"I think he's just adapting to circumstances – like we all are. You know, if you're lonely, you should come to dinner sometime. We have a full house, but there's always enough to eat and you'd be welcome."

"Yeah?"

"Yes, definitely."

Warmth flushed through his body.

"I'll think about it. You're about even with the potatoes."

She paused with her hands out to the shelf of olives.

"Of course. Why olives?

"No idea. I stock what they bring me. I'll help you carry everything to your car. Thanks for stopping by." Yeah, go for it. "Feel free to do it anytime."

"I won't need to shop again for a while."

"Who says you have to shop?"

Her cheeks pinked. They giggled nervously and the moment passed. He definitely needed to visit her house near dinnertime sometime soon.

Information Exchange

Sullivan B&B, Jericho Springs

Grant eased his arm in its sling while Francene Maracle debriefed. She explained she knew him by reputation.

"You may be the only former government official I can trust."

Trust being an operative word. Grant mused that for 20 years he'd been no more trustworthy than his fellow intelligence operatives. He'd done his job – keeping the world safe from democracy. Now that he was making up his own playbook …? Alaska had resources his family would eventually need and if he could pay for them with information, why not?

"So the United States was a lynchpin and the world is spinning right now. Who do you think will shape into the next lynchpin?"

"Hard to know. If they don't go to war – the EU – or whatever it is calling itself these days will likely take that role. The Chinese economy was far too dependent upon American consumer goods. When they stopped paying their workers, a revolt formed and now they've got widespread civil unrest. That's the one thing the CCP couldn't handle. They've lost control of their Belt and Road farce, their agents going native while the natives are grabbing whatever they can." She checked her socks where they were draped over the woodstove.

"Who do you think will become the stabilizer in the United States?"

She sat back down on the sofa, extending her long-toed bare feet toward the heat.

"The fall was inevitable. Dotson tipped us over into insolvency. Congress was in secret negotiations about what to do next. The strongest argument was to grab the retirement accounts and 'repatriate' all that hoarded cash. That would have sent us into a spin. Dotson's solution was to get us into another war that we couldn't win and blame them."

"As if getting Americans addicted to opioids from Afghani poppy fields wasn't bad enough?"

They called her Frankie and he could see that. She must have been such a tomboy before puberty made her beautiful. He tried to see Eden in her features. Similar eyes, though hers were blue and Eden's were light brown. Frankie adjusted her glasses. It was his turn.

"Someone was also fomenting civil unrest around the country."

"Antifa?"

Grant snorted.

"You know Antifa was just a loose collection of useful idiots incited by a few voices who were coordinated from somewhere else."

"I do. And, truthfully, Dotson was worth fighting against. Anyone behind him, that you know of?"

"Very likely." Grant wanted to trust her, but the searing pain of a bullet wound reminded him that trust had to be earned after thorough vetting. "Why don't you want to be president?"

"Of what? The Disunited States? No, thank you. I never wanted to be two heartbeats away from the presidency. I was flattered when they made me Speaker until I realized that I was meant to be a sacrificial lamb. I should have known better. I should have learned better after that VP run."

Grant scanned her face. Selling information was a new concept for him, but he saw the opportunity in it now.

"You know you won that election, don't you?"

Her chin came up. Her smooth forehead crinkled and then she laughed, shaking her head.

"My ego isn't that big."

"You won the election – your ticket did. Forty thousand constitutional votes were all that separated you from Lang."

"The Electoral College --."

"Relies on the popular vote in individual states. They tampered with county-level votes, just a few thousand in a few key counties in a few key states. That's happened before. Our analysis showed you won the election by a few hundred thousand in Pennsylvania and Michigan. They were more subtle in a few other states. It doesn't take much to sway a close election."

She crooked a half-smile at him.

"So, he lost the popular vote too?" She mocked him and Grant smiled at her.

"Yes."

She blinked, stunned.

"Wow! More than a decade ago and I still feel it." She shrugged, her bulky sweater hardly registering the movement of her shoulders. "Well, thank you for that, but I still don't want to be President. The Republic died. Let's admit that and hold the funeral. Alaskans were never really enamored with the old order anyway. Any chance that election was rigged too?"

"It was before my time, but every election is potentially suspect under the right conditions. Regardless, statehood was a lousy deal for a small-pop state. Gave up your autonomy for three votes in Congress and a once-in-four-year placebic vote for President. Although I think what emerges after this winter will be a much easier federal government to head – you'd mostly be the State Department."

"There's symmetry then. I'm the Commissioner of Foreign Relations in Alaska now."

"Do you think Alaska can really go on its own?"

"Yes. We already have. Our National Guard and some of the regular Army is sticking with us. We've already established trade relations with Korea and Hawaii. We're working with some smaller energy countries that don't like OPEC. Russia and China are both sending embassies to us. We already impaneled a commission to look into writing a new constitution. Some of us want to adopt portions of the old federal constitution. I think we'll see that here in the Lower 48 after the weather breaks."

"No doubt, but I expect war. My tech guy is talking with Sergeant Llewellyn. We're going to set up a secure channel."

"Good. I'd like to be able to continue to communicate with Ren Sullivan securely as well."

"We can work on that. What he did in Wichita was some savvy statesmanship. I think we've completed all the questions I had. You?"

"We heard a rumor that American forces bombed the Shalamar Province."

"That's true."

"Why? It seems unlikely the Miristani were involved in such a coordinated attack."

"We don't know the why. Now, if you want to buy information – as a free agent, I'm not opposed to selling it."

Frankie laughed wholeheartedly.

"I'm assuming you work for food and fuel just like Mayor Delaney?"

"You can't eat gold."

"I don't speak for Alaska on this mission. I'll get back to you. If you can provide useful information, I'm sure we can work something out."

"How's the weather there now?"

"It's been a mild winter. You guys got all our nasty."

"Seems fair." She nodded, smile broadening. "How's your husband?"

"Healed. Do you know about it?"

"I have suspicions he was assaulted to get you out of Washington. Does that track?"

"Two snow machines running him down on a remote trail. It happened so fast all he really saw was black Polaris. Nothing unusual about it except they seemed to want to kill him. Why would they want to get me out of Washington?"

"Whoever did this might want a figurehead."

"Yeah." She chuckled. The nervous quality made his eyebrows rise. "I've been warned." She smiled, but her hazel eyes were flat.

"And you weren't going to tell me that?"

"I figured you knew."

"Suspicions are not knowledge. What was the nature of this discussion?"

"Discussion?" She laughed. "*Discussions.* Some people threatened me if I tried to become President and some threatened me if I didn't. All foreign sources except Ren Sullivan who didn't threaten me so much as warn me that I'd end up dead if I tried to become President."

"Is he speaking from knowledge or wisdom?"

"I'm not sure. Has he told you?"

"We only met briefly when he dropped Eden and Travis here. Speaking of which, I think we've given them enough time to think about it. Travis really shouldn't stay here if she goes. I know it's awkward with them being so young, but we can't give him the care he needs."

"Don't worry. If he's having sex with my daughter, I consider them married already and that means he's a member of the family. Travis'll be going with us." She rolled a warm sock over a long narrow foot.

"How do you know he'll choose that for sure?"

"Eden is very persuasive, and we won't give him a choice. It's not like he can fight back, right?"

Grant thought Frankie and Emily's mother Madalyn would have enjoyed one another. They were both strong women who brooked no nonsense. He didn't doubt that Travis would agree to go and think it was all his own idea. That's just the way Francene Maracle would play it.

Breathing

Andrew Bennett Farm, Jericho Township

Thank God for old books. Andrew Bennett thought that as he installed a piston that would move Matt's bed on the added curved rockers. The family took turns because the bed's action simulated breathing. At first, it had just been a supplement, needed once or twice a day, as Matt weakened, but the last three days, someone needed to rock it at all times. During a two-hour shift of being Matt's diaphragm, Andrew came up with the idea of the piston that could do what the family was doing. He also admitted that the rotator cuff repair he'd had last winter might not have been wholly successful.

Matt's lips and fingernails looked bluish by the time Andrew actuated the piston. The bed rocked forward, dragging Matt's organs down so he could inhale. His eyes opened as drool ran down his chin. The piston cycled down, and the bed rocked backward, causing Matt to exhale. Andrew watched it through a handful of cycles, watching as Matt's lips pinked up. Hopefully, his nailbeds would follow soon.

"Drew, there's someone here to see you." Colleen called up the stairs. She had to come up here several times a day to care for Matt and she no longer stood on politeness.

Luke smiled at Andrew. He'd done the second shift last night and dark circles under his eyes spoke of exhaustion.

"It's working."

"It is. Thank you for helping me with it. Stay and watch your brother. Yell if the piston stops working or if he starts to go blue again."

"I'm going to roll him on his side, so he doesn't choke on his spit."

"Good idea."

Andrew headed down the stairs to find Nevada Randolph standing in his living room with a canvass-wrapped package.

"Sorry I underestimated it by a bit. The more I looked at it, the more I realized what you first brought me wasn't going to work. I talked to Hiram and we came up with a better idea."

She opened the canvas wrapping.

"It's half the weight and the problem with loss of muscle mass shouldn't be so big."

Beautiful metal work combined with leather bumpers and pierced with two valve portals. Luke looked up when they entered the room.

"Matt, we've brought something that might help a lot. I have to shut off the bed, but I promise we'll work quickly."

Andrew timed the halt on the inhale so Matt's lungs would be full while they arranged the straps on the bed and then rolled him onto his back. His eyes reported terror. Andrew rocked the bed several times before shutting down again to complete the process. The cuirass fit over the boy's chest and the straps pulled tight for a snug fit. Luke rocked the bed several times while Nevada helped Andrew connect the hoses and start the pumps. Matt's chest rose with the inhalation cycle and fell with the exhalation cycle.

"That is amazing!" Nevada glowed like she witnessed a birth. Matt's lips pinked and as they watched, his fingernails followed suit.

"Better?" Andrew leaned over Matt, who blinked once, his only remaining form of communication.

"Thank you so much, Nevada." Colleen stood near the door, out of the way, but beaming, tears running down her cheeks. "We're blessed the windmill didn't go out in the Pulse, but that wouldn't have saved his life without your help."

"I think he'll be able to sit up with this once the headache goes away." Luke grinned. "He's going to get bored lying in bed all the time." Matt's eyes closed against the light and sound in the room.

"We'll be able to take care of him easier without that bulky design."

"I just wish we had a 3-D printer. It would go so much easier than hand-forging old car body metal. But he looks like he's doing okay there."

The boy did seem to be adjusting to this new method of breathing, which might mean he'd live until his body remembered how to do it for itself. He walked Nevada to her car.

"Max loaned you his 4-by, I see."

"My van couldn't manage the deep snow any longer."

"You two managing okay?"

"Yeah. We've actually become quite good friends."

The wind suddenly blushed both her cheeks with pink.

"I guess that's the best you can hope for."

"Um, yeah, don't know about that. Anyway, if you need any more help…."

"You'll be the first on the list."

She smiled, gaze turned toward the house.

"I'm glad I could make that happen before it was too late. I think we've had enough death of late."

"Absolutely. God willing, we won't lose any more kids to this encephalitis."

She got into the 4x4 and turned east to head home.

Overwatch

Lufgren Farm, Jericho Township

They laid down boards on the catwalk to make the cold more bearable, but the wind still whistled past their elevated position, sucking the warmth out of their bodies and rendering them both cold and cranky.

"I've got something that pretends to be coffee." Keri pulled a thermos out of her backpack. "I brought an extra cup."

"Great! Thank you!" Jazz glassed the makeshift runway. The pilot looked to be doing maintenance. Shane said 70-year-old aircraft maintained well could be as good as new. She didn't know enough about DC-3's to know if this one qualified, but it made it from Alaska, so it probably was the working beast Shane described.

She took the cup from Keri and let the scope dangle from its strap. Keri picked up her own.

"Shane say what we are looking for?"

"Does he ever?"

Out here on the western edge of town between Beulah Ridge and Mara Wells, a long expanse of mostly unbroken snow stretched toward the Rockies. From their high elevation, Jazz could make out the grain siloes at Donovan and what she supposed might have been the top of the water tower in Mara Wells. Why hadn't they heard from anyone in Mara for weeks? There had to be at least one ham operator in Mara but so far Shane kept picking up ghost channels where they couldn't make out the words. He'd turned out to be better at tuning the radio than Click who was more interested in broadcasting anyway. The "coffee" didn't taste like what it pretended to be, but it was warm and pushed back against the wicking wind.

"Take a look."

Keri pointed a gloved hand and Jazz caught up her scope to pan the southwest horizon. It took a bit to locate what had Keri's attention. Black, green and white, squat to the snow. Jazz held her breath to keep from wavering and soon enough she spied movement. She watched without blinking until the movement occurred again – an arm with a cigarette. She watched as steam billowed up into the late afternoon. There was a brief pause and then more steam, punctuated now, billowed out. A moment later, another source of steam issued closer to the front of the military vehicle.

"Do you see it?" Keri whispered as if they could hear her more than a mile out.

"Two men talking."

"And a rocket launcher."

Jazz ran the glass over the truck again.

"I don't see it."

"It was like one of those from Red Dawn."

"An RPG?"

"Yeah. I don't see it now."

"One of the two people out there might have put it in the truck. I'm not sure if they're affected by the cold, but it might pay to keep it warm. I'm going to call Shane so he can get this information to whoever needs it."

Jazz tossed back the warm beverage and dug her radio out from under her coat. Shane took his time answering her, making her worry that he'd overdone and collapsed in exhaustion, but he finally came on the line.

"You okay, Maverick? Over."

"Yeah, Music Box Dancer. I've got a guest. What can I do for you? Over."

"Keri spotted a military vehicle about a mile west by southwest, outside the wire, and she thinks she saw an RPG. Over." There was a long pause before Shane asked his next question.

"She using Alex's spotting scope? Over."

Jazz glanced at her friend who stuck out her tongue, quickly retracting it to prevent frostbite.

"She is. Over."

"Then maybe she's got enough clarity that far out to spot an RPG. Cai's scope isn't as good." Keri laughed silently and flashed Jazz a thumbs-up sign. "I'll have Vint and the pilot take care of that. Can you see to the southeast? Over."

"South of the wire? Over."

"Yes."

"I can just make out Schoenfeld's most-western turbine. Over."

"I bet it's still not spinning."

"None of them are, in this wicked wind. Such a waste. You want me to climb one to try and look for anyone out there? Over."

"No. I can get someone else to do that. You and Keri keep eyes on the plane. Thanks for doing this. We just don't have anyone else who can shoot accurately at the distances you two can. Over."

Shane's realism intruded on what would otherwise be an honored assignment. The possibility that she might have to kill someone rode side by side.

"This is what community does, right? Over."

"Something like that. Stay safe. Over."

"Don't overdo. Over and out."

Jazz stuffed her radio into her inside pocket and turned to see Keri still glassing the prairie.

"It's the only one out there."

"That we can see. You have to wonder where they came from."

"We're not equipped to handle them, are we?"

"What I wouldn't give for an M107 50-cal right now."

"They're out too far even for a 50-cal."

"Not if I fired artillery style. If nothing else, I could scare the crap out of them."

Keri laughed. Her cheeks flushed a pretty rose and she was one of those lucky women whose nose didn't run in the cold.

"You two will be good together." Jazz raised an eyebrow. "Cai mentioned. Kind of wondering why my best friend hasn't been waxing poetic about her latest love … or any love."

Jazz took a deep breath, then coughed from icy air knifing her throat. Keri laughed at her while she got herself under control.

"It's new and he's …." How to explain Shane? She hadn't sorted out her feelings about him yet. She wanted to know him better and at the same time felt like she'd never known a man so well. She breathed through her nose to warm her throat.

"I think he likes you too."

"How can you tell?"

"He gets prickly when Alex teases him about it. If it weren't true, he'd just stonewall him."

"He's so paradoxical."

"He knows who he is … or did. He's a little less comfortable in his skin right now. Helplessness is not a good fit for him."

"He also accepted Christ."

Keri shot a glance at her before turning her scope south once more.

"Alex said he thought so, but I wasn't sure. Typical Shane, he doesn't tell us. How'd you figure it out?"

"He gave up fighting out there on the prairie and something changed while he was healing. And he's admitted it to me since."

Keri laughed. Jazz slowly glassed the southwestern horizon. She saw three snowmobiles following one another in a stream bed toward the southwest. She posted their progress with a pointed hand.

"Wow, he's quick. I knew Murphy commandeered some snowmobiles recently, but I didn't know they were prepared to leave the wire." Keri refocused her scope toward the mysterious truck and then tracked back to where Jazz was pointing.

"You two are going to be good together. Made for this new world."

"You think so? Shane keeps trying to warn me that I'm going to eventually need to kill someone."

Keri didn't speak for a long moment.

"I won't pretend it doesn't stay with you. It does. The thought that you've deprived someone of all their tomorrows. It lingers. If Dad and Jacob are any judges, it never goes away. Some people probably can't handle it even if they know it's part of life. I think when it happens to you, you'll carry it like the hero you are."

Jazz turned to stare at her.

"I'm no hero."

"You are. You are a total badass babe who totally deserves my brother's love."

"We're not there yet." Uncomfortable, Jazz returned to following the snowmobiles. They were reaching the end of the scope's clarity, so must be getting near the truck. There they were, stopped. Beyond, three shadow figures crept along the stream.

"Good. Fine wine takes time."

"You should come see this."

Keri focused where she indicated.

"I'm going to watch south."

"Don't bother. There are too many trees and structures. Shane's right about Schoenfeld's turbine. Probably should have put someone up in there from the outset. Well, that explains it."

"What?"

"Why the truck is hard to see. They parked in the stream bed like a hide. Our guys are sliding up to them and they probably don't even know it."

"Can you tell who?"

"By the outerwear, two National Guard guys and one from the Army."

Jazz scanned back to the plane which had powered to the end of the runway. Now the wider areas at the two ends made sense. The plane barely cleared the high snow walls as it turned and then aligned with the runway once more, backing up until the tail nearly touched the snow wall at the end. Glassing along the runway, Jazz saw Vint had started the plow and was making his way to the east end. Meanwhile, trucks and snowmobiles pulled up and people piled out with shovels and roof scoops.

The sun sank toward the southwest so that they couldn't watch in that direction without burning their retinas. They focused south and east, though the view was far from clear. A long way off, Jazz heard gunfire and both women swiveled to see what was going on, but neither could. A single flare wobbled into the sky.

"What was that?" Jazz pulled her radio out. "Shane – Maverick, you got ears on?"

Again, the delay terrified her, and then Shane's rich voice came over the air. The quality of the sound suggested he was using a handheld.

"Over, Music Box Dancer. What's to report? Over."

"Something's going on out there. Gunfire and then they popped a flare." She waited a second. "Uh, over."

"That's why I'm on the handheld. They radioed about five minutes ago that they'd be going in. I want to keep the base clear. Can you see anything? Over."

"The sun's in our eyes. Over."

"Does Keri have a radio? Over."

Keri shook her head. Jazz relayed the negative. Just then, the radio transmission broke up.

"Music Box Dancer, you got ears on? Over."

"This is Dancer. Report. Over." Click came up with the idea for code words since they were using an open-radio system and Shane suspected someone might be listening. She didn't know this voice, so wisdom said not to trust it.

"This is Brandenberg. Target eliminated. Relay to base. Two down and equipment secured. We're mopping up and coming home. Over."

"Eyes on, Brandenberg. What's with the flare? Over."

"Suspect they were signaling someone. Base, can you get Greyeye's Raven to check out to the Northwest? Over."

Now Shane's signal was clear, so she knew he was on the base.

"Jones, I already asked the militia to dispatch a couple of their guys. They're headed to Donovan right now. Over."

In the background, Jazz could hear an engine toiling.

"They came from the northwest. Tracks are clear as day. Over."

"That truck worth bringing in? Over."

"Yes. We should be on our way in five minutes or less. You copy, Music Box Dancer? Over."

Jones had practiced with her and so knew he didn't want to be in her sights.

"Eyes on. Flash before you come. Over.".

"Will do, Dancer. Over."

"Over and out."

At the runway site, the shovel crowd and dozer cleared the frosting off the snow.

"What are they doing?"

"I'm not a pilot, but I think they're giving the plane a bit more runway."

"Why?"

"Um, maybe something to do with the prevailing wind. I know Jacob always paid attention to that."

"It's out of the west and they landed from the east." Jazz stared at the runway, glassing back and forth. "Okay, so Shane had them dig those turnarounds at both ends. Do you need more runway to takeoff opposite the prevailing wind?"

"Ask your boyfriend. I never really wanted to know. I'd go up with Jacob occasionally because he seemed to get so much joy out of it, but I never wanted to fly the plane. That was always Shane's thing. Jacob was letting him take over when he was eight and he needed to sit on a box to see over the cowling."

"What did your parents say about that?"

"Mom went ballistic. Dad tried to stay out of the free-fire zone, but he did extract a promise from Shane not to solo until Jacob said he could and then Vi extracted a promise from Jacob not to teach Shane how to take off until he was at least able to see over the cowling without the box. Shane was gangly, so he unofficially soloed at 12."

"Crazy. So Delaney!"

"So. Anyway, whatever they're doing is probably necessary."

"Music Box Dancer, you got ears on? Over."

"Maverick, no signal yet. Over."

"Spotter at Schoenfeld's says there's no sign of ground-to-air that way. Still waiting to hear from Donovan. What's the progress at the runway? Over."

"I'm not sure what I'm looking at, Maverick. Do you want to educate me? Over."

"Not on an open channel, no. I'll pretend I believe Vint can do math. Over."

"Flash to the west." Keri pointed. "Three long – two short – one long."

Jazz keyed her radio.

"Forward, Brandenberg. What is your intended entry? Over."

"Lufgrens. Over."

It was another test passed, although Shane recognizing Jones' voice was better.

"Alex and Josiah Bennett are the guards there." Keri bent to pull out her thermos again. "Another warmup?" Jazz nodded, switching to the border patrol channel.

"Alex, Si, you got ears on? This is Music Box Dancer. Over."

"Good evening, Dancer. This is Hearing Ear Dog. Over." Keri always smiled when she heard Alex's call sign, based on an old joke about being the only hearing member of a Deaf family.

"Jones will be at your gate sometime soon, driving a military vehicle, probably with snowmobiles too. Make sure he doesn't have a gun to his head. Over."

"Will do, Dancer. How's my bride? Over."

"She looks beautiful half-frozen and it is so not fair. Over."

"Yeah, but I'd kind of forgotten she was a natural brunette. You girls and your parts these days. Over."

Keri leaned into the radio and Jazz keyed it for her.

"I'm just going back to my roots. Over."

"I like earthy girls. Over and out."

"He's in so much trouble when I get home."

Jazz laughed at her friend and scoped the southwest. The truck's headlights were on, but no snowmobiles followed.

"Brandenberg, this is Music Box Dancer. Where's your wingmen? Over."

"They're chasing that backtrail, Dancer. Over."

"That's off orders." Keri straightened.

"That's not unusual for Murphy's crew. The Army guys want more chain of command." Jazz didn't like the tightness in her gut. *Trust your gut. Always trust your gut.* She switched to the border patrol channel.

"Hearing Ear Dog, you got ears on? Over."

"Hello, Music Box Dancer. What can I do for you? Over."

"Not trusting the guys coming in. Question them about what tune I play? Over."

There was a long pause before Alex's voice returned.

"Five by five, Dancer. Over and out."

"Jazz?" Keri looked concerned. "It's just the two of them at that gate."

"Yeah." Jazz switched channels again.

"Maverick, you got small ears on? Over."

"And large ears, Dancer. Already got Vint sending some people to join the patrol. It'll be fine. It's just in case. I've already talked with the two that are following the trail. All's good. They're just learning to think for themselves is all. But your instincts are great. Over."

"Out of curiosity, where are your father and brother? Over."

"Pathfinder's handling the VIP. I'm not sure where Darrow is. Why? Over."

"Just nerves, I guess. Going outside the wire doesn't seem to work out well. Over."

"Pays to be frosty. Thanks for being the western outpost. Over and out."

Keri already had her rifle balanced on the water tower railing, tracking the truck. Securing her radio in her pocket, Jazz followed suit as the sky began to blush with sunset colors.

Beulah

Beulah, Kansas – County Seat

The APC wallowed through the snow as Lieutenant Daglin steered down the desolate backroad into Beulah. The houses here stood dark against the deep winter snow and there were few tracks to any doors. The sun hung lower than Cai liked. Maybe it was superstition, but he preferred not to go outside the wire when it was dark. The airlift had been the priority today and it had taken until now to free himself from the tasks involved there. They delivered the groceries to Huffman's and the plane should take off within the hour. Click Michaels decided his reporting duties were done and he asked to join them.

This trip could have waited for the morning, but Daglin and Brad showed up at noon expecting to go. After roping them into the grocery security team, he'd permitted them to come to Beulah after they were done.

"Looks like someone's been using the church." Brad pointed through the gathering dusk. Cai didn't have the heart to tell him that the fine old wooden pews had been cannibalized for firewood. The paneling might be gone by now too.

Daglin steered toward a pall of smoke hovering over an intersection. The houses here were small and squat, low-slung bungalows that might have been first-time homes for young couples or rental units. Wood smoke hung heavy in the frigid air, issuing from four chimneys.

"You think someone had a falling out?" Daglin asked.

Cai shrugged and Daglin shut down the APC. Click slid out the back, stomping to circulate blood to his toes. The APC sucked the heat out of the living bodies inside.

"Wait here. Be ready in case we need to bug out."

Brad double-taked and then grinned.

"What?"

"You're starting to sound like you served in the military."

"I don't think that's a good thing."

After spending a week in slavery in an Army camp in Hutchinson, Cai frankly had a hard time being civil to military types. He needed Daglin and Murphy, but he didn't like them and saw no reason to emulate them. Brad sobered and stopped walking. Cai turned. Brad had been his pastor since he was in high school and he didn't hold his military service against him.

"You and I should talk about what happened to you."

"Yeah, probably, but not now. It's freezing out here and we don't know who might have rifle sights on us."

Cai turned to trudge toward the screened porch. The crunching snow behind him testified Brad felt the cold too. The hinges swiveled in eerie quiet as the torn screen flapped in a blast of wind that swirled the woodsmoke around the APC.

Win Reese slid his 45 into a back holster after closing the door.

"Brad? Nice to see you."

He limped toward the kitchen table and sat. Cai remembered him as a slightly overweight middle-aged mechanic who used to work with Rafe Conopher, but hunger transformed them all. Cai was on the last notch of his belts and he'd put his wedding ring on a chain around his neck because it no longer stayed on his finger. Win might have found a pantry, but he must be rationing the food.

"How's my family?" Cai glanced at Brad, who had come along for just this purpose. Win was no fool. "The kids, Donna?"

"They're fine, but –" Brad sighed, shoved his hands into the pockets of his heavy coat. "With you gone – I know you left them behind because you thought it would be easier on them – and I took a food box to them soon as I could. Donna – well, she doesn't have any skills and – Jason Breen pays pretty well."

Win's gaze came up to look Brad in the eye. The pastor didn't flinch. He'd lived through combat. Life today had that element to it, but without the gunfire – usually.

"She's putting out?" Brad nodded. "The girls?"

"No. Donna says she won't do that to them. They're still staying at your place. Donna goes home every day. And they're eating. Like I said, Jason pays."

Win nodded, rubbing a chapped hand over his rough-shaved chin.

"Okay. That's good — better than starving." Denial hung thick in the small kitchen with its white cabinets and black and white checkered floor. "I'll move on when the weather breaks. My leg's about up to it now."

"Win, your family --."

"Was doomed the minute I let Mace talk me into storming Conopher's place. Donna pushed me to do it. And she was right. We were starving and I didn't have a way around it." Win sighed. "I just wanted my girls to survive. Donna's got it covered and I couldn't."

"And you're okay with that?"

Win snorted.

"Nah, but they took away my choices the day they set off those bombs. My back won't let me do the hard farm work and I couldn't feed my family. So I'm going. Maybe I'll find a place. If not, at least I'm not taking food out of my kids' mouths."

Brad settled a hand on Win's shoulder. They stood there nodding to each other. Cai felt like a third wheel.

"I need to check on the other houses. What do you know about them?"

"Yeah, I guess they multiplied since the last time you were here. I don't know any of them. One house is Beulah residents who don't want to give up." He pointed. "They were here last time too, yeah?" Cai nodded. "The others just sort of showed up. I think one's a family." He pointed. "The others — well, guessing, marauders who ran out of gas." He pointed.

Cai considered the odds of surviving knocking on that door and decided to skip it, trudging through the snow across the long shadows of the snow-choked trees. Click followed. Daglin waved at him from the APC as he headed toward the new family. He'd talked to the Beulah family last time and suggested life would be easier in Emmaus. If they chose to disagree, he wouldn't waste his breath.

The man who answered the door at the fourth house looked nervous, which was to be expected of squatters. He opened the door a gap and Cai acutely felt the gun that was no doubt aimed at him. Nobody answered the door to strangers today without a gun.

"I'm Cai Delaney, deputy sheriff for the Emmaus Police Force. I'm just checking on people here in Beulah. This is Click Michaels."

The man's dark eyes flickered behind heavy lashes, then he glanced over his shoulder. Surprisingly, he opened the door all the way to allow entry, his hands in view. Cai stepped into the kitchen, doing the same. Heat filtered in from the living room and a single lantern on the table provided light to the space. Cai could smell something spicy on the stove. Click smiled at the man who had stepped back by the table. Cai's gut tightened a second before the man drew his gun and then he heard the safety come off the second gun. The woman stood in the opening to the living room.

"Hey, hey! Just take it easy!" Click blanched white as snow. "We're just --."

"You are not taking my wife, Delaney!"

"What? Why … I don't --." The adrenaline twisted Cai's voice to high tenor. "What?"

"It's not him."

The woman didn't lower her gun, but she and her husband stared at each other.

"You sure?"

"Who are you to Sheriff Delaney?"

"His son."

"No. His name was Shane, not – not --."

"Cai. Shane's my brother. You meet him at the wire?"

The woman and man vibrated with tension, guns still trained on their visitors.

"You were one of the USDA officers, weren't you?" Click's hands reached for the ceiling, but he didn't look nearly as scared as Cai felt. "You were the last leader standing after the execution, right?"

Her jaw bunched as she considered answering Click's question.

"You are not taking my wife!"

"No, I'm not." Cai looked at the man to assure he told the truth and then looked at the woman. "That was a – fracked situation and I wasn't here for it, so I don't have any anger about it." Well, he did feel anger when he heard what happened to Gary Carter. And Dick Vance. And David Vance. And Kitty Vance. Okay, maybe he was a little angry. "Shane and you have bad blood?"

"The USDA hung him, so of course he was pissed." Click's voice stayed steady. He'd been unarmed as a combat reporter and apparently, he trusted strangers with guns trained on him more than Cai did.

"I didn't do that!" The woman sounded peeved. "Things got out of control and Rumsdale should have been removed from power, but I was on the other side of town."

"Galena?" The flicker of her expression said he'd gotten it right. He'd read it in Jacob's coroner's report. "Can you please lower your guns so we can talk? I promise we can work this out."

They exchanged glances. The man put his gun on safety and slid it behind his back. She lowered hers, but continued to hold it near her thigh, her finger outside the trigger guard. Cai took a deep breath, trying to settle. He glanced at Click, who nodded.

"We're just here to check on folks right outside of our borders." The reporter had done some border patrol mainly for the newsworthiness and knew the general mission.

"We know this looks like we're squatting, but when the winter hit --." Cai nodded at the man.

"It's fine. We closed our borders to protect our resources. If you can figure out how to live out here, it's not our concern, except we don't want hostile forces at our borders and we want to offer succor when we can, for people who will enrich our community. You part of the crowds from up north?"

The woman scratched under the edge of her bright blue beanie.

"We passed by Emmaus in that last vanguard." Her voice rang altogether too flat. "Then the snow hit and Ian got sick. We had the owner's permission to stay, but she'd already been poisoned by drinking the water. We'll go as soon as the weather breaks if we can get a car."

"Car?" Click sounded perplexed.

"Not a lot of those working these days. Walking is probably best." Cai shrugged. He couldn't deliver that news more kindly.

"We can't." The husband shifted against the table he leaned on. "Our boy --." His voice wavered. "He's got polio or something."

Cai felt his expression relax toward the woman.

"It's a consequence of the flu. Did you all have it?" They both nodded. "It doesn't seem to affect adults, but – adolescent boys – that's the theory so far. My wife and her partner are doctors trying to find out how to treat it. If you came to Emmaus, they'd see him."

"We can't move him," the husband said. "The headache finally stopped a day or two ago, but he's still incredibly dizzy and he can't move his legs."

Cai sighed.

"I can try to bring one of them here. Has the fever broken?" They nodded. "Any breathing difficulty?" They shook their heads. "Then, if he follows the pattern, he won't get worse and he might get better. It could have gotten a whole lot worse. We've had some deaths."

"Jesus!" Galena put her free hand to her face.

"We can't help you with food, but it might be easier to get some if you're in Emmaus. There's ways to earn it. We could help you move."

The expression Galena exchanged with her husband sent a chill down Cai's back. Her breathing quickened as she glanced sharply at Cai, who held up his hands to show he remained harmless.

"Shane can be intimidating."

"He promised to kill me if he ever saw me again."

That sounded like his brother.

"How'd you end up back here?"

She sighed.

"I was hiking to Omaha and I found Seth and Ian in a crowd of people headed south."

"And the rest of your group?"

"They peeled off in different directions toward their homes. Some of them continued east after I joined with Seth."

"And you came back here?"

"We had no choice, so we went south with everyone else. I didn't realize where we were until we passed your town borders. We both started to feel sick. The lady who owns this house gave us a place to stay. When the military poisoned the town well, she died. We didn't drink the water, so --."

"It's fine. Sounds like she would have welcomed you staying on."

"Did you know Gladys?" Seth seemed to be relaxing with them.

"Not that I know of, but I know Kansans and she took you in. But you can't live here once the snowmelt isn't available. Galena, you have law-enforcement skills, yes?" She frowned at him. "And, you?" Cai looked at Seth.

"I was an engineering professor at University of Nebraska."

"Engineering?"

"Ag."

"Seth Carboy?" Click frowned again. Seth nodded. "You went to University of Chicago, yeah?" Again, Seth nodded. "I interviewed you for a hybridization project you were working on." They did look about the same age. "The farmers would love him."

"On the assumption that rescue is not coming, we have to boost production on our own, true."

"I can't go to Emmaus. Your brother will kill me."

Cai grinned. That sounded so like Shane, but he could try to talk sense to him. Maybe he'd listen.

"I can talk to him. No promises, but I can try. And I'll get one of our doctors to come to visit your son. The medical care is *gratis*. Joining the community means agreeing to work with the community police force."

"Yeah, but – Shane's probably not the only one who would like to see me dead."

"That's why I'm not making promises, but it's worth a try. How are you feeding yourselves?"

"She had a good pantry." Seth glanced toward the basement door. "So we could feed ourselves if we came to Emmaus – until about May anyway."

"Good. Every family is responsible for themselves. Galena, for what it's worth – you seem to know what happened was wrong."

"Doing our job wasn't an excuse for what happened. I know that."

"Good, then I don't have to make the case that hanging the ringleaders was righteous or that banishing the rest of you was better than the alternative."

"I get that your father was making it up as he went along. We've met a few of the people he's banished. Low tolerance for stealing." She almost laughed.

"It's a tough stance. There are people in our community that want him to use firing squads, but he can't see himself drawing down on someone he played softball with. Question, we've been around a few times and didn't see you here."

Galena looked at Seth who answered.

"We hid before. It was a warmer day and I was cleaning the woodstove when you arrived, so our chimney wasn't smoking, so we just sat in here until you left."

Cai thought it felt like the truth. In desperate times, desperate people did desperate things. The whole country was desperate right now. Emmaus had just gotten a shipment of food. That might keep people from hostility for a while. He could hope.

Forgiveness

Delaney House, Emmaus

The ghost channel drove him nuts. He could hear voices amid the static, but not well enough to understand the words. Tonight, maybe he could skip off the atmosphere and pull it in. At least these days he was doing some of the peddling for the batteries, mostly using his arms since his hip still hurt if he did more than a minute or two of any activity. His shoulder became stronger every day, though it still hurt if he pulled it back too far. He figured another month before it was back to normal. His hip…he had no idea.

He mainly fiddled with the radio to give himself something to focus on while mulling over what Marnie told him about the B&B and the ramifications of unauthorized people within the wire. He'd known Rigby was keeping something to himself, but the truth stunned him. Well, not really. The B&B represented the old government and resistance against the old order was bound to arise now that it was no more. He expected a battle royal come spring. He'd have to talk to Rigby directly tomorrow. For now, he just needed to sort out all the details Marnie had given him and decide if he was prepared to believe them.

As for the news from Donovan….

A chill ran up his back as the kitchen door opened and closed. Glister trotted over to greet whoever it was so Shane didn't need to wheel over to grab his 9mm. He turned off the radio to save the batteries and turned to greet Cai.

"Hey, how are you feeling?"

"Tired, but it's a good feeling. Finally had a completely productive day."

"Good. You need help lying down?"

"No. I've got it and I'm not really that tired yet. I laid down for a while when things were quiet. How'd Beulah go?"

"First, how'd the plane go?"

"Good. Jason and his crew lit the runway with moonshine torches."

"Inventive." Cai actually sounded impressed. "Click will be sorry he missed that."

"I'm sorry I couldn't see it. Jazz promised me a full description when she gets home."

Another shiver ran up his back and he wheeled around the back of the couch to throw some wood into the fire.

"I could have done that for you." Cai started dressing in indoor clothes for the evening.

"I know, but it's good therapy. So, um – what happened at Beulah."

"I ran into Win Reese."

"You mentioned that last time. It's good. That whole banishing people thing – it's necessary but we don't have to be rabid about it. I'm amazed Jason's guys never thought there'd be pantries in Beulah."

"Yeah. I haven't told him yet. Anyway – kind of a delicate subject here."

Shane stared at his brother as Cai fiddled with the tie on his sweatpants.

"What have I done lately that requires that look?" He figured it was better to keep a sense of humor about whatever had Cai mincing about.

"Not you – well, not really. How do you feel about the outcome of the Cow Cop Rebellion?"

"Is that what we're calling it now? I like it. Catchy. We hung a few people and that – you were right that it potentially could come back to bite us. If the US government survives anyway. The execution was righteous, but people hold grudges."

"People?"

"Maybe the people we banished."

"Who you threatened to kill if you saw any of them again?"

Shane felt a mischievous grin play across his face, but a Spirit check pricked his heart, so he sobered.

"Yeah, I don't know if I could do that now. It feels like a different person did those things."

Cai sat down on one of the couches and stared at him for far too long. Shane didn't comply with long probing silences. He moved to get his book to read.

"What if one of them came back just by accident?"

"The cow cops?" Cai nodded. Shane left his book where it was, executed a seat lift, and sighed, giving himself a moment to consider the question.

"Not looking for revenge?"

"No. I think she gets why we had to do what we did."

"*We* didn't do anything. You were in Hutchinson. But yeah – um, this person have a name?"

"Galena Carboy. She and her husband didn't mean to come here and now their kid has the encephalitis."

Oh, man! Shane stared at the door of the woodstove for a long moment, surprised by the flood of prayer that rushed through his mind.

"I don't want to hate people anymore. How bad is her kid?"

"Seems to be turning the corner. I'm going to take Marnie or Ami there tomorrow to examine him."

"Good. Ami was saying she needs new victims. I don't know where they'd stay, but yeah."

"What about other people?"

"Better run this by Dad, but she wasn't the problem which is why we let her group live. What are their skills, by the way?"

"She could work out on the community patrol – or even border patrol if you agreed. And, her husband is an agricultural engineer."

"Introduce Alex to him. They got food?" Cai nodded. "Sharon McLaughlin still has rooms and she's said she's willing to take in boarders. She's not optimistic to make it to spring and she wants to have folks for Danny for when she passes."

"That's so unfair. It's completely treatable."

"Yeah. So's my hip *if* – but *if* doesn't exist so – I guess it's one of those life lessons about leaning on God that you used to always try to lecture me with."

"And it is amazing to hear my words reflected at me from you."

"Not yours." Shane picked up his Bible and transferred it into his lap. His hip complained at the weight, so he shifted it to his left thigh. "I'm not a big person for following other people, right."

"Right. A Berean Christian if ever I met one."

Shane wheeled to the radio table and turned the unit back on.

"What are you doing?"

"Trying to bring in this ghost channel. Can you do me a favor and ride the bike?"

"Sure. Let me just fill the hopper with corn and I can kill two birds with one stone." While Cai filled the hopper and set a bowl under the outflow, he asked questions.

"So, Daglin heard there was some activity out west of the runway?"

"Yeah. A military vehicle, two guys with three handheld rocket launchers, and six missiles. They got them. A couple of the militia guys and a couple of the National Guard group tracked it to Donovan. There were people there who bugged out in a hurry before they got there. They headed west, but it was getting dark. Ed says he'll take a group to scout it in the daylight."

"Why?"

"To make sure there's no threat to us."

"No, not …. Why do you think they were there?"

"I'd guess to bring down the DC."

"*After* they'd offloaded the food?"

"Yeah. I don't think they – whoever they are – sees us as the enemy. It was who was on the plane that they want."

"Do you know who was on the plane?" Cai stood in the dining room entry, clearly forgetting his assigned task. Shane sighed. Cai frowned. "You don't know, or you know from the B&B and can't tell me?"

"Do you know?"

"I saw her, yeah."

"Francene Maracle. There was a lot of radio skullduggery today. Rigby said he'd text me, but he hasn't."

Cai frowned, then shrugged like he'd decided to obey one of the other Indians on his shoulders.

"Did you know that her daughter was at the B&B since Christmas?"

"I've been mostly unconscious since Christmas and Rigby doesn't tell me stuff I don't need to know. So Maracle was on the plane? Rigby knew they were coming to get the daughter, but he didn't know if Francene was coming too."

"Mama and daughter both on the way out. And somebody else, but I don't know who. Dad might know."

"Yeah. It explains someone wanting to take the plane down." Shane shifted in the wheelchair, his hip twingeing. "I want to try to pull in this ghost before I collapse in exhaustion."

Cai disappeared from view and a moment later the battery meter spiked. Shane started fiddling with dials.

"Bravo 6 Forward...." Static filled the air. "...location? Over."

"Bravo Actual, 39.7 N, 94.8 W." Static erupted from the speaker and Shane tried to bring the transmission in with his left hand while he wrote down the GPS coordinates with his right.

"Sit rep, Forward."

"Dig...quiet. Rads elevated ... acceptable. ...rete curing. Over."

"Signs of activity? Over."

"No. River's ... sent squad ... no activity. Over."

"No sign of Cheyenne forces? Over."

"Hardly sign of people. The region's a ghost...."

"Send more scouts. Need to be sure before.... We ... secure forward position ... May. Over."

"Five by five, Actual...." The static blurred the voices again and after about two minutes of trying to get the signal again, Shane admitted defeat and turned the radio off. Cai came to stand beside him.

"What do you think that's about?"

Shane glanced sideways at his brother, always marveling at how he still expected the best from the world.

"Could be preparation for an invasion of this region by whoever that is. Um, that's why I need you to lay off the B&B."

Cai frowned.

"They're suspects in a murder, Shane. A murder that would have implicated you if you hadn't been hurt."

"Can you trust me that they weren't involved?"

"How do you know that?"

"To the extent possible, I've done my own investigation. They are hiding something. I know what it is, but I can't tell you and it doesn't affect Jericho Township."

Cai sighed, shaking his head.

"I don't trust them."

"Yeah. You don't have to. Can you trust me?"

Cai growled.

"I know I should."

Shane snorted.

"Good. And trust me, we're not going to want to have a hostile relationship with them if war is coming our way. Their vision goes beyond the horizon, giving us time to prepare."

"Why would there be a war, Shane? We're all part of the same country."

Wow, Cai could be so naïve!

"Are we? Seems to me like the USDA came in here as if they were invading a foreign country. Should we want to be a part of that?"

Cai's frown reminded Shane of someone sitting on a toilet after a week of eating MREs.

"It's the country we were born in." Under the certainty of his tone, Shane sensed uncertainty in the wings.

"And we're still here, but the government dissolved four months ago. What's left is like a spastic limb without brain control. Think about what happened when the US government had you in their custody? Do you want more of that?"

"Well, no." Cai might not be a natural realist, but he edged closer every day. "We're not in any shape to go up against anyone, much less the US Army."

"True enough, but that's why we need the B&B, to even the playing field."

"That's not an excuse for murder."

"They didn't do it."

Cai sighed. Before he could say anything more, they felt a breeze from the kitchen as Rob and Jazz came into the house.

"I'll think about it."

Shane nodded. He couldn't ask for more and so he didn't.

Event Review

Stinson House, Emmaus

The National Guardsman lived in the Stinsons' house. To the extent possible without running water or electricity, they kept it scrupulously clean. The house sat just down the street from the Delaneys, so Murphy or Jones would come for a bucket of hot water whenever it was their turn to clean the kitchen and they'd done a pretty good job using elbow grease and whatever passed for cleanser this week. Murphy solicited Cai or Rob to tour the house every few weeks to assure that his guys were keeping the bedrooms clean. They were grateful for the housing and doing everything they could to show it.

The wood stove kept the living room uncomfortably warm. The Stinsons probably hadn't ever had this large a group in their house and Jones apologized.

"I still don't know how to balance the stove right."

Murphy watched avidly as Cai adjusted the dampers to allow more heat to go up the chimney rather than overheat the room.

"Sometimes it's not about saving wood and retaining heat." Cai sat down on the blanket-covered sofa. "Anders, you're up."

As the head of the City Council, Anders McAuliff, owner of the local salt mine, led many of the meetings. His mine guards played an integral role in border security. He also had taken over keeping minutes and recording them since Jacob Delaney died in November.

"Tell us what happened out on the western prairie."

Jones considered the ceiling for a moment.

"Okay, two men in the vehicle you passed on the way in were hunkered down in a stream remnant between two fields. They had multiple rocket launchers and M4 rifles with ammunition and two days of food."

"We snuck up on them." Paulson took up the story. "They resisted and we had to kill them. Then me and Barker followed their backtrail to that town with all the silos. There were fresh tracks of someone bugging out to the west. Can we keep the food?"

"Yes, of course." Rob nodded. "Point for future reference – try to leave them alive because it's really hard to question dead people. Marnie and Cai are going through their gear and clothes in the morning. Any idea how long they'd been there?"

"I'd say they got there last night, based on the number of MRE packets."

Rob glanced at Cai.

"That would make sense. Alaska contacted us via radio yesterday afternoon, saying they were headed our way. They might have been radio monitoring."

"But why would they bivouac there?" Murphy looked around the group.

"Shane thinks they wanted to get whoever was on board." Rob caught Cai's gaze. They hadn't discussed it, but Cai was smart and understood they needed to keep Francene Maracle's identity close for now.

"I guess we shouldn't ask who that was." Jones grinned to himself. "I assume whoever it was was in the wire and that they were on that plane."

"Safe assumption." The wood stove didn't have a stack thermometer, but Rob could hear the metal getting warm. He popped up to adjust the damper to tamp it back.

"It was getting dark or we would have followed those tracks. I'm curious if they lead in or out of the wire."

"I am too." Cai sighed. "I know, stay in my lane."

"No, with your brother down, you're doing a great job of trying to fill the gaps." Paulson stretched his feet out toward the woodstove. "I'm grateful Daglin contracted with you rather than some other community. This whole voluntary thing is...uh, weird...but it seems to work."

"Always surprises me too." Anders laughed.

"Anyone want a cup of warm water?" Nobody had coffee, but you took your comforts where you could and Murphy tried to be a good host. Everybody said 'yes' and there was a bit of distraction while he gave them cups of steaming liquid.

"How long was Donovan inhabited?" Rob preferred to keep to the topic because you never knew what might be sneaking up on you while you were chitchatting.

"I don't know." Paulson wrapped his big hands around the cup. "They didn't leave enough to make a guess. We're mainly going with the tracks they left. There were either a lot of them or they were there for a while because they beat down a path to the latrine."

"A while?" Anders' pen hung poised over his notebook.

"Don't know. I'm not a tracker."

"You're doing the best you can. I'll head out that way in the morning." Rob's CB handle was Pathfinder because he was a good tracker.

"I'd like to go with." Paulson leaned his elbows on his knees, still caressing the cup. "We need to learn how to do this stuff, right?"

"It's a good idea, yeah. What --."

A knock on the door snapped the entire group to attention. Murphy sauntered into the kitchen with a hand on the gun in the small of his back. He returned a moment later with Ed Greyeyes, who was wiping his mustache with the back of a snot-back glove.

"Hey! What brings you out this late?"

"I heard the radio transmissions. Donovan's on my way home. You share some border with the Rez, so Shane didn't get crazy about guarding it and that intersection by Donovan has been down for a couple of months, easy to go over with a snowmobile, so sometimes I take that way instead of going through the checkpoints."

"And you didn't tell me that?" Rob raised an eyebrow.

"You don't have the manpower to cover it all and you know it. The Rez has been keeping an eye out, but we're all exhausted, hungry, and cold. Anyway, I was through there about two weeks ago and it was nothing. Abandoned. There are no trees around there to burn for heat. I assume the folks that lived there moved in with relatives."

"Probably."

"Anyway, I didn't go through there this morning, but when I heard the radio transmission, I went there. Hard to tell in the dark, of course, but I'd say they'd been there at least a week. Long enough to settle in. There was a table with rubber transfer, suggesting maybe a radio. They tapped into the electric system and they left behind the wind turbine they were using for power. I'm snagging that in the morning for my payment, by the way."

Rob laughed and indicated he should go on as Murphy handed the big Indian a cup of hot water.

"That all?" Cai sipped his beverage. Rob just enjoyed the comfort of it in his hands.

"No, of course not. I followed the trail."

"In the dark?" Murphy frowned.

"Sure." Ed smiled at the National Guardsman, barely suppressing an irreverent smirk. "There were four people. One of them might have been a woman. Could have been a small man. I ended up at Mara Wells's northeast checkpoint. They wouldn't let me into the town."

"What?" Rob set the cup down, concerned.

"I didn't recognize any of the men at the barrier and they were all wearing fatigues, but --."

"Crap!" Paulson grunted.

"What do you know?" Paulson shook his head to Cai's question. "Did they tell you anything?" Cai frowned at Paulson before asking Ed the question.

"I tried to talk my way into it, but they were hostile. Might have been me. Who wants a six-foot-two guy who looks like me showing up out of the dark? Right? So, I chose not to go Wounded Knee on them and circled to MacArthur Dairy. Mac tells me the town hired this rogue Army unit after the flu knocked out their defense force. They got that paralytic thing too."

"What do you know?" Cai stared at Paulson.

"Daglin says there's a lot of those units out there. Some of them are just doing what we were doing – trying to survive. Others are after what they can get for themselves. After Beulah, the units scattered. I guess we know where one of them went."

"But Mara and Emmaus are on the same side." Anders' brown eyes looked troubled. "What does this mean?"

Rob took a swallow of the warm water.

"I don't know. I'm tempted to head there and find out, but it's dark and red flags are waving."

"I did see the mayor's kid from a distance. I think it was him, anyway."

"Randi or Paul?"

"Paul. I asked to speak with him, but they acted like they had no idea what I was talking about. Mac said these guys are kind of jackbooted. So, I don't know all the story. Shane maybe can find out." Ed tossed back the last of his water. "I should be headed back to the Rez."

"Thanks for doing that, Ed."

"Course. We're all friends here – cousins, even. Let me know if there's more I can do. The Rez is eating okay, so if you need personnel, just ask."

"Thanks. Maybe I'll swing by and see if you'll take more cider for something other than corn."

"Yeah. It's a smart investment, cider."

Ed headed for the door and Rob sat back on the sofa and considered the toes of his boots.

"What do you think, Dad?"

"I don't know. Doubt I need to do anything about it before the morning."

"You're okay with secret enemies on our western flank?" Murphy scratched his beard which was longer than regulation.

"No, but I need more information than I have right now and I'm tired. It's been a long day. And there's almost 20 miles between us, so I don't think we need to worry about tomorrow. My son has information sources we don't have, so…. I'll let you know."

Murphy didn't agree. Rob could tell by how his mouth tightened, but he knew how to take orders, and he didn't argue. Rob rose from the sofa.

"I say we all sleep on it. If you remember anything more, please let me know. I need some sleep."

He donned his coat while others sorted themselves out. Cai and he crunched toward their own house, wind at their backs.

"What do you think, really, Dad?"

"Logically, just wait and see. My gut says we may be in trouble. Let's go see what Shane says."

Shane, of course, was asleep, passed out on the couch with Belle the cat curled up to his side. It had been a long day for all of them and so the Mara Wells situation would have to wait for dawn.

January 27

Blessings & Curses

Lufgren Farm, Jericho Township

Poppy stared at the stick, her abs twitching. She turned sideways to look at herself in the mirror. Her stomach maybe was a little rounded compared to what she normally saw. Certainly, she'd been nauseous and achy lately and her sense of smell became almost overwhelming.

Timing. The timing for this was – odd, miraculous, crushing. She didn't know. She donned a bra, noticing that it was a bit tight now, and then slid a t-shirt over it. She pulled on her jeans and stepped out into the hallway, surprised to see her brother with her husband's limp and emaciated body in his arms, descending the stairs to the lower floor.

Pete's lips turned blue that morning as Mark and Alex tested the pumps and proved the wooden lung would do the job they designed it to do. Poppy knew they'd move him downstairs to the long-unused master bedroom before the day was out. Alex and Mark had been possessed with urgency when Pete woke up yesterday unable to swallow and by the end of the day, he couldn't speak.

Poppy wiped tears from her cheeks while the Ramirezes and Alex got Pete situated in the wooden box, settling all the closures. She stood by the door where she could see what she couldn't hear, and Keri signed what they were saying.

"*He blink yes no, he. Breathe easier. Box works. Lips pink.*"

With Keri at her side, Poppy went into the room. They'd replaced the queen bed with a single so someone could sleep in with him. Pete's eyes rolled around in his sockets, terror-filled. Alex signed.

"*Takes time to adjust. Lips pink. Good look.*"

Poppy leaned in, her lips brushing her husband's dry hot cheek. His remaining muscles twitched in reaction. The other four withdrew to leave them alone. Poppy waited until Keri closed the door and then leaned back to Pete's ear, putting a hand to her throat to gauge how loudly she spoke.

God, let me get the sounds right.

"*I'm pregnant.*" she whispered. "*You must get better, Daddy.*"

She eased back to look at his face. His facial muscles were mostly slack, and he couldn't turn his head at all, but he stared at her in shock, lids blinking slowly. She could only hope that truth would keep him fighting.

Choices

Beulah, Kansas – County Seat

Beulah hadn't changed much since he'd been here last.
A blizzard rolled in the morning after the DC-3 left, closing
Emmaus off house-to-house and from the outside world
while the storm raged. This was the first day they could
leave Emmaus and Ami had readily agreed to drive her
Land Rover into the hinterland. Covered with an extra layer
of snow, the lone inhabited corner resembled pictures Cai
had seen of prairie towns back in the 1880s. There'd been a
big snow then with snow eight feet deep. Rob had remarked
that their house seemed to be warmer now within the
insulating blanket of snow. They planned to shovel the roof
tomorrow. Shane had done it last back in December and it
was getting deeper than any of them liked.

It looked like another house was occupied. There was
only a single set of prints going to the door, so it might have
been a Beulah resident just back to check on their property,
decided to build a fire and spend the afternoon. Or it could
be a new squatter. Either way, it wasn't Cai's concern and
he meant to keep it that way.

"How do they manage without at least some access to
water?" Ami stared around at the snow-clogged street. They
had plenty of time before dusk so Cai didn't fear attack, but

he scanned the streets in all directions before they got out of the Subaru. Cai secured the keys in his zippered pocket. The curtain in the kitchen twitched ever so slightly as they started up the walk which was fairly beaten down by foot traffic. Seth Carboy met him at the door again.

"This is Dr. Ceylon."

"Not worried about a woman, man." He held the door open, gesturing them in. The room felt over warm and Seth's nose glistened with a sheen of sweat.

"Women are equal to men when they are armed." Ami set her bag on the counter so she could strip off her gloves, scarf, and coat. She glanced at Cai. "This is what Javi has taught me – along with how to use a gun. I'm richer for this knowledge. More dangerous too."

Seth's gaze flickered from the darkly pretty doctor to Cai and back again, now a little scared.

"Now, may I see the patient?"

"This way."

Chavez, in a bizarre show of what passed for affection among ruthless mercenaries, insisted Cai not let Ami out of his sight. Cai supposed it was a show of respect that Chavez hadn't chosen to come with them. That level of trust seemed out of character. Cai could only assume Ami really packed heat. With the bulky sweaters everyone wore these days, concealed carry might be universal.

The house wasn't large – kitchen, living room, and two small bedrooms and a bath off the living room. Given the age of the structure, the basement also served as a storm shelter/utility room/root cellar. He'd seen the lump in the snow that might have been the bulkhead cover as they walked up. It would be a nice place to winter if there were running water.

The boy lay in bed in one of the bedrooms. About 13, he winced at the light while Ami examined him, and he answered her questions in whispers. Cai stood outside of the room, listening for sounds outside the house. He'd never noticed how much noise snow made. Shane's hypervigilance might be wearing off on him. He hoped that was a necessary life skill and not some deep psychological damage that would haunt him throughout his life.

"What is this disease called?" Galena held her son's lax hand, stroking the knuckles with her thumb.

"We've just been calling it encephalitis. We're not entirely sure that is what it is. That would normally be diagnosed with a lumbar puncture and an MRI. But Dr. Kletti – a, uh, retired neurologist thinks it's encephalitis, perhaps triggered as an immune system response to this particular variety of flu."

"It's very specific." Seth leaned against the wall by the closet. "Males who are adolescence. My original course of study was botany and that just seems unlikely to occur in nature."

Ami continued to draw blood from Ian.

"We just don't know enough. If we could generate enough power, I could use my electron microscope to get up close and personal with this virus. That would answer a lot of questions, but I haven't been able to make that possible yet."

"It's a power need?" Seth straightened. Cai walked to the living room window because he heard a vehicle crunching snow in the street. He watched the truck go by and went to the kitchen window to watch it turn into the garage across the street. He continued watching until Galena slid up beside him.

"Those are our neighbors. Three men. I think they were Army. They're nice guys, but they get nervous if you mention the town well."

"Imagine that." They smiled at one another. "We've got someone in Emmaus willing to house your family."

"Do they know?"

"Yes. Sharon was part of the security team, so she would know, and I figured that would be best. Fewer complications. She has a good-sized house. Her foster son can help you move. And, well – Sharon has Stage 4 cancer, so she won't be with us much longer and she's worried about her foster son after she's gone. She would welcome the company and give you folks legitimacy with the town. She's known to be a hell of a judge of character."

"You seem pretty certain we'd agree to this."

"You can always say 'no'. I'm not going to force you."

"That's what Win told Seth. That notwithstanding the whole hanging thing, bossing people around is not a Delaney attribute."

Cai wondered if that part of his personality came from the Faradays. Shane showed it too, but in much more specific circumstances.

Galena scratched under her beanie.

"I could sure enjoy a shower."

"I think Sharon has running water when she wants it."

Ami and Seth came from the bedroom. Ami held up a card.

"Low hematocrit. Do you know his blood type?"

"O Positive," Seth said.

"All three of us," Galena added.

"Can I get a unit from one of you?"

Seth held up his hand.

"We've found that it does seem to mitigate the symptoms." Seth nodded. "Can we get these folks moved to Emmaus in the next few days?"

"If they're willing."

Seth and Galena exchanged glances and then he answered for the both of them.

"Yes. Time we came in from the cold."

Ami grinned and followed Seth to a recliner where she could take his blood.

"Seth estimates the well should clear by midsummer. I could almost live here if I didn't think the Apocalypse was nigh."

"It's a nice house. Perfect for three. And who knows how that whole property ownership thing works now. I guess that'll have to be decided when we've worked out how we're feeding ourselves."

The fact they laughed said they'd crossed into undiscovered territory and were becoming comfortable with it. Cai mourned his old life at the same time recognizing that

Shane was right. You adapted or you died. Cai meant to adapt.

Homecoming

Garden City, Kansas

Southwestern Kansas lay flat in front of him, not a tree, not a house, not the slightest ripple in the snow. The GPS Sullivan insisted he take with him said he trended toward Garden City, but it would be easy to get lost without it. The wind ran unrestrained over the field before him, whipping snow devils that danced from one grey horizon to the other. The sky melted into the ground so his equilibrium felt disconnected from its gyroscope.

Scott City had shown signs that people might still live there, tracks to some of the low-lying buildings, a curl of smoke from a chimney. The city started in the 1880s as homestead land, so it was possible to live in this area without plows or Tuckers, but Kris Lawson never wanted to live here. Flat, unwelcoming, windy as hell – who would want to call this place home? Until the Bombs went off. He'd wanted to come home every day since.

To his right, a cell tower stuck up through the snow like a periscope. He gauged the snow to be at least 10 feet deep here. He'd maybe seen three feet in his lifetime. He'd passed a couple of barns along the way, buried in snow, looking abandoned. The Tucker didn't zip along, so he'd been traveling since before dawn and was worried he'd not reach his folks before sunset. The grey sky rendered time a dodgy concept, but his wristwatch said it was three. Funny how the minutes used to matter and now – why?

He recognized another farm by the wizened windrow tree sticking up from the snow like skeletal hands. A snow dune beyond might have been a barn roof. It was possible to keep a farm operating under those conditions. He remembered his grandfather telling stories about how his dad had dug a snow tunnel between the house and the barn back in the Great Depression. He doubted anyone at this farm was still alive, but he hoped he was wrong.

A grain silo's conveyor stuck up from the snow some distance on. Kris could see no silo. It seemed impossible that the snow could be that deep, but flakes were starting to fill the gusty air. In Oakley, he spied the top of a concrete silo punched up into the air. The wind must have scoured the area pretty good recently. The overpass was clogged with packed snow, but the Tucker just climbed the drift anyway.

He knew he'd reached Garden City because someone had run a grader down Highway 83, leaving maybe a foot of snow in a canyon of snow. The Tucker just barely cleared both walls, so he didn't enter the slalom at all, but followed the GPS across the prairie toward his parents' farm. Eventually, he had no choice but to risk the road because it turned out a few roads in Garden City had been plowed, including the narrow lane leading up to the house and barn which like most buildings in GC were to their eaves in wind-packed snow. He parked the Tucker out by the road, planning to walk up to the house rather than risk damaging anything he couldn't see under the mantle of winter. He was pulling the distributor to assure nobody could steal the venerable machine when headlights swept his perch. He turned, reaching for his gun just in case, and found himself staring in his father's face and noting the shotgun in his right hand.

"Bout time you came home, boy. That daughter of yours forgot what you look like."

They embraced, the shotgun held out to the side like a wing. Jasper Lawson's weather-beaten face needed a shave, but his smile beamed like a spotlight.

"Where you been galivanting to, boy?"

"I'll tell you later. I really need to see July and Lynette."

"And you will, but you know, we gotta walk up to the house and this here museum piece'll disappear if we leave it here. Folks are all drooly like over any working bit of machinery these days. What is it?"

"It's called a Tucker – or a Snowcat. It's like a forerunner of the snowmobile – for groups."

"Nice! This thing got a heater?"

"It does. Not a great one. So what's the safest way up to the barn?"

"Just parallel the drive. You might crush a fence or two, but that's no never-mind before spring. I'll meet you there."

"It'll be a couple of minutes while I reconnect the distributor."

"Smart. If'n our neighbors didn't have tractors, it maybe would work. You got great timing. Your ma's cracked a jar of snap beans and I butchered a hog last week, so we're eating a roast with potatoes. You felt kind of skinny. Anorexics need not apply."

Kris laughed. He'd missed Jasper's sense of humor.

"Food was short in Wichita. I ate pretty good in Emmaus, but everybody's rationing these days."

"Yep, round here too, those that don't live on farms."

The wind had been sighing among the treetops, clogging the branches of the tough cottonwoods that formed a windrow here, but now a strong gust blasted into them, scattering ice into their faces, numbing Kris's fingers as they worked the screwdriver on the connector. He thought he got the last one set. He'd have to check it better tomorrow. The Tucker started at least and that was the mission.

The gates had been dug out and left wide open. Just beyond the commodious entrance, the driveway narrowed to where the Tucker couldn't clear the canyon walls, so Kris just drove up the bank and across what was normally potato fields. Thanks to the proximity to the Arkansas River and the Great Eastern Ditch, Garden City grew a lot of crops in a dry climate. Most of his dad's fields were in wheat, but he ran some cattle and hogs too.

"So where'd you get that thing?" Jasper asked.

"My employer loaned it to me. Let's get inside. That wind feels like knives of ice."

They pushed into the back door after walking down a shoveled-out canyon higher than Kris's head.

"Emma, I found this vagrant out in the snow. Thought we could feed him, maybe have him run off with July and Lynnie.

Kris's mother turned from the stove, her eyes widening with surprise.

"Oh, my!" Emma embraced her son, tears rolling down her cheeks.

"Hey, Ma."

"We thought you were dead."

"Now, Emma, don't get the boy all wet. *She* thought you might be dead. *I* knew you got too much of her in you to die from a little cataclysmic event."

"I'm okay, Ma. I'll tell you all about it later tonight. I hate to be one-track, but where's July?"

As the words left his mouth, movement in the doorway between the kitchen and the living-dining room caught his eye. July's full lips pursed as tears welled in her big brown eyes. Emma let go and Kris wrapped July in his arms.

"Oh, baby!" Her whisper feathered the whiskers on his cheeks. "Oh, my god!"

"No fuss." He always said that whenever they'd been apart, even after a fight – especially after a fight. He'd learned it from his parents and July had adopted it. "We're all here and we're all fine. Right?" They all nodded and wiped tears. "We'll get caught up at dinner. Where's Lynette?"

July wiped her dusky cheeks. He'd been fascinated by her biracial features the moment she poured him a cup of coffee in the diner where they met and now he traced her slender elegant nose and caught a tear as it rolled down her narrow chin. His parents hadn't rejected her. He'd misjudged them.

July shook herself like a retriever coming out of a spring pond and turned toward the living room end of the large main room. He could see a playpen set up near the woodstove.

"She's great and she's been the best little girl I could hope for. Come on, Daddy. See your daughter."

Lynnie learned to sit up during the plus-four months since he'd left home for Kanorado. Her dark curls still lay close to her perfectly round head and he gasped when she stared at him with blue eyes.

"Wow! Are they supposed to stay blue so long?"

"They probably will. She's only a quarter."

July picked up their daughter and handed her over to him. Lynnie's face screwed up and Kris feared she might bellow, but she rubbed a sticky hand through his scruff instead.

"Yeah, I should shave that, shouldn't I?" He looked at July. "Oh, baby, I'm so glad to be home and to find you here."

"Yes. It's a miracle we're all three here together." She started to mist up again, but then took a deep breath and turned toward the dining area. "I was setting the table. You spend some time with your daughter while I put out an extra plate."

Jasper and Emma startled guiltily from where they'd been watching from the kitchen door and then they all three left Kris to hold Lynnie. Overcome with emotion, all he could do was cuddle her to his filthy coat and weep for joy while trying to ignore the memory of a fellow soldier calling him a traitor.

Power Up

Delaney House, Emmaus

Rob walked around the truck, viewing the turbine from all angles while Ren stomped his feet and blew into his gloves. It was an interesting design, the blades shrouded like an oscillating fan. Ren said McArthur liked birds, so he decided to make it a little easier for them.

"I appreciate you're thinking of me, but there's places that need it more."

"I figured you'd say that but hear me out. It's not big enough to run City Hall, so you'll still be working from here for the time being. I'm putting one on the radio station so Click can start working toward region-wide broadcast and as a listening station. I'm giving one to the medical center. Anders is looking forward to powering the mine again. We're running low on salt, so it's timely. And, then I'm powering the cottage. It could run the Shack, but I can't heat it, so I'll wait for spring for that. McArthur says he'll make more now that he's gotten his initial investment back. I'll have materials brought in by truck, although the train should be rolling as soon as the snow melts. By next winter, I hope to have the whole town independently powered."

Rob sighed.

"Mayor shouldn't get special treatment and I've got nothing to give you in exchange."

"You know I don't need anything. I'm a billionaire."

"Are you still?"

"Remember that big to-do about my off-shoring some of my business? Well, that turned out to be a good thing and not just for my bottom line. And when was the last time the City paid your salary."

Rob wished he could come up with another excuse, but he couldn't. The City of Emmaus owed him about $12,000.

"I don't know anything about wind turbines."

"That's fine. Jace Welton is happily getting paid in food and salt."

Rob hunched his shoulders against a blast of wind.

"Yeah. Have him put me at the end of the list."

"You bet. These things don't weight that much, so you want to help me drag it around to the back?"

"Let me get Click and Cai. They're young and strong. Our old backs don't need to be doing this."

Ren laughed.

"Thanks for being sensible. We need to show people that we're trying to return to normality. It gives them hope. Yeah, you feel like you're being privileged, but you watch. People will start lining up asking to charge stuff and then they'll want one of their own. Summer's coming. It'll help us hang on to then."

"Maybe. You got a food delivery coming?"

"I'm trying. There's not a lot left in the United States and the sea weather stinks this time of year, so it takes time, but, yeah, we're still moving. Got to figure out what to do about marauders, though. I think the train will fix that ... I hope." Rob nodded. "You out?"

"Getting there. We're down to Pa's storage food. We'll be okay. Alex is very generous with milk and eggs and Jill's still making bread."

"I've got pantry items I can give you."

"No. You might need that food. I might change my mind in a few weeks."

"That's the spirit. I promise I'll come through if you ask. Got it?"

"I do. Thank you."

They shook hands before Rob went in to get Click and Cai. Entering the house by the front door, he could hear the whir of someone riding the exercise bicycle, no doubt grinding corn and charging batteries. Ren was right. They needed this.

Connecting

Conopher Farm, Jericho Township

Kix's gaze followed Dell while he walked from the window to the bedside chair. His left eye turned in toward his nose and the lid remained drooped, but the right eye seemed clear and in his control.

"Doctor's coming out in a day or so to see how you're doing. How are you doing?"

Kix's lips twitched, but he didn't so much as grunt. His right arm moved across the blanket, fingers curled, wrist at a strange angle.

Brian the physical therapist explained that the twisting of Kix's right arm and leg was called spasticity. It looked bad, but he was moving his limbs, which meant some signals were getting through. Dell put a hand on Kix's, gently straightening the arm at the elbow. He could feel muscles weakly tightening and relaxing. The left-side limbs lay completely limp. Brian was right. Signals were getting through.

"It's January. You missed Christmas, but that's fine. Things were pretty low-key this year. Can you squeeze my hand?"

Nothing happened right away, for long enough that Dell thought Kix couldn't answer, but then his thumb tightened, and he grimaced as if in a smile.

"Can you feel that?" Dell ran his ragged thumbnail along the back of Kix's hand. Slowly, the fingers tightened. "So you are in there just figuring out how to reach out?"

Kix seemed to pause and then his thumb came up in an awkward thumbs-up gesture.

"Well, we aren't in a hurry or anything. I've only got a whole farm to take care of."

Kix grimaced again and a light grunt issued from his throat.

"Seriously, your mom needs help with the dishes."

Kix grimaced again. A sense of humor was a sign of intelligence, so Dell figured the kid was mentally intact. Dell could see the hand starting to tighten up. Brian said tone would be a common consequence of effort at least for a while.

"How's your headache?"

Again with the awkward thumbs-up. The elbow started to flex, the fist moving up toward his chin.

"That's probably enough for right now. You got a lot of time to rebuild your strength. Besides, I came up here to read to you. Do you remember the rabbits?"

Kix's hand convulsed, but then the thumb came up again. He was still in there, Dell knew it.

Brothers in Christ

Delaney House, Emmaus

The Dinty Moore cans gave the situation away. It seemed like every time they got stocked with food, they started to run out in a day or two. Click hadn't even brought home rabbits recently, so they were at the bottom of the pantry, reliant upon Alex's milk and eggs and Jill's bread for breakfast, corn mush for lunch, and salty flaccid stew for dinner. Cai sighed and headed toward the living room. He'd been out all day on body duty, and he shouldn't even be hungry, but near-starvation diets didn't allow for nausea. Besides, he'd stopped caring – mostly.

Shane's guitar noodling resolved itself into a tune Cai recognized as an old favorite. The beat was half-time, but he was pretty sure.

"What if I stumble, what if I fall…." Shane's eyes widened, but he picked up the pace on the notes and Cai finished the refrain. "What if I lose my way and make fools of us all. When the walk becomes a crawl, what if I stumble, what if I fall."

"Thank you! That's been an earworm for days and I had no idea what song it was."

Cai laughed and sprawled on the couch. His shoulder popped. Shane's gaze flickered over him and behind him before he bent over the guitar again.

"So appropriate to my mood today." His voice barely registered, conveying the vulnerability riding the words.

"You okay?"

Again, the green eyes moved behind a veil of lashes. Shane sighed.

"It's a day of the dead."

Cai resisted the temptation to look behind him as the hair flowing down the back of his neck stood on end. He covered by rubbing his shoulder that felt the presence more than his neck did.

"Right now? When I'm in the room?"

"Yeah."

"I thought that was getting better."

"It is – it was. I still have PTSD but it's not every day all day now. And it hasn't been all day since New Year's. But today –. Got anything you need to do for the next hour?"

"Yeah." Cai watched the imperceptible slump to Shane's shoulders. "Hang out with my brother and keep him safe from the past – much as I'm able and he'll let me anyway."

Shane cast him a grateful look.

"Thank you. I know I say I'm fine by myself – and usually I am – but I'm feeling a little fragile today."

"Any particular reason why."

Shane played the opening notes to Fer Elise, paused, and continued forward with the next movement.

"It's two years ago today."

"Since?"

"Sarna." Cai didn't know what that was, so he just stared at Shane. "The village – " Shane sighed. "The village where I shot that woman."

"So you're seeing her now?"

"I guess it's her."

"What does she look like?"

"Black hajib. I haven't seen her in a while. It's mostly just been Mike lately. I guess I lulled myself into thinking she'd gone on to haunt someone else."

"Another Greyeyes?"

"Dad tell you?"

"No, Vi did. After Marie died. I used to see her."

"Used to. How'd it stop?"

"I'm not sure. I would even see her in Lawrence. It was – surreal. The first few times, it actually sucked me in. I ran around a corner trying to catch her and I socked a store window reaching out to her another time. Lucky the glass didn't break." Cai laughed at the memory. "But it just gradually stopped. It's been years."

Shane took a deep breath and let it out slowly.

"So, you don't know how you fixed it?"

"I said I wasn't sure. I bathed it in a lot of prayer. I started going to AA for a while. I talked to a Christian friend. I got a tattoo to engrave the guilt into my skin. I apologized to Marnie. And then I fell in love with Marnie." Cai laughed at the ridiculousness of that turn of events. "Not sure where along the way that the guilt eased, but it has been years since I've seen her."

"I guess that means the legend isn't true."

"Legend?"

"That she only bothers the dark Greyeyes?"

"That's not what Vi told me. She never said that part. She said that giving it power would make it stronger and that I needed to lay aside my guilt or it would destroy me. So I went about doing that."

"And I let it build until it nearly killed me."

"But you're here now and you're working on it. And you know, you never had Jesus before, so prayer and," Cai almost giggled, "fasting help."

"Ah, yes, fasting. I wonder if Mom and Marnie would let me now."

"I don't think they're going to have a choice. We're nearing the bottom of the pantry."

Shane set aside the guitar and stretched his legs out straight, using his hands to support his right hip.

"Is this helping?"

"It is." He looked around the room. "I think she's gone, for now. Thank you."

"Sure. You feel up to praying or is that still taboo territory?"

"It's not taboo, so long as you're the one doing it aloud. I still feel like – yeah, praying in my head is getting easier, but I feel like a phony when I try to do it aloud."

"Yeah? You pray in pictures too?"

"What?"

"Um, Keri – she prays in pictures, so she always feels like she's praying wrong when she prays aloud."

"Wow. Yeah, kind of pictures and words mixed. Is that normal?"

"I guess so. There's no right or wrong way to pray. I just have conversations with Jesus. Sometimes I tell Him jokes. Sometimes I pray in pictures too. It's how I purge body detail, for example."

"Yeah? That's not going to become PTSD for you?"

"It hasn't so far, but Dad says it didn't hit him until he got back from Vietnam, so -- ." Cai shrugged. "I'm not giving it power until I get there and then I'll deal with it."

"I wish it were that easy."

"I get that. So I'll lead a prayer and if you feel like praying aloud great and if you don't, that's fine too."

Cai prayed Shane would find peace with his past and that this demon would be driven far from him. In the end, he allowed a space of silence for Shane to pray and Shane whispered "Thanks, Lord" and straightened. "' Put your burden on the Lord and He will sustain you.' Any idea?"

"Psalm 55:22. That Bible has a good cross-reference, so it'll get you to the parallel passages."

Shane opened his Bible to the verse. Cai wondered how he'd learned his way around the Bible so quickly, but then, he'd had a lot of time on his hands since his injury.

"Wow! Hard to believe that thousands of years ago God knew I'd need this message and wrote it down."

"Yeah. It is amazing how an ancient book can speak such wisdom in our time." Cai sniffed. "Oh, yummo!"

"We should probably just be grateful."

"We should. Do you need to crash for a while? I guess I noticed you were more restless than usual last night."

"I am tired, but dinner's not long from now."

"What were you dreaming?"

"Mike driving Alicia's papa's truck and singing to this Eagles tune."

"Mike had the worst voice."

"He did. And he absolutely didn't care if I thought so."

"Me either What song?"

"*Well, I'm running down the road, tryin' to loosen my load. I've got seven women on my mind.*" Shane stopped singing. "But Mike never would have sung that in Alicia's dad's truck. He was true blue to her."

"Dreams are weird. They mix up memories sometimes."

Shane nodded, sighed.

"I guess. Maybe it's just another stage to grief."

"And it would make sense that you would relate it to music because that's how your brain works."

"Maybe. Thanks for walking me through it."

"Oh, hey, do you recognize this?"

Cai dug the ring out of his pocket and handed it to Shane, who rolled it around in his palm and then held it up to the lantern to read the inscription around the stone.

"It's a class ring."

"That's what I thought too."

"And you're asking me about it because …?"

"I found it behind the hotel, right near where we found John Doe."

Shane rolled closer to the lantern on the dining room table and stared harder at the inscription.

"It looks like a class ring but there's no high school or date listed. This is – I think, jasper, which is a weird choice for a ring you want to last forever. It's been worn. You can see some scratches."

"What else?"

"That's it for me. What about you?"

"The med-alert bracelet traces to the militia. Ren contracted with one of the teenagers there to split some wood for him. It's got nothing to do with the case, so I returned the bracelet. Besides that--."

They heard clattering in the kitchen and then Jill came to the opening between the living room and dining room.

"Cai, can you set the table?"

"Sure, Mom."

"I can help. Silverware's not that heavy."

"Sure. Thank you for talking to me. Maybe we could be friends going forward?"

Shane gave him an odd sideways glance and then grinned.

"Sure. Not really sure why we never were before."

Uh-huh? Cai rubbed the back of his neck, uncertain how to answer. Shane laughed.

"I know, completely my fault."

"No, not true. I was arrogant and pushy, and you don't like to be condescended to by pushy people, so we were oil and water. I'm sorry for my part in that."

"Me too. Believe me, when all you have to do is think, you spend a lot of time navel-gazing. I have enough to regret without regretting my family relationships." Shane held a hand up to shake. Cai met him. His shoulder popped again. Shane frowned and touched his own shoulder. "That wasn't mine. It's still out?"

"It comes and goes."

"Yeah? Brian can maybe help you with that."

"I talked to him. I'll do it again."

Shane held up the ring.

"I'll put this with the rest of the evidence. Something is tickling in the back of my mind, but I don't know. It's probably just some random thought and those are elusive since the concussion. We better get this table set."

Shane cast a ready smile at Jazz who was hanging up her coat in the mudroom. She joined Jill in the kitchen, hauling a bowl of mashed potatoes into the dining room.

"Hmm, the fine fragrance of mustang, the perfume of the western lady."

"Not all of us can enjoy bed baths." The girl smiled at Shane.

"I'd love a real bath but getting me in and out of the tub would be ridiculous."

"We could manage it." Cai counted the number of plates. "You could even be first." Shane's forehead creased. "You know, we now do serial bathing, drawing straws on who gets to go first."

"A lovely family activity." Jazz leaned down and whispered in Shane's ear. Cai supposed he'd noticed them drawing closer in the last few weeks. Shane no longer seemed determined to hold her at arm's length. Cai knew it had been Jacob's hope the two would discover one another. The old man was a matchmaker and prophet.

"Yeah, if Mom and Marnie are okay with it, I'd be willing to try. You guys just can't drop me."

"How about holding you under?"

"Nope, not that either."

"Well, then where's the fun in any of this?" Jazz giggled, hand trailing along Shane's shoulders.

"Fun and hygiene – not the same thing."

"We definitely have to find some bubble bath." Jazz's green eyes were wide and laughing as she met gaze with Cai.

"Horse soap bubbles."

"You two!" Jill set the big tureen of stew in the middle of the table while Jazz went to collect the bread. Rob and Click came in the back door then and Alicia lumbered up the basement steps. Marnie appeared from somewhere and slid an arm around his waist.

"Wow, we're all here."

That felt like something of a good omen and the Dinty Moore stew wasn't so bad when you were really hungry.

Love

Garden City, Kansas

His childhood bedroom seemed really small with three of them. Lynnie slept in a playpen crammed in the corner and Kris patted himself on the back for buying himself a full-sized bed when he was in high school. At least he wouldn't have to sleep on the floor. July closed the door before starting to strip off her clothes. The big woodstove in the living room barely heated this room under the eaves.

"Baby, I'm so glad you managed to get here."

"Me too. I was scared your parents would send me away, but I didn't have a choice after the Army took over in Wichita. I tried to wait, but it just got so out of control so quickly."

"What happened to your mom?"

July shook her head, tears welling in her huge brown eyes. Kris pulled her into his arms, humming to soothe her. He tangled his fingers around his class ring that she wore on a chain around her neck.

"I was out looking for food. Mama had one of her headaches, so I took Lynnie. I was going to leave her with her. It was like a God-thing. I came back to the apartment trashed and Mom gone and the few neighbors who were still there saying the Army took everybody for sedition."

"Sedition?"

"Yeah. Mama? Sedition? Makes no sense."

"None of this makes any sense, honey. How'd you get here?"

"Hitchhiked. I started with Mama's car. Mine was dead, but hers still worked, but not good. All the food was gone, but Mr. Beuchamps gave me some baby food and formula leftover from their kids." Kris smiled because the Beuchamps had teenagers. "I loaded up the stroller out of habit. When the car broke down about a hundred miles out of Wichita, I put what I could in the stroller and a backpack and just started walking. People gave me rides and food along the way. The last leg a woman drove me 100 miles out of her way to get me here. And I still didn't know if your parents would accept me."

"I guess I misjudged them."

"Your mom hugged me and cried. I didn't know what to think. Your dad wanted to know where you were, but it wasn't like unfriendly. He was worried about you. I hated that I had to tell them I didn't know."

"I survived. I needed to make sure you and Lynnie were okay.

Kris kissed the palm of her hand, his lips caressing calluses.

"They have you working hard?"

"No harder than they do. They have to do most things by hand now."

"Yeah. They're going to hate that I can't stay, but I made a deal to borrow the Tucker."

Her eyes glittered in the lantern light.

"How long?"

"A few days and then I've got to head back, but I promise I'll be back in the spring."

July pushed her back against the wall.

"Oh, honey, you know you can't promise us that. If you go out into the world, this world might just eat you."

He opened his mouth to protest but closed his lips because he heard the truth in her words.

"We can't run away from the world. It's going to come to us whether I go or not. But I will do my best to come back."

She wiped tears and he kissed them away, then pulled her down on the mattress and made love to her.

February 1

Maintenance

Seattle

Cassidy and Sherwin came most often to sit beside his bed and keep him updated on the outside world. Cassidy read to him. They were halfway through *Ulysses*. His hearing might have improved a little over the long days in this dark world without true sensation. He still lost words when people didn't speak directly in his ear or if background noise interfered. Despite Sherwin's accent, he was the easiest to understand – a deep voice that didn't speak too fast. Cassidy's higher tones alluded him often, though he hung on every word.

Geo supposed the doctors talked in his presence because they thought he was a vegetable and he admitted to being the next closest thing to a Brussel sprout a man could be. Stitching together the story had taken some time, but he knew he'd been shot in the back of the head with some sort of advanced weapon that had disrupted his nervous system. A bullet still rested in his brain. Until that came out there was no chance of improvement. He had no way of keeping track of time, but he sensed surgery would be soon. There

411

seemed to be less concern about his heart rate and there'd been no discussion of fever lately.

He assumed from Duke's presence that he wasn't in a regular hospital. His caregivers were always the same, three women and a man who were charged with keeping him alive. That seemed no easy task. He couldn't breathe on his own, couldn't move, couldn't feel. They mentioned his blood pressure a lot. He'd never had a problem with blood pressure before, but now his head throbbed with his pulse whenever they were worried about it.

The voices across the room spoke so low he couldn't grasp the words, but they didn't sound like the doctors. More boisterous and yet subdued. He supposed they would be, entering the room of a half-dead man. He'd given up hope of opening his eyes, but he still strained to hear what people said across the room even when he knew he couldn't. He'd always had such good hearing. He wondered if the surgery would repair it or if he'd need hearing aids.

"Sleeping, huh?" He knew that voice though the name eluded him. "Man, you're more screwed up than I was when I came back from the Box. But they're saying if this surgery goes well, they might be able to fix you up with some new tech."

Zapata snapped his gum.

"You in there, man?"

Geo tried to open his eyes, twitch a finger, make a grunting noise. Nothing. The bed moved and he sensed but didn't feel the change of position.

"Of course, he's in there," Marek grumbled. "Don't be a Debbie Downer. He needs to know we believe in him."

"I do. They get that bullet out of his head and I think he'll be back in no time. Much as he can be."

"Does he know?" Tanner asked.

"If he's able to hear, yes," Cassidy replied.

Geo knew, but he didn't believe. When he'd been shot, he'd spun around and landed back first in the bottom of the canoe, breaking his back. His future looked dark and not just because he couldn't open his eyes.

"So, tomorrow," Tanner said. "And then you move toward getting back to life. It'll be better than they're saying. I have faith."

Geo appreciated Tanner's optimism. It reminded him of his parents, who also had faith. He wondered where they were in all this chaos and hoped Knights Industries would let them know if he died. He didn't particularly want them to see him like this, but he didn't think they should be left to wonder for the rest of their lives.

Everybody said goodbye and Geo thought he could slip away into sleep, but then he heard the squeak of a rubber-sole on tile.

"You'd be better off not waking up from that surgery. The world would be better off if you couldn't tell what you know."

The man's voice moved from his ear to somewhere up above his head.

"Put you out of your misery right now."

The whoosh-hiss stopped and a second later an alarm began to sound. He couldn't breathe, couldn't even struggle with it because he was completely paralyzed. He felt the world slipping from his grasp as people ran shouting into the room and then the whoosh-hiss started again and his mind cleared.

"His blood pressure is spiking. Valium now! Geo, calm down! You're risking a stroke. You're okay, just relax." Geo tried, but he couldn't communicate with his body, and he only relaxed on a tide of medications. Before he settled into darkness, he tried to remember where he'd heard that voice before, but it didn't come to him and then he slept.

Leave-Taking

Garden City, Kansas

July leaned into his arms, breathing slowly, tears wetting the collar of his shirt. He waited, wishing he could freeze the moment and remain here forever.

"I know you have to go." She pulled back, wiping her cheeks. "I shouldn't do this. It's not fair. I'm just scared we'll never see you again."

"You will. I'll come back. I'm really motivated."

They were in his bedroom while Lynnie slept in her playpen. He wished he could pick her up and hold her, smell her sweaty curls, but he knew that would unnecessarily complicate the leave-taking.

"I'll pray for you every night." He'd been surprised to discover she'd become religious while they were separated. It didn't bother him as much as he thought it would. He sometimes actually prayed now himself – unsure of who or what he was praying to, but Jasper pointed out that there were no atheists in foxholes and the whole country was a foxhole currently.

"You should go and I'll stay here. It'll be easier that way."

"Oh, baby."

They hugged one last time and then he stiffened his spine and headed downstairs.

The wind still blasted hard from the west, piling up a dune on the side of the house. The Tucker percolated in the yard, awaiting his leave-taking, which would have to wait on his mother releasing her grip from his arm. She knew he had to go, but she didn't have to like it and Kris understood that.

"Woman, let the boy go now." Jasper shaved for the occasion and the hat he wore showed a logo as compared to omnipresent grease. Emma wiped her eyes with the back of a work-worn hand and wrapped her arms around Kris's neck.

"You stay safe out there. That little girl needs her daddy."

"Yes, ma'am."

Emma turned resolutely and stalked off to the living room. Kris blinked tears from his own eyes. He and Jasper paused on the porch. Despite the wind, it was a crystal clear day with a hard blue sky and the sun glowed with a double sundog.

"Ren Sullivan's a good man."

"I think so."

"No, he is. Always admired how he seemed to know the economic future."

"I don't think he was prepared for this."

A long silence settled on the porch until Jasper laughed.

"Who could be? Insanity don't make sense." Kris laughed. It was true. "So the women want you to be safe and stay here, but I know you can't. I just want you to be smart. Stay alive. You can't come home if you're dead. In fact, if you come home dead, I'll kill you." Kris grinned. It was funny even if macabre. "And don't worry about them. I'll keep a roof over their heads and food in their bellies while I can, but guys like you – we're going to need resupply and that's your job."

"Yes, sir." They embraced briefly and when they pulled apart, Kris thought he saw the glimmer of a tear in Jasper's eye. They didn't talk about it. Leave-taking required bravery and a dollop of denial. Kris climbed up into the Tucker and got ready to go. July stared down at him from the bedroom window. He stripped off his glove to flash the I-love-you sign to her. She returned it. They held it a second before he steeled his backbone and threw the Tucker into forward gear.

Turning Point

SullCorp Hub, Columbus, Ohio

Europe proved elusive and Julian's neck and head hurt. He'd assailed the firewall all day long, thought he'd had it a few times, only to find another layer of encryption. His best hacking skills hadn't been tested this thoroughly since he'd hacked into a Department of Defense website and spent years in prison for it.

A breeze touched the hair on the back of his neck and as he reached to rub his aching neck, he encountered a hand. Bellowing, he turned to ward off an attack and found his hands wrapped in Andi's jacket. Her hazel eyes flared wide with surprise as she swung from his hands by her clothes. He pulled back to settle her on her feet.

"Bad idea?" She sounded apologetic.

"Yeah, sorry. Survival skill. What are you here for?"

"It's past nine. Didn't even see you at lunch. What are you up to?"

"Trying to get through a government lock-key to access Europe's Internet."

"The infamous kill switch?"

"Indeed. But you're right. I stopped being productive at this a couple of hours ago. Take me home soon as I close this out."

Laughing, she sat down on a nearby office chair, tucking her legs up so she could rest her chin on one knee.

"What were you up to all day?"

"Sorting food stocks. They got another shipment this morning."

"Well, that's good. The food's been less than fresh lately."

"Don't expect much change. It was a half-ration. I think there's not much left out there and every shipment may be the last."

"Spring's coming." He scanned a pop-up under one of his windows. Andi straightened and he shot a look at her. "Something?"

"The Daily Earth is in Augusta, my grandmother's hometown. Do you mind?"

He pushed back so she could roll up to his workstation and read the screen. The article detailed the execution of a slave for refusal to obey. Her eyes swam with tears as she pushed back from the screen.

"Did you know him?"

"A cousin. Oh, my god! I didn't really believe what you said about how things were going in what's left of Georgia."

"I'm sorry. I tried to warn you, but you didn't want to see the video, and – I didn't want to see the video."

She wiped her cheeks clear of tears.

"There's no home to go to now."

She took a steadying breath. She wasn't a woman who cried easily, which was how she'd survived Pittsburg. He put an arm around her shoulders, squeezing her bicep. Meanwhile, his gut jigged a happy dance because she had no reason to head south without him. He knew it a perversity that he was actually rejoicing at the death of a stranger because it pushed Andi into his arms.

She turned her face into his shoulder, shivers running through her muscular body. Her breathing slowed and she straightened in the circle of his arms.

"I came to tell you something." She pulled her sweatshirt sleeve from her jacket to wipe her cheeks dry. "Are there any tissues?"

"Butt roll."

"That'll do."

He reached behind Murat's monitor and tore off a couple of loops of toilet paper. Andi blew her nose and Julian pointed to the trash can while he shut down his workstation.

"What did you need to tell me?"

"She's pregnant."

"She?"

"Katharine."

"Wow! She's – really?"

"Yeah. I kind of thought she was – like since way back at the quarry. It never occurred to you?"

"I'm the youngest. I was never around for a pregnancy before. Are all women as hissy as her?"

"I'm not sure and I don't want to talk about the past because it'll make me cry again."

"Of course. Let's head home."

He turned off the lights and settled his arm behind her back as they walked down the corridor toward the stairs that would lead across the truckyard to the maintenance barn they lived in. As they neared the suite of former offices that formed the infirmary, a scream echoed out of the door. Julian's prison sense said to not get involved, but the thought of Derry lying in there helpless caused him to overcome his reticence and barge into the infirmary. Carmen's arm dripped blood where Chris swung a pair of scissors at her. Julian caught Chris's wrist. The boy writhed, kicking at Julian, who tightened his fingers on the boy's wrist until he triggered the reflex that caused the scissors to clatter toward the floor. Julian felt Andi grab up the scissors as he held the boy at bay.

"He needs to be restrained. Are there straps?"

Carmen looked around the room where other children were crying. The oldest boy swung himself into a wheelchair and rolled over to a cabinet while Andi righted a chair to help Carmen sit down. The boy joined Julian at Chris's bed.

"Hold him down and I'll set these up. They should have done this earlier. I didn't sleep last night because he was threatening us."

"Nobody wants to believe a 12-year-old can be violent."

Julian lifted the kicking Chris onto his bed. When Chris tried to bite him, Julian slapped him.

"You can't hit kids."

"When you try to kill people, I don't have to treat you as a kid."

"She's the devil here to eat our souls."

"And, that's not scary at all." The younger of the two paraplegics had been on the floor but dragged himself up into a wheelchair to join them. He helped the older boy get each of Chris's feet into the leg loops. Chris roared swear words and flailed his head back and forth while Julian restrained him from behind. By the time they tied his good arm down and put a gag in his mouth to quiet him down, Andi finished bandaging Carmen's arm. Carmen's hands shook while she filled a syringe with a sedative to drug Chris.

"You were amazing!" Carmen cast a grateful look at Julian. "How did you ever learn to do that?"

Four months ago, Julian would have avoided telling her the truth about his past, but surprisingly he no longer cared.

"Prison." She raised an eyebrow. "The government objects to their websites being hacked."

Andi snickered. The oldest boy held up a palm to high-five.

"Colm and I think it's cool. She'd have been dead before I could have gotten to them and I'm not sure what I can do with these."

He gestured to his withered legs before pulling a blanket off his bed to settle over them.

423

"I threw the chair at him." The other boy grinned. "And tossed myself right out onto the floor."

Theirs was a shared experience that Julian didn't know. A SullCorp security officer bustled in the door.

"Everything taken care of here?"

"Tragedy averted." Carmen briefly described what happened. "Can you inform his parents?"

"Of course. Fred needs to decide what to do. I'll take care of that too. He's fine?"

Connie and Parker pushed in behind him and rushed to Derry's bed. The boy looked agitated and his face gleamed with tears, but he seemed uninjured. Andi plucked at Julian's sleeve.

"We should go."

Julian looked at Carmen and she nodded. His heart rate still thundered in his ears as he followed Andi down the stairs.

"You okay?" The crisp wind sliced right through his jacket and numbed his lips.

"Yes. Wow!"

"The longer we stay here, the more chance of stuff like this."

Julian stared at her in the glow from a yard light.

"You think so too?"

"I know we can't go anywhere until spring, but we need to start preparing because – I don't know – I just feel like this is a trap. Don't you?"

He nodded, too overwhelmed to speak. They stood in the blasting wind for a moment, holding one another.

"Let's go. Perry will want to know about this."

Brother-in-Laws

Liberty Trucking, Jericho Township

Cai never expected his father-in-law to conspire on his behalf, but Jason Breen liked to keep people guessing. He muscled Josh into his office and closed the door. Cai heard the lock turn and knew they were either talking or starving.

Josh smelled like a man who had access to a shower occasionally, evidence of his association with the B&B. Briefly, Cai remembered the feeling of hot water washing over his head and the smell of modern shampoo. He would kill for a shower. Well, no, but he'd push a little old lady out of the way.

"What do you want?" Josh looked older than his 23 years. Prison aged people, McAuliff said. Marnie was the only Callahan-Breen sibling to take up smoking, but she'd stopped smoking at 19, so her face didn't show the lines smokers usually developed. Josh just looked older.

"I know you sometimes meet with Grant Rigby behind Shane's hotel. You know we found a body back there at New Year's?"

"I heard. I know nothing about it."

"When was the last time you two met back there?"

"Before Christmas. It got too cold for outside meetings, so we meet in the house now."

"And, there were no dead bodies the last time you were there?"

"No. I'd have noticed that and not a lot gets past Rigby."

"Who is he, really?"

"Ask your brother. How's he doing, by the way?"

"Getting around with crutches some now. Not walking yet. Swinging."

"Well, that's good then."

"I thought you didn't like him anymore."

"I'm pissed off about going to prison, but – it's just best we stay away from each other. So, are we done?"

Josh walked around the desk and tried the cabinet behind it.

"Damn, the man knows me!"

"He locked up the coffee and booze?"

Josh sighed and Cai laughed.

"I'm still trying to figure out this murder. You hear anything?"

Josh sat down in one of the chairs.

"No, but – haven't you pretty much asked everybody in town?"

"I have – now that we're talking. I even talked with Lufgrens. It's like this guy fell from the sky."

"He didn't. Nobody just appears like magic."

"You have a theory?"

"Maybe. Am I really a better detective than you, Darrow?"

That hurt, but Cai recognized Josh hit near the truth.

"You might be. I'm open to suggestions. I've interviewed everyone inside the wire and I'm no closer to a solution than I was on New Year's Day."

"Wow, Sherlock wants his name back, man. You haven't interviewed everyone inside the wire. Days are warming up, snowpack is settling."

"You're suggesting I go to Mara Wells? But who there would want to implicate Shane?"

"Ah, that's why we're having this conversation – because you think I would frame your brother."

"Wouldn't you?"

"And then have Shane or Chavez me? No, thank you! I might probably have killed Shane if he were always armed when I first got back to town, but I'm beyond that now. The whole survival thing – I just don't want to anymore. So, I don't think the body was dropped there to frame Shane – not necessarily anyway. Still, after you've eliminated all the possibilities and you're still looking for answers, then you have to look for another answer."

"Mara Wells?"

"Or the Rez. They come in and out of the wire all the time. But I'd guess Mara Wells."

Cai nodded. He knew he couldn't go to Mara Wells now. It would mean a long trip on an open snow machine putting along at 20 mph. No, he needed to stay home until the weather improved, but the game was afoot once more.

Curly Problems

Delaney House, Emmaus

Shane shifted in the wheelchair, trying to reduce the ache in his hip while still staring at the evidence arranged on the table. He heard the floor creak behind him and looked over his shoulder to find Jazz crossing the living room, dressed to stay in. Lately, as he grew stronger, he was alone more often. He didn't mind solitary activities now that his mind wasn't turning to dark caves. Still, he enjoyed time alone with Jazz.

"What are you doing?" she asked.

"Still trying to figure out who killed John Doe."

"I thought Cai gave that up as a lost cause."

"Mostly, but I got bored and decided I could either tune the piano or look at the evidence and until it warms up and stays that way, the piano would be a waste of time." He gestured at the array of evidence. "What do you think? Anything jump out at you?"

She leaned over the photographs, stared at the boots and fingered the clothes, then picked up the ring.

"It doesn't have a school name on it."

"No, which is weird, right?"

"Yes and no. It's homeschooling."

431

"What?"

"Some of the kids I grew up with who were homeschooled still wanted a class ring."

Shane noted that in his notebook while she stared at the stone intently.

"This is jasper."

"Is it? I thought so, but I'm not a rock-hound." His gaze lingered on the crease between her eyes. "Something?"

"Geo has a jasper ring. He and some friends all chose it as a sign of friendship."

"Homeschoolers in that group?"

"Yeah. There were five or six of them. Geo's ring had Mara on it, but Trey was alternative school."

"Trey?"

"Conopher." Shane stared at her, so she gave more information. "He lived with their uncle over in Mara when he finished high school. Him, Geo, Paul, Tommy used to hay together, and then they'd party too."

Shane held the ring up. He remembered Trey Conopher. They'd ran track against each other as freshmen, and he'd been one of Shane's cannabis customers. He'd then dropped off Shane's radar for the last part of high school. Must have moved to Mara when things became hard at home. Shane vaguely remembered Old Man Conopher and he didn't blame Trey.

"What are you thinking?"

"That I'll tell Cai about it and don't worry, I'm not going to Mara to investigate."

He set the ring on the table and reached for her hand, using his other hand to swivel the chair. She stopped him from drawing her onto his lap.

"You know it will hurt you." She giggled and pulled a chair out from the table. She'd barely sat down when he pulled her into a kiss. They had only kissed once before, back during the Cow Cop Assault when he'd not had time to follow up and now he was in no shape to finish the course. She braced her arms on the rests of the chair, but eventually, they both felt the strain. His back and hip blazed with fire. He sighed.

"They made me promise when you moved in that I wouldn't have sex with you in their house."

"Is that where you think this is headed." She pulled back to look into his eyes. Uh, yeah, his mind had gone that way. He felt his cheeks grow warm.

"Not something I could do right now, but I was enjoying kissing."

"And you're in pain."

He shrugged, sighed.

"Maybe we could go sit over on the couch and I could untangle your hair."

"That bad, huh?"

"It is, but it's also something we can do together that doesn't violate my promise."

"I'll get my comb."

"No, I can do it without. The Miristani have curly hair and the men spend times in the evenings untangling their women's hair and braiding it. I never did it, of course, but it looked…."

"Sexy?"

"Romantic. I'm not really up for sexy and – yeah. I did some really stupid things when I was a teenager and I'm trying to live that down."

He stopped at the couch and swung himself across to it. She sat down at his feet so he could slowly work the knots out of her curls. Her hair grew exceptionally quickly, so it was already past her shoulders.

"You always straightened it, didn't you?"

"I did. And, I bought good product. Now that yours is growing out, I bet you wish you had clippers."

"I used to have hair down past my shoulders and I embraced my curls. But I had great product too."

"So what happened? You were practically a skinhead when we met."

"Hey, I wasn't that bad! South America was too hot, and I met Mike who owned a pair of clippers. And…." He sighed. The desire to confess roiled in his chest, but he feared she'd reject him.

"What happened?" She turned so she could see his face.

He rubbed an eye.

"Would you believe I killed a guy?"

Her green eyes shifted back and forth like she read his mind.

"Yes. You were a soldier."

"Not. Mercenaries aren't soldiers. We are, but …." He rubbed his temple. "And it wasn't like that. This isn't an excuse. I shouldn't have done it. He was a guy in our outfit and a serial rapist. He'd done it before and some of us had told him to stop, but he did it again, so I followed him to *el banjo* and killed him." He couldn't speak above a whisper or lift his eyes from his hands. Briefly, he remembered his torn knuckles where he'd battered Brikowski to death. Everybody knew and nobody reported him because they all knew Brick deserved it. He'd dumped the body near a bayou and he assumed a croc had disposed of it. *God, how do You forgive that?* Then Jazz's hands closed on his. He looked up and her green gaze held no judgment. "I met Mike that night. I was really drunk when he showed up and polished off the bottle and got drunker than I was. I took him back to his place and the next morning, I cut my hair. The kid I'd been was dead and I needed to change to show that."

A long silence ensued and then she squeezed his hands.

"He would have done it again. What you did wasn't right, but what he did was more not right."

"No shades of gray. I can't excuse my actions. I wasn't doing God's work, that's for sure."

"And you also can't redo the past." She smiled up at him and the wad of guilt in his chest dissolved. She ran the fingers of one hand through his short curls. "Do you want a haircut?"

"Maybe, but not now. I need to finish your hair." She turned back to let him work on her curls. He settled his hands on her shoulders. "So you're okay knowing that about me?"

He liked that she didn't answer immediately.

"Yeah. It makes sense now."

"What?"

"When we were first training for the border patrol you mentioned that killing someone was a game-changer. I didn't really understand then and now I do."

He teased out a substantial knot. The strand curled like a spring. He set it aside to continue working the same knot.

"When was the last time you did this?"

"Weeks. I sort of gave up, figured I'd have to cut it. How do the women in Miristan keep their hair from tangling without conditioner?"

"Oh, yeah, they do something. I've seen their men dip their fingers in oil and do what I'm doing now. I think Mom would harm me if I used even a teaspoon of her cooking oil at this point."

"I have moisturizer."

"Yeah, that might work." She got up to get it and then he started working on her knots, rubbing small bits into her hair and slowly working each strand loose.

"So tell me something about yourself. We've known each other for months and I feel like I don't really know you."

"Like what?"

"Uh, did you do sports in high school?"

Her slim shoulders quaked with quiet laughter.

"Yes. Shooting, track, and dance."

"Right. Forgot about dance. Shooting? So biathlon?"

"Match shooting. I did pretty well there. I was a decent runner. Wasn't going to set any records like you."

"Don't want to talk about me. How come those sports?"

"Too little to compete with girls six inches taller than me and I like individual sports. Dance was always my true sport, but you know how kids are in high school."

"Judgmental stone-chuckers. I remember." He finished one tangle and moved on to another, fingers caressing the lighter hair by her scalp. "So you're a natural redhead?"

"Yeah. Not the Nicole Kidman milk-white skin kind. I have pigment. But the red is definitely dominant. I've used the rinse for years to keep it in check."

"It's lovely. I liked the darker color too, but I like the natural too. And the natural curls."

"You are incredibly gentle."

"Guitar fingers. Turn to the left, so I can get the other half." As she turned, he leaned down to capture her mouth with his lips. She giggled, kissing him back. He heard the back door open and close and straightened. She blushed. He returned to teasing knots out of her hair.

"Oh, good, you aren't just sleeping." Jill bustled in to pull house clothes out of her bag. She straightened and stared at them. Shane felt heat coming from Jazz. "What are you doing?"

"Detangling her hair. She's got curly problems."

Jill touched her part where the grey and brown were overcoming the red dye.

"You found the right guy to help you out, Jazz. I'm going to go get cleaned up and start dinner. Will you be able to stay up, Shane?"

"Maybe. Depends on how long it takes, but you know, a nap doesn't need to be long."

He became an expert on naps weeks ago. He listened for her to pass into the kitchen and then pulled a face at Jazz's smothered expression. She snorted and that set them both to laughing.

"I heard that." Jill leaned around the corner to the dining room. "And, I'm also aware that you two don't sit six inches apart when I'm not around."

"Is that permission?" Shane slid around so he could look over his shoulder.

"No. When you're strong enough to leave this house, you two can do whatever you want … not here."

"Aye, aye, *capitana*." Shane turned to Jazz as Jill disappeared from view. "This gives me an incentive to endure the pain of therapy."

She grinned and he ran long fingers through her now untangled hair.

"I'll braid this for you and then, unfortunately, I probably do need a nap." He cast an embarrassed grin her way.

"Thanks. I should probably help Jill with dinner anyway." Her hand gently caught his wrist, pulled his hand to where she could kiss his palm. "This was very romantic."

She caught her pink lower lip with her front teeth and cast him a coy glance from under her surprisingly dark eyelashes.

"Good. And, it's probably best this way since I need to be different going forward."

She rose from the floor and planted a kiss on his cheek.

"Take a nap."

"Yeah. Can you put the evidence back in the bag?"

"I will. And I'll tell Cai about the ring if you're still asleep when he gets here."

"Thanks."

With a big yawn, Shane used his hands to pull his weak leg onto the couch and pulled a blanket over him. Within minutes, he'd drifted off to sleep, savoring the memory of Jazz's kisses.

Escape Planning

SullCorp Hub, Columbus, Ohio

Perry, Joseph, and Katharine listened to Julian's account of what happened in the infirmary. Outside the window, another snowstorm blanketed Columbus and so Julian's last pronouncement fell on unconvinced ears.

"We shouldn't stay here. Sooner or later, they're running out of food here or something else like what happened in the infirmary will happen."

Silence. It wasn't the absence of sound. He could hear them breathing. He waited.

"No, you're right." Perry tended to the quiet side unless he needed to be loud and he didn't need to be yet. "Food is getting scarce. Fred says shipments are being beset by highwaymen." Katharine made a scoffing noise. "His word, not mine, but close enough. Guys with guns who stop trucks and take what's in the containers. Which is what will happen to us if we head out on those roads too soon."

"So, we just wait for the inevitable?" Andi's delicate brow crinkled.

"No, we start planning. I know about the food stores you've been hiding on our behalf. We need guns and ammunition and a plan. We also need roads that are not feet deep in snow."

"And maybe more than one vehicle." Joseph Sullivan hadn't felt great since he'd had pneumonia, but the forced inactivity seemed to have made him more contemplative and therefore smarter.

"A larger group, perhaps." Andi scanned around the group to see if they agreed.

"Why?" Katharine frowned at her.

"There's safety in numbers." Perry scratched an eyebrow. "Greater numbers cause complications, too, but extra vehicles are a good idea and maybe people in them also works. We can consider it. Assuming the weather's going to warm up and melt the snow off the roads soon, I'd say we have another month, maybe less. Andi, can you get us more food?"

"I can try."

"Why don't I just ask for it?" Joseph had learned to defer to Perry, but he occasionally seemed to remember he was the heir to SullCorp.

"When we get ready to go, yes, but I don't think we should be too open with our plans."

"Why not?"

"Because they might try to stop us?" Katharine's view of the world was much less rosy than her husband's.

"More or less." Perry and Julian turned to look at the door a moment before the knock fell. Andi rose to answer it.

Connie and Parker waited in the small hallway outside the apartment.

"Come in." Andi stepped back.

"What brings you folks out in a storm like this?"

"What happened in the infirmary?" Parker stared at Julian.

"Chris lost it, went after Carmen and I walked in to stop it."

"That's what Derry was trying to tell us." Connie nodded as if affirming something to herself. "I know you're planning to leave soon. We want to go with you."

In the act of taking a sip of water, Julian choked and coughed.

"Um, I don't know." Perry glanced over his shoulder at the rest of the Sullivan group.

"Listen to me. My family is at risk if the Republic of Afrika pushes north and Dr. Ibrahim said Derry's stable. He can travel. Parker's got our old truck working well and it has a camper. We'll figure out fuel and food. Please, let us go with you."

"To where?" Katharine demanded.

"Anywhere. You're going to Seattle, right, Julian?"

"I don't know. I'm going to Emmaus first. That's in Kansas."

"That sounds good to me." Parker nodded in agreement. "It's just not safe here."

"The Republic of Afrika is a long way away." Perry eyed them skeptically.

"But others like Chris are not." Parker returned Perry's frown. "I've been asking around. About 1 in 30 of the encephalitis patients becomes violent. Chris was also affected physically, but some of these kids are still quite

443

physically capable and they're apparently banding together and assaulting people out in the city. Plus, I'm hearing rumors about a war of reunification planned come summer."

"What does that have to do with us?" Joseph demanded.

"Supposedly there is a government forming here in Columbus."

"Where are you hearing this?" Perry's expression said this wasn't good news.

"I've been picking up day labor in the city and people are talking. I thought it was conspiracy theory at first, but the more different people I hear it from, the more I think there's meat. And, Connie can make any computer sing while I can fix anything on wheels."

Perry stood and stalked to the kitchen counter to stare out the window. They all spent what seemed like a long time just breathing.

"The weather will keep us here for a while yet, but yeah, you can convoy with us when we go. Keep it quiet, though. We don't want such a large group going with us that we can't control it."

"Right." Parker looked down at Connie and smiled. "We'll start gathering what we need. Thank you!"

The couple excused themselves and the Sullivan group all eyed one another. Katharine stood.

"I guess we've made a decision and all there's left to do is plan and schedule. Let's go to bed, Joseph."

He followed her meekly to the bedroom. Andi moved to wash the dinner dishes, which didn't exactly leave Perry and Julian alone, but they were the only ones left by the sofa.

"I'm sorry this forced your hand." Julian hoped Perry wasn't too upset.

"Not your fault. Eventually, we're going to have to tell Fred our plan, but for now, under wraps." Julian nodded. "And, just to be clear, I've known about the bezerks for a while. Since the hospital, but then I asked about it. Fred says we're safe here in the compound, but sooner or later, someone is going to lose control of this situation, so --."

"Do you know about the government?"

"I've heard rumors too, but we don't know anything for sure. So, figure out a way to get us intel headed out west if you can."

"Right. I'll do that. You think life is ever going to go back to normal?"

"A normal? Sure. Like what we knew? Maybe we'll see traces. But, yeah, better to be places where sane people are in control."

"Who is in control in Emmaus?"

"I'd guess Joseph's father and the mayor, Rob Delaney. Sane people. And that's probably the best we can hope for in these circumstances. Hey, Andi, you two get the bed tonight. Let me finish those dishes."

"I've only got a few more."

"And I can do them. Go on."

Perry shooed her away from the sink and Julian swept her into the bedroom. They'd been on the foldout in the living room last night, so Andi started removing her clothes as soon as the door was closed. Julian paused her hands as she unbuttoned her jeans.

"Are you coming with us?"

"West?" He nodded. Her mouth twitched with an almost-smile. "Yeah. I thought you already knew I'd go with you."

"You kept talking about Georgia?"

"I miss my family, but they're gone and – well, you should know how I feel about you."

"Don't assume I have self-esteem."

"Yeah, well – Kansas, huh? I thought Seattle."

"I don't know. But –" He knew it was time to be brave. "Anywhere with you."

She mugged a face.

"Georgia?"

"Anywhere sane with you."

"Good. Now shut up and undress me."

Dinner Out

Conopher Farm, Jericho Township

Rafe Conopher was a jerk, Jos decided. He kept making comments that Jos thought were meant to rattle him. Did he not realize that everybody went armed these days? If he pulled anything, Jos had the means to answer him. He was so used to wearing a gun now that he'd not even thought of leaving it in the car. Since he was concealed, nobody would know until he needed the gun.

The Conophers chattered over their meal of potato gnocci and pasta sauce with green beans as a side. They still had electricity because they had a windmill for irrigation which produced electricity too.

"It's enough to keep the freezer going and we each get a shower once a week." Dell seemed nervous and Jos wondered why. He'd heard dads didn't like it when boys came around their daughters, but Dell didn't seem hostile. He was just talking more than Jos had ever seen before.

"There's turbines going up at a few places. I'm planning to take some trade goods to MacArthur's to see if I can buy one."

"Get out of the 1880s on an individual basis." Leisha – she had insisted he call them Dell and Leisha – smiled at a gnocci speared on the end of her folk. "The lessons this crisis is teaching us are vital."

"I've half a mind to go with you. Our windmill works, but it's inefficient. A more modern turbine might work better."

"Or we could just get those big turbines working." Silver spoke around a mouthful of crusty bread.

"Someone was working on that, but Jace Welton says we need special tech to make them work."

"Those big turbines were never a good idea." Rafe finally said something intelligent. "They only work when the wind is blowing and they can't operate when the wind is blowing too hard. They cost more to make than they offset in a decade and they kill birds. They were a greenie idea that made people like the Sullivans happy, but they didn't do anything."

"I wish we had them now." Leisha's tone said this was an old argument and she was done with it. Jos didn't know the Conophers very well, but they seemed like very honest people. Honest and nice, except for Rafe.

The Conophers' Aussie shepherd came padding in from the living room, looked at Leisha and whined. Leisha tossed her napkin beside her plate and left without a word. Jos looked at Gen, who had made an effort for this meal — washing her hair and wearing a nice dress.

"Something with Kix." Dell offered the bread plate to Jos. "The dog decided Kix is one of her lambs."

"How is he?"

"Getting better. It takes time to rebuild strength after a coma, but he's doing okay. If Leisha says it's okay, I'm sure he'd like to see people his own age."

Jos felt a weird chill up his back, but Granmae would say "It's not about you."

"Sure, if he's up for it."

Leisha came to the door.

"Dell, I need you."

All seemed calm, but Dell got up quickly and followed her. Jos glanced at Gen.

"He probably had a seizure. It makes a mess. He won't be up to a visit tonight."

Jos concentrated on cleaning his plate up with the hunk of bread. Nobody wasted calories these days and food not from a can was a luxury for him.

"Wow, that's got to be hard."

"For him more than us."

"Cady, are you staying here tonight?"

Rafe stared at his wife with seething anger. She looked at him with what Jos thought looked like fear.

"Yes. You've been drinking again."

"What if I have?"

"I'm not putting the kids through that. We'll talk in the morning."

Rafe slammed out the back door a moment later. Had the door not already been repaired with plywood, the window surely would have broken. Jos finished the last bit of food on his plate while the Conophers stared at their plates in embarrassment.

"It's none of my business but – you know Mayor Delaney's an alcoholic. It's been a long time since he drank, but maybe he could talk to him."

Cady nodded, stood, started collecting plates with shaking hands.

"Let us do that, Aunt Cady." Gen stilled Cady's hands. "Jos said he wanted the full domestic treatment. Washing dishes sounds fun, right?"

"Sure. I normally eat my food right out of the can and so I have no real dishes, but yes, sounds like fun."

The whole family relocated to the living room while Jos helped Gen clear the table.

"Sorry about Rafe."

"Not a problem. Lots of people are tense these days."

They poured hot water from the bucket on the coal stove into the kitchen sink. Gen dumped a cup of salt into the water and then used a sponge to soap up each dish.

"Where's the soap coming from?"

"There's a chunk in the sponge. Mom, Cady and Ms. Thomas made it with wood ash and boiled fat. Oh, it was horrible!"

Jos picked up the bar of soap from the back of the sink. Compact and grey, it smelled of nothing.

"This is the best soap I've seen. Whose recipe?"

"Um, Ms. Thomas had made soap before. I don't think Cady and Mom had. Why?"

"Soap is a commodity. I'll talk to her. I know times are tough for her. Maybe manufacturing soap will help more than doing laundry."

"She's lucky her mother-in-law was a collector, so she has an antique washer that doesn't need electricity. We're scrubbing by hand."

"Yeah, me too."

"Sorry to rope you into dishes."

"It's fine. I like doing things like this. It feels … normal."

"Yeah. Wouldn't normal be something lovely?"

"It would. When we talk about the good ole days when we're your parents' age, we'll really know what that meant."

"You don't think it's coming back, do you?"

"Some of it will come back. We're manufacturing turbines ourselves now. But it won't be the same."

"Yeah – that's what I think too." She sighed. "I don't think Kix will ever be the same. He's getting stronger on his right side and that's great, but he can't move anything on the left. He'll need help for the rest of his life."

"He's got family. You guys will take care of him, right?"

"Of course. It just – that's a future I wasn't expecting."

"None of us were expecting this future."

The rinse water was so hot the dishes actually hurt his hands as he put them in the drying rack. Should he? Could he?

"So, sometime – wow, yeah – I don't know what there is to do these days, but would you go on a date with me sometime?"

Gen smiled and turned toward him, hands dripping.

"Yes. Maybe we could just meet with James and Kim, play a board game or something."

"Yeah, that – where?"

"Kim's mom is cool. We could probably it there. Or if it warms up, we've got a kind of rec room above the barn."

"Sure. That sounds like fun. I look forward to it."

"When?"

Jos tilted his head toward the kitchen window over the sink.

"Looks like wind's picking up, which might mean more snow, but by next weekend. Sound good?"

"It does. Weather permitting. I'll let Kim know."

"Sounds good." She blushed and Jos felt his own cheeks warm. For the first time in months, Jos felt hopeful.

February 14

Not Immune

Delaney House, Emmaus

Jill woke before dawn with a fever and crawled out of bed to retreat to the kitchen. Rob rolled over and saw Marnie's spot was empty. He stocked the woodstove as quietly as he could, but Shane's eyes still opened.

"She okay?"

"I'm going to check now."

"Being pregnant, there's not a lot she can do about it, right?"

Rob tilted his head, confused. As Shane healed, he woke more easily. Maybe Rob missed something by being able to sleep through the standard activities of a group sleeping arrangement.

That's when he heard the coughing. He headed for the kitchen where Marnie and Jill sat on opposite sides of the table, wrapped in quilts.

"We're both sick." Marnie's teeth chattered with cold. "It's probably the flu."

"What's your temperature?"

"Just over 100." Jill tossed off her blanket, wiping sweat off her face while Marnie resumed coughing. "That's hers. Mine's 101. We need to be isolated and then you need to bleach-wash wherever we've been. Shane shouldn't move around until that's been done."

"Bedrooms are still too cold."

"That would feel good right now." Marnie tossed off her own quilt. "But staying warm is better medicine. We're going to need to --." She paused to cough into her elbow.

The stairs by the back door creaked and Rob looked over his shoulder to see Click ascending from the basement.

"Alicia's clearing her space so you guys can isolate there. I'm going to make up a bucket of bleach water. Rob, you haven't had the flu yet, right?"

"No. Actually, this is the first flu we've had."

"I had a mild case of it when I was still living in the shelter and Alicia had a really bad case when she was in Santa Fe, so we should be the ones to take care of them. Aren't you supposed to head to Mara Wells today?"

Rob sighed.

"Yes, but the timing sucks. I've got Jace Welton coming today to install the turbine and that leaves Shane to honcho everything."

"Shane's fine so long as it doesn't involve walking." Jill's voice croaked. "He's back mentally."

"And if Jace needs help, he can't."

"It'll be fine. You're just jonesing for electricity. If it happens next week, we'll be just as fine."

Rob felt torn between hugging his wife and not wanting to get within 10 feet of her. Alicia came up the stairs. She had grown quite big in the last couple of weeks.

"We're ready downstairs. Rob, you and Cai should go take care of things in Mara. Click and I have this."

"Are you sure? Aren't you due soon?"

"Yes, but my mother went over by two weeks with every pregnancy and Marnie and Jazz both examined me a couple of days ago and I'm nowhere near delivering. Just have Jazz back here by three days."

The glass in the mudroom window shook. Rob put his face close to the kitchen window to stare out at the lightening back yard. It looked like it would be clear and windy today.

Cai came into the kitchen, rubbing a hand through bedhead.

"I'm fine. Don't you dare come near me." Marnie held up a shaking hand. "I already checked the baby's heart rate and he's fine too."

"When you consider how many people we've treated this winter, it's surprising we didn't get this earlier." Jill stood. "Let's get downstairs."

Marnie followed her down the stairs.

"I've got a bad feeling about this."

"Don't do that to yourself." Click tested the water in a metal bucket he'd put on the coal stove. "It's the flu. She survived the southern version." He indicated Alicia who emerged from the pump room with a container of water to take downstairs. "They're both healthy. Most of the people who died here were also starving. So just go do what you need to do and let us take care of thing. This is what family does, even shirttail relatives."

"You and Alicia are family, no shirttails involved." Cai sucked in a deep breath and turned back toward the living room. "Better get ready for the day."

Rob moved toward the pump room which they all used as a hygiene center. He knew he needed to trust other people to take care of things when he needed to be somewhere else. He'd always struggled with delegation. He knew he couldn't be in two places at one time and they needed to satisfy this murder mystery or at least give it a last shot. Besides, not hearing from Mara Wells all winter didn't speak of anything good.

Skeleton Crew

Delaney House, Emmaus

It hurt some to put weight on his leg but advancing it to walk involved so much pain Shane felt like hurling. He didn't let it stop him from making his slow way across the living room to the dining room. Brian shadowed him, occasionally correcting his step, reminding him to breathe, and asking him if he felt dizzy yet. Meanwhile, his cell vibrated on the end table. Eventually, they reached the table. Shane clung to the walker, shivering with exhaustion.

"Okay, that's enough. Tomorrow, you can try walking back to the couch, but we don't want to overdue today." Brian brought the wheelchair over so Shane could settle into it. It took an entire week to get to where he could stand without almost fainting. He'd used crutches, swinging while supporting his sore leg for a few days and then yesterday, the pain restricted him to one or two steps, but he'd managed 17 today and that felt like a milestone. Shane accepted the bag of snow and cozied it against his hip and then poured himself a more than generous glass of cider to ease the pain a little. He blotted sweat from his neck as Ami came into the dining room from the kitchen.

"It's definitely the flu. Mayor Delaney was right to quarantine them."

"Both of them?"

"Yes. Where is he?"

"Gone to Mara Wells to find out what's going on there." Shane picked up his phone.

GRANT: It's just one of the rogue units. Renfield was a decent officer when he had a high command. Not the type to foment an insurrection against the Constitution.

Well, at least Rob wasn't walking into an ambush. Shane rolled to where the handheld radio was, hoping Rob hadn't left range yet.

"Pathfinder, you got ears on? Over."

A burst of static screeched from the radio and then Jazz spoke.

"Pathfinder's driving. This is Music Box Dancer. What's up, Maverick? Over."

"It is the flu, for both of them. Over."

"No harm to the baby? Darrow wants to know. Over."

Shane glanced at Ami. The cider kicked in, not taking the edge off enough to make him drunk, but he didn't feel his hip quite so bad now.

"Baby's fine. It's past the stage where a fever will cause a miscarriage."

Shane relayed that information.

"GR reported back. A sergeant Renfield should be in charge of that unit. He still doesn't buy that he's connected to the group that tried to bring down the plane. Over."

Rob's voice came in next.

"Good to know, Maverick. We'll keep you informed. Over."

Shane wanted to tell Jazz how much he was going to miss her, but it was only for a few days. She planned to visit Michael and then come home. Shane's heart felt stretched by 22 miles. He knew he couldn't go, but he so wanted to.

"Who is taking care of them? Over."

"Mom and Marnie? Alicia and Click. I don't think I can manage the stairs just yet. Over."

"So, we don't need to come back? Over."

"No, we've got it covered. Over."

The radio static made it hard to hear what Rob said next.

"…keep … batten … see later … Over and out."

"Over and out, Pathfinder."

Shane set the radio on the end table and used both hands to readjust his leg and then to settle the icepack.

"You need help lying down?" Brian asked.

"Yeah, maybe. Of course, once I'm down, I can't probably get back up."

He glanced over at Alicia as she came into the dining room.

"They're both sleeping. I'm going to make some lunch. You should lay down."

"How are you feeling?" Ami asked. Alicia did look pretty flushed.

"Like an elephant, and my back is killing me, but other than that – pregnant."

"I'm sorry I can't stay, but I have rounds and that holds a special meaning when you do house-calls."

"I also have to get going. You want the couch or the bed?" Brian seemed overeager to put him to bed.

"I can do it myself."

"Na-huh. I don't trust you."

Shane sighed and rolled over to transfer onto the couch just to show he could. He arranged himself and settled the icepack on his hip.

"See, I'm good."

Jace came in the front door without knocking. His skills for keeping anything "modern" still running were in high demand, so he ate regularly, though like everyone else, he'd lost his extra pounds.

"The turbine is up, but I'm coming back when it's not so windy to do the connections."

"Thanks, Jace. We're all looking forward to electricity."

"You okay?"

"Yeah, just being fussed over by medical professionals." He made a face at Brian, who mugged a face back.

"Like I said, I'll be back. See you then." Jace waved nonchalantly as he closed the door. Shane got back to the business at hand.

"You guys be careful out there. The snow is melting quickly, and Dad says the roads are slick in the shady spots." Wind buffeted the roof of the house. Over the howl, he heard Jace Welton coming down the ladder from the roof. "And listen to that wind scream."

"You stay in bed for the rest of the day, okay?"

"I make no promises, but if it's like it's been, I will."

"And, you make sure to wash your hands before you go near him." Ami finished zipping up her bag. "He doesn't need to catch the flu. I'll swing by tomorrow. You stay down, understand?"

"Yeah, yeah. And the flu seems to not like Delaneys and Greyeyes."

"I suspect so, but a natural resistance might not be protective when you're putting this much stress on your body. Be sensible."

"Taking a nap now."

Alicia saw them to the door.

"Where's Click?" Shane tried to settle into a more comfortable position, but the throb came and went like a broken strobe light.

"He's gone to inspect Carl's house and then he's meeting with Ren Sullivan about the radio station. The latest component arrived with the food shipment last night."

"I'm starved. What's for lunch?"

"Tuna fish sandwiches."

"Seriously?"

"Seriously. And tomato soup. We only have about a week's worth of food, but your dad said to make sure you eat."

"I think Jazz decided to go to Mara Wells just to take some burden off the pantry."

"You two are cute together."

"We're still pretty new."

"And that's what's sweet about it. Don't be so afraid of losing her that you don't let yourself celebrate."

"That obvious?"

"Yeah. It took you so much to mourn Sera's death. But it's time to move on."

"I agree, but it scares me. I don't want to let her out of my sight, but I can't go with until I can walk."

"That's coming. I'm going to get the food now." Alicia stood up and then, clinging to the chair arm, rubbed the small of her back, groaning. "Get your foot out of my spine, *mija*."

Shane watched as her hand moved around to the underside of her swollen belly. Spanish swear words came out of her mouth.

"You okay?"

"It's Braxton-Hicks. I've been having them off and on for m – oh, *Dios Mio*."

"You sure that's not labor?"

She stuck a pretty pink tongue out at him.

"It's just my body getting ready to give birth."

She started for the kitchen to get lunch, but before she got to the dining-room door, she paused to look down between her knees. Shane heard the trickle of water and pulled himself up to sitting to look over the back of the couch.

"What is it?" Alicia looked panic-stricken.

"I think your water just broke. You were saying?"

Correlation

Conopher Farm, Jericho Township

Ami watched as Kix Conopher awkwardly maneuvered a spoon from a bowl to his mouth. As with Dylan, when the fever broke, the worst of the symptoms dissipated very quickly, but they left residual disabilities. His right arm had been deeply spastic during the fever, he possessed use of it now, though the stronger muscles fought against the weaker ones, resulting in difficulties with fluid movement. He'd overcome that with practice, Nick explained. Same with his leg, which was weak and tended to stiffen, but his parents reported he could help with transfers.

His left hand lay splayed on a pillow, unmoving. Brian scored both limbs on that side at 0. Nick said that wasn't a good sign for the future. Brian would work with him, but Kix probably wouldn't walk again.

"Doc-cor Cey-won. Ell my modder I'm dohn."

Leisha came in from the hall to clean up the bowl, tv tray, bib, and Kix's chin. The feeding tube wouldn't be needed for much longer. His swallow reflex returned. He just needed to regain strength and coordination so he could feed himself.

A wide strip of fabric kept him upright in the chair as he struggled to right his head against the headrest. He looked at Ami, his right eye straight and focused, his left eye slowly moving to the center position before slowly turning back toward his nose.

"Will that right itself?" Leisha asked.

"I don't know. We're learning as we go."

"Do you know what turned the corner for him?"

"I have theories, but I won't share them until I've had more study."

Out in the Land Rover, Ami scanned through her notes, looking for any similarities among her patients who were also the first cadre in her test program. Too soon to make correlative observations. She couldn't even be sure this was the same disease because the pattern of paralysis varied so much. She now had 10 patients. Only two, Matthew Bennett and Pete Ramirez, showed the same pattern. What did it mean? She didn't know. She'd had two recoveries of a sort. Except that both were hemiplegics, she wasn't sure they resembled each other.

She stopped at the Vance farm to check on David. His remaining deficits were stable. He walked a little better every visit and seemed to understand Alison and his family better, but he still couldn't say anything but "hi" and nod his head to "yes-no" questions. In some ways, it was nice to work with a known ailment in his case. Nick and April called it "global aphasia" and neither held out much hope that he'd ever speak again. The Cow Cop Rebellion as the town called it happened before she and Javi arrived, but she didn't particularly care for those who had done this to David. She tried not to connect the Carboys with it, but there was a perverse part of her that saw symmetry in their son's condition. The paralysis had stopped at his hips. Ian had uncertain control of his bladder and bowels, but some movement in his hips, so he might be able to walk with braces eventually.

The afternoon sun bumped along the western horizon as she pulled into the Bennett farm, having stopped at one of the Lufgren farms to note that their son's fever had taken the use of his left leg. The leg had been weak when she stopped by a few days ago. Now it was completely paralyzed, and he remained unable to cope with the pain and, the most concerning symptom, not communicating in sign. His hands worked, so it wasn't a physical disability. Dylan's aphasia might not be isolated.

Ami ran a battery of tests on Matthew who seemed to be adapting to the cuirass. He still could blink to answer questions, although the headache made it hard for him to pay attention. Pete Ramirez had lost that ability a few days ago.

Anemia? It made sense. Probably half the population of the town had nutritional deficiencies. The Bennetts all had resources – they'd planned ahead better than most – but Ami was still not surprised to see the hematocrit level. She scanned through her notes. Dylan had turned a corner after she treated his anemia. The Shore kid had never been tested for anemia. Marnie treated Kix for it. Intriguing. Ami went downstairs to ask Colleen if anyone in the family had the same blood type as Matthew.

"O positive?" Ami nodded. "Me. The other kids all take after Andrew. What do you need?"

A unit of blood might not do anything other than improve Matthew's immune response, but it was worth the test to eliminate a provisional theory. Ami had one more place to stop before returning to the B&B. She wondered if she'd find a low iron level. It was worth investigating. Although she now had an electron microscope, the power situation meant she couldn't pursue actual virology experiments just yet. Grant and Jim worked on something for her, but for now, she had to concentrate on old-fashioned doctoring and trial and error. And maybe that would yield the answers she needed. She could hope.

Solving a Mystery

Mara Wells, Jericho Township

The wind whipped hard as they traveled west, grabbing the bed of the truck and trying to pull it to the right. Rob kept both hands on the wheel, fighting to stay in his lane. Cai fiddled with the Geiger counter.

"It's hard to tell. I think it's elevated, but with the wind, it's hard to tell." He set the counter down by his feet. "Wow! The lion is early."

"Huh?" Jazz cast him a bemused sidelong glance.

"In like a lion, out like a lamb. That's March. It's early."

"It's blowing the snow away."

Rob felt the tires sliding across the slick-as-snot pavement.

"Not entirely. Another storm's on the way. I can feel it." Cai rubbed his left shoulder.

"And you're worried rain will be more radioactive than snow?"

"Yeah. Maybe some PTSD there." Rob fully admitted that he was terrified of rain after the Bombs.

"I'll be glad to be warm again. I don't feel like I've ever completely warmed up since that night with Shane."

"I could lay on a hay bale in the middle of Shoenfeld's field for any afternoon." Cai smiled almost as if he'd been in the memory. "I'd probably sunburn as badly as I did in Hutchinson, but warmth – God, that would feel so good."

Rob remembered more trees as they approached Mara Wells. People cut down 130-year-old live oak to heat their houses in the winter and it wasn't over yet. A pall of smoke hung over the town as a soldier raised an arm to tell them to stop.

"Mayor Rob Delaney from Emmaus to see Stan Osimowitz."

The soldier gave the three in the truck a narrow-eyed examination before speaking into his radio.

"Wait here."

The roadblock was just barrels and men with rifles, but Rob wasn't encouraged to argue. He and his passengers talked about plans for the warmer weather until the soldier came back to them.

"Drive directly to the mayor's house."

"We're dropping this young lady at her parents' house."

"Who?"

"Jessica Tully. My brother Michael is there."

"Oh, Mike. Yeah. Okay. Just go to the mayor's house after that, please. We're trying to keep things orderly within the wire."

Rob promised he would and then rolled up the window.

"I can't imagine Stan let this get this bad."

"Yeah," Jazz whispered. She gave him directions to her parents' house. As they drove, Rob noted how few people were on the streets and the ones that were kept their eyes down. Quite a few houses had a vacant look, like blind faces that had stopped trying to see. Several had caught fire in the Pulse, and nobody had the energy to do anything about them. They pulled into the Tully driveway and the curtains twitched. A moment later, the front door opened, and Cai let Jazz out to hug her little brother who towered over her. Rob got out to join them.

"I was beginning to wonder." Michael hugged her again. "I haven't heard from anyone all winter. Mac said Ed Greyeyes dropped by a few weeks ago and said everything in Emmaus was okay and that you were alive, but I'm so glad to see you. Thank you for taking care of her, sir."

"She takes care of herself. We just gave her a roof to do it under. We can't linger. What's up with the soldiers?"

Michael's blue eyes flickered as if he made sure nobody could hear them.

"They showed up after the Pulse. At first, they were manning the wire and then Stan Osimowitz got sick and suddenly they were manning checkpoints toward Emmaus."

"Who's in charge?" Cai kept his voice low.

"Not sure. Sometimes it seems they are. Sometimes it seems Paul is. Or Randi. And Stan, lately, but I'd really not know."

Rob nodded.

"I don't like leaving you here."

"I'm fine. Michael will keep me safe. Come back day after tomorrow?"

"Barring another storm, sure." Rob hugged her as if she was his own daughter and Cai gave her a sideways hug. The wind lashed her curls around her head.

"I'll keep her from getting into any trouble," Michael assured.

Rob and Cai got back into the truck.

"What do you think?"

Rob shrugged.

"Let's go talk with Stan."

Fragile Lifeline

Seattle

Color broke the gray sometimes. He assumed some of his caregivers or visitors wore bright clothing. He couldn't focus his eyesight, though his eyes sometimes opened involuntarily, at least for a crack. The surgery went well – maybe too well. Sounds now echoed loudly, slamming into his tender ears. He couldn't turn away, couldn't put his hands up to block out the sound. When others were in the room, he felt assaulted by their clamor. Even Cassidy's reading aloud hurt him.

The return of his recent memory proved a more beneficial side effect of the surgery. He remembered Kenmore. Something about the entire episode stank. How easily they were accepted and allowed free range, treated like valued partners. What if whoever disconnected his respirator had been in contact with them all the time? What if they'd been betrayed?

"Hello, Geo." He distrusted voices he didn't recognize. "It's Carlindo. They tell me you're awake some of the time now and can probably understand us. Can you blink or move a finger – anything?"

No, not anything. He felt Cassidy touch his scalp yesterday. He supposed it was yesterday, but he was in and out so often he couldn't be sure. He thought feeling his scalp might be an improvement. He wanted more, but healing would take time. He hoped healing would occur.

"Cassidy says she thinks you know more than she does about Kenmore. If only you could tell us. Do you feel that?"

No, he felt nothing. The bed's changes of position still registered as sensation not feeling. He only remembered bits about Kenmore – holding Cassidy in his arms, cleaning a rail gun, a file room. He couldn't imagine what he might know that Cassidy didn't.

"I promise, we're going to get you moving again. It means another surgery and you're still weak from the last one, but soon. They're excited by your labs. Not everyone qualifies and it's such new tech. We need to know what you know."

He didn't think he knew anything. Hadn't it been Cassidy that knew something? What had he known that she didn't?

Distantly, he heard a whistle. Somewhere outside. And then a thud. A distant memory of a sere landscape stirred in a far-corner of his swiss-cheese memory.

"What the hell?" Carlindo turned on what Geo imagined was a swiveling stool that shrieked like a banshee. He heard footsteps slap on the tile floor, the jarring clatter of blinds. "Jesus!"

What's happening? Geo tried to focus his eyes on his boss, but he mostly saw gray shapes. He could hear too well, but his sight was still not good. Again, the distant whistling and now he remembered the sound. Artillery. *Shit!*

The enemy barraged the city and here he lay completely helpless. A shuddering thud hit the building again. Carlindo spoke on a radio.

"They're targeting the power stations. Federal Way was hit first. The second one went wide of its mark. We've got helicopters aloft to hit their location."

Geo heard the whistling again. Power stations? His life depended on power to operate the respirator. Fear clutched at his chest. Don't let the power go out!

The next whistling blew out the windows to the room and the whoosh-hiss of the respirator stuttered before it stalled.

A New Suspect

Mara Wells, Jericho Township

Stan Osimowicz never carried a lot of weight, but he looked like a walking skeleton now – cheeks hollow, jeans clinging to his hipbones from a cinched down belt. His daughter Randi's clothes hung from her shoulders as she led them to the living room. A handsome girl who favored her mother, Randi avoided eye contact in an unusually pensive attitude for a girl Rob remembered as bold. She barely spoke above a whisper.

"I'll be in the kitchen if you need anything."

Rob returned Stan's hug, his own throat choking up as he heard Stan swallow hard.

"Stan, what's going on here?"

"We've been out of food for a couple of weeks. You doing any better?"

"People are responsible for themselves in Emmaus. Some folks were out some time ago, others aren't. We're down to our last two days of food and then we're eating Alex's eggs and milk."

"Good for you. I screwed up. I had a handle on it for a while, I lost control of it when I got sick around Christmas. By the time I was better, the food was gone, a month earlier than I anticipated. People butchered their livestock, even their dogs. But we're all starving now—well, maybe not MacArthur's. He never did cooperate with me." He closed his eyes as if pushing back horror. Rob nodded sympathetically.

"That's why I didn't take food god on as one of my tasks. I do what I can to keep the food coming in, but people are responsible for themselves."

"You warned me. I always did have a bigger ego than you – at than sober you."

"God knows I'm a narcissist when I drink, no doubt." They sat there nodding, thinking about the mistakes they'd made in line. Meanwhile, the wind growled around the eaves, reminding Rob that they needed to head back before they got caught by another storm.

"Stan, do you – this isn't an accusation on you. I'm sure you had nothing to do with it and you would have been sick when…when. Do you know anything about a dead body that cropped up in Jericho Springs around New Years'? A black-Asian man whose operative name would have been Qualls."

Stan pulled his head back, reminding Rob uncomfortably of a turkey vulture.

"Is that what happened to him? I wondered."

"Who was he?" Cai leaned forward to drop his elbows onto his knees.

"Show'd up with the second Army unit. He wasn't their leader, but he was something special to them. I got sick and then when I was up and around again, he was gone, and they wouldn't tell me where he went."

"Second Army unit? So, when did they show up?"

"Thanksgiving. The first unit showed up right after Beulah and it was a don't-ask-don't-tell arrangement. They were good. Maybe Renfield was never a bad guy and he just couldn't stop what happened in Beulah or maybe he reconsidered after that. They took up border duty and sent out scavenging parties. Then this second unit showed up right after the first snows. That was weird – it didn't make sense, but they brought food. Couldn't turn that down."

"And Qualls?"

"Like I said, I didn't know him. He hung out on the edges, observing, but a few things happened that made me think he was more important than the unit commander.

"You mind if we ask folks some questions about Qualls?" Rob looked from Stan to Cai who barely nodded.

"I don't mind, but others might."

A floorboard creaked behind him and Rob looked toward the stairs.

"Someone else here?"

"Not that I know of." Stan frowned at the stairs.

"Any idea where I can find Trey Conopher?" Cai continued looking toward the stairs.

"Paul might know."

"Is that who's upstairs?" Rob rose from the couch.

"I thought he was out." The advantage of knowing someone since high school is knowing their tells.

"You're a lousy liar." Cai followed Rob as he climbed the stairs. Stan's house was old-fashioned, with narrower stairs than in Rob's house and wall enclosing the stairs on the second level. A blasting wind washed down the hallway from an opened window which Paul tried to climb through to the roof. Cai was at the end of the hallway in three strides and dragging him back by his collar.

"You're under arrest for suspicion of murder."

Tragic Circumstances

Lufgren Farm, Jericho Township

Low hematocrit! It was becoming a coincidence that didn't feel so coincidental. Pete's arm didn't so much as twitch as she slid the needle into the vein. His eyes showed how much pressure his brain was under. Nick said it stayed low-level but Pete's seemed the worst of the patients she'd seen today. To keep herself from blurting out that she didn't think he'd survive, she changed the subject.

"How did I not know that you are O-negative?"

Keri Lufgren paused in switching the bottle under Pete's breathing box.

"I don't really like needles, so I haven't volunteered." She chuckled nervously and finished what she was doing. "How's he doing?"

"Still a high fever and his neck is rigid. I wish we had the equipment to see what's going on inside their brains, but for now, we just have to guess. How is the rest of the family doing?"

Keri put the bottle by the door.

"His wife is pregnant."

"Oh! Is that a pleasant surprise?"

"It's a surprise. It makes his condition more tragic."

483

"It does. Might give him a reason to fight. Does he know?"

"We think so. He lost consciousness a few days after she told him."

"Well, hopefully, we'll figure out how to treat this."

"Is it true this only affects boys?"

"As far as we've seen, yes. Boys between the age of 12 and about 21."

"What kind of disease does that?"

Ami knew from Samira's recordings that this flu had been designed in a lab and the secondary effects were planned. But she knew almost nothing else. Patterson had been unable to break the encryption for one of the files on the disc. She supposed the answers might be in there. She supposed the passcode was something personal between her and Samira, but they hadn't been close friends.

"We don't know." Ami wished she could share what she knew, but she really didn't know much and her giving out information might result in influencing other people's thoughts. She might be the only virologist in Emmaus, but other people might be the source of out-of-the-box thinking she needed to solve the mystery.

"It almost seems like someone designed it to do that." Ami met gazes with Keri and smiled. The younger woman blinked. "You think so too." Ami nodded. "But you don't know how to cure it?"

"I hope to find a cure, but right now, I'm just trying to find a way to treat it. That might go a long way toward turning the corner on this. Well, I should be along. Do consider giving blood at the medical center in a month. Every little bit helps, especially since I'm planning to test this anemia theory across the whole town."

Keri smiled tightly, laughing nervously, and followed Ami down to the kitchen where she dumped the bottle while interpreting the questions of her young sister-in-law. Ami asked about the pregnancy and the girl told her she didn't need her help. There was nothing to argue. People could make their own choices and Ami had plenty of other work to do.

Encryption

Sullivan B&B, Jericho Springs

"Ddddog." Dylan's finger enthusiastically came down on the picture of a terrier wagging its tail.

"Good." Grant peeked at the next page, covered the top half with a piece of carboard and revealed it. "Can you read that?"

Dylan grimaced. He put the same finger under the word printed beneath the hidden picture. His lips twitched. Grant remembered working with him in a similar fashion when he was maybe three or four. Back then, his abilities seemed limitless.

Dylan shook his head. Grant revealed the picture.

"C-cat." Dylan rubbed his forehead. "Words."

"They'll come back. What about this one?"

They'd been working on Dylan reading the concealed word for several days. He frowned at the word. His throat muscles rippled.

"Cow."

"See, you're getting there. It's about 20 words you can read now."

Dylan didn't appreciate being patronized and he shook his head.

"Well, then I'll get you going on this."

Patterson hacked a speech therapy website and downloaded a program that supposedly would allow Dylan to work on his own. When Grant opened the laptop, Dylan scanned the home page. He settled his unaffected hand on the mouse and maneuvered to an icon he'd used a few times now. Ron Patterson originally set up the laptop with the speech program, but he reported that yesterday Dylan stumbled on an old code challenge. Grant watched while Dylan opened it and began filling in the blanks. It was a warm-up challenge and pretty basic. Grant could probably work his way through it. He knew Miranda could. Dylan did it faster than either of them could. And suddenly, the little string figure at the bottom left of the screen began to dance. Dylan smiled.

"I'm glad you still have that, son. The rest will come back."

Dylan cast him an annoyed look, but then he went to another icon on the screen and stared at the page. Grant recognized it as Dylan's cryptography app. He held his breath waiting for grief to strike, but Dylan merely scowled at the page before maneuvering to a dialogue box that asked for a password. Dylan angled the laptop so he could use the keypad with his left hand and closed his eyes. He inputted four numbers, opened his eyes to read the screen, closed his eyes again, inputted four more numbers and hit enter. The page progressed to another page with another dialogue box.

Grant turned his head at a tap on the door. Because Dylan didn't like cross talk, he went out to the hall to talk with Patterson.

"You decided to try that code-breaking app. Good."

"It's too dense for someone who can't read."

"You think? He still has numbers and 1s and 0s. And, he's the original writer of that program, so it's possible some of it looks familiar. That's what April said, anyway."

There was a grunt from the bedroom and a drawled "Dad." Patterson followed Grant into the room where Dylan smiled at a page with a map on it. "Nneed – um, type."

He'd entered a long string of numbers, letters and special characters into a box. Grant didn't understand.

"Why not hit Enter?"

"No!" Dylan used his unaffected left hand to grab his spastic right wrist. "Hands."

"You need both hands?" Patterson stepped to where Dylan could see his face. Dylan nodded. "Which keys?" Dylan pointed at Control and then keys H, Y, P. "Same time?" Dylan nodded. Patterson did as instructed. The laptop bleeped and the screen went blank.

"That's enough." Grant worried Dylan would get frustrated.

"It's too much for the laptop, but if he got here once he can take me to it again and I can write down his codes. Right?" Dylan nodded. He pantomimed taking information from his brain and giving it to Patterson. The laptop continued to spin for a moment longer before it timed out. Dylan pushed a notepad and pen toward Patterson. They were items that so far were useless to Dylan. He could make simple sketches with it but couldn't even copy letters and numbers. He knew Patterson could.

They started the painstaking process of writing cryptography code down. For some reason, Dylan could type it into the computer keyboard, but not write it down. Because Dylan got distracted by too much activity around him, Grant withdrew. He found Javi in the basement glaring at a computer screen.

"Something wrong?"

Javi pulled the earphone from his ear.

"It just started."

"What?"

"Chattering numbers and letters. And something was flashing across the screen, but I couldn't tell what."

Grant went over to his station and entered a few codes. A string of Spanish letters and numbers issued from his speaker and the image of a Mayan Temple appeared on the screen.

"Was that it?"

"Yes. How's your math?"

"This is a code challenge. Why in Spanish?"

"Don't know. You ready for the translation?"

The math was algebraic equations which once translated had to be solved and then the answer submitted to the portal. Grant had entered three layers by the time Patterson returned from upstairs.

"Your kid unlocked this, by the way. I found it yesterday and couldn't get past the first key."

"You're telling me he can still code."

"At least some and this is pretty high level stuff."

"It's a puzzle." They both looked at Javi. "It's stopped with the equations and it's asking a riddle in Spanish. What makes no sound when no one is around?"

"A falling tree." At Patterson's suggestion, Grant entered it into the portal. There was a shift of screens. "That was too easy."

"There's another one." Javi listened to the riddle. "What can't be unraveled?" Grant and Patterson stared at one another. "You've got a count down. Sixty seconds and three chances."

"Rip-stop nylon?"

"No. I don't think so. We'll try it last."

"Gordian knot." Javi looked as if he was trying to read their expressions.

"Maybe." Patterson and Grant continued staring at one another.

"30 seconds."

Grant entered Gordian knot. Password error. Rip-stop nylon had the same result.

"15 seconds."

"Throw caution to the wind." He typed frantically. "The ties that bind us."

The screen shifted and opened another dialogue box, surrounded by a street scene. Javi listened to the audio.

"Find all the dogs in the photo."

Grant clicked on all he could see. The Spanish speaking voice then gave him another 60 seconds to work out a quadratic equation. With one second to spare, he entered the answer and suddenly found themselves in a directory. Oddly, the file names here were all in English.

"Ron, can you transfer that to our servers?"

"Yeah. You know your servers are filling up, right? I went looking around town and the college had servers in an underground basement. Near as I can tell, they still work. The question is if we can work out a good deal for them."

"They don't belong to either of us, which I don't have a problem with, but you can't extort goods from me for something I could just go pull on my own."

Patterson laughed.

"That's true. I guess I just won't charge you for that land."

"What land?" Javi asked.

"Are you interested in becoming a farmer?" Patterson stared at the information on his screen. "Wow ... that's ...."

"Make sure the VPN is in place. Download it and we'll analyze it offline."

"How did Dylan access this?" Patterson finished the download and Javi set aside the earphones. "A lot of this is listening in on Santa Fe, but in a way more sophisticated way than before."

"He remembers coding."

"Yeah, that's – okay. But, if this is an entirely new thing, how did you know the codes?"

"Ah, yes. Well, I suspect this is a CSA crypt and Dylan might have been the architect of the security system."

"I'm not sure about that, but what we were working on upstairs was his password breaker and I think I can now get into a lot of places we couldn't before. Boss, I think we maybe just cracked the safe. It's too bad he doesn't have the energy or mobility to come down here and help because he's still brilliant even if he can't talk."

Javi grunted.

"I could get him down here if he wanted."

Grant remembered the smile lighting Dylan's face and started to contemplate the possibilities.

Interrogation

Osimowitc House, Mara Wells

"I don't know who killed him." Paul repeated himself for the fourth time. Cai and Rob dragged him downstairs to the living room where Rob showed him what Vietnam had taught him to do and Cai started acting like a district attorney.

"How'd his body get to Jericho Springs?" Cai asked that question for the second time.

Paul glanced at his father, uncertain of the man's mood. Rob still had hold of Paul's thumb, but he didn't apply pressure, waiting for the answer instead. Stan had been an interrogator in the Nam. Rob knew just enough to know that the fear of pain worked better than pain did.

"We moved his body, okay. But we didn't kill him."

"We?"

"Trey Conopher and I. But we didn't kill him."

"He was bashed in the head and then smothered."

"Not by me and not by Trey."

"Then why'd you move his body."

"You can't just leave dead bodies lying around. They make a mess." Paul winced as Rob pressed his thumb back.

"Ow! Look, I figured it would cause Shane some trouble, but that you guys would protect one another, so no big."

That sounded a lot like the relationship Shane and Paul had. Paul absolutely would think that. As if Rob hadn't noticed when the Costco shipment began showing up in Huffman's Grocery. If he'd ever doubted his son, he'd stopped when he saw the evidence. It still brought them no closer to solving the mystery of John Doe Quall's life and death.

"What about the class ring we found on him?" Cai leaned forward, intimidating the weaselly petty criminal with his height and the familial relationship he had to the man threatening to break Paul's thumb. "No school, just the year you and Shane graduated. Jasper stone. A lot like the one you're wearing."

Paul's eyes twittered. The door to the kitchen swung open and Randi stood there, brown eyes rimmed with red.

"Stop. It was me."

Stan frowned at her.

"You what?"

Her gaze flickered toward her father. Paul might be useless, but Randi made him proud...until now.

"I killed him. I smothered him. His head was bashed in. He wasn't going to live. You could see his brain. So, I put him out of his misery. And, I've regretted it every moment since. If you want to arrest me, hang me, banish me – I'm ready."

"Here?" Cai glanced around the room to indicate the house.

"No. City Hall. I don't know who did that to him, but that's how I found him. Maybe he tripped and hit his head on something, but it was back here, so --." She gestured toward the area behind her ear. "I thought he was pretty much dead when I put the pillow over his face, but um, well, he reached out and grabbed my chain, I guess. I didn't notice until after Paul and Trey took him away."

"Your chain?" Stan frowned, perplexed.

"Trey and I have been dating for a while and he gave me his ring as like a not-yet-engagement."

"You and Trey? He's still freeloading off his uncle."

Randi shook her head, wiping her tears.

"Any idea who would want him dead?" Rob let Paul go and shoved his hands in his pockets. Either they stayed on subject or he'd be driving back to Emmaus in the dark and he hated that idea.

"Almost everyone." Paul rubbed his thumb joint. "He wasn't a nice guy. That whole crew --. The first group – Renfield's group -- were okay, did what they were told, went out marauding for food. But this second group – they – I don't know."

"They don't feel like soldiers." Stan rubbed a shaggy jaw. "I don't have proof, but they remind me of the mercs we used to run into in Cambodia. And, son, I would leave this alone, because solving the mystery of who killed him might get you killed." Stan's gaze rested on Cai.

"He might be right, Cai."

Cai didn't like it when his father treated him like he was 12. He'd survived slavery in Hutchinson, for heaven's sake.

That's what he would say at home in Emmaus, but here he acted like a professional.

"I should at least talk to this Renfield fellow. Who is the commander of the other unit?"

"Goes by Blackburn. I don't think that's his real name, but you know, nobody is who he says he is today."

"Where can I find Renfield?"

"Am I under arrest?"

At Randi's question, Cai and Rob shared a glance and Rob answered for both of them.

"We're more interested in finding out who killed him than in finding out who eased his suffering. For now, you can stay here. It's not like you're going to go anywhere in weather like this anyway. We'll be back for a fuller statement. Cai, we need to head back to Emmaus and talk to Renfield another day."

"He'll be at the border. He was probably there when you came through earlier." Stan stood. "Paul and I will go with you, see if he'll talk if I'm there."

Rob nodded and they moved toward the door. Brother and sister touched arms as they passed, very much as Rob would have expected Keri and either of her brothers to interact after such a deeply-bonding event as laying an unloved man to rest.

Ghosts

Delaney House, Emmaus

Alicia bellowed as another contraction tore through her. Shane stripped a blanket off one of the beds and spread it in the corner between the china cabinet and the wall.

"Can you come over here? It's warm and soft, a great little nest for a baby."

She muttered Mexican swear words at him, as she waddled over to him.

"I can't have this baby without help."

"Yeah. I sent out a distress call. No answer. Not from anyone. I'd guess the tower's detached and the house next door might be on the other side of the moon for all I could reach it. Hang on. I've got an idea."

He wheeled through the dining room, shoving chairs out of the way. In the kitchen, his mom had a step stool stashed in a corner. He settled it on his lap so it wouldn't get away. It was then that he smelled the scorching tomato soup. He transferred the pan to the metal drainboard next to the sink and wheeled back toward the living room as Alicia screamed again.

"That's about three minutes apart," he calculated, breathing through his own pain as he put the stool beside her. While he got the stool, she'd stripped off her shirt. Surprisingly, after the first double-take, her nudity didn't distract him from the task at hand. He'd seen her naked before…on a beach in Cote d' Sol. "I have zero experience birthing babies, but I did see a birth room in Miristan and they used a stool for the woman to squat. It's easier against gravity. Horses stay on their feet until just before they foal."

Alicia's legs already shook with exertion. When the next contraction hit, she knelt on the stool, clinging to the side of the china cabinet, praying to saints Shane had never heard of.

"I can't do this."

"It's a little late for that." Shane laughed nervously. He wasn't sure he knew how to deliver a baby. He knew a caesarian was beyond his skills. "This baby is coming, and you and I can't stop it. We just need to deal with it."

"You don't even know what you're doing."

"No, but since when has that ever stopped me from living in reality." Alicia grimaced. "Another one coming? I think this is when you're supposed to push." Alicia's hand clamped down on his as she bellowed a deep, visceral cry. Blood-tinged water washed down her legs.

"What the hell?" she cried when she could breathe again.

"If you were a horse, I'd say it's more amniotic fluid. For them, when the water breaks, labor speeds up and if there's a second gush, it really speeds up. Hopefully, we're done soon."

"You want to rush my baby?"

500

"Hell, no, darlin'. I just need this to be over while I still have the strength to help you."

"Ah, *Dios Mio!*" Her back arched and she squatted, clinging to his hand and the china cabinet. A staccato string of mighty vile Spanish words came out of her mouth. "Where is my epidural?"

"I don't know what that consists of and the woman in Miristan didn't have one."

"Let's have babies, he said. I should have cut off his --. Oh, God!"

She knelt in front of Shane in the wheelchair, both hands squeezing his hands so hard he wanted to yell as loudly as Alicia. When the contraction stopped, Shane bent sideways to feel what was going on below the round of her belly.

"It burns."

"Yeah. You're crowning. I think one or two more good pushes."

"I can't do this!"

"You *are* doing this, *chica.*"

She sounded like a cat in heat being drilled by a big male and Shane feared she'd break his elbow where she squeezed as a slimy body slid into his hands. It didn't look real, kind of blue, with fuzzy dark hair. Was it dead? No, foals took a moment to go from interior to exterior. Alicia settled back on her butt with her back against the wall, holding her hands out for her baby. Shane handed it over and straightened at the sound of movement in the living room, a heavy tread like Rob or Cai, coming his way. He leaned back in the chair to reach a stack of towels while Alicia wiped slime off the baby who gave a little hiccup as Alicia cuddled her daughter to her chest. Shane, in the act of handing her towels, looked toward the dining room again. The world spun as Mike's ghost smiled at him.

"You look done in. Back up so I can finish this thing."

Heat flushed through his body, followed by a thundering cold, and then fog closed around Mike as Shane slipped into unconsciousness.

Hijacked

Arkansas

A lashing rain blurred the road in front of him, already cast in shadow as the sun settled into the horizon. Lawson kept a sharp eye out for the brake lights of the truck in front of him. He glanced at the rear-view mirror. Beyond the long box of the semi, the dark road concerned him. There ought to be at least two more trucks behind him, but he hadn't seen one in more than half an hour. Bryson, his partner cozied into the passenger seat, snored loudly enough to be heard over the squeak of the windshield wipers. The lack of a National Weather Service began to tell. Now people were at the mercy of the next storm. The convoy of eight trucks left Gulfport yesterday morning. Thanks to rough roads, they took refuge at Jackson last night. They planned to drive through the night and hopefully roll up to Wichita in the morning. That became a faint hope when the storm caught them. Conditions improved over the last hour. The road no longer ran inches deep in water.

The brake lights in front of him disappeared and he slammed on the brakes as the headlights picked up a fallen tree blocking his route. The slick pavement didn't favor rapid braking, but he managed to stop before the tree punctured the radiator and he avoided jackknifing the rig.

Not bad considering he was more of a mechanic and security specialist than a truck driver.

"Carlson, you got your ears on? This is Lawson. I'm stopped by a downed tree. Over."

Nothing. Bryson sat up, rubbing a big hand over his bearded face. The static from the radio seemed to oscillate like it sought any signal. There'd been a movie about that once – something to do with aliens.

"Great." Bryson found his cap on the floor. "We're on our own."

"We've got a come-along. Take your gun --."

Bryson opened the passenger door and dropped out into the rain, his gun still on the central console. Lawson grabbed it and climbed out of the cab himself. Rain pounded from above and his left as he rounded the front of the rig. The pine seemed to reach out to him with living fingers, plucking at his clothes as if still alive. The headlights didn't illuminate the shadowy ditch, so he couldn't see if it had uprooted or snapped off.

"Bryson, we need to get the come-along and get this thing off the road." His voice seemed dampened by the thundering rain and he turned down the side of the rig, surprised to see Bryson on his knees in the dark shadow cast by the rig. "What happened, man? You trip?"

And then he felt the cold metal at the back of his head.

"On your knees. This rig is ours now."

Will the Real Bad Guy Stand Up?

Mara Wells

Approaching the border from the other direction, Rob's mind swirled with questions. The soldiers were indistinguishable from one another. They could all be killers. Correction, all soldiers are killers. It's what they're trained to do. From the radio tech to the guy walking point, they could all be killers. Eenie, meanie, minie, moe …. His gaze landed on a very young soldier who looked like he needed food more than Stan did. Probably wasn't him. Or maybe. Rob gutted a Vietnamese boy when he was only 19. Had he seemed dangerous then. The kid hadn't thought so.

Stan slid out of the car Paul drove and spoke with some of the soldiers at the checkpoint. One of them, older than the others, argued with Stan, but then called to his soldiers to let them drive through. Stan and the officer followed them on foot, so Rob and Cai got out of the truck. The icy wind whipped around them while the sun dropped toward the southwestern horizon.

"Cai, this is Simon Renfield." Renfield looked just as hungry as Stan. His fatigues not only hung on him but were fraying at the cuffs.

"Captain. Thank you for talking with me."

Renfield's gaze wandered around the area. Rob didn't like that they were having this conversation in the open. The soldiers at the barricades stomped their feet and blew on their hands, joking among themselves. He hoped they were frostier on the checkpoints that protected actual borders.

"I do what I'm asked, but I can't help you. Qualls wasn't part of my unit and I have no idea who killed him."

"This second unit – how did it get here?"

"Showed up in three military vehicles. They seemed legit at first, but the longer they were here, the worst it became. I'm frankly nervous to talk with you about it."

"Was there a helicopter involved?"

"A Kiowa?" Cai nodded. "I don't know if it's connected to them or not, but yes, we've seen it. It goes west by southwest and then back toward Emmaus. If it's landing around here, it's been subtle."

Cai frowned.

"Okay, so Qualls, you didn't know he was dead?"

"I didn't. He just disappeared."

"He came in with the second unit first thing?"

"No. I first saw him in December. That's part of what bugs me about this second unit. The members change. Qualls was here maybe two weeks and then he disappeared which I've seen with other members of that unit. I'd swear they swap some people out every few weeks."

Rob didn't interrupt the interview, but he filed the statement away. Military units sometimes did that to keep members fresh and on tender hooks, but he couldn't imagine where they might get reinforcements.

"That was around Christmas?" Cai pulled up his hood to screen some of the wind.

"I saw him last – hmm, Christmas Day. He and Blackburn were talking."

"Where?"

"They were going into City Hall. Son, I suggest you let this go. Blackburn is a dangerous man."

"I'm coming back day after tomorrow to collect a friend and hopefully we'll have food to share. If you have any ideas come to you – other people who know anything …."

Splat, bang, splat …. Rob's reflexes snapped into place, identifying the threat from the shed, and rounding the truck to seek cover, drawing his weapon as he moved. The soldiers at the barricades turned to stare at a shed across a field before diving for cover behind the barrels. Rob trained his 9 mm at the shed – a derelict with peeling paint and a broken fence. A figure moved to run, and a shot rang out. Despite his weakened condition, Stan had leapt to grab the AR15 in Rob's truck rack and smoke rose from its barrel. The figure on the ground by the shed didn't move, but neither did Renfield who lay eyes wide open to the sky, not moving, his neck blasted open from the M4 the shooter fired. Rob stood, glancing around for Cai, only to see him lying on the ground in a spreading pool of blood.

A Taste of "Worm Moon"

Mara Wells

Stan Osimowicz stood shoulder to shoulder with Paul, wishing sanity would replace the crazy thoughts in his head.

"I don't know him," Cabot said. "He could be new second unit, but I've never seen him before."

Stan's bullet had landed precisely, not like the one the dead man had fired at Cai Delaney. His spinal cord severed, the shooter had collapsed immediately and bled out in under a minute. Too bad all that blood was wasted, leaking into the snow.

"You two start interviewing. Bring them by here one by one and ask them if they know him." Stan shifted the lantern from hand to hand. He felt so weak. "Renfield was a good man. He didn't deserve this. Find out who is in charge now that he's gone."

"I'm probably highest rank." Corporal Cabot rubbed his jaw. "Not that they'll honor that."

"Second unit?" Cabot nodded. Stan tried to banish the vision of his oldest friend in the world trying to stop his son from bleeding out. No, that one would stick for a while.

"What do we do with the body?" Paul wiped snow with the back of a glove.

"What have we been doing with them?"

Cabot and Paul exchanged glances.

"Piling them up in the Costco building. Not more we can do these days."

Stan frowned at his son. Paul had always been a liar – telling fibs to stay out of trouble when he was little, lying about his whereabouts on high school weekends – just a liar. He held no records for it. Stan usually caught him, partially because he could hear the stresses in his voice when he lied.

"What aren't you telling me?"

"Naw, nothing."

"Cabot, you in on this."

The young soldier's nose was red and then his whole face flashed cherry.

"Just out with it."

"Um, yeah, about the bodies. I – uh – don't think any of us did it until we'd been without food for a week."

"Two." Paul stared resolutely at the wall of the shed. "It wasn't an easy choice."

"What are you talking about?"

Paul let his gaze drop to the dead body at their feet and suddenly Stan realized they'd been doing what he was contemplating just minutes before.

"Dear God, help us! You're eating people?"

"Strangers." Paul shrugged and Cabot looked like a kicked dog.

"People."

"Oh, c'mon, Dad. You were thinking about it when you were examining the body. This is where we are. We either eat or we die."

Stan swallowed convulsively. He'd had nothing but water all day and so there was nothing to throw up, but the thought. He stared down at the body and realized Paul knew him as well as he knew his son.

Other Lela Markham Titles

Transformation Project

Life as We Knew It

Objects in View

A Threatening Fragility

Day's End

Gathering In

Winter's Reckoning

Watch for "Worm Moon in 2022

Daermad Cycle

The Willow Branch

Mirklin Wood

Watch for "Fount of Wraiths" in 2021

Other Books

Hullaballoo on Mainstreet

Gateways (Anthology)

Encountering Jesus (Testimonies)

Echoes of Liberty (Anthology)

Unbound (Anthology)

Fire & Faith (Anthology)

Overmorrow (Anthology)

Whisker Rebellion (Upcoming Anthology)

Other Great
Breakwater Harbor Books

Moscow, 2138. With the world only beginning to recover from the complete societal collapse of the late 21st Century, Zoya scrapes by prepping corpses for funerals and dreams of saving enough money to have a child. When her brother forces her to bring him a mysterious package, she witnesses his murder and finds herself on the run from ruthless mobsters. Frantically trying to stay alive and save her loved ones, Zoya opens the package and discovers two unusual data cards, one that allows her to fight back against the mafia and another which may hold the key to everlasting life.

www.breakwaterharborbooks.com

Waste Energy Resources Company
werc-u.com

My friend Bern Sliney, featured in *Winter's Reckoning*, has invented a system to take the hot water in a humidity pot or vat sitting on your woodstove and conduct the heat throughout your entire home using forced hydronics.

Want to know how to do it yourself? Bern is offering access to how-to invention videos for a $5 subscription at woodstove.locals.com, where you can help build a community around this innovative technology.

Meet Lela Markham

Hi. I was raised in a house made of books in Alaska and told tales from the time I could talk. A teacher eventually made me write one of them down. I hated the exercise, but it was the spark that ignited a fire that has never gone out.

My daring husband, two fearless offspring and I live the adventure of a lifetime here on the Last Frontier where the midnight sun encourages wandering the wilderness and the long dark winters favor reading, writing and staring at the northern lights ... hence the moniker Aurorawatcher.

It's all about the aurora watching!